SHADOWS
OF THE
TREES

by

SUE BRIDGWATER
and
ALISTAIR MCGECHIE

First Edition 2015

ISBN 978-0-9927472-8-2

Original Maps © Alistair McGechie
Cover design & artwork © Jan Hawke

Published by Eluth Publishing
in association with DreamWorlds Publishing
Printed by Ingram Spark

Contents

Map of the far West

FOREST
LANDS

Saracoma

Kiril

The Outer
Mouth

The
Inner
Mouth

The
Neck

Telan

Nork

Telk

Mil

Ipple

Drelk

Pelk

Imman

Imm

Drent

Sen-Mar

Esmil

The
Western
Isles

ISSKOR

Preface

Eluth Publishing is pleased to present here the second of the tales of Skorn to be published. *Shadows of the Trees* is set in an age so early in the history of Skorn, that to the characters of *Perian's Journey* it is mythological, ancient beyond reckoning.

Here the Immortals walk the world, learning of the love, loss and pain that mortals must bear.

Once more, very special thanks go to Jan Hawke of DreamWorlds Publishing, who continues to be a stalwart mentor and supporter in the work of Eluth Publishing, now establishing itself as the home of the Skorn stories. As before, we have had the help and support of our friends and families, and are particularly grateful to Caitlin Hudson-Jenkins for a meticulously close reading of the text and the scooping-up of minute typological errors.

We wish you an enjoyable journey across further realms of Skorn...

Sue Bridgwater and Alistair McGechie, 2015

Derren

*I*n days long ago the Immortals walked freely among the people; and there came a day when Iranor wandered alone upon the white sands of the Isle of Esmil. She strolled along the beach, picking up shells, stopping to watch the seabirds diving, enjoying the warmth of the sun upon her face. Rounding a headland into a quiet cove, she came upon a young fisherman repairing his nets, who sang as he worked. Then the Lady stood still in wonder, for it seemed to her that she had never seen any of humankind so fair as this young man. He was tall and strong; golden curls tumbled about his brow, and when he looked up at the Lady she saw that his eyes were bluer than the summer sky. She smiled at him as he rose to his feet.

'Greetings, My Lady Iranor,' he said.

'Greetings to you, fisherman.' Iranor drew nearer and inspected the huge rents in the fishing nets. 'You have great labour here.'

'It has been a bad night, My Lady, for us fisher folk. Two men died in the storm—and one was my brother.'

'Your brother? But that is terrible—how brave you are to go on with your work, to sit here beside the waves, and sing.' She laid a hand on his arm, but he pulled away angrily.

'Do you not know, My Lady, what song it was I sang? No, how would an Immortal know about mourning and lamentation? That was Seren's funeral song, and I sang it here by the sea because I may not lay his body to rest in the earth; and I sang over my work because now I must work twice as hard to provide for our mother and for Seren's widow and child. But these are things you would not know!'

Iranor stood shocked and silent as the young man turned

9

away from her and began to gather up the nets. Although he tried to hide his face, she could see that there were tears in his eyes. She moved closer to him again, gently touching his shoulder. 'What is your name?'

He did not answer. 'I am sorry that I have hurt you—please tell me your name.'

He looked over his shoulder at her, and muttered, 'Derren.'

'Please listen to me, Derren. I seek only to help. You and your people are my charge and my care; I feel for your sorrow and share your grief.'

Derren shook his head, turned to face the lady, and spoke quietly. 'Oh Lady Iranor—I do not doubt your care. But you speak to me of the sea and of storms, of the immortal mother who moves in the waves, and there is no comfort for me in such great themes. My brother is dead, My Lady—Seren is gone, and I shall never hear his voice again or see him smile. His wife lies weeping in the bed they shared, my mother is silent with misery. You cannot truly understand this, you whose children live forever and rule all the lands of Skorn. You do not understand.'

Before Iranor could think how to answer him, he went on; 'You come into our homes, you share in our festivals and we love you for it. But there are troubles in our lives, pain that you do not truly share. We cannot feel you among us when we stand beside the graves of our dead.'

She stretched out her hand towards him and Derren stepped forward to meet her. She was quiet and serious, and looked into his face with sombre eyes. 'Forgive me, Derren, and help me.'

'I? How can I help you, Lady of the West Wind?'

'You have done so already, by your words to me; but tell me

more—tell me, Derren, what is it to be mortal?'

Derren's profound silence lasted for only a moment. Then he burst into a gale of laughter, startling Iranor so that she jumped backwards away from him, and stood staring in amazement.

'What—Derren, what are you laughing at? What can you be laughing at?'

'I am sorry—it is discourteous of me. But can you not see how foolish this is? Did you not, lady Iranor, shape our mortal flesh out of the shadows of the forest trees? For so the old wise women of my village tell us as they weave their cloth and their tales. How can you ask to learn of me?'

Iranor took his hands in hers and spoke eagerly. 'Yes, Derren, I am asking you. For you were right to tell me how little I know. I am old as the world of Skorn, yet I know nothing of love, of mortal birth, of death – of the things you know. You must teach me; come with me now and we will be together on the Isle of the West Wind, so that I may learn from you.'

Derren frowned. 'But what of my mother and my widowed sister? Who will care for them if I am gone?'

'Have no fear: they will be cared for. And you will return.'

'Then—if I have your promise, Lady—I will come with you.'

Iranor folded Derren in her arms and bore him away with her to the Isle of the West Wind, and the people of Esmil mourned him as dead, not knowing what had become of him.

So for many years Derren lived with the Lady Iranor on the hidden Isle. At first they talked of death and sorrow, then of the daily lives of Derren's people, their joys and their work. But on the enchanted island, the two were far from these things, and time did not touch them. Derren forgot about his home and family and began to speak to Iranor less of the ways of his world, and more about herself, her beauty, and his growing love. Iranor loved him in return, and they became lovers. Two fair children were born to them, a son whom they named Drewin, and a daughter, Saranna. Derren and Iranor played with their children and walked hand in hand at evening along the quiet beaches. Iranor delighted in these children more than in any of her immortal offspring, and would have dwelt content forever with them and with Derren.

In the world beyond the island, the days and years passed by unheeded by Iranor. The fisher folk and those who worked the land prayed to her, for there was less bright sunshine and fewer gentle warm winds than they had been used to, and they feared that they had angered the Lady. Year by year the harvest from land and sea diminished and, when they gave to her the first fruits of their toil, the offering was less, and poorer. It seemed that she had turned her face away from them. At last in despair the peoples of the islands gathered together and went down to the sea. Together they made a great barrel that they filled with ale, and together they took the barrel down to the surf. There one woman from each island bore it into the water and poured the ale into the sea in offering to Ellanna the Maker. She heard their voices and awoke in the depths. When she understood their prayers she grew angry, and sent huge waves lashing against the coast of the Island of the West Wind. Iranor came to the shore and saw the waves and heard the voice of her mother, the maker of all things.

'Do you not hear the cries of your people? Why do you neglect them?'

Then Iranor begged her mother not to be angry, but to relieve her of the great burden of care that would keep her from Derren.

'You cannot abandon the people, my daughter. I gave this world into your hands and you made the people to live in it. There is no one else to care for them. Send your lover back to his proper place.'

Iranor knelt at the water's edge and wept. 'I will do my duty to the mortals, but I will do it better with Derren by my side. Let him stay and I will do as you ask.'

'You must know that he cannot stay with you: he is mortal and belongs with his own kind. You do him a great wrong by your selfishness.'

So Iranor walked sadly through the groves of the island until she came to where Derren was. He sat beneath an ancient tree, carving a fanciful wooden fish from a piece of driftwood. As Iranor drew near, he looked up at her and smiled, holding the carving out for her to see. 'A gift for you.'

Iranor closed her eyes as she reached her hand towards him. Her fingers touched his hair, and she heard the clattering sound of his knife falling to the ground as he fell into an enchanted sleep. She knelt beside him and kissed his brow, then brought a blanket to wrap him in. Taking him in her arms like a sleeping child, she bore him swiftly on the wind to the Isle of Esmil. Weeping, she laid him gently at the door of his mother's cottage and wove a spell of forgetfulness about him. When Derren awoke the next day in his own bed he remembered nothing of the Lady and their love, but the Lady Iranor, first among the Immortals, never forgot Derren. And by her loss she learned at last the pain of mortal sorrow.

Fatherless

*M*ore than a century and a half passed like waves of years over the lands of Skorn; Derren of Esmil and all his generation were laid to sleep in the earth and forgotten. In the city of Sen-Mar by the northern shores of IssKor, a son was born to Berget, a young woman who lived in a small hut in the poorest part of the city, making her living by weaving. In IssKor the Lord Jaren is worshipped and besought for mercy by all the priests of IssKor; he has small love for his people, it seems. The greater part of that land is dry and fruitless, and only in the South does the River Jar give green life, and only by the coast do the people wrest food from the sea. Among the nomads of the inland desert, a hardy race of goats is herded, and from their rough coats is woven a harsh but serviceable cloth. Some of the most skilled weavers, of whom Berget was one, learn to work also with the finer wools imported from more temperate lands where sheep are raised.

As a baby Kor-Sen played at her feet with old shuttles and fragments of bright-dyed thread. He slept in a corner of the single room, on a heaped pile of the softer scraps of fleece. Berget was a kind and loving mother, and although she was always busy with weaving, cooking, cleaning or washing, would spend as much time as she could with the growing boy, cuddling him, talking to him, singing and laughing. They were very happy together in their little home. But as Kor-Sen grew older he began to play in the narrow, hot streets of the city with other children; and from them he learned the word 'father.'

'My father says I'm not to play with you, you're a dirty fatherless foreign brat!'

Kor-Sen, a skinny eight-year-old, was pinned by both arms against a crumbling mudbrick wall, held by two large henchmen of the plump, well-dressed speaker. For months he had been trailing after the other boys—young girls did not play in the streets of Sen-Mar—and had been allowed to join in their games from time to time. He would be allowed to make up a team if they were one short of a side for the eternally popular pastime of pursuing an inflated goat-bladder up and down the twisting streets. He might be allowed to carry something particularly heavy for one of the wealthier boys. One of them might now and then grant him a sweetmeat or a sip of sherbet from their purchases when they decided to impress the poorer children by spending their own money—bronze or even silver coins—at the market stalls. He was usually the one left behind to take the blame when the rush and tumble of their games caused the collapse of a stall or the scattering of some household's washing, and in this way he acquired many bruises. Yet until this day he had been happy. Until this day when the two big boys, poor and dirty boys like himself, had suddenly grabbed him on the orders of Sal-Mor, fat and oily Sal-Mor whose father owned half the weaving sheds in the artisans quarter, and whose rents gave a sorry double meaning to the word 'fleece'.

Fatherless. While Kor-Sen was struggling with this word, Sal-Mor grabbed him by both ears, twisting and pinching, dragging his head up so that the bright sun blazed into his eyes.

'My father says it is time we let you know your place, little brat, and that you should not think yourself equal to decent women's sons.'

Kor-Sen wriggled; the other two boys were squeezing his

arms mercilessly and now Sal-Mor let go of his ears, only to amuse himself by tweaking Kor-Sen's nose. 'Back to the gutter for you, little brat. Back to the dirty gutter where you and your dirty mother belong.'

With one enormous heave Kor-Sen broke free of his captors, and leapt forward screaming. Sal-Mor's eyes grew round with fear in his round greasy face, and he tried to move backwards. Kor-Sen was too fast for him, and flattened his plump nose with one furious punch. Bright red blood flowed across the rich boy's elegant robes and he sprawled in the mud of the gutter to which he was so eager to consign Kor-Sen. 'Get him!' Sal-Mor howled.

Kor-Sen vanished like a shadow, lost in the alleyways of the city before the pair had time to think of catching him. He ran and ran until he came out to the place of the tombs, the quiet avenues of the dead that lay on the edge of the city. Here he flung himself to the ground and sobbed and sobbed until he had no tears left. Exhausted at last, the child fell asleep, and woke to find that night was drawing near—the brief dusk of IssKor was deepening around the tombs. Again he ran, this time towards home, reaching his mother's hut just as the first stars sprang out in the darkening sky. But the hut was gone.

Berget stood silent and stiff in the narrow street, watched by an equally silent crowd of the people who lived nearby. A man with a sword stood next to Berget, while three other men smashed up her loom. A fourth destroyer was methodically breaking up pottery, jugs and bowls and platters, and had even smashed jagged holes through the bottoms of Berget's one copper dish and one brass pan. To one side was a bale of woven cloth, and Berget's whole store of wool. As Kor-Sen watched, the men finished their work of destruction, gathered up the cloth and wool, and walked away into the night. Everyone else drifted away, their entertainment finished. Berget did not move.

'Mother.'

She turned very slowly, and smiled wanly at him in the dim light from someone's house-door. 'Child, what have you done?'

'I broke his nose. He said you were dirty. What is 'fatherless'?'

They slept that night huddled together for warmth in the angle between two houses. At dawn, a man came out of one house and chased them away; but as they passed near his door, his wife rushed out and pressed a loaf of bread into Berget's hand. 'Quick, before he sees you! Go!'

They wandered through the streets, sharing the bread as they went and stopping to drink from one of the public fountains when they came into the richer part of the city. Here, on the edge of a great square where the chariots and carriages of the wealthy thundered over stone-laid roads, they sat down in the shade of a tree. Kor-Sen looked up into the branches; he had seen few trees in his life, for only where the rich and important people lived was there enough money to provide trees and the servants to water them.

'Well, my son, what shall we do?' Kor-Sen looked bewildered, and Berget hugged him. 'I am sorry, little one. It is not your fault. Come on, there is somewhere we can try.'

They got to their feet, and Kor-Sen said, 'But mother—you have not told me what 'fatherless' means!'

Berget set off across the square so rapidly that Kor-Sen had to run to keep up. He grabbed at her arm, and stayed close to her while they wove in and out between the rolling wheels. At the far side of the square, they turned at once into narrow streets like the familiar ones of the weavers' quarter. 'It is a meaningless word,' Berget said suddenly.

'What?'

"Fatherless! It means without a father, and no-one is without a father, so it is a word without a meaning.'

'But am I not without a father?'

'Of course you are not!' But after that she would say no more, and Kor-Sen had to be content with following her and looking about him. The twisting, torrid streets were busy and full of traders with and without stalls, noisy and smelly. Little girls and old women peeped out of doorways, boys ran whooping everywhere, and no one took any particular notice of the pair.

'I thought it was along here—ah!' Berget turned in through an archway that led into a courtyard, quieter than the street but still hot and bright in the midday sun. Scrawny fowls scratched in the dusty shadows that filled the corners, and the doorways of many dwellings opened off the yard, some on an upper storey reached by a rickety stairway. Berget headed for the stairway, and Kor-Sen trailed after her until she paused by an open doorway.

'Dal-Nen! Are you there? May we come in?'

From inside came the sound of a shuffling step. Then the head of a very old man peered round the doorway. 'Berget? My sweet girl, can it be you?'

The owner of the head came out into the sunlight, and Kor-Sen saw that he was bent and twisted, his body leaning to one side and one leg shorter than the other. His hands and arms, however, looked strong, and his face kindly. Twinkling eyes regarded the visitors, from under brows as grey as his hair.

'Good-day to you, Dal-Nen. I hope you are pleased to see me.' Berget's voice was trembling.

'Of course, child; and your boy, too. Come inside and tell me what you are doing so far from home.'

'We have no home,' Berget replied, and burst into tears.

Raising an eyebrow at Kor-Sen, Dal-Nen put an arm about her shoulders and led her inside. Kor-Sen followed, expecting the room to be as dark as all the houses of his old quarter. All the weavers had worked by lamplight, and many of them grew blind early in life. But in the far wall of Dal-Nen's room there was an opening, a window with hinged wooden shutters that were now drawn back against the inner wall, so that a bright shaft of sunlight fell upon the worktable that stood there, covered with bits of leather and bright tools. While Dal-Nen led the weeping Berget to a seat, the boy dashed to the window and knelt upon the stool beside the table. Leaning out, he saw to his delight that he was looking out of the archway over the entrance to the courtyard. Down below him the busy life of the street went on, donkeys and boys, merchants and beggars, all unaware that Kor-Sen was watching them. Fascinated, he forgot all about the earnest grown-up conversation that was taking place behind him. When he began to feel thirsty and hungry, and turned round to tell his mother so, he heard the little old man saying, 'Berget, my dear, I am glad that you have come to me. Stay here, and welcome, you and the boy, and never think again of what has passed. Down these streets we are mostly free of landlords and priests; there are people here from all over the lands of Akent, and you may live safely among us. I can give you both a home for as long as you need it.'

'Can I have some milk, please? And I'm hungry,' said Kor-Sen.

A few days later, Kor-Sen leaned out of the window to watch his mother come through the archway and set off down the narrow street towards the market. He waved until she was out of sight, then turned to watch Dal-Nen at work. Soon the old man said, 'Shall we have some milk?'

'Yes!' Kor-Sen scrambled down from his perch on the window-seat and came to help Dal-Nen get milk from the pitcher and small sweet cakes from the jar in the cupboard. They settled down at the worktable, clearing a space amidst the leather and thread and tools.

'I wonder you are so thin, the way you put milk and cakes away.'

Kor-Sen grinned. 'That's what mother says.'

'Mind you, you'll be putting on weight all right soon, if you stick in here all day, every day.'

The boy frowned, and buried his nose in his mug. When he emerged, he said, 'I don't like the streets much.'

'Why is that?'

He looked up at Dal-Nen, and tears sparkled in his eyes. 'You know.'

'Yes, I think so. You are afraid?'

Kor-Sen nodded. 'The other children call me names, and hit me.'

'They used to do that to me, too. They used to call me demon's child, and run away from me.'

'What did you do?'

'Nothing. I refused to cry, scream, or let them annoy me at all. Eventually one or two of them started talking to me, and before long they had all forgotten about my funny shape.'

'But I have no father; or that's what the boys said, mother

says I have.'

'You will find that matters much less over here than where you used to live. We have all sorts here, including people who know much less about their fathers than your mother knows about yours. Now, out into the courtyard with you; fresh air you shall have before the end of today, or I'll know the reason why!'

'But...'

'Never mind 'but'—GO!'

Giggling at this poor attempt at ferocity, Kor-Sen scuttled out of the room, around the gallery and halfway down the courtyard steps almost before he realised it. Then he stopped and peered cautiously around. Only sleepy dogs and scratching fowl were to be seen; but he could hear a child's voice singing, and somewhere two other voices squabbling. Slowly he came down the rest of the stairs, and out into the courtyard. He stopped by a recumbent and aged dog, and stooped to scratch behind its ears. 'Good boy, nice doggie.'

Out of the corner of his eye, Kor-Sen saw the two boys approaching. He noticed that the singing had ceased. One boy was bigger than him, one about the same size. Behind them stood a small girl.

'Hello,' Kor-Sen squeaked.

'You're the new boy,' asserted the girl. Kor-Sen nodded.

'What's your mother's name?'

'Berget.'

'What's your father's name?'

'Don't know.'

'Why not?' asked one of the boys.

'Because I've never seen him.'

'Oh.' Silence fell as the two boys drew near and stopped. The old dog had fallen asleep and its back leg jerked as it dreamed.

'Don't you want to know my name?' The girl spoke again.

'Yes, if you like—what is it?'

'Garnet, isn't that pretty? Do you love me?"

Startled, Kor-Sen looked at her properly for the first time, hearing the two boys smother their laughter. 'Well – I've only just met you.'

'Doesn't matter—I love you.' Garnet stepped over the snoring dog, and planted a wet kiss on Kor-Sen's cheek. Then she seized his hand and stood close to him, smiling sweetly through her missing upper teeth.

'That sets me free,' said the smaller of the two boys, smiling. But Garnett frowned at him.

'Well, I don't love you at all, Gal-Den, you're horrid to me.'

'No I'm not.'

'Yes you are, you are.' Kor-Sen's new sweetheart abandoned him at once, and pursued Gal-Den about the courtyard, shrieking.

The older boy smiled and said, 'I am Kal-Men. Gal-Den is my brother, and sometimes Garnet wants to marry him, and sometimes me. It seems you have joined us.'

Kor-Sen smiled back. 'I've just come to live here, with Dal-Nen. Me and my mother.'

'That's good. There's only us three here to play with—I hope you're staying.'

'Yes—I am.'

'Good.'

Sometime later, Berget came back laden with vegetables, bread, cheese, meat and all the other produce of the market. She paused inside the threshold to rest, and was rewarded with the sight of her son wrestling energetically in the dust of the courtyard with Gal-Den, while Garnet and Kal-Men yelled encouragement and the dogs woofed in alarm at this disturbance of their peace. Kor-Sen did not notice Berget at all.

After a few weeks, Berget found work in a large emporium at the heart of the market, an imposing building of mud-brick. Its owner was one of the richest women in that part of the city, and traded in all kinds of manufactured goods, including cloth and a few ready-made garments for the better off. Berget's lifelong knowledge of weaving and cloth soon won her promotion, and she became solely responsible—under the eagle eye of old Dorket—for purchasing cloth, and overseeing its sale. She was busy and happy, and Kor-Sen saw very little of her, spending much of the time with Dal-Nen or with his three new friends. One day, soon after the weather had changed from the blistering heat of IssKor's summer to the slightly less unbearable warmth of its 'winter', Kor-Sen went out into the courtyard and found Garnet there alone, teasing chickens.

'Where are the others?'

She looked up at him with the kind of scathing expression she was so good at.

'School!'

'School?'

'Yes. Why aren't you?'

'Well, why aren't you?'

'Girls don't go to school, silly—the priests say they mustn't. Only Dal-Nen says he is going to teach me soon, because that's all foolish.' She whispered the last few words, looking about her furtively. Kor-Sen was puzzled.

'What shall we play, Kor-Sen?'

'What—oh, no, I am sorry Garnet, I can't play today.'

'Why not?'

'Oh—Dal-Nen wants me. Sorry.'

'Beast!'

Kor-Sen ran up the stairs and into the little room where Dal-Nen sat by the window, stitching. 'Dal-Nen—please—what is school? What happens there? The others have gone to school—what for? What does teaching mean, that you're going to do to Garnet?'

'Shhh! Not so loud about that! Come and sit down and I'll tell you—but let's get some milk and cakes first.' When they were settled at the table, Al-Nen went on; 'Learning and teaching are things we all do, all our lives. You have watched your mother weaving, and helped her with some of the jobs that involves; so she has taught you, and you have learnt. When you were a baby, every word she spoke was a teaching, and you learnt to talk. When you help little Garnet to tie the strap of her sandal, showing her how to make the knots, then you are teaching and she is learning—do you understand?' Kor-Sen nodded.

'Now the reason for having schools is that there is so much to learn, such a great store of knowledge in the world, that we cannot hope to just pick it all up from those around us. In schools, the pupils learn from their teachers all about runes and writing, number and measuring, the busyness of the bees, what the stars are saying, music and song and story—and more besides.' Al-Nen refreshed himself with a draught of milk. 'Here in IssKor, there are few schools and very few that are good—at least not to my way of thinking. The Temple School is the biggest, run by the priests, who hold much of their knowledge to themselves so that their power may be greater.

It is forbidden by the edict of Jaren to teach girls and women. All this is foolishness, to me. Here in the Southgate, at small schools like the one your young friends go to, boys are taught to think and to ask questions. But even here we only dare to teach in secret if we teach our girls to read. Bah!'

Kor-Sen sat enraptured, a cake growing sticky in one hand and a mug of milk wavering perilously in the other. 'Could I learn things too? Could you teach me to read too?

Dal-Nen was startled. 'You cannot read, boy? Why then of course I shall teach you! You and Garnet shall start tomorrow.'

Early the next day, Garnet and Kor-Sen seated themselves at the table by the window, and Dal-Nen placed before each of them a slate and a pencil. Taking up a piece of charcoal and a scrap of parchment, the old man made several scratchy shapes upon the surface, then turned it around to face the children. 'See if you can copy these runes—and then I shall tell you what you have written.'

Carefully, holding his breath, Kor-Sen made his wobbly copy of the mystic shapes. He was finished long before Garnet had made the first shape properly. 'Good, good, excellent. And what does it say?'

'I don't know, Dal-Nen; don't tease!'

'This top row makes 'Kor-Sen'; and this bottom row, 'Garnet'. You have written your names—that's a good start for a young scholar.' By midday, little Garnet was worn out with all her new learning, and Dal-Nen sent her home. But Kor-Sen would not stop.

'Can't we do some more runes?'

'You must stop and eat, boy.'

'Well—can we go on after that?'

'I have bags and shoes to make, too.'

'I'll help you. Just let us learn some more, please, Dal-Nen, so I can go to school with the others.'

The old man nodded. 'Yes, yes. Of course you must go to school, and quite a scholar you will be too by the looks of things. People must just wait awhile for their orders, that's all.'

When Berget came home, her son flung himself upon her and tried to tell her everything he had learnt. He drew runes and letters and short words all over his slate. 'Slower, slower, little one. I cannot read more than a few words.'

'Sorry, mother. But I do like it so much, I want to do more and more and as soon as I can read properly I can go to school with Gal-Den. I want to know everything about everything, about the stars and the world and—oh, everything.'

Berget laughed. 'Then you shall go; I can pay for it now, and one day, who knows, you may be a great man.'

'Why might I?'

'Well, if you have all this learning in your head, it is bound to do you some good, is it not? At least you might become rich, like –'

'Like who, mother?'

'Oh, nobody—I mean, someone I used to know, that is all.'

The daily lessons went on, half a day for Garnet and many more hours for Kor-Sen, who within weeks was reading fluently and tackling the precious scrolls and books that Dal-Nen kept locked in a small cupboard. He owned three books and seven scrolls, all hand-written and delicate. Dal-Nen watched with delight as the small hands opened and handled his treasures with a natural reverence that touched his heart. 'The boy is a born scholar,' he told Berget.

'But what does that mean?' It was late at night and she was sitting with Dal-Nen, mending clothes and sharing a jug of wine.

'It means that he has a great mind, that he will be a thinker, a teacher, a wise man.'

'Will that make him happy?'

'Oh, Berget—who can foresee that? But I tell you, we must do everything in our power to get him the best possible education; if his mind is not allowed to go on learning now that he has started, it will be a tragedy. It will be his passion all his life, to learn; to know; to find out; to understand.'

Berget laid down her work, and looked at Dal-Nen silently. At last she said, 'I do understand, Dal-Nen. I have sometimes felt in myself the need to know more, to do more, to be more than I am. I want whatever is right for my son. But I fear his life will take him to places where I cannot follow.'

'That is true for all mothers, I think.'

'Maybe. But my heart tells me that my boy may journey very far away from me—farther perhaps than most.'

One bright morning a week or so after this conversation, a trembling Kor-Sen set out early with Gal-Den and Kal-Men, carrying a smart new leather satchel which contained a slate, a slate-pencil, fruit, bread and cheese, and a letter from Dal-Nen to the Master of the school. Speechless with a mixture of fear and eagerness, the boy followed his two friends along streets and alleyways that he scarcely saw, until they led him into a small house at the end of a short cul-de-sac near the Southgate of the city. Here rows of boys of all ages were sitting on the floor before a kind-faced man, who stood up and smiled as he saw a new face.

'Hello! What have we here?'

Kor-Sen tried to answer, but blushed and fell silent.

'He's Kor-Sen, sir, he lives near us. He's got a letter, get the letter out, stupid!'

Kal-Men dug his brother sharply in the ribs; the whole school laughed while Kor-Sen scrabbled about in the shiny new satchel and dropped his lunch everywhere. Gal-Den helpfully retrieved the food while Kor-Sen thrust the letter at the Master.

'Thank you,' he said gravely. 'I hope you can read more fluently than you talk. You can talk, I suppose?'

Kor-Sen nodded, and all the boys laughed again; he flushed angrily. 'Yes, I can read—Dal-Nen taught me.'

The Master smiled again and laid a hand on Kor-Sen's shoulder. 'Don't be cross. And you should call me 'Sir' when you address me. My name is Karenoran, and I come from another land to live among these ungracious louts and teach them—teach them manners amongst other things!' He turned on the giggling school, and silenced it with a fiery look. Kor-Sen's heart warmed to the big, golden, deep-voiced man, and he overcame his fears.

'Thank you, Sir. I hope you will let me come to your school, when you have read Dal-Nen's letter.'

'I hope so too. Now you may go and find yourself a seat by Gal-Den for now, and I will talk with you later.'

Everyone settled down again, and Kor-Sen copied the other boys, who were all getting out their slates. Then one boy from the end of each row—they were seated together according to age—got up and went to a set of wooden shelves that lined one wall, and from this each took a larger slate, already covered with writing, and stood still until all the others in his row got to their feet. Then, with a minimum of fuss, the rows of children moved until each group could settle down in a circle with the large slate placed so that all could see it. Gal-Den whispered to Kor-Sen, 'This is what we do first each morning, after a Prayer to Jaren (we missed that today, you walked so slow). We have to copy the writing onto our slates as neatly as we can, all the letters properly shaped and all the words clear to read. Then the master goes to each group in turn, because the littlest ones have easy words and the oldest very difficult, you see.'

Kor-Sen nodded, already moving his pencil dextrously across the slate. He knew the text, because Dal-Nen had written it out for him a few days before. Gal-Den shrugged, and settled down to his own work. Meanwhile Karenoran was reading the letter, and looking up from time to time at his new pupil. When he reached the end of the paper, he folded it carefully and put it into his desk. Then he sat watching while Kor-Sen worked, nodding to himself as he saw the boy's absorption in his task. Beside Kor-Sen his friend fidgeted, sighed, stretched, put down his pencil and then his slate, flexed his fingers, picked everything up again, wrote a little more, looked around the room...—and as Karenoran too looked around at his pupils, he could see that no-one else was working with Kor-Sen's intensity of concentration.

He called out, 'Put down your pencils Class One. Bring your work to me.' He worked his way through the classes, coming to Kor-Sen's halfway through. The neatness and clarity of the boy's script pleased him at first sight. After commenting on each boy's technical achievement in shaping the letters, Karenoran asked, 'And who can tell me about this piece—what is it, what does it mean?'

There was a lot of shuffling and looking down and muttering. Kor-Sen looked at his classmates in surprise. 'It is a poem, Sir. An old poem about the people of the desert.'

'Go on, Kor-Sen.'

'Well—the poet says that the people are like the stars of the desert sky, wandering over the empty sands just like the stars move across the empty night. And he says that their lives are fierce and harsh like the desert sun; and they are brave and strong as the desert lion, and secret like the hidden springs, and the words are beautiful, Sir.'

Karenoran smiled. 'Is that right? You, Kan-Den, do you agree?'

'Me, Sir? I—I didn't know it was about people—I mean, it doesn't say it is, does it?'

'Kor-Sen?'

'It's a metaphor, Sir—it is really about the people, but it's written to compare them to all these other things. That's a metaphor.'

'So it is. Learn that, all the rest of you, and today will have been well spent. Now take the two younger classes out into the yard to play, while I deal with Fourth and Fifth Classes.'

After the morning break there was drawing, something Kor-Sen had done very little of with Dal-Nen, and which he did not think he was good at. Gal-Den's designs seemed to him fine enough for a lovely Temple, to some kinder god than Jaren.

At noon they stopped work and ate their lunch, then after a rest took up their slates again and worked out many calculations which had appeared on the big slates while they were out of the classroom. Then at the end of the day, Karenoran settled them all down in their tidy rows and began to tell them a story.

Kor-Sen fell at once under the spell of that voice, and listened with all his ears and all his heart. Karenoran told of the magic island far away and long ago, where the great Goddess lived who cared for all the world, she who was the Mother of all the Immortals, though the priests of Jaren denied that she existed. 'In the West Wind she speaks to us, in the waters of fountains and springs, in the cool skies of evening she comes to us...'

Kor-Sen was lost, swept away beyond the walls of the room, the walls of the city, beyond the western sea to the magic island. When Karenoran's voice fell silent the boy felt as if he were being shaken awake out of a lovely dream. He sat motionless while the others leapt up and got ready to go home, laughing and talking. He could still feel the cool winds of the island, still hear the swish of the waves that fell on its shore –

'Get up, dreamy, Sir wants you.' Gal-Den was kicking him gently in the behind.

Kor-Sen sprang up and rushed forward to the Master's desk. 'I should like to talk to you for a while, if you can stay?'

'Yes, Sir—but Dal-Nen -'

'I have a letter here for him to explain that you will be a little late. Perhaps Gal-Den will take it for us?' When they were all gone, Karenoran looked at the worried face peering across his desk, and smiled. 'Why so anxious, young man?'

'Please Sir—I want to know if I can stay at your school. I like it here, Sir.'

'Do you? Good. Yes, Kor-Sen, I should like you to stay here, for a while at least. But not, I think, for very long.'

The boy hung his head, and tears showed at the corners of his eyes. 'No, no, boy, don't be foolish, but listen. The work you have done today has pleased me very much.' Kor-Sen brightened up at once. 'Is it true that you have only studied for a few months, with Dal-Nen?'

'Yes, Sir.'

'And what do you like best?'

'Everything, Sir. Well, I can't do drawing or play music, but I like numbers, and the things you said about the rocks that Skorn is made of, but best I like words and runes and stories, Sir.'

'Well, don't think you haven't a great deal to learn, because you have. But I think you will learn quickly, and well. Will you stay with me for a while, and study in Class Five, Kor-Sen?'

'Five, Sir?'

'Yes, Five, Sir! There is no reason to waste time; as I said, you have a long way to go. How does that sound?'

'Oh, Sir!'

So Kor-Sen went to school, a small figure amidst the tall young men of Class Five, absorbing everything he was given to learn, herb lore and the names of rocks and stones, the history of IssKor and all the lands of Skorn, poetry and tale, number and measure. At last Karenoran began to teach him separately, indeed secretly, the hidden lore of the Runes and their true power and the names of the Immortals, all the things that the Priests of Jaren wished no-one to know but themselves. Never before had Karenoran revealed to any young pupil that runes were anything more than a writing script. And at the end of a year Karenoran walked home with his pupil one day, sat down across the table from Dal-Nen, and said, 'What are we to do with this boy?'

Exile

On the island of the West Wind Iranor's children grew; their mother played with them and told them tales; of mortals—their foolishness and joys and sorrows; of her mother Ellanna and the making of the world. And she told how she herself had made the runes for her children. 'There are eleven runes, and these are their shapes,' she said, drawing the outlines in the sand. The two children quickly learnt the shapes and sounds, and were able to put them together to make all the words they knew.

'What clever children you are!' said Iranor, delighted. 'As a reward I will do for you what I did for my other children: I will invent runes for you that will call up the sounds of your names for all time, for eternity beyond the end of Skorn itself. For the runes are immortal as you are, and you and each of your runes will exist together forever.'

She made new marks in the sand: marks never before seen. The first was made of two curved lines, down and to the left. 'This is 'Orth', and it is yours, Saranna.' The second was a line upwards and one to the right. 'And this is 'Ord', and it is Drewin's.'

The children looked in wonder at the marks in the sand. 'Mother,' said Drewin, 'are they really ours? Are they really new?'

Iranor smiled and hugged both her children to her. 'Yes,' she said, 'they are yours, and only yours. I have made them and given them to you, and no-one can ever change or destroy them.'

In a quiet glade Iranor and Derren had built a little house of stone and wood, and there the children slept and ate and kept their treasures. Saranna would collect leaves, twigs, stones, feathers, shells, anything at all, Drewin said, as long as it was useless. He himself always looked for useful things. He started by collecting sharp stones that could be used for making marks or cutting; then he tried to make implements from wood or stone. But one day he found a small wooden bucket that had been washed up by the tide, and so he spent a lot of time on the shore searching for strange objects.

One day Saranna came running to him as he paddled in the sea. 'Drewin! Drewin! she shouted. 'Look what I have found!' She showed him the small object in her hand. It was made of metal, very rusty, and pointed at one end.

Drewin examined it carefully. 'Is it something useful?' Saranna asked.

'I don't know: we must ask Mother.'

When Iranor returned, the first thing the children did was to fetch their find and show it to her. She took it in her hands and looked at it closely, then she turned pale and spoke sharply. 'This is a fisherman's knife. Where did you find it?'

Saranna answered, 'In the wood under the big old tree.' Her mother sat down on a stone holding the knife and seemed to go into a dream. The children watched, puzzled.

Finally Iranor spoke. 'It is your father's knife: he dropped it under that tree before he returned to the world. When he had it, it was bright and shining, but now it is dull.'

'Can we keep it, Mother?' Drewin asked.

'Yes, I think Derren would have wanted that.'

So Drewin took the knife and cleaned and polished it until it was bright again, and it became the most treasured possession in his small store of objects. He kept it sharp and taught himself to carve the white driftwood from the sea. Saranna used to sit and watch him carving, or cleaning the precious knife; sometimes there was a frown of discontent on her face.

Then one afternoon Drewin awoke from a brief rest to find that Saranna had disappeared, and that his knife was gone from the top of the flat stone he used as a workbench. He hurried out into the woods to look for her, but searched uselessly for a long time. He called her name, but she did not answer. Drewin began to feel afraid, because Saranna had never hidden herself from him, and he could not think what was wrong. At last, as he drew near the beach, he heard a faint sound that he did not recognise. It was a rhythmic, gasping sound, something like the dragging of the waves on the sand. 'Saranna, is that you?'

The sound stopped abruptly.

'Saranna—where are you? Why don't you answer?' Drewin walked on; behind a great rock he came across his sister, huddled on the ground and clutching her left hand with her right. Beside her on the sand lay Derren's knife, and there were sticky red stains upon the blade. She looked up at Drewin and he saw with wonder that a clear liquid was welling from her eyes and running down her cheeks. He went over to her and touched it carefully. 'Water is coming from your eyes – why is that happening?'

I don't know – something bad happened to my hand, and then the red stuff came, and the water. Drewin, look, I don't like it, it's bad!'

He cried out in shock as she showed him her left hand; the skin and flesh were opened up and red fluid came from the

35

opening. 'It was your stupid, nasty knife, it made my hand like this!'

'I'm sorry—but why did you take the knife? Mother gave it to me.'

'I wanted it. And now I don't, I don't like this.'

Sobbing noises and flowing tears started again, and Drewin said wonderingly, 'That is crying—that's what mortals do. I wondered what it was like.'

'Stop it! Make it stop! Stop saying silly things!' Drewin helped her gently to her feet, took up his knife, and walked slowly home, supporting Saranna with one arm about her shoulders. He had no idea what to do about the opening in her hand, and it was a great relief to him when Iranor came home that evening unexpectedly. She cleaned and bound up the cut, showing Drewin how to treat it, and laid Saranna down to sleep with a gentle touch that soothed away the sadness from the child's face. Then she turned to Drewin.

'I am sorry. I never thought that this knife from mortal lands might have the power to hurt you or Saranna. I suppose that the mortal blood in you is vulnerable to the mortal works of the people.'

Drewin nodded wisely, although he did not quite understand. He had more urgent matters to ask about. 'Mother, why did Saranna speak loud to me, and sound like—like a gull that loses a fish, screechy and sharp? Why did she say 'stupid Drewin, silly'?'

'Because of her pain and fear—these are terrible afflictions, Drewin, and Saranna was so shocked by them that she became angry with you, cross and accusing.'

'But I did not do the pain—I would not want to pain

Saranna."

'I know, dear. But just for a while she did not know that.'

'Will she be—angry, did you say—will she be like that always now?'

'No. Do not fear, when she wakes tomorrow the hurt will be healed and you will be friends again. All you must do is remember in future to take great care with that knife—we don't want it to do any more damage.'

Another day, as the children ran on the beach Saranna found a small piece of wood cast up by the sea and brought it to Drewin. 'Drewin, Drewin, look at this. What a funny shape it is, like two circles stuck together.'

'Thank you, Saranna, it is beautiful. I will see what I can make from it.' So for several days he carved and polished, hiding his work from Saranna until it was finished. Then he showed her what he had done. The two circles were separated and from each of them Drewin had carved a perfectly regular ring. Patterns of twining leaves adorned the rings, while at its centre each bore a carving of a Rune; one Ord, and the other Orth. Drewin had cut out the shapes with such skill that the back of each carving was as smooth and attractive as the front, and looked at from the rear they each displayed their rune in reverse. The wood was now polished, and glowed like satin.

'Oh Drewin; how lovely. Such pretty things; may I have one?'

'One is for you, little one. See, I have carved here Orth for Saranna, and Ord for Drewin. And we shall wear them forever.'

Saranna reached eagerly for the Orth-rune, saying, 'I shall look just like Mother, with her beautiful fish necklace.'

'Now look at this,' Drewin said. He showed Saranna what

he had fashioned from the rest of the driftwood fragment. An oval of wood like the link of a metal chain, skilfully hinged so that it opened or snapped shut easily. As Saranna watched, he fastened the two amulets together with the link. 'See, if one of us wishes to leave our rune with the other to care for a while, the two may be joined safely.'

'That is good,' said Saranna, and reached her hand out again for her amulet. So Drewin showed her how to plait a strong cord of fine leather strips, and from that day they wore the disks all the time. Drewin kept the joining link safely on his own leather cord.

Saranna and Drewin wandered one day onto the eastern shore of their island, and looked towards the lands where people dwelt. Not for the first time, they began to talk of those lands.

'Drewin, what is it like, do you suppose?'

'What is what like?'

'Being mortal. Living on those islands and fishing and farming and growing old and dying.'

'I don't know.'

'They fall in love, too. I should like to know what that is like.'

'Why?'

Saranna did not answer at first. She ran her fingers through the sand and let little piles of it build up beside her toes. At last she said, 'Because mother did it, once. She fell in love with father.'

Drewin grunted and turned over onto his stomach in the sun. 'Well, I cannot imagine what it is like. Nor do I wish to. From Mother's tales, it all sounds very foolish to me.'

'What do you mean?'

'All that clasping of hands and gazing at each other sighing and whispering. I do not see the point.'

'Oh Drewin—I think it sounds sweet. Exchanging love-tokens, swearing eternal loyalty; here—like this.' She leaned over and removed Drewin's rune from about his neck, replacing it with her own. Then she put his around her own neck. 'Here, you can have the little fiddly bit, I don't like it.'

Drewin frowned, taking the link from her and fastening onto the chain he now wore. 'Are you certain that is all right? These are not just ordinary necklaces; mother said the runes made them special.'

'Drewin, do not be so serious! This is only a game; we are playing at what mortals do. We'll change them back again soon. You can be so silly!' She seized a handful of sand and threw it at him. Soon they were both laughing, and they ran happily into the sea to swim and splash. They forgot all about exchanging the discs. When evening came they left the beach, hand in hand, and walked through the shadows of the trees towards their home.

Iranor came home, weary from her wanderings across the face of Skorn, to the little house where she had lived with Derren. There she found Saranna and Drewin, peacefully sleeping on the smooth lawn before the dwelling, warmed by the gentle sun that shone into the clearing. Her tired face softened as she smiled down at them and watched their regular breathing. Then suddenly she frowned, and stooped closer to Saranna who lay nearest to her. Iranor peered at the rune-disc lying on her daughter's breast. 'No! No, this cannot be true. No!'

Her shout woke the startled children, who saw their mother

towering above them like an angry dragon, her fists clenched and her face anguished. 'Miserable brats! Stupid, mortal children! What is this you have done? How dare you misuse my greatest gift to you?'

Drewin cowered away from her; Saranna stood up and asked, 'What is it? Dearest Mother, what have we done?'

Speechless, Iranor pointed at the Ord-Rune Saranna wore.

'But—but I don't understand. You said that we might wear them; just as you wear the wooden fish that Father made. You praised Drewin's skill... -'

Iranor reached out a hand to each of them, seized Drewin by the hair and Saranna by the arm, so that both cried out with pain, and dragged them towards each other until they stood face to face. 'Look! Just look at what you have done in your foolishness! These are Runes, Runes of power, Runes that shall endure beyond the falling of the last star; not fiddling trinkets to be exchanged or given away or dropped in the sand like trinkets from some mortal market. Oh!'

Drewin spoke, hesitantly. 'I am sorry, Mother. Shall we exchange the discs again? We did not mean to anger you.'

'Ellanna give me patience! No, stupid boy, it is too late to exchange them again. The Mother alone knows how much damage you have done already by your meddling. You are not fit to share the knowledge of the Immortals! Not one of my elder children would have been so foolish, so wicked... -'

Iranor swept suddenly up into the air, crying aloud the name of Ellanna. While Saranna and Drewin huddled together in the glade, Iranor's anger took form and shape and a great torrent of wind and rain and storm swept across the world. Ellanna, answering her daughter's summons, woke the slumbering fires of the mountains so that great rocks and hot lava were cast into the air. Iranor in her fury seized one of the fragments and would have hurled it down upon her cowering children; but Ellanna, filled with pity, wrenched her daughter out of Time by her own immeasurable power, and in the earliest dawning of Skorn Iranor cast the rock instead into the sky, where it circles still. Such was the birth of the Moon that lights the night but hides one week in six, remembering the transgression of Drewin and Saranna. Iranor grew quieter then, and returned to the Island.

In the clearing her children stood motionless, clinging together. 'Mother,' said Drewin, and took a step towards her.

'Keep away,' she warned, and stretched one hand out to ward him off. Saranna began to weep.

'But mother, what is happening? What do you want us to do? We will do whatever you ask, only tell us how to make you happy again,' Drewin pleaded.

The Lady turned away from them, crying bitterly. 'Go down to the sea. There you will learn what you have brought upon yourselves.'

They went stumbling and crying down to the shore, where they found a boat. As they stood beside it, looking fearfully about into the strange dusk that was falling rapidly upon the sea and the shore, the voice of Ellanna came to them in the waves, full of sorrow, but nonetheless angry. 'You have shown yourselves unworthy. You have misused the Runes of Power, the great creation of Iranor my daughter, and now we see that you are not fit to dwell with the Immortals and share their joys. You must leave now, and never see this island again. From this time you will live in the years as mortals do, and you will know death.'

'No!' Saranna cried, 'No. Ellanna, Grandmother, spare us. Spare our mother.'

'You gave no thought to your mother when you betrayed her trust.'

'But we didn't know! We didn't know!' Drewin shouted furiously into the wind. There was no answer. The waves surged up the beach and behind them they heard the grinding of the boat against the sand. The tide sucked at Drewin's feet so that he stumbled and fell onto his hands and knees in the water. Saranna grabbed at him, screaming. Stumbling in the bitter waves, they helped each other into the boat and at once it moved away from the shore. Behind them, carried by the wind, they could hear Iranor weeping. The untimely dusk was deepening, and soon night closed over the island, and they saw it no more.

Two nights and days they drifted on the tide. There was a small store of food and water in the boat, but neither of them could eat for misery. Through the stormy night Drewin held Saranna close to comfort her, but when dawn came and calm returned she pushed him away and sat huddled in the stern, staring down into the green depths of the sea. Drewin scanned the horizon, wondering if he might contrive to steer the boat somehow to one of the islands where mortals lived, but despair overtook him and he too sat helpless. The boat drifted on. So still and quiet were the two that a fishing cormorant came and perched on the prow, close by Drewin, and stayed for most of their first sorrowful day. The next morning they were surrounded by a family of grey seals, who poked their curious noses almost into the boat, blowing softly and grunting at the silent woman and the desolate man. But neither Drewin nor Saranna noticed them. Then on the second evening a vast whale rose to the surface so close to their boat that they were almost swamped, and Drewin fell with a cry into the tumbling waters, and was gone before Saranna could call his name. She jumped to her feet, almost toppling into the sea herself in her terror. All around her the surface of the water seemed unbroken, save for a few small patches of foam. There was no sign of either Drewin or the whale.

The Temple of Jaren

*D*al-Nen laid down a soft blue leather purse, and looked over at the Master and his pupil. 'Yes—it is time we thought seriously about your future, young fellow. But we must wait until your mother can join us. Will you take supper, Karenoran?'

So the table was cleared and set for a meal. Kor-Sen busied himself with preparing the food, bending over the fire and stirring the pots, while the two men broached a flagon of wine and sat facing each other by the window, watching the dusk deepening rapidly outside, and talking in low voices. Kor-Sen was absorbed in his task, and heard little of what they said until a sudden shout startled him. Looking up, he saw Berget standing over the two men, her hands on her hips, her face red.

'Never! Give my child over into their evil hands? Never!'

'But Berget...'

'Hear us...'

'No! I will not! How can you even ask me to send my son to the priests? Did they not speak the words of the Curse of Jaren over his cradle? Is it not they who say that I am accursed and outcast, because... ' She stopped suddenly, and looked round at her son, standing stricken by the hearth with a dripping ladle in his hand and the rice starting to burn behind him. Berget rushed to rescue their supper, then stood behind Kor-Sen with her hands on his shoulders, and glared at the two men.

Dal-Nen spoke gently. 'At least let us eat together, now that the child has worked so hard to prepare our meal. Come, Berget, sit down and welcome our guest, take a goblet of wine, and we shall see if we can think things through with more reason and less passion.'

Slowly Berget relaxed, patted Kor-Sen's shoulder, and went over to the table. They talked only of everyday matters while the food was being eaten, and all praised Kor-Sen's cooking. At last Karenoran, pouring Berget some more wine, said to her, 'We have been talking about Kor-Sen, my dear lady, because he is the cleverest boy it has ever been my pleasure to teach.'

Berget looked gratified. 'Go on, Schoolmaster.'

'There is no telling what this boy might achieve. He has a great mind. Please try to understand that we are only seeking the best for the child!'

Berget nodded, and was about to speak when a dry young voice butted in. 'Do you not think, oh respected elders, that it might be a courtesy if you were to inform me of your secret plans for my future?' All three turned to look at Kor-Sen, sitting up and grinning cheerfully at them.

'Yes, the boy is right,' said Dal-Nen. 'Listen, Kor-Sen; Karenoran and I want you to seek admission to the Temple School—your mother is angered by the very idea. What do you think?'

'I do not like the sound of the priests. Why do you want me to go to them?'

'Because,' said Karenoran, 'whether we like it or not, the temple school is simply the best in this land. It is the only hope a poor boy has of making anything of himself. If he is very clever indeed, they will train him for the priesthood...' Berget shook her head vigorously, but remained silent as Dal-Nen laid his hand on her arm. Karenoran continued.

'Others they will train for the service of the King, to carry out the work that the Nobles are too stupid to manage for themselves.'

Kor-Sen giggled, and then became more serious. 'What do you think, mother?'

She shook her head, and Kor-Sen saw with distress that there were tears in her eyes. 'Is there no other way? None? Dal-Nen, I know we said that his way in life might take him far from me; but if he becomes a priest, or a servant of the court, what price his great learning then? He will be forbidden by the edict of Jaren to speak to his own mother! He will learn to look with contempt on us, the rag-tag dwellers in the Southgate—am I to look forward to this for my child?'

'Oh, mother, no, don't cry, please!' Kor-Sen was almost in tears himself.

'Let us all have some more wine,' suggested Dal-Nen hastily; in his agitation he served Kor-Sen as well, splashing wine into the boy's beaker of goat's milk. Kor-Sen thought the mixture quite pleasant.

'Now, we are not thinking clearly at all,' explained Karenoran earnestly. 'What is to say that the lad must needs become a priest or a pen-pusher for the King, just because we extract from the servants of Jaren, a decent education, such as his genius—yes, genius, mark my words—deserves? You see, Madam—perhaps I may call you Berget? You see, Berget, for the higher branches of learning, the Temple is the place. If I were to go on teaching the boy myself, and they found out, I would be exiled, or even killed. Learning must be subservient to the priests, so that we may be controlled by them. But Kor-Sen, having learnt all he can, may escape IssKor altogether, and make his way in the wider world, beyond Jaren's cruel grasp.' He drained his cup, and Dal-Nen hastened to refill it. Kor-Sen gazed at his teacher in admiration.

'Please, mother,' he whispered to Berget, 'Karenoran says there is no better schooling I can have, not here in IssKor. And I won't stay there, truly I won't, I will seek out the wider world and make use of my learning there. I will miss you, you know I will, but it is only a few years. Please?'

She smiled down at him. 'Very well, my son. If you can make use of these priests and their school—you have my blessing. How is he to win his place, Schoolmaster?'

'Please—Berget—my name is Karenoran. Twice each year the priests hold open examinations for boys from every part of the city; you need only go to the Temple, and submit yourself to their tests.'

'And when will the next test be?'

'Tomorrow, Berget; they are holding a test tomorrow.'

The next day Kor-Sen was up early, having hardly slept all night. Berget insisted that he eat some breakfast, while she ran round to the shop to get permission from her employer to go with Kor-Sen on his journey to the temple.

Dal-Nen fussed about, brushing the boy's hair several times, and shooting questions at him to see how he would fare when the priests got to work. Kor-Sen was calm under this treatment, until at last he said, 'Dal-Nen, will you and Karenoran be very distressed if the priests do not take me in? I know mother will not mind it.'

'But they are sure to take you, child!'

'Are they? But what about my father?'

'Your father?'

'Yes – the one I haven't got. They will know who I am and they may not let me in because of the curse and all that.'

'Oh! I see. I wonder why Karenoran has not considered that.'

'It is not the sort of thing he would think of. But what am I to do if they say that I am not worthy?'

Dal-Nen smiled his inscrutable smile, and beckoned the boy closer. He leaned over and whispered in Kor-Sen's ear for several minutes, while the boy's smile grew wider and wider.

'That is wonderful, Dal-Nen!' He hugged the old man tight, and then went back to his breakfast with a better appetite.

Soon Berget came in, with Karenoran whom she had met on the way. As the four descended the stairs to the courtyard, Garnet, Cal-Men and Gal-Den rushed to follow them and a little procession wound through the lanes of the Southgate. When they came around one last corner into the great square they all halted, and looked out across the smooth paved roadways where the chariots of the rich bowled along, and elegant young noblemen were carried in litters by sweating servants. Slowly the little party made its way across the square towards the temple, making for the Paupers Gate. At the centre they paused beneath the shadow of the huge statue of Jaren the Terrible, fashioned as a mighty Man who towered forty feet above his subjects and gazed sternly down the Avenue of Jaren towards the sea. Kor-Sen stared up at the fierce, angry face of the God, and shivered. 'Lord Jaren does not look as if he gives much thought to us.'

Berget looked down at him. 'No—he does not care for people like us. And I should not be here, with my head all uncovered and no cloak to wrap me round; I will offend the sight of the nobles. I had better go back.'

'Oh, Mother!'

She stooped down to look into his eyes. 'My son, think. I cannot come with you, through the Strangers Gate. Even the

Court of the Unclean is denied me. It will be better if I go back now; I will be waiting when you come home.'

Kor-Sen turned to the two men, who both nodded solemnly. So he kissed his mother, and watched her slowly cross the square, turning to wave once before disappearing back into the narrow streets. He sighed heavily. The diminished party set out again, and came to the Pauper's Gate, a high, wide archway whose massive doors of wood stood open. No one challenged them as they passed under the arch and came into the wide court. The place was full of men and boys, and most of the boys looked nervous. Moving among them were the black-robed figures of priests, mainly novices by their youthful faces and their sleeveless gowns. Kor-Sen was surprised to see that some of their young faces were cheerful and friendly; although most were composed into a stern expression that looked as if they had modelled it on that of the great statue.

One of the stern ones came up to their party. 'A candidate?'

'Yes, Worshipful One. This is the boy.' Dal-Nen pushed Kor-Sen forward; the priestling's stare seemed to the boy to imply that he was not a very impressive sight.

'Very well. Take him up to the wicket gate there'—he pointed—'and the Holy One will tell you what to do next.' Kor-Sen and his supporters moved towards the narrow gate. A senior priest, bearded and haughty, waited between two of the temple guards to question each candidate in turn;

'Your name?'

'Your father's name?'

'Your teacher?'

When Kor-Sen heard these questions put to the boys in front of him, he clutched at Dal-Nen's hand.

'Courage, child—remember what I told you.'

They came before the Priest. 'Your name?'

'Kor-Sen, Holy One.'

'Your father's name?'

'I do not know, Holy One.'

The august personage looked down, astonishment lending his face for a moment a more human aspect. 'What?'

'I do not know, Holy One. I am Kor-Sen, the Fatherless.'

'Well—then your teacher's name?'

'Karenoran, Holy One.'

The schoolmaster bowed even lower than he had to the novice.

'Greetings, Holy One of Jaren.'

'Silence, foreigner!'

The priest turned to Dal-Nen. 'And you?'

'Dal-Nen the leatherworker, Holy One, the boy's sponsor.'

'And by what right do you dare to bring into the Courts of Jaren the Terrible, a Fatherless One who bears the curse of Jaren—may his name be praised—and who has been taught by a foreigner and known heretic?'

Dal-Nen bowed so low that Kor-Sen thought he would fall over. 'Most merciful and Holy One, on this day of all days it pleases our Lord Jaren—praise his name—to open wide his gates so that none whose talents may be used in his service, shall fail of his chance. Holy One, let the boy have his trial— for the wisdom of Jaren is surely inscrutable to us his servants.'

The priest drew himself up. 'You argue well, leatherworker, and with due respect. Very well—the boy Kor-Sen may enter.'

The two men bowed again and turned away; the guards thrust Kor-Sen through the gate, so hard that he bumped into another boy and knocked him over. 'Oh—I am sorry!'

'That's all right. Wasn't that awful—I heard what you and the Holy One said. But do not fear – Lord Jaren is merciful.'

Kor-Sen looked at him, and saw that his eyes were shining. 'Do you want to be a priest, then?'

'Oh yes—if only I am worthy.'

'I am sure you will be.'

Kor-Sen turned away and surveyed the Court of Jaren, a sight not often viewed by the common people, but now visible beyond the palings of the domestic yard where the poor boys were gathering. By contrast with the bare dust and plain walls of the Court of the Unclean, this place was floored with marble, and filled with fountains and flowerbeds and little trees. Towards the centre of the space clustered a small group of boys, richly dressed and attended by servants, who had already been admitted to the inner Court by way of the Court of the Nobles. Beyond them, a group could be seen in the Court of the Faithful, sons of artisans from the north of the city.

There was a long wait while the sun grew hotter and the Courts stuffier. Finally, the last boys came through the inner gates, and three priests followed them, one from each gate. There was a sudden blast of trumpets, and the three priests, each now flanked by two guards and followed by a double line of novices, processed solemnly towards the Sanctuary. Here they were met by an even older and more impressive priest, to whom they all bowed. This priest raised his hand in blessing, and the silence deepened. The ancient one spoke. 'I am Jar-Dal, he who works the will of Jaren.'

'Praise his name,' all the priests, novices, and some of the boys responded.

'Let the candidates come forward!' Jar-Nen-Dal turned, and marched towards the open area of the Court, between Jaren's sanctuary and the Priests' private yard. The priests followed in their turn, then the novices, then the boys, still divided by rank, in three long lines. Then the servants of the wealthy boys were turned out by the guards of the Nobles Gate, to wait in the square for the return of their young charges.

Inside the Priests' Court, the procession swept around the Well of Jaren, an ancient construction of mud brick said to be the work of the God's own hands, and covered with an elaborate iron lid. The priests at the head of the procession drew up in a more or less orderly fashion before a dais, hung with black, grey and brown cloths and banners, that stood before the Holy Place of Jaren the Proud. The boys assembled less tidily between the dais, the well, and the sanctuary, some trembling with fear and awe at the sight of the holy places and of the two mighty priests who stood upon the dais and were now joined by Jar-Nen-Dal.

The tallest priest addressed the assembly. 'I am Jar-Nor the Voice of Jaren! Hear me, and tremble!'

An audible murmur of fear swept through the boys, for this was the High Priest of IssKor, the one to whom Jaren spoke in the darkness of the Sanctuary. 'You have been greeted by Jar-Dal, who is Master of Boys and Novices in this holy place; here at my other hand is Jar-Men, he who measures the wealth of Jaren. Your testing will now begin.'

The three Great Ones seated themselves beneath a canopy of black, and the trumpets sounded again. Out from the houses built against the wall of the courtyard to the south, came a stream of priests to join the gathering. Each man collected a small group of boys around him, and the first round of questioning began. After an hour, the priests and novices touched the shoulders of every boy who was to stay for the next test; about half of each group from the artisans and the poor group. But Kor-Sen saw that the rich boys of the noble caste, who had been tested by elder priests rather than novices, were all sent away, wreathed in smiles, and each bearing a rolled up scroll of parchment, a written promise of a place at the school. All the rejected aspirants from the lower classes were sent home, some weeping bitterly. When the remaining candidates were gathered together, about forty boys, Kor-Sen saw that the earnest youngster who wished to be a priest had survived for the next test. Slates were issued for an examination of writing skills and knowledge of runes.

By now it was past noon, and the heat was tremendous. The boys were offered no refreshment, nor did the priests take any. Five youngsters fainted, and were carried away by the guards to be returned, rejected, to the outside world. Of the thirty-five remaining, fifteen were retained for the next test, including Kor-Sen and the earnest boy. They were made to stand, in the full glare of the sun, silent and still for one hour. Two more fainted; some of the others wobbled, or made a small sound; seven remained to be tested. These were called to the foot of the dais, where they stood while Jar-Dal addressed them. 'Jaren is merciful! He has allowed you to survive thus far. In some years he is pleased to welcome as many as ten or twelve boys into his precincts; but this year, since the remaining count is so small, there will be only two. This, then, is your final chance.'

All seven boys realised that they must keep silent and not show their dismay; yet each was convinced that he would be one of those rejected. Kor-Sen felt himself sway just a little on his feet, and thought he would faint. Then he pulled his attention back to the priests, and gritted his teeth.

There followed a long session of questions and answers, the boys desperately trying to please the three priests with their replies, while a silent row of novices sat on the ground behind them and observed the proceedings. The feeling of being stared at was very uncomfortable. Kor-Sen spoke up clearly and at length, and when the questioning suddenly stopped he found that five boys, exhausted and weeping, were being led away by novices while he and the earnest one stood alone before the dais. 'Kor-Sen the fatherless, and Mal-Den son of Mor-Ken; Jaren shows you favour.'

'Praise his name,' whispered both weary children.

'Mal-Den; great is your love for Jaren our Lord, and you shall be given our official seal upon a letter to your father; you shall be welcomed into the School of the Temple in six weeks time.'

The boy knelt, and bowed his head; tears of joy slid down his cheeks. Kor-Sen stood absolutely still.

'And you, Kor-Sen the fatherless, child of the accursed, fosterling of foreigners; in spite of all, Jaren has granted to you great gifts of mind.'

'His mercy is great,' murmured Kor-Sen, and the priest nodded in grim approval.

'Yet we seek for a sign, Fatherless One, that it is indeed the will of Jaren that we admit you to the great treasuries of learning that are stored here by his command. Speak! Can you win this place for yourself?'

Kor-Sen raised his head, and looked boldly into the High

Priest's eyes. Still holding that implacable gaze, he sank to one knee. 'Most Holy One of Jaren; I have a question for you.'

The three priests stirred and muttered like angry bees. 'Ask it!' snapped Jar-Den, his voice cold as death.

'Most Holy Ones, can you name for me the Father of Jaren the Mighty?'

A dead silence fell. It was followed by a period of muttered conversation among the priests. At length the High Priest spoke again, his voice slow and heavy. 'None knows the father of Jaren; he is oldest, and—fatherless.'

Kor-Sen ducked his head, to hide the fierce triumph in his face. Steadying his voice, he replied, 'Then I, being Fatherless also, may serve him.'

Silence. The priests were all nodding at him; and he thought he saw the ghost of a smile upon the face of him who is the voice of Jaren.

The evening came that would be Kor-Sen's last at home. A farewell supper was held, at which the guests were Karenoran, Gal-Den, Cal-Men and Garnet. Much wine flowed. Dal-Nen made a sentimental speech, Karenoran a mellifluous and impressive one on the virtues of Learning (with a capital L), both of which affected Berget to tears, in which she was joined by Cal-Men, who suddenly realised that he would not see his friend again for years. 'Years and years! It is dreadful!'

Garnet slipped her hand into Kor-Sen's, and said nothing. But at the end of the evening, she hugged him fiercely before setting off down the stairs to her home. Berget chased her weary son into his bed. When he was tucked in, she sat down beside him and took his hand, smiling a little sadly. 'Kor-Sen, my dear boy. What shall I do without you?'

'I am sorry, mother. But I will make you proud of me, I promise.'

'I am proud of you now, and always shall be—and I wish for you all that you desire, with much love and happiness besides. But now, before you leave our home, I must tell you what you have wanted to know for so long. Forgive me for finding it so hard to tell you; I must speak about your father.'

The boy clutched her hand tighter. 'When I was young and life seemed easy, I met a young trader from the Isle of Imman, far to the west across the sea. His name was Mannen, and he was sent by his father, a wealthy merchant, to buy our cloth. I liked him from the first, and soon I loved him. He said he loved me too, and when he went away he promised to return, and said we would be married—but he never came back. He does not know that he has a son called Kor-Sen.'

'But why? Why did he not come back? Was he lying to you? Didn't he love you?'

'I don't know, little one. I think I shall never know. He was kind and loving while he was here; and you are like him in many ways. But I fear our paths will never cross again.'

Kor-Sen sank down into his blankets, and was silent. His mother leaned over and kissed him, then blew the candle out and left him to sleep. For a while his mind turned over and over the things she had told him; but at last he slept, to dream of the baking hot precincts of the temple of Sen-Mar, crowded with boys in grey tunics, who all changed into seabirds and flew squawking away to the west, vanishing into the blue sky that brightened outside his little window and woke him to the first day of his new life.

Esmil

Saranna stood gazing about as the boat drifted on, but soon darkness fell and left her without hope of finding her brother. 'Drewin! DREWIN!' Her voice startled the homeward-flying gulls above her. 'Drewin!' She spoke more quietly. 'Are you gone, then? Are you dead so soon?'

She sat down and wept, then lifted her head and shouted into the depths. 'Ellanna, will you kill me now? How will I live without him?' The only answer was the sound of the waves against the side of the boat. Saranna lay and stared into the darkness, and stayed huddled in the bottom of the boat as nights and days followed each other, until she did not know whether she had drifted for days, or months, or years. Then one bright morning a freak wave cast the boat ashore on an island, and the girl climbed out to drop exhausted on the sand. She was woken by the sound of a strange voice. 'Wake up now, you're not dead yet.'

Saranna opened her eyes to find a large smiling man standing over her. He spoke kindly to her, and led her along the shore to a small settlement and into one of the little cottages. Here gentle hands led her to a warm seat by the hearth, and spooned broth into her until her strength began to return.

'Where am I?'

'This is Esmil, my dear. The house of Gartten, who found you on the shore.'

She blinked at the woman. 'Esmil? I know—I think— Esmil? Oh, is my father here? Is Derren the fisherman here? Take me to him.'

The islanders looked at one another.

'What is it? Why won't you answer me?'

A grey-haired man spoke up then. 'Derren – my poor little one, Derren cannot be your father. His name is known to us from tales we heard as children – but he died long, long ago.'

Saranna looked around, slowly, at the first aged and careworn faces she had ever seen. Then she fell to bitter weeping, and the islanders watched her helplessly. Suddenly the door opened and closed and an old woman came to Saranna. 'Now, what's going on here, then?'

'I was coming from my nets and found her on the shore, right by the big rock there,' Gartten answered.

'Where's she from? Who is she?'

'She isn't from these parts, and she was talking all odd, about Derren. What's it all about, Eddarr?'

The old lady put her arm around the weeping Saranna. 'There, there, my pretty. What a state to be in, and none of these people with the sense to lend you a hand. What's the matter with you all? Standing about gawping at her, poor thing! She's cold and tired and hungry and lost. There, there.'

Saranna wailed even louder and leaned against Eddarr's comfortable bosom.

'I give her some of my soup, Eddarr,' said Gartten's wife Allarr. 'She's not been here all that long, we've not had a chance to ask her anything.'

'That's right.'

A babble of voices broke out, all asserting that they had been just about to give their strange visitor everything she could need.

'Oh, whissht, the lot of you! I'll take her home with me, and she can sleep in my poor dear Morrarr's bed. Just think if she had lived, or if one of your daughters as you love so much, had travelled far away. Wouldn't you want someone to care for them? So we must care for her. Come you with Eddarr, dear.'

Saranna followed Eddarr out of the house and along the shore to the tiny cottage where the old woman lived alone. Several of the villagers trailed behind, making sympathetic noises.

'It's true, she's only a child really.'

'Poor soul, she does look done in.'

Eddarr took Saranna into her home, and shooed everyone else away. From that time she took tender care of her, preparing the best food and drink she could, bringing flowers, sea-shells, feathers and leaves to show her, and talking endlessly about the affairs of all her neighbours and of their ancestors for several generations. Although Saranna never responded, the old woman refused to be discouraged. Since the deaths of her own daughter, and of her only sister, she had been lonely in her cottage, and welcomed the chance to care for someone again.

The rest of the villagers were less certain about Saranna. Some of them feared her, and few of them could understand her. The little she said seemed to them mere folly; or perhaps she was mad. She did not join in their work or in their play, but sat by the hearth staring into the fire and only looking up now and then to accept a little food or drink. Eddarr noticed that Saranna clung always to the wooden disc of driftwood that she wore, but did not ask any questions.

Several months passed in this way, until one evening in late summer when Eddarr was sitting with one of the village women on a bench outside the cottage door. The sunlight and summer air streamed into the house, but Saranna was not tempted out;

she stayed in her corner by the hearth.

'You have poor company in that one.' The woman jerked her head in Saranna's direction.

'She's quiet enough, it's true. But I'm glad to have someone to look after again.'

'Small thanks you get for it, Eddarr. She's not much of a daughter to you. Your Morrarr was such a lively, pretty thing, always singing and laughing.'

'I want no thanks, Marek. She's a poor lost thing and someone must care for the lost. We may hear her sing one day, when she comes back to herself.'

Marek leaned closer and lowered her voice; yet Saranna could still hear. 'Is it true she's crazed, do you think? Look what she was like when she came, going on about islands and Gods and somebody's grandmother giving birth to the moon. Whatever was all that about?'

Eddarr drew herself up. 'Crazed is not a kind word, Marek. It's my belief she's seen some great trouble that holds her tight. She'll break free of it in time, with kindness.'

Marek snorted. 'Now would be a good time, then, when every able body should be helping with the harvest. It's a fine life to sit by the hearth and be waited on hand and foot.'

The two old women sat on in companionable silence for a while, watching the slowly darkening sky. Then suddenly a gentle voice startled them. 'Eddarr. Eddarr, please may I take a drink of buttermilk? I can fetch it myself.'

Eddarr turned, a smile lighting up her wrinkled face. Saranna was standing just inside the doorway. 'Of course you can child. And perhaps you will bring some for us?'

'Yes. Yes, I will.'

Marek almost choked on her buttermilk, trying to drink it while staring at Saranna. Soon she hurried home to spread her news, and Eddarr smiled up at her ward. Saranna smiled back. 'Good night, Eddarr,' she said.

'Good night, my dear.'

For two more years Saranna lived with Eddarr on Esmil. She learnt to live as one of the people, planting, harvesting, baking and brewing; mending nets and gutting fish for salting; singing the strange sad songs of the women as she joined in the spinning and the weaving. Her body grew strong and her hands were roughened. Her hair was whitened by the sun and wind and her skin burnt a deep brown. Slowly she learnt to laugh and joke with the other young women. 'S'rannarr' was their name for her, the nearest they could manage to her true name in their own speech. They were rough, but kind, and they became her friends.

'S'rannarr, come and fetch the goats in. I don't like to go alone.'

'All right, Marr. I'll get my shawl.'

Across the summer green of the island they would walk, chattering and cheerful. 'Old Eddarr all right, is she?'

'Yes, very well. Though I do wish she would do a little less work now she's got me to help.'

'She was always a one for hard work. Specially after Morrarr went. Not like some of those lads, now.'

Marr meant the young men who worked the fishing boats.

'It's Krann you mean, no doubt.'

'Oh, S'rannarr, don't tease! I didn't mean anyone particular!'

'Oh, no!' laughed Saranna, jumping quickly to one side to cut off one of the goats. 'I suppose that's why you always happen to be on the beach when his boat's coming in!'

'S'rannarr! I do not!'

'You do!'

'No I don't!'

Still, whenever a storm rose, when the wind howled and the sea lashed at Esmil as if in anger, Saranna grew afraid and hid in her cupboard bed in Eddarr's house, refusing to come out. Eddarr would sit by her, talking and soothing, and when the storm had passed, all would be well again.

But Eddarr was growing old. Soon she became frail and needed Saranna's care. As the old woman grew weaker, Saranna nursed her night and day, washing and feeding and cleaning her, barely sleeping, caring for the house and the patch of garden and the hens and goats. The other women helped, but Saranna would not leave Eddarr's care to anyone else. Eddarr was in a hazy dream, thinking that Saranna was her own lost child.

'You're a good girl, Morrarr, to come back to your old mother now that I need you.'

'Yes, mother. Rest now, don't talk, I'll be here with you. '

'Sit down with me and let me look at you.'

And Saranna would stay with her, catching up on all her work while Eddarr was asleep.

Eddarr grew weaker as the spring days went by and early one morning she slipped into a brief, calm sleep and died with her hand resting in Saranna's. Saranna went quietly to call Marek and some of the other women, and they helped her prepare Eddarr for burial. Throughout that day and the next, Saranna kept herself apart from the villagers: she sat silently with Eddarr. Not until the men had laid the body in the earth and begun to cover it with soil, did she show any sign of grief. Then she wept again as on the day she had first come to Esmil, and the women gathered about her, trying to comfort and console her. 'Come now, child, and rest yourself. You did all that was needed, no daughter could have done more.'

But Saranna shook her head, saying, 'We used to wonder about death.'

For two or three weeks after Eddarr's burial, Saranna went quietly about her work. She continued to live in Eddarr's little house and kept it clean and fresh. The garden was neat too, and the hens and goats well cared for. The villagers approved. 'She's a good girl,' they said. 'It will be best if she marries soon. Some young man will be after her before long, wait and see.'

One wet, cold morning, Saranna was baking in her cottage. There was a good fire in the hearth and she had loaves in the small stone oven built into the chimney. She was kneeling by the griddlecakes, and singing as she worked. The little house was warm and neat and cosy. Just as the scones were cooked, the door flew open with a crash and Saranna looked up, crying out with surprise. At first she thought the wind had risen, but then a stranger came through the door and stood just inside it looking at her. He was a big man, roughly dressed and dirty, and he dripped rainwater onto the clean cottage floor.

'Who are you? What do you want?'

He advanced towards her. 'Kerren's the name, my pretty. And who might you be?'

'I am called Saranna. What are you doing here?' She got up from her knees and moved to put the fresh scones down on the table. Kerren grinned and seized a handful of them. He ate them greedily, ignoring Saranna's cry of protest.

'Any ale?'

'No—only buttermilk. And I say again, who are you? How dare you come in like this?'

He sat down on Eddarr's old chair by the hearth, and smiled again. 'Well, now. I might ask you the same question. What are you doing here?'

'I live here—this is my home.'

'Ah. There it is, you see. I live here too—or I do now. This is my house.'

'How—how can that be? This house was Eddarr's, and I lived here with her.'

'Fair enough. But I, you see, am the old woman's own sister-son. And this here is now my very own property. And here I am all the way from Drent to claim my own. I'm a fisherman, I am, but this nice little place is a better bet than a third-share of a leaky old tub on Drent. Boat here too, isn't there?'

She nodded. Kerren got up and came to the table, where he ate the rest of the scones. He made a lot of noise and a great deal of mess. Saranna watched him silently.

'What am I to do?' she asked when he had finished.

He shrugged. 'Have to find somewhere of your own, my dear. You've no claim on me, you know.'

Saranna lowered her head and began to cry. He leaned across the table and touched her arm, so that she leapt to her feet and backed away, glaring at him. 'All right, all right. Keep calm. I won't hurt you. Sit down again, for goodness sake.'

He sounded a little less menacing now, and Saranna eventually returned to her seat. 'Now,' said Kerren, 'how about this? I'm going to have a lot on, with the land and the boat and all. How would you like the idea of working for me? Keep the house and feed the hens, and all that?' He smiled, lowering his voice carefully. 'You've kept it all very nice, I can see that.'

Saranna looked at the trail of mud and water across the cottage floor. Kerren saw the look and blushed.

'Well, look, I'm sorry. I didn't mean to startle you and mess the place up and that. I suppose I seem a bit rough to you, such a quiet little thing you are. How about giving it a go, eh?'

After a long silence, Saranna nodded.

'Good,' said Kerren 'Now, can I smell burning?'

'Oh!' she cried, and ran to rescue the bread.

It was at the beginning of summer that Kerren came to Esmil. Through the long hot days, he and Saranna got on well enough. He left her alone to care for the house as she had always done, and he was out in his boat a good deal, sometimes by day and sometimes by night, at the mercy of the tides. Even in his leisure hours, Kerren was little trouble to her, preferring to seek the company of the other unmarried men and sit for hours drinking firemilk, than to stay at home with her. Had it not been for the amount he consumed at each meal, and his rough clothes and dirty linen that fell to her care, Saranna might have felt that she still lived alone.

And so the days passed until the autumn and the first storms. As the sun cooled and the days shortened, the people brought their flocks down from the high moors at the centre of the island, to be near the settlement. Rain fell more frequently. The islanders called the rain 'Rannarr's tears' and the storms 'Lannarr's voice.' Saranna heard them and shuddered. She remembered how Iranor had wept as her children drifted away, and how the voice of Ellanna had come to them; she thought of Drewin and felt lost and lonely. The winds rose and became colder and cried more harshly around the little houses by the shore. The sea darkened from blue to leaden green, and flung itself at the rocks and sand.

'Lannarr speaks,' said the people, and went singing down to the beach with wreaths of rough heather, which they cast upon the waves in offering to the Mother. Saranna hung back at the edge of the crowd, gazing fearfully at the waves and the darkening sky. Kerren came and spoke to her gently. 'What is it, girl? What are you afraid of?'

'The sea frightens me,' she answered, turning away.

Now the islanders began to gather in the evenings in each other's houses, to talk and sing and laugh and drink. Wrapped in the warmth of their companionship, they forgot the harsh winter that was deepening around them. Some sat and knitted, some carved driftwood, they all passed the firemilk round; and Kerren came into his own as a teller of funny tales. At one of these gatherings he was keeping the company entertained with all his best stories, and laughter and fellowship filled the room: but Saranna sat alone in a dark corner away from the fire. Kerren came over to her. 'Come on, have some fun for once. You work so hard, now's the time for play,' and he tried to lift her up out of her chair. She pulled away from him.

'No, Kerren, leave me. I'm all right here.'

'Come on, girl, come and have a dance. You've never danced 'til you've danced with Kerren!' He grabbed her by both arms and hoisted her into the air.

'No!' she screamed, 'put me down!'

Kerren dropped her in surprise. 'I'm sorry, Saranna. I didn't mean to upset you, I really didn't. Say you forgive me?'

'No; I am the one who should be sorry. But I cannot dance with you.'

The days passed quietly until the next big gathering. Saranna and Kerren went together, and for a while Saranna seemed content. As the evening drew on, however, Kerren looked up from his drink and caught sight of her across the blazing firelight.

She was sitting in silence, staring into the flames. Her face was tense and her body held stiffly on the low wooden stool. Now and then she turned her head slowly to look out at the black sky through the small high window of the cottage. Kerren saw her shudder, huddle towards the fire and draw her shawl up over her head.

He got up and tried to push through the crowd towards her.

'Shh! Sit down!' people hissed at him. Marne was about to sing, and all talk stopped for Marne. Even Saranna was gazing at the slender young girl as she began her song;

When first you sailed away,
Alone to roam the sea:
Lonely the waves
on the winter shore
of the quiet island.

When you did not come home
I waited by the trees:
Silent the leaves
in the empty grove
drifting down to earth.

When they first said that you
Would not come home to me:
Quiet the tears

that streak my face
when I think of you.
When I think of you alone
Far away from me:
Sore is my heart
when I hear your name
and you are not near me.

Now I cannot speak your name
There is no-one to hear
Silent my grief
as the falling leaves
in the empty land.'

Marne sat down quietly and the room was still. Then suddenly Saranna jumped to her feet, overturning her stool. She screamed like a wounded gull, broke away from the hands of those who reached to help her, and fled from the room. The heavy door crashed back, letting wind and rain into the warm house. The room grew darker and colder, and the slight figure of Saranna disappeared into the blackness outside. Everyone sat stunned and fearful, except Kerren, who rushed after her, calling her name into the howling wind.

At last he caught up with her on the sloping shingle, stumbling on the rasping stones. He fell, staggered up again, and struggled to where Saranna was fighting to drag a small boat down to the waves. He seized her by the shoulders and turned her round. 'Saranna! Are you mad? What are you doing?'

'Let me go,' she screamed, 'let me go!' The wind had torn her shawl away, and her long hair blew wildly about her. Her clothes were wet through, beaten against her body by the ceaseless force of the wind.

He yelled at her, 'Go? Go where? You can't put out to sea in this!'

'She is calling me, and I cannot stay. Can't you hear her? Let me go!' She struggled against his grip and pulled away from him.

He was weeping now. 'Saranna, what is it? I can't hear nothing! Stay with me. Don't you know I love you?'

She broke away, pushing at the boat again. The rising sea had almost taken it when he pulled her back and tried to hold and kiss her. 'Let me go!'

'You'll be killed. No-one can go to sea in this!'

She stopped struggling for a moment and looked at him. 'Kerren, the Lady calls me, and I cannot stay. I hear her in the wind.'

They stood together, listening to the wild wind that tore at them, that sent the sea crashing up the beach, dragging the shingle from under their feet and drenching them with foam. Saranna stood with her eyes closed and her face turned up to the sky; Kerren bent his head, shivering, listening for a voice, but hearing only the wind.

Saranna pulled away from him and he grabbed at her. Springing into the boat, she stood and stretched her arms towards the sea. 'I am coming!' she called.

A huge wave curled under the boat and lifted it away from the shore, away from Kerren and Esmil, and out into the wind. The terrified fisherman watched as the boat was carried beyond his reach. He stood helpless hearing across the waves the sound of her weeping. 'Saranna!' he called again. But she could no longer hear him.

Leartenda

Coldness closed over Drewin's head and he was caught in a swirl of water around the vast bulk of the whale. His mouth was full of bitter brine as he was thrown about by the frothing sea and he could not breathe. He thrashed his arms and legs about, trying to reach the surface, but the more he struggled the further he sank, at the mercy of the water and the whale. Down he went, deeper and deeper, the weight of the whale, the weight of the sea pressing him down into the darkness. His feet plunged into the soft sea-bottom and the whale floated upwards. It circled him three times, gazing emptily at him with one giant eye, then swam away into the darkness. Drewin wallowed in the mud and tried to look about, staring intently to penetrate the clouded water. He tried to clear the swirling shadows from in front of his face, but waving his arms about only made it worse. Eventually he realised the futility of trying to make the mud subside and waited patiently for the water to clear.

After some time the clouds began to settle and he could see, in the distance, a faint green light that seemed to grow slowly brighter as he watched. He took a step towards it, only to sink deeper into the silt and send up another muddy cloud around him so that he floundered about and lost sight of the light. He waited until the cloud had dispersed, then tried to walk towards the light again; but before he had taken two struggling steps his leg was gripped by something so soft and slimy that he launched himself away, half swimming, half crawling to escape from it.

He succeeded in freeing his leg, but in his frantic writhing his elbow hit something solid and he collapsed, clutching his wounded arm. Again he lay still until the water cleared. Cautiously he crawled towards the hard object that had hurt him. He felt it with his hands: it was smooth and large, and flat on top. Drewin climbed out of the mud onto its firm surface and looked once more for the green light. He soon spotted the glow and took one careful step towards it, testing the ground with his foot before putting his weight on it. His first step was on hard rock, and his second. When the third and fourth also found firm ground he stepped forward with greater confidence. He seemed to be on some sort of road about four paces wide that led straight toward the light. He walked along the middle of the road keeping his eyes fixed on the green glow. At first the glow seemed to be getting brighter as he walked towards it, but after a while it started to fade and appeared to be moving away. Drewin stopped and watched it intently. It continued to fade until it became so dim that he thought that it would disappear completely, but then it started to grow stronger and he could see it clearly. He set off once more towards it.

From time to time the light would fade and then he would stop and wait until he could see it clearly, before proceeding. He carried on in this way for hours but he did not seem to be getting nearer to the source of the green glow. Drewin stopped walking, sat down on the road and closed his eyes. His feet were sore, his eyes were stinging and his body ached with the cold. Around him there was no sound, no movement except the gentle strong surge of the sea pushing this way and that. He rested his head on his knees and fell asleep. When he opened his eyes he found that he was buried almost up to his waist in sand, and small brightly-coloured fish were nibbling inquisitively at his hair and ears. He struggled upright and the fish darted away in all directions. Drewin found that he felt much less stiff and weary, and decided he must have been asleep for a long time. He looked towards the light, far off in the distance, and set out along the path in the hope of finally reaching it. After he had trudged for hours with only the wandering shoals of fish for company, the light looked brighter, more blue than green, and it flickered and danced in swirling patterns that confused the eye. Drewin moved forward, his eyes confused by the turning patterns in the light that now seemed to surround him. His legs carried him into the midst of the confusion then stopped. Shapes dived and danced about him in the dark, half seen in the hazy blue glow. He turned to right and left trying to gain a clear view of them, but when he looked they were no longer there. He stepped back but they followed him, coming so close that he could feel the disturbance they made in the water. Once or twice he felt a cold touch on his cheek and there was a sound that might have been laughter. He spun round to avoid them, he waved his arms about to fend them off, he shouted soundlessly at them, but it made no difference and finally he closed his eyes, fell to the ground, and covered his head with his arms. But this had no effect: his tormentors carried on their furious dance. Feeling around in the dark, Drewin found something solid. It was a thick strand of seaweed. Grasping it tightly he suddenly leapt to his feet and flailed blindly about. The maddening motion ceased and he opened his eyes to see what had happened. Everything was still and the blue glow was steady. In its light Drewin could make out eleven figures suspended in the water ahead of him. Their green and scaly bodies undulated in the ebb and flow of the sea-current and long white hair streamed out behind their pale faces. They were pointing at Drewin: they seemed to think him very funny.

Enraged by their laughter he advanced on them holding his seaweed club ready. The glittering beings drew back in mock alarm, then danced a pattern in the water weaving and swirling, and laughing all the time until they had arranged themselves in a straight line across Drewin's path. Huge silver swords appeared in their hands and they loped forward frowning fiercely. Drewin faltered, but as soon as he stopped the swords turned to seaweed and the white-haired dancers burst into uncontrollable laughter once more and threw away their weapons.

Then they turned away and swam towards the blue light, beckoning to him to follow them. They moved slowly through the water so that he could keep up with them. Occasionally one would execute a little dance, darting ahead of the group or looping overhead and arriving behind Drewin, then swimming quickly past him to one side or the other or even above his head. They seemed to delight in their skill and no longer laughed at Drewin in spite of his slow and clumsy progress through their element. At last they came to their destination; an opening in a wall of rock that rose from the sea floor to a great height. He peered up at the massive barrier, but could not make out how high it was. The entrance arched far above him as he passed through it with his companions and a few stray fish. He found himself inside an enormous cavern that stretched as far as he could see. Everything within it gave off a bluish glow that Drewin found dazzling after the darkness of the sea outside, and the water felt warmer. His guides floated gently to the ground around Drewin and waited, smiling, as he admired their home. He was not aware of them as he tried to make out the details of this new world stretched out before him. The high roof of the cavern sparkled with small shiny fish darting about in flowing waves that reflected the pervasive blue light; below this display was spread a city built of rock formed into fluid organic shapes that sprawled over the floor and soared up into towers and pinnacles. Between and above them, through them and out of them swam all manner of creatures: some looked like fish and some like human beings, and some like both; they had arms and tails, or fins and legs, and some sprouted tentacles; some were blue and green, some were orange and red, and some were all the colours of the rainbow.

'Welcome to Leartenda, honoured visitor. We, the guardians of the entrance, greet you in the name of the Leaa.'

Drewin was startled and returned his attention to his guides. 'You can speak! I can hear!'

They all smiled at this, and the one who had spoken before, a tall creature, whose scales were orange and purple, answered him. 'This place is not of the sea outside, which is cold and silent and dark. Here there is warmth and sound and light. Here there is laughter and music and joy. Here you are an honoured guest. I will conduct you to the palace while my friends guard the portal. Come.'

The guardian took Drewin's hand and led him down into the city. He followed, as if in a trance, along a tortuous route between the flowing shapes of the dwellings of Leartenda. There were no straight roads and most of the inhabitants travelled by swimming above the roofs of their houses. In spite of this Drewin often found his path obstructed by the fishlike beings who stood singly or in groups all about the place: some were deep in conversation, some were singing, some were dancing, some lay across the way and some stood on their heads. The swimmers hurried this way and that in the water above.

'There seems to be great agitation here. Is there some trouble?'

'They dance the dance of life, as all creatures do. This is a time of haste. Come, we must hurry too.' With this the being pulled Drewin onward, and rushed faster than before in and out of the narrow passages, under rippling arches and past all the living obstructions. Drewin often failed to keep his feet but he was nevertheless pulled along at an ever-increasing pace. The sights of the city became a blur and he had little time to take in the scenes that passed by, and no time at all to ask questions.

They rushed on through the bewildering spectacle until they reached some tall buildings that Drewin had seen from the gate. Here they stopped and Drewin looked around. He was in a broad open space, the only one he had so far seen in Leartenda, with a tall thin tower in front of him and shorter more massive ones on either side. His companion, who had been watching him approvingly, took him by both hands and smiled. 'I am called by my friends Reva-mal. Please call me Reva-mal. How are you called by your friends?'

'I am Drewin. Thank you for taking me as your friend.'

'I can see that you admire our Meeting Place, Drewin. Is it not the most wonderful place that you have ever seen? Are these not the tallest houses that you have ever seen? Tell me what you really think, Drewin. But is this not a marvellous place?'

'Truly Reva-mal, I have never seen such a place as Leartenda.

And in Leartenda this Meeting Place is the most wondrous I have so far seen.'

'You really think so? That is your true opinion? It is the most remarkably extraordinary place you have ever seen?'

'Yes, that is my honest opinion.'

'Good. I am glad. This always seems the most wonderful place to me, and I am glad that you agree. But now you must meet Arnuma-leaa. Come.'

Reva-mal hurried towards the tall tower and Drewin followed at a trot. The entrance to the tower was high above the ground and was approached by a long ramp of shallow steps. Reva-mal ran swiftly up while Drewin followed more cautiously. At the top the Leaa stopped and waited for Drewin to catch up. 'This is the High Door. We could have come in by the Low Door but this is grander don't you think? Look at the view!'

Drewin turned to look then quickly turned back. 'We are very high here. Can we go inside? I think I would feel safer.'

His companion laughed. 'This is not high! You wait! Let us go in, I cannot wait to show you.'

They stepped in through the narrow entrance and onto a smooth hard surface that sloped up to the right and down to the left. A faint pink glow seeped through the walls creating the effect of sunset on a misty evening. There was nothing to be seen but the wide sloping floor that curved round a central column, the outer wall fused to the edge of the floor and, up above, a curving sloping ceiling that echoed the form of the floor. While Drewin was taking in this scene Reva-mal watched his face with a look of delighted expectation. 'Amazing! Is it not amazing? Come, there is more.'

Drewin followed his guide up the curving ramp. The way was steeper now and while they climbed neither of the companions had breath to speak. As they neared the top of the tower the passage narrowed and the ceiling became lower, but there was still enough width for them to walk side by side and plenty of headroom. It was a hard climb and Drewin began to slow down. 'Is there much further to go? Shall we rest?'

'No. Nearly there. Come on.' Reva-mal grabbed him by the arm and pulled him up the final slope and into a wide chamber that occupied the top of the tower. Drewin collapsed onto the level floor, exhausted, while Reva-mal bent over him holding his hand and looking concerned.

Then a loud voice echoed round the chamber. 'Who's there?'

Reva-mal released Drewin's hand, stood up and looked around. 'Are you there, Arnuma-leaa? I can't see you.'

'I am here. Where else would I be? I couldn't be anywhere else but here could I? Now I have answered your question, but you haven't answered mine. Is it too difficult?' If anything the voice was louder than before, but the speaker was not visible.

'It is only me, Reva-mal. And I have brought the outsider. But I cannot see you: where are you?'

'I am here,' the voice boomed, 'do I have to tell you everything twice? Would three times be better? I am here, where I am and I couldn't be anywhere else, could I? Can you be somewhere where you are not? Even if you can, I can't.'

Drewin was standing beside his guide now and trying to work out where the voice was coming from. The two visitors went further into the room and started to look behind and under the various objects that were scattered about the floor; a battered rocking-horse, three large soft cubes of some spongy material, a huge chest made entirely of exquisite mother-of-pearl, a rolled-up carpet and several things that Drewin could not recognise at all. No further clue came from Arnuma-leaa until they had given up and joined each other near the middle of the dome.

A pink structure rose up from the floor, turning as it rose. When it had risen to twice the height of Drewin, its top opened like a flower to reveal Arnuma-leaa seated on a crystalline throne, laughing.

'Welcome! Welcome! Welcome! Come, sit and talk with me.'

Drewin looked up at Arnuma-leaa in amazement. The figure on the throne looked similar to Reva-mal except that its scales were golden red its the hair was green, but the face that gazed down on him was the face of a monstrous fish with round staring eyes and a mouth full of sharp thin teeth that gave the impression of a permanent predatory grin. 'Sit down. Sit down. No standing on ceremony here. Sit and tell me your story. Why are you here? Where have you come from? How did you get here? Where are you going? What is your name? Tell me all.'

Drewin and Reva-mal sat down on low stools nearby and Arnuma-leaa lowered the pink throne to the floor. 'My name is Drewin and I come from above the sea. I ...'

'Above the sea, you say. We know of this. Oh yes, you may think we are ignorant down here in the depths, but we know many things. Is that not so Reva-mal?'

Reva-mal turned to Drewin and spoke earnestly. 'It is true Drewin, my friend- we know many things.'

'I did not think that you did not,' protested Drewin. 'Shall I continue?'

'Drewin did not think that we did not,' Reva-mal reported.

'I am glad to hear it, Reva-mal. I am glad to hear it. Very glad. Now Drenn will you answer my questions? Nobody answers my questions these days: they used to, but they seem to have got out of the habit.' Arnuma-leaa blew out a stream of bubbles and the two staring eyes closed slowly and stayed closed for several moments. Suddenly they opened again and fixed Drewin with their hypnotic gaze. 'Go on. Tell your story, Drenn, if you can.'

Drewin made a fresh start. 'It is quite simple. I...'

'Simple is it? Good.'

'Yes. You see, I was...'

'No I do not see. I cannot see the past. If I could see what you were telling me I would not ask you to tell me, would I? Don't answer that, tell me your story.'

'We were in a boat when...'

'Are you royalty then?'

Drewin hesitated and turned to Reva-mal for some explanation. But Reva-mal was staring into the distance apparently unaware of the conversation. Drewin turned back to the figure on the throne.

'You said 'we were in a boat'. There is only one of you. It takes two to make a 'we', does it not? Only royal ones are 'we', in my experience. I told you that we know things in Leartenda. We know that! I sometimes use 'we' myself, when I am feeling grand, because I am royal. But you say you are not. Explain.'

'My sister and I were in a boat when...'

'Sister? What is that? Is it a person? You must not make assumptions. We do not know everything you know.'

'My sister is the woman-child of my mother.'

'Ah! I see! Now tell me: what is a woman and what is a mother?'

Drewin looked puzzled, then answered slowly. 'A woman is one who can bear young and a mother is one who has borne young. Do you not have these words?'

'We have no need of useless words. Since all people can give birth to children, why should there be special words for them? One might as well have names for those who swim, when all people can swim.'

Arnuma-leaa started to chuckle then burst into noisy laughter. Drewin waited for the noise to die down before speaking again. 'But where I come from not all people can bear children. I cannot, for I am a man.'

At this, both Arnuma-leaa and Reva-mal stared at Drewin in horror. Reva-mal spoke first. 'You cannot bear children?'

'No. Where I come from only half the people can do that: women. I am a man.'

Arnuma's eyes closed and then opened again slowly. 'Man and woman?'

'Yes. May I continue my story? My sister Saranna and I were in a boat on the sea above here. You know what a boat is?'

'Boats? Yes. A nuisance: they litter the land all about us. Make the place most untidy. Now stop asking me questions and get on with your tale.'

'There is not much to tell. We were in a small boat when suddenly a great whale came up out of the sea and I was thrown out of the boat. As I struggled to swim back to Saranna the whale came on top of me and pushed me to the sea bottom. I saw the light of Leartenda and came towards it. Then I was met by Reva-mal and brought here. That is the whole story.'

Arnuma gazed at Drewin for a long while before speaking. 'No—that is not the whole story. A story is not just the what, it must also be the why. You say a whale brought you down here? Well, there is a reason for that. We must find the reason. What could be the reason? Do you know, Drewin?'

'No. I do not.'

'Yes you do.'

'No I don't.'

'Yes you do. You may not think you do, but you do. Tell me, why were you in this boat? What passed before you were in the boat, before you met the whale?'

'We lived together on the island of the West Wind.'

'Then you are under the care of Iranor? You see, we do know many things; we know of Iranor.'

'She was our mother, but she cast us out. We may not return to our home, and we will die.'

Arnuma leapt up off the throne with a great cry. 'This is it! Here we have a reason! If Iranor, beloved of the islanders, cast you out with your sister you must have done some great evil. You have been brought here for a reason! Tell me, what did you and your sister do? What crime justifies such punishment?'

Drewin bowed his head before the accusing look of Arnuma and the shocked expression on the face of Reva-mal. The chamber was still and silent, waiting for Drewin's answer. 'I love my sister. My sister loves me. Our crime was to show our love for each other by exchanging runes.'

Arnuma interrupted. 'What are runes?'

'Oh—they are a sort of letter or sign. Like this.'

Drewin showed Arnuma and Reva-mal the carved disc he wore, and Reva-mal studied it closely, exclaiming at its beauty and delicacy. 'My sister has the rune that belonged to me, and this is hers. It is the law of the Immortals that each must guard one rune, and never give it into the care of another. I do not understand why, but Ellanna herself told us that we had done an evil thing and so it must be true.' Drewin stopped speaking and waited fearfully for the response to his confession. Reva-Mal looked bewildered, but Arnuma-Leaa shouted, 'All mad! I knew it – they are all mad!'

Reva-mal added, 'Poor Drewin – you must be so sad and lonely.' Then he sat down on the floor and went to sleep.

'I know!' roared Arnuma, 'You must find out about us. I dare say you find everything strange here. Ask us some questions and we will answer them. If we can! Ha!'

Arnuma started to walk up and down the room impatiently while waiting for Drewin's first question. 'How did this land come to be? Why is it not known in the world above?'

'Some above know of us—some fear us, and a few look into the depths with love and understanding. But those few are looked on as mad by their fellows. As for us, we are content enough as we are: we do not seek out those of the world above but some come to us as you have. And they are welcome, as you are welcome.'

'Thank you for that, Arnuma-leaa, but you have not told me how this land and its people came to be.'

'A good question, and an important one, I think. This land and all its people is the oldest land of Skorn: we came to be as Ellanna descended into the sea to rest from the making of the world. Ellanna herself cares for us now.'

'Do you think, then, that Ellanna has brought me here deliberately?'

'Undoubtedly! That is why I thought your question was important. But what now? What now? Where is Reva-mal?'

Arnuma walked back to the middle of the chamber and stood over the sleeping Reva-mal. The ruler of Leartenda watched quietly as the figure on the floor slowly awoke. 'That's right. Time to wake up. Time to take our guest to find somewhere to stay.'

Reva-mal rose wearily from the floor and blinked at Drewin. 'Come, I have a surprise for you.' The guardian took Drewin's hand and led him to the far side of the chamber where there was an opening in the wall. There was no stairway or ramp leading down to the city below, just a vertical drop. Drewin pulled back, but Reva-mal gripped his hand firmly and leapt through the gap. They floated downwards while Arnuma watched them from above. Reva-mal released Drewin and start to dive and swoop through the water with his arms outstretched, laughing. 'Guide yourself with your arms. Pretend you are a fish!'

Drewin flapped his arms and succeeded in turning himself upside-down. He closed his eyes and screamed in terror, but Reva-mal came to his side and showed him how to control his swimming.

Gradually, Drewin learnt to glide and swoop like a bird above the city, and he was able to follow Reva-mal down to a safe landing on the roof of one of the buildings. Reva-mal landed in front of Drewin and bowed. 'Welcome to my home! This way. Follow me!'

Drewin followed his host down a ramp into the dwelling below where he found a single comfortable room enclosed by curved translucent walls. 'Sit down, Drewin. Make yourself comfortable, and I will get some food. I expect you are hungry after your long journey.'

Drewin sat down on one of the chairs and sank into its soft

covering. 'I am. Hungry and tired. I had forgotten my body, here in Leartenda.'

Drewin sat and talked as Reva-mal cut and arranged fish and sea-plants into elegant forms. 'It is so peaceful here. I had forgotten everything, but now it comes back to me: the cold, the sea, the whale. And where is Saranna? She will not be able to manage without me. I promised mother I would look after my little sister, and now she is alone and lost on the open sea, while I sit safely here.'

'Do not blame yourself, Drewin, it is clear from your story that this was all the work of the whale. And the whales are Ellanna's creatures too: they do her will.'

The meal was soon ready and the two companions ate it quickly in friendly silence. Drewin was the first to speak once the food was finished. 'That was delicious. I have never before tasted such food. Everything in Leartenda seems to be new and wonderful: a delight. But Arnuma said that we should find me somewhere to stay. Is that difficult?'

'I don't think so. Do you like my home? Say yes and you can stay here.'

'Thank you. That would be wonderful.'

'Good. That's settled then.' Reva-mal showed Drewin a small chamber that he could use and gave him some cushions and other things to make him comfortable. 'Now I must show you round the city: this time we go more slowly.'

They left the house through an arched entrance that opened onto a narrow passage between buildings of different sizes. As they walked along it, the path widened and narrowed chaotically, sometimes wide enough for ten people to walk along side by side and sometimes so narrow that Drewin and

Reva-mal had to walk in single file. The route they followed weaved in and out between the houses so that sometimes they seemed to double back and sometimes go round in circles, Drewin was bewildered. He stopped and looked back to see if he could get his bearings on some landmark, but there was nothing he could recognise. He tried to recall the way back to Reva-mal's home, but without success. He tried to find the tall towers of the middle of the city, but his view was obscured by the surrounding buildings.

Finally he gave up and turned to follow Reva-mal; but Reva-mal was not there. Drewin ran down the path that he thought Reva-mal had followed and found himself in the midst of a jostling and noisy crowd. He turned back and tried to find the place where he had stopped, but when he thought he had reached it everything was different. He ran to where he had seen the crowd but found himself in a wide empty street. He listened for the noise of people, but everything was quiet. He was lost.

He peered along each of the paths that led away from where he stood. There were four of them, each was different from the others, but none of them gave any indication of where it led, he looked again: there was no reason why he should go down one rather than another. Drewin walked aimlessly along one of the paths and at each junction he came to he chose a direction at random. Sometimes be found himself at a place that looked familiar, and tried to pick a different route, but he could never remember what his original choice had been and so he went round in circles. He became aware of this when he came, for the third time, to an open space with a statue at its centre. He walked towards the statue and then round it. When he reached the far side he nearly tripped over a small creature lying on the ground gazing up at the stone figure. He jumped back in surprise.

'Oh! I did not know that you were there.'

The being, which looked more like a fish than a person, looked at Drewin coldly. 'Why should you?' it murmured, and returned its attention to the statue.

Drewin waited for some further response, but none came. 'I wonder if you could help me. I am lost.'

The creature continued to stare at the statue and spoke as if to itself. 'Do you? Are you?'

Drewin nudged it with his foot to attract its attention. 'Will you help me?'

'What do you think of this statue?'

Drewin stepped back and looked up at the statue for the first time: he let out a cry and backed away, staring. It was the perfect image of Saranna. Every detail was correct; her hair, her eyes, the texture of her skin, the way she held her head. The creature looked at him languidly. 'It is good, isn't it?'

'It is my sister!'

'Is it?'

'Why, how, is there a statue of my sister here?'

'Why not? How not?' the creature asked, and returned its attention to the work of art.

Drewin approached the statue and put his hand to its cheek to feel the familiar contours of his sister's face. He let his hand move slowly over the smooth, cold stone, touching the brow, the nose, the mouth, the throat, until it came to a plaited cord, cunningly carved, and a medallion, decorated with leaves, that bore the rune Ord. His hand went to his own neck, pulled out the matching amulet, and placed it beside the stone carving. The copy was perfect; every leaf, every line was just as he had carved it.

'What does this mean? It is as if Saranna had been frozen into stone and placed here. How can it be?' He turned to the preoccupied figure lying on the ground.

'You! Tell me. Who made this statue? Why is it here?' he shouted.

The art lover tore its gaze away from the object of its adoration and looked at Drewin curiously. 'How should I know?'

Drewin knelt down beside the creature and jabbed it with a finger. 'Who are you? Why do you answer my questions with questions?'

'What business is it of yours? Who gave you the right to go around poking people with your bony fingers?'

'I am sorry,' said Drewin, standing up, 'but I do not understand how these things can be. Who can tell me?'

'Why not ask your sister?'

Drewin turned back to the statue and gazed at it for a short while before answering. 'But I have lost her. I do not know where she is. Do you know where she is?'

'Why not ask your brother?'

'I have no brother.'

The creature lifted itself lazily from the ground and swam towards Drewin until their noses nearly touched. 'Haven't you?' it asked, and swam up and over the surrounding buildings, leaving Drewin alone once more.

Drewin stood lost in thought, looking at the image of his sister.

'If only you could speak to me.' The stone Saranna seemed to return his stare, with its empty, lifeless eyes. 'What does this mean? Why do you stand there? It is impossible that you have been here before me, but if not how do you come to be here now? Speak to me, little sister.' The statue's silence was absolute. Drewin ran at it and grasped its hard unyielding arms. 'Speak to me! Why do you not speak to me? Are you alive or dead? Should I seek you?' Suddenly he came to himself. He stepped back and looked once more at the cold figure of Saranna.

'No. You are dead. That is what this means. I am alone, and must find my own way.' He looked around to see if he could work out which way to go, but all the roads looked the same and he had forgotten how he had arrived there. Then he looked up and saw the creatures of Leartenda swimming about in the water above his head.

'Of course! There is no need to be lost here when I can swim up and see the whole city from above! Why did no-one tell me?'

Forgetting about the statue, he swam up until he was higher than the roofs of the houses, then higher still so that he could see the whole city laid out before him. Wearied by his effort he trod water, hovered above the bustling scene below, and looked for some landmark. He soon spotted Arnuma's tower and at once started to swim towards it, quickly arriving at the entrance to Arnuma's chamber at the top of the tower. He landed on his feet inside, relieved to see something that he recognised at last.

'Ah! There you are, Der-en. I was wonder you had got to. Where have you been?'

'I was lost in the city. I got separated from Reva-mal and came across something wonderful. It was a statue....

'Lost? That should not happen. Are you sure that you were lost?'

Drewin hesitated before answering. 'Why, yes. At least I think so. Yes, I was definitely lost: I did not know how to get to where I was going. But eventually I remembered that I could swim up, and so I came back here. I want to tell you what I have learnt.'

But Arnuma was not listening to him: he was walking around in little circles and looking puzzled. 'Oh dear. I do not understand this at all. It is impossible to get lost in Leartenda because there is nowhere to go. How did you know that you were lost?'

'I did not know which way to go.'

'Oh dear! And where were you trying to get to?'

'I don't know. I lost Reva-mal and so I tried to go where we had been going.'

'And where had you been going?'

'I don't know. If I had known I would not have been lost.'

'But there is nowhere to go. Do you not see that? You cannot get lost if there is nowhere to go.'

'What are you saying, Arnuma-Leaa? It does not make sense.'

'Sense? What has that got to do with it? Here in Leartenda no one can be lost. As the saying goes: 'Heart is where the Home is'. Only those who turn away from the love of Ellanna can be lost here.'

'But you said that I was welcome here! Now you are saying that I am not. It is not my fault! I did not choose to leave the island: Ellanna abandoned us and withheld her love.'

'Yes. Yes, I can see that. And that means you should not

be here. I was wrong to greet you as I did. It is clear that you are not at rest; you are going somewhere. That is why you were lost. You were going somewhere. Now the question is: where are you going?'

'I do not know.'

'Then you must find out. Go back down into the city and find your way; you will not get lost again.'

So saying, Arnuma turned and walked away. Drewin stood watching the ruler for a moment, expecting him to speak again; to say some words of farewell and encouragement. But when Arnuma's back remained resolutely turned, Drewin went to the opening in the wall and launched himself out over the city. He swam in ever widening circles, until he approached the edge of the cavern and the rocks that surrounded the city. He swept past the opening that led to the cold outer sea and saw the guardians at their posts. From here he noticed what had been hidden from him on his arrival at the gateway—a pair of heavy stone doors was folded back against the inner wall of the cavern. Drewin could just make out the carved patterns on them. He allowed himself to drift down until he was swimming a little above the roofs of the houses. As he did this he drifted away from the portal and found himself heading for the opposite side of Leartenda. He was now looking at the base of the soaring rock wall as he circled round, and could see that it was not natural: there was a difference in colour that showed that the wall was made of a different substance from the rock of the cavern floor. Drewin floated down, landed next to the wall and started to look closely at the smooth rock.

'Is it not wonderful?' Drewin jumped at the sound of Reva-mal's voice. 'It was made long ago by our ancestors. A monumental enterprise indeed. Is it not?'

'Yes, but how? No mortal beings could do such a thing.'

'No; but they were no more mortal than you and I; and they had the aid of Ellanna. It is good to meet with you again, Drewin.'

'Yes indeed, Reva-mal. How do you come to be here?"

'It is my duty to be here. I am a Guardian of the Gate for the time being.'

'But the Gate is on the far side of the city, over there!' said Drewin, pointing towards the portal.

'Oh yes, the Seagate. But we Guardians watch over both the entrances.'

'You mean there is another Gate?'

'Oh yes. Come, I will show you.' Reva-mal turned and hurried away, and Drewin trotted behind.

'You will see that the wall ends soon, and natural rock takes its place. See?' Reva-mal stopped for a moment and pointed to a place where a join could be seen between the wall and the rock. 'This is where Leartenda is linked with Akent, the land. We lie between the sea and the land: we are the link. Here is a refuge from the sea beyond—Leartenda; and a refuge, too, from the land—arakent. For you, since you came from the sea, we are Leartenda: if anyone should come from the land, we would be Learakent. It is all quite clear. Here is the gate.'

They stopped by a pair of massive stone doors covered with elaborate carvings, similar to those on the sea gates. Drewin ran his hands over the carvings.

'Why are they closed, if all strangers are welcome?'

'Are all strangers welcome? I do not know. But it is my duty to watch over the gate and to welcome those who come to us. I, at least, have never turned anyone away, but I suppose I might, if it was the correct thing to do. '

'I am turned away.'

'What? Oh no, Drewin, you are welcome. I welcomed you myself. '

'But when we were separated in the city I was lost. If I belonged here I would not have been lost. Arnuma-Leaa said so.'

'But you are found now! Now you are found, it is all repaired. Everything is all right now!'

'I think I know why that is. I am in the right place because this is the way for me to leave Leartenda.'

'You cannot leave. No-one ever leaves. Please stay here and share your life with us. Is this not a beautiful place?' Tears welled up in Reva-mal's eyes.

'Yes, it is, my friend. But I fear that I do not belong here. For me this is the way to somewhere else. I am not immortal as you are, l am not beloved of Ellanna as you are.' Now Drewin wept and the two friends met in warm embrace, their tears streaming down their faces.

Reva-mal slowly pulled away, held Drewin at arm's length, and looked into his eyes. 'If this must be, then I must accept it, though it breaks my heart. I am the guardian of this gate, and it is my duty to greet those who enter and to say farewell to those who leave. It is my duty, but I take no pride or pleasure in it.'

The Leaa turned away and touched a section of the rock-face close to the door. A small panel opened to reveal stores of food, some of which Reva-mal packed into a bag for Drewin. 'This is my gift to you; I wish it were more worthy of our friendship. But the bag at least you may keep to remind you of

Leartenda, and of me.

Drewin took the bag, wondering what gift he could give in exchange. Then he thought of his carvings, and took the hinged wooden link from the thong about his neck, thinking that he would never need it to join Saranna's amulet to his own; he would never see her again. 'My gift for you, Reva-mal; I too wish that I had more to give as a reminder of me.'

Reva-mal was delighted, and hugged his friend again before saying sadly, 'Farewell, Drewin. May peace attend your path.'

Drewin looked one last time on the face of Reva-mal, then turned away and pushed at the doors.

Academy

*I*nto the harbour of Drelk on a bright, spring morning a merchant ship sailed, laden down with cloth of IssKor and wine from Mardara. Also on board was a passenger, a young man in a coarse-spun robe such as the desert wanderers of IssKor wear to shield themselves from the blistering sun and the parching wind. He stood on the foredeck, gazing up at the town that climbed above him on its three hills, holding ready in his hand the one small, battered leather satchel that was all his luggage. His thick black hair was whipped by the breeze, his slight frame balanced easily as the ship crested the diminishing waves, and the crew looked askance at him as they had throughout the voyage.

'Think he was coming to the Lady's isle, the look on his face.'

'He's a dreamer—or two knuckles short of a fourteen, more like. Schooled by them priests in that benighted land—can't be right, like, can he?'

'Sssh! He's coming this way, he'll hear.'

'Not him—got his head in the clouds, that one. Some kind of magician, I shouldn't wonder. Uncanny, that's what I say.'

As they came alongside the conversation was cut short, and the object of it, all unaware, placed himself amidships, ready to be first out and away. Before the ropes were made fast, he was over the side, landing nimbly on the jetty and setting off towards the town without a break in his stride or a backward glance. The busy sailors soon lost sight of him, nor did they ever again trouble themselves over the fate of Kor-Sen of Sen-Mar.

Kor-Sen himself found his fate pleasing enough as he strode though the busy market streets of Drelk. The town was busier and noisier and happier than his native city, and the people were brightly dressed and prosperous-looking, going about their business with more cheerfulness than in priest-ridden Sen-Mar. Some called out a greeting to him as he passed, and if others looked down their noses at his homespun robe and worn leather sandals, that was no trouble to him. He wandered happily about for some time, looking at everything as if he were new-born into a world of delights; then he paused for refreshment outside an inn that had benches and tables spilling over onto the roadway outside its little tap-room. Children materialised like magic at his feet.

'Got a spare coin, Sir?'

'IssKor money, Sir?'

'How do you know that I am from IssKor? I might be a wandering fiend from the northern wastes, come here to eat up wicked children.'

He thrust his face towards them and growled, scattering them all screaming in every direction. One girl stuck her head back round a corner to hiss, 'Smelly old goat-hair—must be from IssKor. 'Smell like a goat and stupid as a donkey, do what the priest says, OR YOU'RE DEAD!"

Kor-Sen roared with laughter as she vanished, and made a mental note of the rhyme. He was becoming interested in the beliefs and stories and legends of different peoples; indeed, he was becoming interested in everything.

He settled his bill. 'Which way to the Academy, Landlord?'

'Carry on up this hill, young man. But I warn you, they won't take just anyone up there, if it's a job you're after. I hear all the servants' jobs are filled for the moment.'

Kor-Sen laughed again. "I thank you for your advice, kind sir. But such was not my object.'

He whistled his way up the hill, up steeper and steeper streets where the houses crowded together as if for support. Kor-Sen thought that if you were to remove the lowest house, then all the others would tumble down the hill and splash into the harbour. The mental image cheered him still further, so that when he reached the top of the hill and found himself crossing a broad square towards a grim, grey building, he was full of confidence.

A high, imposing arch pierced the long frontage of the Academy; Kor-Sen stepped boldly under it and was making for the inner courtyard thus revealed, when a stern voice cried, 'Hey! Where do you think you're a-going of, without so much as please-may-I?'

Kor-Sen turned, and saw an indignant old man dressed in livery, who had just come out of a door set in the side-wall of the archway.

'And who might you be, my crusty old friend?'

The porter's face grew purple. 'None of your impudence!' he spluttered. 'You can't come a-marching in here like you owned the place! This is the Academy of Drelk, this is, which I doubt you knew, young ragamuffin. And I am the porter on duty, and it is my job to ensure that none don't get in here as has no business here. So! Either state your business—which I doubt you have any—or be off. '

Kor-Sen bowed, a deep and courtly bow that startled the porter and nearly overbalanced him. 'Most reverend keeper of the portals of learning, I am Kor-Sen, Scholar of the Temple of Jaren in the land of IssKor, come to bestow the benefit of my wisdom upon this humble establishment. My business is with the Convenor and the Council, and is, I submit, urgent. They will not thank you if you allow this opportunity to slip away, while you cavil on the doorstep. I might decide to endow my learning elsewhere.'

The porter's confusion was deepened by this speech. He was further discomfited by the laughter of several students, men and women just a little younger than Kor-Sen, who, passing through the gateway, had stopped to watch the battle of wits.

'Better let him in, Moran. Sounds as if he could tie the Convenor up in knots, let alone you.'

Kor-Sen bowed to the speaker, and winked at the women, who smiled at him.

Moran spluttered again, but then made up his mind. 'Well, Aspirant Coren, if you would stay here and have an eye to this—person—I will go and enquire.'

Gathering the remnants of his dignity around him, he set off across the court, the laughter of the students following him. They all clustered round Kor-Sen and asked him eager questions, but he replied only briefly, contenting himself with mysterious smiles.

Soon Moran the Porter returned, more flustered than ever. 'That way—straight across the court—past the fountain—centre door. Knock and wait, if you please.'

Kor-Sen, with one more deep and silent bow, obeyed.

'Enter!'

Kor-Sen pushed open the heavy wooden door, and found himself in a small ante-room, furnished as an office with desk and carven chair and shelves full of scrolls and sheets of parchment. The room was occupied by a harassed-looking man of middle years, who seemed slightly dusty and a little frail, as if himself made of aged parchment.

'The foreign student? Kor-something? Well?'

Kor-Sen bowed a less exaggerated bow than the previous ones, and admitted that he was indeed the person referred to.

'Well—the Convenor and Council will see you now. I hope you appreciate your good fortune, it is not at all in order, walking in off the street and making demands and so forth.' He twitched his drab robe closer around himself.

Kor-Sen murmured appreciatively. The secretary sniffed, and knocked at an inner door, thrusting his head inside the room in response to the answering summons.

'The peasant-lad from IssKor, Sirs and Madam.'

This silenced Kor-Sen effectively until he was inside the inner room—a large, impressive chamber heavy with wooden panelling—and seated on a chair before a polished wooden table, behind which sat a stern old man with a shiny bald head. He was flanked by two other men, rather younger, and at one end of the table a woman, about thirty years old, was seated. All these people regarded Kor-Sen with steady, unreadable gaze. The oldest man spoke.

'Greetings, young traveller. I am Cren, Master of the Division of Thought, and Convenor of the Academy. On my right is Master Torran of the Division of Number, and on my left Master Danel of the Division of Language. The lady Igrade is master of the Division of Form. Together, as the Council, we govern the Academy. What is your purpose here?'

'Greetings to you, most learned Masters. I seek to enter the Academy as an aspirant.'

'In what division?' the Master Igrade asked.

'All of them—it should not take me long to master the Four Branches,' answered Kor-Sen cheerfully.

Cries of protest came from the Council.

'My dear young man—how old are you, by the way?'

'Twenty-five years, Lord Convenor.'

'Really? I should have supposed you to be younger. No matter, it would take you twenty years to master ail the Divisions, it has never been done. Each aspirant must elect to study one Division, or branch, of learning, and must study for five years to earn the appellation, Master. Then the most gifted may stay to teach, to continue their studies, and then by right of seniority, to sit upon the council. What you propose is impossible; none has ever sought to master more than one Branch.'

'Nothing less than the whole tree for me, though,' said the irrepressible candidate. 'I do not much like Division, a negative sort of notion, I feel. I shall start in the fifth year of language, then do the fifth years of each of the others in turn, so I will easily be Master of them all in four years. And then I would like nothing better than to teach the rising hopefuls below me.'

He beamed at them all, while they stared first at him and then at one another.

'I don't believe you could do it!' Torran slapped his hand down on the table. 'I do not believe it!'

'Nor I—the fellow's mad. What is the Temple of Sen-Mar, that he should dare to come here challenging us in this way? '

Cren turned from Torran and Danel, and looked inquiringly at Igrade. She was studying Kor-Sen thoughtfully, and he was reurning her stare for stare. Then she turned to the Lord Convenor.

'I say try him, Master. There is a certain air of—confidence about him. He obviously believes he can do it. Let him try, then; it is he who will be a laughing-stock if he fails.'

Kor-Sen rose, and bowed.

Cren sighed and shook his head. 'I do not see him prospering here, not at all. He looks like a peasant, and his manner lacks all respect.'

Kor-Sen nodded his agreement, and Igrade laughed aloud, stifling the laugh hastily when Torran glared at her.

'Nevertheless,' the Convenor continued, 'our purpose here is to further the cause of Learning; and we should not deny him his opportunity. Aspirant Kor-Sen, you are admitted for a trial period of three months to the Division of Language, year Five. May the Lady support you, and curb your arrogant ways, and show you the true paths of learning.'

'Thank you, Lord Convenor.'

'Now leave us, and Secretary Dollan will show you what to do.'

Kor-Sen departed, with one last secret smile for Igrade, which left her very uncomfortable. As the door closed behind the new Aspirant, Danel repeated, 'I do not believe such a thing can be done—I will not believe it.'

'You may have to, Master,' replied Igrade; and blushed under the indignant stares of the three men.

Yet Igrade was right—Kor-Sen was quite capable of carrying out his boast, and in fact gained the title of Master of Language within ten months. He then proceeded to master the other three divisions before he had been at the Academy for three and a half years.

But his position was not altogether a happy one; although

Igrade became his friend, he was not popular with the other Masters, who resented both his brilliance and his casual attitude towards the learning and the Academy they all took so seriously.

He was the darling of the younger Aspirants, and when he began to teach, his lectures were always crowded with students from every Division, regardless of his subject. To the annoyance of his colleagues, he was quite happy to mix with the Aspirants socially, drinking and talking with them until all hours of the night. Add to this his immense success with women and his resultant dubious reputation in the town; and it was no wonder that he did not fit comfortably into any group.

He was a friend of the Aspirants, but he was not one of them; he was one of the Masters, but lacked friends among them. Yet those who knew him in those years remember him as cheerful and contented.

By the time Kor-Sen had been at the Academy for ten years or so, he had become a renowned scholar; shelves and shelves in the vast, dim library were stacked with scrolls and leather-bound books of his works. Some were in his own hand, some lovingly copied by admiring disciples. Scholars travelled from all over the islands, and from all the lands of Akent, to consult him or to study his writings. He began to be received into the wealthy society of Drelk's merchants, attending balls and dinners and receptions, and became quite rich himself by tutoring their children at exorbitant rates and by accepting munificent gifts from his patrons. The fame of his charm had preceded him, and he received a good deal of attention from the merchant's ladies.

One evening he was enjoying a splendid reception at one of the greatest houses in the city; feeling himself rather too well fed, he slipped out onto a terrace that overlooked the harbour and the western sea. It was a late summer evening, warm and still, and the sun was sinking towards the distant horizon. Kor-Sen stared idly at the little island beyond the cliffs that sheltered Drelk; Vodor's isle. He must go and investigate it sometime, he though; curious tales were told of the tower that stood there, by sailors who swore that the sea-folk came and danced around it and by old wives who told stories of a God who dwelt there and built the tower, in times forgotten.

'Master?'

A soft voice behind him. Turning, he saw a beautiful young woman, scarcely more than a girl, hesitating at the open window that led onto the terrace. He smiled his charming smile, and swept a bow.

'Madam?'

She laughed delightedly, and came towards him. 'Master Kor-Sen; I have heard so much about you, and so much wanted to meet you.'

'I am flattered to be sought after by such a beautiful young lady. But now that you have found me, you are sure to be disappointed.'

'No—no, not at all!'

She spoke with a youthful intensity that embarrassed him, and he turned back to look at the view. The girl came and stood beside him.

'I am Maressa. I should like to go to the Academy and study, but my father says it has cost him enough to send all my brothers—I have five, you see, and I am the youngest child. He says women do not need education to be good wives. I tell him I might as well live in Sen-Mar—at least, I did once, but he got very angry. I'm sorry, I am talking too much.'

'No, not at all. I like to hear you. What would you most like to study?'

'Language, I think, but I wish I could know everything about everything.'

Kor-Sen looked at her more closely, touched to hear his own childish words from her lips. She was looking up at the first stars in the dusk, and said, 'I suppose you know all about the stars. I wish you could teach me!'

She turned her earnest gaze upon him again, and he could not help himself—he took her in his arms and kissed her, and she relaxed into his embrace with a sigh. Many kisses were exchanged as the darkness deepened on the terrace, and hours passed before they realised that it was late, and the guests were going, and they must also go.

Kor-Sen was thinking how very young she was, and that he should not see her again. She said, 'May I come and see you? At the Academy?'

'Oh, my dear—I do not think it would be wise, do you?'

Her face grew sad. 'Do you not like me, then?'

'I like you very much, Maressa—possibly a little too much. Why, you are only a child, and I am a grey-haired old man.' Kor-Sen's hair had begun to grow silver at an early age, and he sometimes liked to exaggerate his age as a way of adding to his dignity.

'Not so very grey; and you do not seem old to me.' She pressed herself against him again, and several more kisses were exchanged. Kor-Sen pushed her away, and said, 'Come, we must go in, it is growing late. Perhaps we will meet again, I will see.'

Inside the house, servants were rushing about with cloaks

and Kor-Sen found Maressa's for her.

'I must escort you to your father.'

'No, please do not he'll think the worst, I am sure,' she giggled childishly.

'Very astute of him—but you must find him now.'

'I have, I can see him there near the door.'

Kor-Sen looked, and saw a fat, anxious-looking man some twenty years older than himself, richly dressed and obviously looking round for someone. 'What is his name, Maressa?'

'Father? Oh, he's called Mannen, Mannen the Merchant he's known as.'

A rushing sound began in Kor-Sen's head, and he looked back again at the fat little man and saw lurking beneath the fat some of the lines of his own face. He was aware of Mannen's voice saying something to him, but could not grasp the words. He turned from his father to his sister, looking up at him with bright and trusting eyes. A constricting coldness gripped his chest. The rushing sound in his ears grew louder, and he turned away, dashed back to the terrace and flung himself over the parapet onto the steep, thickly-grown slopes below. No-one saw him again for three days.

When he was a very old man indeed, Kor-Sen was given to relating the story of those three days as a descent into wild debauchery unequalled in the history of Skorn. Be that as it may, the first person to set eyes on him when he returned—the new porter, Grenal—saw the change in him at once.

'Master Kor-Sen! Good to see you back, sir.'

The Master slouched past Grenal without a word, and staggered up the stairs to his rooms, where he growled fiercely at a few students waiting to see him and sent them away. 'And don't come back for a week!'

Next, he sent a servant out to order a vast amount of wine.

The next day, he went down into the town and spent a day searching through old records in the Registry of Lands and Buildings. When he had traced the owner of Vodor's isle, he went to the man's home and insisted upon buying island, tower and all. The day after that he hired a boat to take him, together with his barrels of wine and other supplies, to the island; the boatman came back with a garbled tale of having landed the Master on the far side of the island, on a narrow strip of dangerous rock, whence—so he said—he intended to scale the cliffs. The sailors were to land the supplies on the beach below the Tower, and go.

'Well, that's the last we'll see of him,' was the general opinion in the town and in the market-place. But one week later he came back, settled in his room, and shouted at all his students for being behind in their work. He was cheerful or seemed so; but the Aspirants grew a little afraid of him, of a sharpness in his tongue that had not been there before.

Igrade tried to speak to him. 'What did you find to do on that lonely island, Master?'

His eyes were like cold green ice as he stared at her. 'I was thinking, Master.'

'What about? Is something troubling you, Kor-Sen?'

'The wickedness—and the weakness—of men trouble me, Master.'

'What has made you dwell on that? Has something happened to you? If it would help you to speak of it...'

'Oh, Igrade! How can I speak of the wickedness of my own heart? How can I tell you what I found within myself, what I saw as clearly as if I had seen myself in a bright silver mirror?'

'You are talking in riddles; yet I see that something has hurt you very deeply. What is it?'

Kor-Sen took her hand, gently, and kissed it. 'Would you say, dear friend, that I would be capable of murder? Or of lustfully attacking a young woman? Or of any kind of violence?'

'No! By no means! Maybe you can be sharp with those who annoy you, but in general you are the soul of courtesy. Certainly you have always been so to me'

'Ha! So you say. But I have looked upon the face of a fat, kindly old man, and desired to take his throat between my hands and twist his life out of him!'

'Kor-Sen! Stop it—stop!'

'Listen, Igrade—you said that you would willingly help me bear my pain—then listen! For there is more, and perhaps worse. I have looked upon the face of that man's daughter, a young and innocent girl, and I have felt within myself the urge to violate and degrade and ruin her! That is the knowledge of myself, that now I cannot bear.' He turned away from Igrade, and she heard him weeping.

'But...'

He looked round at her.

'But?'

'Kor-Sen, you say only that you felt the desire to do these things. You have not done them?'

He shrugged. 'No—I have not done them. But I grieve to find such evil within me, evil that I believed I had left behind me in the cursed land of my birth. I think I shall never be free of that grief again.'

Igrade held out her arms, and embraced him; she could find no more words to set against his sorrow.

Sanctuary

West and north the tides carried Saranna's boat, while she sat or lay unheeding, until it was swept around the eastern end of the island of Imman. From here it was washed gradually closer and closer to the northern shore, where it grounded on a deserted beach. Saranna lay motionless, while the tide ebbed and the boat tilted over on the wet shingle. At last, towards evening, she climbed stiffly out and stood looking around her, shivering and rubbing her hands in the chill wind. Turning her back on the sea, she trudged up the beach and struck out across the rough grassland towards the south.

That night Saranna slept huddled under a gorse bush in a hollow, shivering with the cold and waking often out of disturbed dreams. In the grey dawn she set out again, stumbling with weariness and faint with hunger, pushing on towards the centre of the island.

The Isle of Imman was like a great dish or saucer, a ring of hills fencing off from the sea a sheltered central valley or plain. On the seaward slopes in the east lived a shy, simple people who laboured to raise goats and toiled to catch sea-fish. The cruel winds and the deadly tides made life harsh and full of struggle. These people offered sacrifices of kids to the Sea-Wife, maker of the world; they rarely visited the kinder lands within the circling hills.

The centre of the island was a lush, fertile plain. Here a great freshwater lake harboured thousands of wild birds and gathered into itself the waters of hundreds of little streams that ran down from the hills. Brown trout swam in it and grew plump. Beside the lake was the market town of Salk, whose people were fat and contented, farmers who raised milk cows and made cheese and butter so rich that they were sold across the sea on Drent, Esmil and Ipple; Nork, Pelk and Imm. At the heart of the island life was pleasant and prosperous. Iranor was worshipped here, Irnor the Mother who cared for the land and the herds and the people.

Towards this haven Saranna staggered through the cold winter morning, dragging wearily down from the hills. She stumbled into a cart-track between hedged fields, where curious faces peered over the hedges at her, and inquisitive lowing sounds came from their owners. The rutted track was frozen and tripped her many times as she missed her footing between the ridges of mud. Her hands and knees were cut and bruised, and she was colder and hungrier every minute; she began to cry.

At last she sat down, exhausted, at the side of the road. A small oak grew there and she leaned back against it shuddering with weariness. The dim sun was climbing higher, and soon she heard voices calling out cheerfully to each other around the next bend in the road. She heard trundling hooves and lowing cattle, the excited barking of dogs. As the sounds grew clearer and the noses of the first cows came into view around the corner she struggled to rise, and move towards the newcomers. But a singing noise grew in her ears, and an empty sick feeling climbed up from her stomach to her throat and into her head. The sky spun and the sun flickered, and she fell before the hooves of the leading cattle. She heard cries of alarm and felt the stabbing pain of a heavy hoof coming down on her hand. Not even that agony could hold her back from unconsciousness.

'How is she?'

'Not well. But she is warm and dry, and the hand is well bound up. I shall find soothing herbs for her as soon as she wakes."

A man's voice, and a woman's. A soft blanket under her hand. Pain. Weak sunlight on a far-off ceiling. Saranna slipped away into sleep.

She woke again with a cry, her hand throbbing and stabbing with pain. Darkness, relieved by flickering firelight and candles, was all around. One of the candles came nearer. She felt gentle hands, and heard a soothing kind voice. She was lifted up and a cup held to her lips. Greedily she swallowed the warm milk, not noticing the sweet, thick taste of pain-easing herbs. Almost before she was laid down again onto the soft pillow, she was asleep.

Her next awakening was to a bright morning. She moved to sit up and heard a voice close to her left ear. 'No, no. You lie still and rest. Tell me what you need.'

Turning, Saranna saw a woman, older than herself and neatly dressed in fine cloth, seated beside the bed.

'My name is Essk. You are in the house of my master, Drenn. Is your hand better now?'

Saranna moved her right hand cautiously. There was a sharp twinge of pain. 'Oh! It still hurts. But I feel much better.'

'Hungry?'

'Oh, yes. Yes, I am.'

Essk went to the door and called. Saranna heard footsteps and a conversation about food. She looked curiously around and noted the great bed with white linen sheets and soft woollen blankets; a fine chamber, high-ceilinged; smooth-plastered walls and polished floorboards. Then a young girl came with steaming bread and milk in a bowl, and after eating it Saranna lay down and slept again. When she next woke, Essk was not there. By the bed sat the young servant girl, sewing by the light of a candle on a little table at her side. Behind her the fire leapt in the hearth, and Saranna lay quietly watching the flames and the flickering shadows. She felt warm and comfortable. Softly she said, 'Who are you?'

The girl rose and curtseyed. 'I am Carr, My Lady. Shall I call the housekeeper to you?'

'Do you mean Essk?'

'Yes, lady.'

'I would be glad of some supper, Carr. Will you tell her, please?'

Essk came quickly and sent for food and milk for Saranna. She helped the girl to sit up and piled pillows behind her. 'There now. You are much better, I can see.'

'Thank you. I will try to get well quickly, so that I shall not trouble you for too long.'

'You are no trouble at all, child. And my master will not hear of your going until you are completely well. You must not worry so.'

'I would like to see your master, and thank him.'

'Indeed you shall.'

Saranna turned her attention to the tray Carr had brought. When she had eaten, Essk came to her again and tucked a warm shawl about her shoulders, straightening the covers on the bed. Saranna heard a step in the doorway, and turned to see a man, younger than she had expected, standing just inside the room.

'Good evening.'

She smiled at him. 'Good evening.'

After a long pause, the young man came further into the room, and looked as if he was about to speak again. Instead he moved suddenly away to the window, where he stood with his back to Saranna. The silence remained unbroken until Saranna asked,

'Are you Master Drenn?'

He turned to face her. 'Yes, I am. I am sorry, I should have given you my name.'

He smiled rather heavily and moved closer to her. She saw that his broad, pleasant face bore a worried look. 'Does your hand cause you much pain?'

'I am greatly recovered—Essk has taken good care of me.'

He sat down in the chair beside the bed, and smiled again. 'She is wonderful, is she not? She knows everything about herbs and potions. Thank the Lady you are not badly hurt. When the men carried you here, all soaked in mud and pale as starlight—I thought at first you were dead.'

'How kind you must be to be so concerned for a stranger. How shall I ever repay you?'

'Oh, that is—no, it is nothing, you must not...—He got up and left without another word. Essk came forward from the shadows, smiling. 'The master has taken to you, I can see.'

'But he did not even ask my name.'

'He was always a shy boy, but as good as gold. And I have been just as much at fault—what is your name, my dear?'

'Saranna.'

'Well, Saranna; we will take care of you until you are quite strong. I think you should sleep now.'

Essk hesitated beside the bed for a moment, then leaned over and kissed Saranna's brow. 'Goodnight, my dear.'

'Goodnight, Essk.'

After a few days Saranna felt well enough to come downstairs into the great kitchen, where she enjoyed the talk and the company. She learned that Essk had been Drenn's nurse, his mother having died when he was born. Now she ruled his household while he ran the farm his father had left him.

Drenn came rarely into the kitchen. Essk served his meals in a small, cosy parlour across the hall, and Saranna thought he must be lonely, without the noise and bustle of the kitchen to cheer him. One evening she asked if she might join him at table. He smiled, and nodded; but at first he spoke very little, keeping his head down. Several days passed before Drenn became a little more talkative.

Gradually Saranna's health improved and she went out to walk about the garden and the orchard. Soon she felt strong and well. At last, one evening almost a month after her arrival at the farm, she told Drenn she must leave soon.

He looked straight at her, and stammered, 'What? Why should you leave us? Where would you go?'

Then he blushed and looked down at his feet. Saranna lost patience with him.

'Drenn!'

He looked up.

'That is better. Keep looking at me. Do you not wish me to go?'

He sat silent, toying with the fringe of his tunic. He crossed his legs, then uncrossed them again, scuffing his fine leather boots against the floor.

Saranna watched him. At last he said, 'Saranna, I would like you to stay.'

'Well. I would like to stay. If you can find work for me...'

'Marry me, Saranna.'

'What?'

'Marry me. Please?'

'Oh, Drenn—you have scarcely spoken to me this past month!'

'But I want you to stay. You are so beautiful. And gentle. I love you.'

'Do you?'

'Yes. I do. I love you, Saranna.'

Saranna got up and crossed the room to him. He put his arms around her and held her tenderly. 'I do love you.'

'I know.'

'Will you stay with me?'

She looked at him. She looked around the cosy room, with its sturdy old furniture and air of calm. She thought of the raging sea that had swallowed her brother. At last she spoke.

'Yes, Drenn, if you will have me.'

On the morning of Saranna's wedding day, the Priestess of Salk made her way to a level place by the lake. Gathering bundles of rushes from the shore, she strewed a carpet three paces long and three paces wide. She cut boughs of blossom from the forest trees and wove them into a canopy that she set high above the rushes on wooden poles. Then she walked three times about the marriage site, singing. As the song ended, a procession approached, Drenn's friends and neighbours from Salk all dressed in their finest clothes, then his household, the servants first, followed by Essk looking proud and splendid in a new yellow gown. Last came Saranna with her hand on Drenn's arm. The guests moved to form a circle about the canopy, while Saranna and Drenn came to stand before the priestess.

Smiling, she said to them, 'Come, for all is prepared. Come and pledge yourselves to one another in the name of the Mother of All.'

She took each of them by the hand and led them under the canopy; at the centre of the carpet of rushes, she halted. Drenn and Saranna knelt, and bowed their heads as she stretched out her arms above them, invoking Irnor's blessing. Saranna was trembling.

She heard the priestess say, 'Drenn of Salk, will you be true to Saranna, in the Name of the Lady?'

'I am the servant of the Lady; I swear it.'

'Saranna of Esmil, will you be true to Drenn, in the Name of the Lady?'

Saranna felt a gentle breeze from the west caressing her face. Her shaking ceased, and she said clearly, 'I am the servant of the Lady; I swear it.'

Then the priestess raised Drenn and Saranna and joined their hands, and all the people cried aloud for joy. There followed three days of celebration, music and dancing and laughter in the quiet old farmhouse and the fields. Essk and the servants had prepared enough food, wine and beer for the whole village, but it seemed as if half the people of the vale were there at times. And now Saranna was joyful and light-hearted, joining in the dancing and the songs. Drenn watched her proudly, smiling at her pleasure. He told her, 'You have brought spring into my house, and into my heart.'

Nowhere seemed brighter to Drenn now than the great bedchamber that had belonged to his parents, where he had slept alone and lonely for so long. Each night when he and Saranna were at last together, snug in the warmth of the evening fire and the glow of a single candle, he would take her gently, hesitantly, into his arms.

'You are so beautiful. I cannot believe that you could love me.'

One blazing afternoon in late summer, Saranna walked slowly along the lane that led to the farmhouse. The fields on either side were deep-gold with ripening corn, and near the house the trees in the apple-orchard, laden with rounding fruit, were bowed almost to the ground. At the gate was Essk, just climbing down from the pony-trap laden with purchases from the market.

'Mistress.'

'Good day, Essk—and what a glorious day!'

'Well enough for those with nothing to do but bother the master with posies and kisses. It was hard work marketing today in this heat.'

Saranna blushed. 'You must be worn out. Let me help you to carry these things and then we shall have a drink of cool milk.'

'I have no time for idling, I must be getting on.'

Turning her back on Saranna, the older woman stumped off up the path to the house, and vanished through the open door. Saranna sighed, and went around the side of the house to the vegetable garden.

At supper that evening, Saranna spoke to Drenn. 'Essk seems so cross with me. What can I have done?'

Drenn reached across the table and took her hand. 'Come here,' he said. He drew Saranna round the table and settled her comfortably on his knee.

'Let's see that frown go away, if you please, wife.'

Then the door opened abruptly and Essk came into the room. The young couple both looked towards her, but before they could speak, she turned away and went out, slamming the door behind her.

'Do you see, Drenn? What can be the matter?'

'It is nothing, my love. You worry far too much. You'll see, Essk will cheer up when the cooler weather comes. She is older than us, and the long summer days are trying for her. Now kiss me again, and let us be happy. '

The next day Drenn and Saranna rode up into the high meadows to check on the growing calves. While Drenn rode about the hillsides inspecting his herds, Saranna rested under a tree by a little pool. Noon was hot, and she fell asleep in the patch of shade cast by the ancient thorn. But she was troubled in her sleep, hearing the sound of the sea, and beyond it the voice of her brother Drewin calling her name, as if from some deep hollow place. She awoke crying and trembling, and Drenn hurried back to her. She clung to him, weeping.

'What is it, my love? What has frightened you?'

'The sea. I heard the sea, and the waves beating on the rocks. He fell into the sea, he must be dead. But how can I hear his voice if he is dead?'

Drenn could get no more sense out of her than this. Gradually he soothed her, bathed her hands and face in cool water from the pool, and fetched food and wine from their saddle bags. In the late afternoon he helped Saranna unto her horse and led her slowly home.

Essk was standing on the threshold gazing down the lane

towards the hills. She watched silently as Drenn dismounted and turned to help his wife down from her mule. Saranna swayed a little on her feet, and then slid to the ground in a faint. Drenn knelt anxiously beside her.

'Essk, what is wrong? Is she ill?' he cried.

'Ill? No indeed, master, not she. Near three months gone with child, I'd say.'

'Child? Child! But why did she not tell me?'

Essk shrugged and turned away. Carr arrived with water, and helped Drenn to revive Saranna. Tenderly he led her inside and put her to bed, sitting by her until, near midnight, she opened her eyes.

'Drenn?'

'Yes, my darling.'

'Am I at home?'

'Yes, you are safe with me.'

'Am I ill?'

'Essk says not, dearest. She thinks—well—she says you may be going to have a child.'

'A child? Oh, Drenn—I thought there might be something wrong with me, but I did not like to ask Essk, now she is always so cross.'

'Well, dear, never mind. It is wonderful news.'

'Are you pleased, Drenn?'

'Of course, my love.'

She turned her head away. 'Then I am glad too. But -'

'What, darling?'

'Oh, I wish my mother was with me. I want my mother.'

Essk was gentler to Saranna now, motherly and kind. The two women talked very little, but there was a kind of peace between them. One day when Drenn was out with the farmhands, securing fences and buildings against the deepening winter, they shared the warmth of the kitchen and talked together.

'Essk, is it long now before my husband will come home?'

'No, my dear, he will soon be here and I have a nice supper cooking for you. Here is a mug of good fresh milk.'

'Thank you, Essk. I wish I could go out for a walk, I seem always to be inside the house now.'

'But it is much too cold for you, little mistress. You must take great care of yourself now, for the child's sake.'

'Yes, I know.' Saranna got up and moved sluggishly to the window, looking out at the grey cold dusk. 'But I shall be so glad when spring returns and my baby is born. Then I shall sit under the apple trees with her, and sing to her as my mother once sang to me.'

'But perhaps you will have a son, mistress. That is what my master would like, I am sure.'

Saranna looked round at her.

'Drenn? Why should he prefer a son?'

'Why, to learn the ways of the farm and to be master after him. That is what all men wish, for their sons to follow in their way.'

Saranna went back to the fire again, and sat looking deeply into its flames. After a while she said, 'I have heard nothing of this before, Essk. I long for a daughter, to love her and be loved by her as once my mother and I loved so long ago.'

Her voice fell until she was almost whispering. Essk came to set her loaves to rise on the hearth, and bending over Saranna she asked,

'Why so sad, mistress? Is your mother dead too, like my

poor master's? You must miss her sorely.'

'No. No, Essk, My Lady mother is not dead—only, only I may not see her or speak to her. She is so far away from me now. '

'A quarrel, then? Is she angry with you? That is very sad, indeed. But you should look to the future, now you have the finest husband a girl could hope for, and the child will come with the spring. Oh mistress, I do hope it is a boy, just such a little boy as my dear master was, fair and sturdy. I can see him now toddling after me about the house and yard.'

'You love Drenn very much, Essk.'

'Oh, mistress, he was like my own child. The old master was always busy. It was to Ess'—that is what he called me when he was tiny, Ess'—the little master came with his hurt knees or some treasure he'd found. He loved me so much then, mistress.'

Saranna stared into the older woman's rapt face, and was about to speak when the door opened to let in Drenn and a burst of cold air. Essk rose at once and began to fuss over her master and fetch warm drinks and dry shoes, while he came to Saranna's side and took her hands, kissing her and gently asking how she was. There was no more talk of sons or daughters.

Soon snow swept over the island. Little work could be done once the penned beasts were fed, and Drenn spent much time with Saranna, watching with delight as she learned from Essk how to knit fine soft wool from their own fat valley sheep into delicate wrappings and coverlets for the coming child. In a small workroom off the kitchen, old Bann the gardener was lovingly mending and repainting the wooden cradle that had been Drenn's and his father's before him. By the roaring fire, the young couple talked together and learned more about each other's lives before they had met.

One day Drenn asked, 'Love, why do you wear that disc of wood, and never take it off?'

All the brightness went out of Saranna's face. She put her work down and looked away from Drenn. He leaned over and took her hand, but she was silent for a long time.

'I am sorry,' he said. 'If it is something private, something painful, do not speak of it.'

Saranna spoke rapidly, trembling a little. 'It is my brother's rune; he made the disc for me. I think he is dead, but I do not know. At times I seem to hear his voice, in the wind or in the stream, or when I am dreaming. I do not know whether he lives or not.' She clutched Drenn's hand.

'What is his name, dearest—your brother?'

'Drewin,' she whispered.

'Drewin? So like my name, how strange. Why, the rune might stand for me, just think of that!'

Saranna turned her head away from him, and saw Essk nodding in agreement by the hearth. But before she could answer her husband , he embraced her gently. 'Sweetheart, I am so sorry for your trouble. But for our child's sake, try to put the past and its sorrows behind you—I will always take care of you now, I promise. '

Saranna looked from Drenn to Essk and back again. She put her head down on Drenn's shoulder; but she did not weep, and so he was content.

The first warm day of spring came towards the end of the month of Ellan. Saranna spent a happy day strolling in the orchard attended by Carr, and shortly after Drenn had returned home for the evening meal, she sat up rigid in her chair, crying aloud with pain.

'Drenn! Drenn!'

He went to her instantly, but Essk was before him.

'What is it Mistress?'

'Pain. Essk, the pain.'

'Yes, little lady. It is the child. Come you with Essk now.'

She raised the younger woman to her feet, and Saranna cried out as another pain caught her. She fell against Essk, stumbling almost to her knees. A rush of water soaked her gown and stained the parlour floor. Drenn rushed distractedly about, calling for Carr and the other maidservants. Essk turned on him abruptly.

'Master! Be quiet now! You may be with her if you are quiet, but not otherwise.'

Saranna cried out again, and Drenn quietened. He and Essk led her to the bedchamber, and then all she knew was the relentless surging of the pain, like cruel waves of the winter sea, tearing at her body while her mind swam between light and dark; the voices of those around her drifted and mingled in her head like rain and wind and the cries of dying birds in winter's shadow. Pain and pain and sweeping light and fearful dark, until a sudden ease came and there was the crying of a thin new voice in the room and the sound of Drenn weeping. Saranna heard Essk say,

'There, my dear young master, your boy, your son.'

She turned her head on the pillow and saw Drenn holding a fair, fat baby, a small image of himself, and she tried to reach out but Essk was there, soothing, pushing her back into the bed.

'There, there, poor thing, rest you now, leave it all to Essk, all is over now, rest you, sleep, and here, drink this, Essk is here, you sleep now.'

And the dark came back, and Saranna slipped into it heavily, until there was no more sound or pain or light.

The boy was named Raðenn, after Drenn's father. For weeks after the birth, Saranna's strength refused to return. Drenn suggested to Essk that they must send for a physician from the town.

'No, master, no need for that. I shall care for the mistress, and the child. Let me be master Raðenn's nurse and feed him on our own good ewe's milk. He will soon be fat and strong, and my young lady may rest free from anxiety. She will be able to grow strong herself then.'

Drenn sat down heavily at the parlour table.

'Saranna will be distressed to think that she cannot nurse the child herself.'

'Yes, of course. But you will comfort her, master. She will soon realise that it is best for the child. Did I not care for you well enough when you were a baby, master?'

He smiled up at her. 'Of course you did, Essk. I am sure you are right. I will speak to Saranna about it this very evening.'

Saranna wept bitterly when she heard of this.

While Essk carried off the fretful baby to her own room, and the servants moved the crib and other things belonging to him, Drenn held his wife tenderly and tried to soothe her. But it was not until after midnight that she slept, and then only with the help of one of Essk's potions.

So through that first summer of Raðenn's life, his mother lay weary and fretful in her bed, swallowing draught after draught of Essk's medicines, but never improving. The baby grew plump and strong and alert, smiling and gurgling up into Essk's face just as Drenn had done so long before. He was now her full-time care, while Carr took charge of the kitchen and larders.

At first Drenn sat for hours with Saranna, trying to cheer her, but there was much to do on the farm during the summer months, and Drenn was by nature an outdoor, active man. Soon he began to stay away from the sick-room except for one or two brief visits each day, and at night he slept in a separate room, since Essk had told him this would be better for Saranna's health. Saranna felt desolate, and began to look forward to Carr's appearance two or three times a day, to administer Essk's prescribed medicines and set the room to rights. Saranna took the medicine eagerly, for it dulled her mind and stopped some of the pain of thinking. She welcomed the night-time, when Essk's sleeping draught brought her complete oblivion, free even of dreams. She began to fear that she would never be well. But when winter came again, Drenn spent more time with Saranna, and she felt cheered by his company. Sometimes he told Essk to bring the child into Saranna's room too. Raðenn was now a big strong baby, and Saranna could hardly hold him. Drenn would sit beside her on the bed with his son in his arms, and they would sing and play games for the baby's delight. These times were all too short for Saranna; soon there would be the sound of Essk's knock on the door.

'Excuse me, master, but it is time for the little one's bath now.'

'Just a few more minutes, please, Essk.'

'No, My Lady, you'll tire yourself, and little Raðenn must have his routine, mustn't you, my pet?'

The little boy would stretch out his arms to Essk laughing and jumping up and down in his eagerness to get to her. This always made Saranna weep.

'There, master, the poor lady is distressed again. Let me take the little one and you can settle her down.'

But one day near mid-winter, Drenn stood up abruptly during one of these scenes, holding the baby close, and said, 'This is enough! We must do more, Essk, we must send for the physician!'

Essk took the baby, looking anxiously at Drenn.

'Oh, master, do not fear. I will have her well yet. I shall try a new mixture of herbs, you will see, I will soon make a difference in her. A few more weeks, master, and all will be well.'

'If you are sure, Essk...—but if there is no improvement by spring, then the physician it must be.'

'Yes, yes master, of course.'

And Essk was gone, calling Carr as she went. That very night she began to dose Saranna with different medicines, and it was soon clear that a change was taking place at last. By the time the spring sunshine began, Saranna was well enough to come downstairs and sit by the fire, to watch little Raðenn staggering up onto his feet and toddling shakily across the kitchen.

The baby's first words were coming, too; first of all he said 'Ess", then 'Da' for Drenn and then 'Dat', for the old tabby-cat that kept the mice at bay. Saranna hoped that she might soon hear him say 'Mama'.

As the days grew warmer, Saranna, Essk and Raðenn spent more and more time out of doors. Essk would take the boy's hand and encourage him to walk about the orchard. She insisted that Saranna should rest on the bench beneath the tall old apple tree that stood nearest the house.

'But I can walk a little now, Essk. Let me take Raðenn for a while. He will tire you out.'

'No, no, mistress, you must rest, you are still very weak. What will the master say if you make yourself ill again?'

Saranna gave in and subsided onto the bench. The garth of trees that sheltered the farmhouse was very wide and deep, so that Essk and Raðenn were quickly out of her sight.

Shortly after Raðenn's first Birthfeast, there came a day of such hot sunshine that Essk suggested Carr should help Saranna wash her long, thick hair, so that it might dry in the sun. She herself seized upon Raðenn and encouraged him towards the far end of the orchard. Saranna, when Carr had left her, sat down in the sunshine, near to the hedge that surrounded the garden and orchard, and began to brush out her wet hair. She recalled the words of a sad old song of Esmil, and softly she began to sing;

Deep rushing sea,
Cold waters of my distant home,
Why did you spare me
Only for sorrow?
Deep rushing sea,
Cold waves upon the eternal sand,
Why did you take him
Who loved me true?
Deep rushing sea,
Cruel tides of bitter parting,
Why did you sunder us
Who breathed as one?'

As she stopped singing, all was still around her. The heat of noon-tide had stilled the breeze in the apple-boughs; Raðenn's bright voice had died away in the distance. Saranna sighed heavily, and reached for the hairbrush she had dropped upon the grass.

'Sweetheart, why so sorrowful?'

She gasped, and sprang to her feet. A strange man was standing looking at her across the hedge, not five feet away.

'Oh,' she said. 'You startled me. What are you doing there? I shall call the servants, what right have you here? Who are you?'

'You need not fear me, pretty one. Nor summon any protectors. My name is Kor-Sen, and I will not harm you. '

He moved to the gate and came into the garden and over to where she stood. His green eyes smiled directly into Saranna's, and the long hair that framed his face was white as the blossom in the orchard. He was plainly dressed, and carried a bundle on his back. Saranna found that she was smiling back at him.

'You do not look dangerous.'

He laughed. 'I did not say that I was not dangerous; only that I would not hurt you. What is your name, fair lady?'

'Saranna. Where have you come from, Kor-Sen?'

'From far and near, over sea and land—what about you, Saranna?'

'I could say the same thing, as far as that goes. But what land and what sea—and what were you doing, looking into my garden?'

'I wanted to see who sang so sweetly—and a lovely sight is my reward, the sight of you.' He stepped closer, and gold light danced in his green eyes; Saranna could see the sun's rays glancing through the long silver hair.

'I like to see you smile,' he said, 'you seemed so unhappy while you sang your song. What troubles you, lovely Saranna?'

She blushed and looked down, but he reached out his hand and lifted her face to his again.

'You are lovely,' he insisted, 'but why so sorrowful? Tell me."

His voice was deep and compelling, his touch gentle and reassuring. Saranna sat down again on her chair, and began to talk.

'I—do not know where to begin.'

'Try the beginning.'

'Well—I was in a boat.'

'Is that where you were born?'

'No! I mean my brother and I—we—went out in a boat one day, and the tide carried us away from the island where we lived. And a whale came.'

'Yes, go on—I am listening.'

'Drewin—the whale—it knocked him into the sea somehow, and I think he must have drowned; surely if he still lived I would have found him—he would have sought me out—I fear he is dead!'

Saranna wept bitterly, and Kor-Sen came closer and seated himself on the grass at her feet.

'Have you never spoken of this before? I can see it distresses you deeply.'

She sniffed loudly. 'No. No-one here knows, not even my husband knows what happened with the whale, though he knows I have lost my brother. And I never told anyone on Esmil.'

'Esmil?'

'That is where the boat drifted to. I lived there for a long time, they were kind to me, but then I—came here and met Drenn and we have been married for nearly two years—we have a little boy...—'

Tears overwhelmed her again and Kor-Sen patted her hand gently.

'Now what is this? Is there more troubling you?'

She nodded, pressing her hands against her eyes as if to stem the flow of weeping.

'What is it? Come, you may tell me. It is quite safe.'

'Drenn—the baby—Essk—oh, everything—everything is horrible, I have been ill for so long and the baby loves Essk more than he loves me and Drenn does not notice—what am I to do!'

'I never give advice, Saranna. Instead you must think and think and when you have thought you must do what you know to be right. And I must leave you now.'

'Why? Where are you going?'

'On down this road, to continue my journey.'

'Oh, but I have told you all my troubles—will you not help me?'

'I have said, lady, I will not advise you. And I have listened long to your troubles. What more can I do for you? You must learn the way to help yourself.'

She stepped forward and clung to his sleeve, looking closely into his face. 'I know it is foolish of me, but I trust you. I feel as if you have been sent to help me. Please say you will come and talk to me again.'

Kor-Sen looked around as if seeking a way of escape. Then he sighed heavily, and said, 'Very well. I shall make my journey to the north-east, where I am going to visit the fisherfolk on their rocky shore. In about two weeks I shall be travelling south again, and I can meet you here if you think it will be of help. '

'Oh yes, it will, I know it will. Thank you, thank you so much.'

'Oh, please do not thank me, lady. You go to your dinner, which no doubt is due soon, and I will be on my way.'

As the days passed, Saranna watched the family and servants, and thought over what had happened since Raðenn was born. Everyone seemed busy and cheerful except for her. At first she could only conclude that some weakness within her made her discontented. But as she grew steadily stronger and healthier, she began to see things differently. She realised that whatever she tried to do, someone else had already done it; or someone else would interfere and prevent her from finishing her task. If she tried to organise the butter-making, Carr would bustle up and say,

'No, no, mistress, I can see to that!'

If she tried to work in the vegetable garden, Bann would be there.

'Tssk, tssk, mistress, whatever are you a-thinking of? You go into the house now; it's too hot for a lady like you to be stooping over carrots and parsley.'

Day by day Saranna's thoughts cleared, as if a stifling veil had been drawn away from her mind. Her senses sharpened, and she took in more and more of what the people around her were saying, and noticed more of what they did and how they behaved. Slowly the truth dawned on her.

One day, about, a week after Kor-Sen's visit, she was sitting alone in the orchard as before, when she was assailed by an inner surge of anger that grew to fury. She jumped up and shouted aloud, shaking her fists in the air and crying out,

'Essk! This is Essk's doing! She has them all dancing to her drum, even Drenn!'

All that day she wrestled in thought and when evening came she felt that surely they must all see the marks in her face of the grief and anger she had been through. But no-one noticed. No-one asked how she had spent the day. That night Drenn settled down beside her, kissed her and said,

'Goodnight, my love. It is good to see you so much happier.' Then he turned over and went to sleep.

By the end of a fortnight, Saranna was in a state of high excitement and felt a permanent turmoil inside her. Even Raðenn could not distract her, and she thought only of how much she had to say to Kor-Sen. For three successive days she waited in the orchard at noon, until at last she heard whistling in the lane outside and saw Kor-Sen approaching the gate.

She stood up as he drew near, and took the hands he extended to her in greeting.

'You have helped me to see the truth,' she said.

'Me?' He laughed. 'I deny it. Not guilty.'

'I like the way you laugh. It makes me feel happier, too.'

'Well, then, that is good. Now let us sit down and talk.'

They sat together on the grass, and when Kor-Sen took her hand in his, she did not object.

'I have been thinking and thinking, as you told me to.'

'Yes.'

'And I think I have seen the truth.'

'Yes.'

'It is not a good thing.'

'No.'

'Oh, goodness, do say something other than 'yes' and 'no'!'

'Sorry.'

She laughed and stood up, moving away a little to lean against an aged pear-tree.

'I think Essk—during the winter—I think she was making me ill, not well, with the potions she gave me. I think she hates me. I think she would have liked to see me die.'

Saranna walked around the pear-tree and back again, twisting her long hair through her hands. 'I cannot fight her; she is too strong for me. But what can I do? This is my home. How can I leave my husband? How can I leave my child? Where would I go?'

'Saranna!'

Kor-Sen got up and came close to her, taking her shoulders in his hands and looking directly into her face. She dropped her gaze and turned her head away as she heard his insistent words.

'Listen to me—for there is more to this truth, and you must see it clearly. You could have overcome Essk long ago; you could have reshaped the life of this farm and made it good—if you had cared enough to fight.'

'Cared? I have cared—I do care.'

'No. You have used this place and used Drenn as a refuge, and now that you are stronger you chafe at the safety you once desired. You have given in to Essk to excuse your own failure. Even your child you would have fought harder for, if he had been the daughter you wanted. Look at yourself, Saranna, if it is truth you want! '

Taking her hand, he led her towards the still pool that lay between the trees in the farthest corner of the orchard.

'Now look!' he said, and she looked into the pool to see her own face reflected there. He said softly, 'I cannot tell you what to do, Saranna. Whatever you do, must be at your own will.'

He released her, turned away, and walked to the gate. There he paused, looking back at her over his shoulder, while the rising West Wind lifted the silver hair from his shoulders.

'I am going,' he said.

'Wait for me,' said Saranna.

She followed him through the gate, and closed it behind her.

Darkness

*D*rewin opened the doors, entered a high-ceilinged chamber, and stopped. It was quite dark: there was no source of light, but as his eyes adjusted to the gloom he could make out the dark shapes of columns to left and right.

'Follow the darkness.' His voice spoke the words aloud.

He went straight ahead into the darkest shadow and came to a large doorway. The door was open and through it was a flight of rough stone steps leading downwards. Drewin leaned forwards and peered down the opening. The darkness was complete, like a dry well.

Drewin felt his way down the stairs, reaching his foot down at each step, and touching the coarse stone wall with his hands. He descended slowly, step by step. He stopped at the bottom and waited until he could see where he was. He could make out the flat stone walls: an empty room about half the size of the chamber now far above.

'It cannot end here. There must be a way forward.' His voice echoed off the hard walls. He examined the walls tapping and feeling them with his hands. Then he got down on his hands and knees and crawled all over the floor. He quickly found what he was looking for; a flagstone in the floor with a large iron ring embedded in it. He stood up, pulled at the ring, and, with some effort, lifted the stone.

'Not so difficult. I seem to be stronger down here.'

Peering into the dark and dimly perceiving another smaller flight of steps leading down into even deeper darkness, Drewin shivered and drew back.

'I must go on.' Slowly, hesitantly, he went down into the

deeper blackness, one step at a time. The steps were narrow; the air was cold. The tiny room at the bottom of the steps was darker than the darkness above, but he could still just manage to see. As he reached the centre of the room, Drewin heard the flagstone fall into place above his head. The darkness was now complete, but he could see one thing clearly: on the floor at his feet there was a pattern of runes which glowed so that it stood out as a deep yellow colour against the darkness of the room. Drewin could make no sense of the words, but he could make their sounds. His mouth was dry and he found it difficult to speak in that lifeless room, but somehow he managed to do it.

'The end is the beginning. Darkness is light. Two is one.'

The words hung in the air, and the room seemed to wait.

Then, out of the centre of the bright inscription came a shining mist that gradually, imperceptibly slowly, formed into a being. It was not human, nor an animal, but something altogether different. It was not solid: the mist swirled within its shape and the features of its face moved about like reflections off troubled water.

The creature's deep strong voice filled the room. 'You have come here because this was the only place to come. This is the place you fear most. You have come here hoping to find answers, but what do you find? An empty dark cold room. And what is in the room? Drewin alone.'

The figure dissolved into the air and the symbol on the floor slowly faded. The room was dark and silent. Drewin was alone.

He turned and felt his way to the stone steps, then up the steps to the trap-door. He pushed at the stone slab that blocked his way: it would not move. It was as if the weight of a mountain bore down on it and Drewin's strength had evaporated. He went down the steps and sat on the floor to think.

There was no way to go back the way he had come, so he would have to go on somehow. He stood up again and moved about the chamber examining the walls, the floor and the ceiling with his hands. There was no sign of an opening, or even a crack. There was no way out.

He sat down again. He sat silent and still for a while, then his body started to shudder, and tears fell from his eyes. He sobbed desperately, until he was exhausted. Then he shouted. At first there were wordless howls of anguish, then words came.

'It's not fair! It's not fair! It's not fair!'

The cold rock said nothing: it watched him, indifferent.

Exhausted once more, Drewin slumped in a heap on the floor. 'If I can't get out then I must stay here,' he said.

He sat quietly doing nothing. For a long time, the only sound in the chamber was the sound of his breathing. Then a voice, strong and clear, echoed through the room.

'There is no solution without a problem. There is no answer without a question. What is the question? Ask the question.'

Drewin looked up, then looked behind him and all round the room. He could see no-one.

'But what question?' he shouted at the walls. 'There are so many questions.' He sank down again and started muttering to himself.

'How many? ...Who? ...Why? ...When? ...What? ...Where?'

He sat thinking for a while, and then sat upright. "Where!' Yes, it must be 'Where?' If I can find out where I am, I might be able to find out how to get somewhere else. Where am I?'

The answer came back immediately, in the same strong voice. 'You are here.'

'And where should I be?'

'That is for you to decide.'

Drewin thought before speaking. 'I must go on.'

Before he had finished speaking, something started to happen: a large patch on the wall opposite him began to look different from the surrounding rock. As he watched, the shape became more sharply defined and its colour changed to a rich brown. He sat watching the slowly unfolding image, until he realised what it was.

'A door!' He stood up and walked slowly forward, his arms outstretched, until he came to the door. His hands touched wood, not stone. It was real. He pushed, and the door swung open smoothly; immediately light and noise flooded the chamber. Drewin fell back, turning away, closing his eyes, and covering his ears with his hands. But he could not keep out the sound of a multitude of hammers crashing in chaotic rhythms. He turned once more to the door and, keeping his eyes half closed, cautiously he edged forward. The noise got louder and the light became brighter as he left his dark prison and entered a vast cavern.

He could make out hundreds of people scattered around as far as the eye could see. They were all working with hammers and chisels on pieces of stone: some of them worked alone while others were in groups of two or three. At first none took any notice of Drewin, so intent were they on their tasks, but as he advanced further into the cavern a few of the stonemasons stopped their work and looked curiously at him. Gradually more of them put down their tools and a group started to gather. There were all sorts: male and female, tall and short, fat and thin. Drewin looked them and they looked at him. Nobody said a word. The group was now quite large, there seemed to be no hammering at all coming from nearby. Then a voice came from the back of the crowd.

'Make way! Make way! What's going on here? Come on, clear a path. Come on there's work to be done. No slacking. Back to work everyone!'

The crowd gradually dispersed until Drewin could see the speaker, who was walking towards him with a determined manner. The newcomer, a tall thin man, stopped in front of Drewin and looked him up and down before addressing him.

'From Learakent I daresay. Tell me young man, how are you called?'

'My name is Drewin and I come from beyond the sea.'

'Well, I am Urbelin, and we know little of what lies beyond Learakent. That is not our concern: we are all travelling the other way.'

Drewin waited for Urbelin to say more. When the older man said no more Drewin broke the silence.

'Can you tell me what work is being done here? Are you constructing a building?'

'We are building a stairway to the light. For many years we have laboured to get out of this dark cavern to the brightness above, and, though progress is slow, I am certain that we are close to our goal.'

Drewin looked to the far end of the chamber and could see men and women labouring on a massive construction of stone blocks. Some of the people worked at ground level while others were scattered over the face of the structure at various heights above the cavern floor: some worked at the very top where their heads disappeared into the darkness near the cavern's roof.

'I can see no light.' said Drewin.

Urbelin laughed. 'That is not surprising, young man, for only from great heights can we see afar. It is as you climb towards the top of our stairs that you begin to see the illumination that comes from above. We cannot see that from here, but up in the light above all is clear, to those who have the eyes to see. Come, I will show you the Archive.'

Urbelin turned and walked quickly away, not towards the stairway where the work was most intense, but to a quiet part of the chamber where there were few people. Drewin followed him. They passed between rows of shelves and cabinets that were full of books and elaborate artefacts until they came to a dark corner where there was an old table covered in dust. Urbelin stopped and waited for Drewin to approach.

'This is where it all started, many years ago. Many years ago.'

Drewin looked at the table and saw a thin book lying at its centre, under the layers of dust. He brushed the worst of the dust away, and opened the book. He turned over a few of the dry brittle pages, examining each one carefully.

'These are the runes of Iranor!' he exclaimed.

'You know of them? Few people do, outside this cavern. In this book is the list of all fourteen runes and the rules for their use.'

'Fourteen! But there are only thirteen! What is this new one?' Drewin looked intently at the page.

'The last rune is Vor, but it is not new. There cannot be a new rune: they came from the beginning of time and they are as old as truth. They are the beginning of our task: for without the runes our forbears could not have found the truth. Without the runes they could not have recorded what they had learnt, and so we would have been doomed to repeat their work.'

Drewin lifted his eyes from the book and stared at Urbelin. 'Forbears? How long have you been building the stairs?'

'I do not know the number of years, but it has been many generations. It started when a young traveller named Vodorian came here and showed us how to measure time so that we knew day from night, and gave us fire so that we could light the days and warm the nights, and he made the gift of the runes, then went on his way. Since then, all our people have laboured to build the way to the light.'

'But what have the runes to do with the stairs? What has writing to do with building?'

Urbelin looked Drewin in the eye and an air of great seriousness came over him.

'The runes were the beginning. From the runes came knowledge, and from knowledge came more knowledge, and from more knowledge came even more knowledge, and so on until we knew there was a light to be found. And once we knew there was a light, we knew we were bound to seek it. To seek it we learnt number and we calculated, and our calculations told us how to build, and the form our labours should take. From language came thought; from thought came number; from number came form; and from these four, language, thought, number, and form together came being. And so we build according to the dictates of the runes.'

Drewin looked at Urbelin, at the dusty book, at all the shelves and cabinets that surrounded them. 'So all the knowledge you have discovered is collected here and you use it to build your stairway?'

'Precisely! You have a quick mind, Drewin. You will be a great help to us. A fresh mind, a quick mind, is just the thing. Of great value to the work. Just what we need! Come, eat with us, and work with us.'

So saying, Urbelin hurried back towards the noise of the builders, and Drewin followed. As they approached, the work stopped and food was brought. It was divided between the workers, and Drewin received an equal share with the others, even though he had done no work. As he ate he talked with those seated by him, and found that they all agreed that building the stairway was the most important thing and that there was no other way to go but up.

'May I climb the stairs as far as they go?' he asked.

His companions laughed. 'You may climb the stairs as high as you can go,' they said, 'but few people can find the way to the top. It is not like an ordinary staircase where the hard work is done by the mason so that others might have an easy passage.'

'And once you get to the top,' said a little girl, 'you have to build the next step yourself.'

As Drewin was finishing his meal, Urbelin came to him. 'Come with me and I will show you the stairway.'

He took Drewin to the base of the massive structure, and Drewin looked up to its top, high above the cavern floor. It was not like an ordinary staircase: the steps were irregular, some very small and some twice as tall as Drewin, some little more than the width of a foot, and some reaching across the whole construction. The whole stairway was very wide at the bottom and narrow at the top.

'It is so confusing, like a maze, or a mountain. How can anyone reach the top?'

Urbelin did not answer immediately, but gazed at the stairway as though on a work of art. His eyes flicked from place to place taking in the details, and a look of pride came over him.

'Few can find their way to the top, and even though it has been built by others it can take years to master. I am one who has climbed more than any other, and sometimes even I get lost at the higher levels.'

Drewin turned to Urbelin, and looked him in the eye.

'May I attempt the climb? For some reason I feel it is important.'

Urbelin smiled. 'I hoped you would say that. Of course you may climb; anyone who has knowledge and skill can climb, but first comes desire. You have the desire, now all that is needed is hard work.'

'May I try now?'

'Such eagerness!' Urbelin laughed with a full-throated laugh. 'Yes, Drewin, you may try now and at any time you wish. No permission is needed: you can do no harm to such workmanship, and you can go only as far as you are able. I doubt if you will get lost.'

Drewin looked up at the massive structure and moved towards it. He stopped at its lowest level and stood for a long while, taking in all the details of the irregular stairs. Slowly, he walked forward and placed his foot on a low step at the centre of the lowest level. He transferred his weight onto that foot and lifted the other from the ground. He paused and looked about him, paused again, then lowered first one foot, then the other, back to the ground. He stepped back from the stairs and looked again at the massive structure. Tears came to his eyes.

Urbelin stood watching this with a look of deep seriousness, almost anxiety, on his face. When he saw Drewin back away from the stairs, the tall teacher moved forward, and stood beside him.

'Do not be disappointed. Do not despair. It is very hard.'

Drewin glared angrily at the stairway through his tears. 'I will not despair. I will climb to the light.'

'Then you have much work to do.'

In the days that followed, Drewin explored the shelves and cabinets in the Archive. He started by learning all that was in the book of the runes, and he made his own copy of it so that he could carry it with him wherever he went. Then he examined each of the dusty shelves, looking carefully at the machines and contraptions, and studying the books. He learnt about Vodorian's four divisions of knowledge: language and thought, number and form. He read tales and legends and histories of ancient heroes. He studied accounts of how people lived in different parts of Skorn, how each people was bound together by language and custom, and theories about why they behaved as they did and how they should live.

He studied ideas and words, argument and rhetoric. In this way he gradually moved nearer to the bright and busy area where the building was being done. Occasionally Urbelin would come and look at what he was doing, but he did not speak, though sometimes he would smile or frown. Drewin seldom saw other people, except at mealtimes, when he would join the other workers for food and conversation.

The little girl who had spoken to him on his first day in the cavern often sat with him to eat. Her name was Elara and while they ate she questioned him about his researches and gave him guidance with the intensity of a concerned mother.

'I think you have some idea of language and thought, but what about number?' she said to him one day.

Drewin frowned. 'I've only just started number, and I find it very hard. I have been talking and thinking all my life, and so I know something about language and thought, but number is very strange. I don't really understand what it is for.'

He took two biscuits from his plate. 'I know that these are two, but what I need to know is whether they are enough to satisfy my hunger, and I find that out by eating them and seeing if I am still hungry. So what use is number?'

Elara thought for a moment, her face fixed in an expression of deep seriousness. 'That is a hard question; good, but hard. I think that you can only see how good number is after you have used it. Then it is like a kind of magic.'

'But I don't know what it can be used for, so how can I use it?'

'Yes, I understand your problem: but it's not really a problem. It's like the connection between thought and language: you can't have one without the other, but they are not the same thing. Only, with number, it's form: numbers make patterns, and things make patterns. Do you see?'

It was Drewin's turn to sit and think with a blank look. Eventually, he came to himself and smiled at Elara. 'No, I don't see. I think I must be too stupid.'

'No, not stupid: you have learnt more in a few days than most of us have learnt in a year.' Elara took a piece of stick and split it down its length. 'Look. Here are two sticks that are the same length: we can see they are the same because they are close together. If they were at opposite ends of the cavern, we could see that they were the same by counting the number of finger lengths in each one.'

She demonstrated by measuring each stick in turn with her finger. 'So each stick is seven finger lengths and so the sticks are the same length. And if one stick were at the far end of the cavern it would still be the same length as the other. A simple pattern. That could be important if you are trying to fit two stones together, or two ideas. Do you see?'

'I think I am beginning to.'

He thanked Elara for her help, and she went to join the others working on the stairway. Drewin returned to the Archive and worked hard until the main lights had been extinguished, and then when the other workers had gone to bed he started again and worked by the light of a candle. In the days that followed he often did the same. Sometimes, when he had become so absorbed in his work that he forgot to sleep, one of his friends would come and tell him to go to bed. But he would wake up before all the other workers, eat a little food, and enthusiastically set to work with the books and machines. He did this day after day, until his eyes became reddened and he was pale and haggard.

One day Urbelin came to him, and instead of watching him silently, he spoke to him. 'Drewin, you have been working hard and long. Stop now, and tell me how you fare.'

Startled, Drewin looked up from the device he had been examining. 'Oh! Hello, Urbelin. I'm sorry: I didn't see you there. Tell me, am I holding this chronometer correctly? I don't seem to be able to work it properly.'

Urbelin took the instrument from Drewin's hands and placed it on a shelf. 'Stop for a moment, and talk to me. I think you should rest for a while: you do not look well. Elara tells me you are making good progress. What do you think?'

'I think I need to work harder. There is so much to learn, and I must climb the stairs.'

Urbelin laughed. 'That you know what you want to achieve is a great advantage: it gives you singleness of purpose and great energy. But the question is whether your energy has been well used. It is some time since you visited the stairway. Come with me and look at it again: that is the true test.'

Reluctantly, Drewin stood up and followed Urbelin through the maze of passages to the stairway. When they arrived, the older man stood aside and watched as Drewin studied the stone structure.

Drewin stood for some time, unaware of all else around him, his eyes moving rapidly as he traced patterns in the structure of the stairway. His face held a look of intense concentration, and the tiredness and strain of recent days showed clearly, so that he looked older than his years. At last he seemed to come to himself, his face relaxed and he turned to Urbelin, smiling.

'I would not have thought that it was possible that the chaos I saw when I was here before could have been transformed into such order. I know that the stairway has changed little since then, yet now it seems to me to be a different thing altogether. Now it seems to be orderly and logical, where before it was a jumble of bits and pieces. Now it seems to be beautiful, where before it was ugly.'

He laughed, and Urbelin laughed with him for a moment, then stopped and looked stern. 'So, now it is easy, and you will climb it quickly, will you?'

Drewin laughed again. 'I did not say it was easy: I said it was beautiful. Sometimes, I think that beauty must be hard, for if it were easy it would be more common.'

'Well, beautiful then. But beautiful or not, will you try the climb?'

Drewin shook his head. 'No, not now: I am too tired. But tomorrow I will climb it.

Early on the next day, before the others had awoken, Drewin arose, washed and breakfasted. Then he put food and drink in his bag and his copy of the book of runes, and went alone to the stairway. He took a moment to look at the structure, and then started the ascent. Steadily and quietly he moved up the steep surface, pausing occasionally to study the route he would take. Sometimes he would climb across to one side or the other; sometimes he would even travel downwards, but with a certainty of movement that never suggested doubt or retreat. Soon he was far above the floor of the cavern, approaching the very top of the stairway, and he stopped at last to look about him.

Urbelin now came to the bottom of the stairway and stood watching. When it seemed that Drewin was unable to advance further, the older man called up to him.

'Do you need help? Shall I come up?'

Drewin turned round suddenly and seemed to lose his balance, but he quickly regained it and peered down towards Urbelin. When he caught sight of him he gave a short laugh, cupped his hands round his mouth and called down, 'That was close: I thought I was going to have to climb all the way up again. Don't come up: I think I must do this by myself. I don't think anyone can help me.'

Drewin returned to his task, examining the steps around him and stepping back as far as he dared to look up to the top of the stairs. He re-examined each possible route upwards several times, then stood perfectly still, looking at nothing, deep in thought. Urbelin watched with no less concentration, his body rigid, his face showing anxiety and expectation.

By now others had gathered at the bottom of the stairway to watch Drewin's progress. They stood in rapt silence, their eyes fixed on the young man high above them. All was still.

At last Drewin moved. Slowly, uncertainly at first, then with increasing confidence, he advanced from step to step to step in one continuous motion, so that he seemed to float over the surface of the stairway. His course was bewildering: he moved sideways, up, and down, in a sequence that appeared nonsensical. But Drewin moved so purposefully that it was clear that each change of direction was deliberate. Gradually he moved nearer to the summit, but the nearer he came, the slower his progress became, and the last stage of the climb was taking longer than all the rest. Drewin climbed tirelessly all morning. Urbelin and the other workers watched in silence.

Drewin worked through the afternoon, but seemed to be getting no nearer to the summit. Occasionally, when the climber stopped to think, Urbelin would move as if to climb up after him or to shout some advice, but would restrain himself. Towards the end of the afternoon Drewin stopped and sat down on a step. He looked exhausted and dispirited, and he was bent over with his head in his hands. A sigh, a quiet groan, went up from the watchers on the cavern floor, for it seemed that, after all, Drewin had been defeated by the problem of the stairway. Disappointment showed on all their faces and they turned away: some of them seemed about to leave.

Only Urbelin stood still and fixed his eyes on Drewin. Only

Urbelin saw Drewin stand up slowly, tiredly, and start to climb again. At each step Drewin paused, thought, then moved. The people became silent again, and watched as Drewin moved remorselessly to the top of the stairway. When he reached the top, he looked up and stared for a long while, then he turned and called to Urbelin. 'No light! No light, Urbelin. Where is the light we are seeking?'

Urbelin smiled sadly and replied. 'Do not fear, Drewin, it is there. We have not reached high enough yet, when we get higher we will begin to see it.'

But Drewin was angry. 'No! You are wrong, Urbelin: this is not the way. There is not even a glow, a glimmer, here; there is more light down there on the cavern floor. It is dark here, darker than the demon's chamber that I escaped from: but I will not come down from here, I will go on.'

Drewin looked up from the top of the stairway, and saw blackness. He stepped forward, beyond the top stair, and fell into dark empty nothingness.

Drelk

*A*s the afternoon grew hotter Saranna began to tire; she had neither eaten nor drunk since breakfast, and her feet in their thin shoes were growing hot and sore. The hem of her gown was thick with dust and she felt as if she were dragging herself along. At last she halted.

'Kor-Sen!

He turned to look at her.

'My feet are hurting.'

She drew the hem of her robe up a little, and he laughed at the sight of the pretty little shoes of thin leather.

'And a silken gown, no less. This was a well-planned escape, was it not? In the morning I shall slip into Mor and buy some more suitable attire for you. Meanwhile... -'

Kor-Sen's pack soon provided for Saranna's needs. A sharp knife trimmed the full, heavy skirt of her dress. A pair of scuffed, worn leather sandals replaced the useless shoes. He also unearthed a small water-bottle and a piece of bread, white and fresh. When she had eaten he gave her his hand, and they set off again down the long dusty road.

After some miles the heat of the day grew less, and ahead they could see the hills that marked the southern coast of Imman. Away to their right the sun was descending, and a welcome evening breeze softly cooled their faces. Suddenly Kor-Sen halted, and gestured toward the wooded slope on their left.

"There is a good camping-place here, sheltered among the trees.' He took her arm gently, leading her away from the road to a hollow where a clear, bubbling stream ran.

'This is the place. Rest now, and I will make a fire. The nights are chill.'

Saranna sat down gratefully and watched while Kor-Sen built and kindled the fire. Then he settled beside her and brought out what was left of his food supply.

'I will replenish my pack tomorrow', he said, and encouraged her to eat the bread and some thick slices of a pale, mild cheese. Kor-Sen ate little, but drank from a bottle of rich red wine.

'Do you often make these solitary journeys, Kor-Sen? Is it not a lonely pastime?'

'No, no,—I find such company as I have need of along the way. I relish the quiet, after three sessions of lecturing, talking, discussing—Lord, how those young scholars love to talk Saranna!'

'Scholars? Oh, then you teach at the Academy—I wondered what you did, and where you came from.' She smiled at him, liking the warm, friendly mood that wrapped them round in the firelight. But they were both weary and soon the silences between remarks grew longer. Saranna began to feel the strangeness of what she had done and of where she was. She saw shadowy trees around her instead of the panelled walls of the farmhouse; through the branches she could glimpse the stars. The sudden scream of a small night creature seized by an owl startled her, and she found that she was crying. Kor-Sen spoke, but she could not answer. 'Saranna? What is wrong? What distresses you?'

'Nothing, it is nothing!'

'Are you thinking of your child?'

'Yes. No, I mean. Oh, yes, I am, but why? He will not miss me. None of them will miss me.' She wept again, even louder;

wet and choking sobs shook her body and contorted her face. Kor-Sen sat quietly watching. As the sobbing began to grow less, he moved closer and drew her into his arms, holding her against him until she fell silent.

'Better now?'

'Yes, a little.' She looked up into his face, her head still resting on his shoulder.

'I think you are very wise, Kor-Sen; wise and kind, strong and gentle.'

He released her abruptly, and moved away, tossing wood onto the fire and keeping his back to her while he answered, 'Now indeed you trust me too much and praise me too far.' Seizing the wine bottle, he drained it, tossed it aside, and began to scrabble in his pack.

'Curse it—I thought there was one more, at least. Ah well, pretty lady, we must resort to sleep. Why are you watching me so solemnly, with those weird eyes so full of wonder?'

'You are a strange man.'

'Oh, Saranna—maybe one day you may learn how strange. Now we must sleep.'

He pulled a heavy cloak from the pack, and shook it out. 'Since we have only this to cover us, we must sleep together, fair Saranna. I promise to behave well. Thus far at least, I assure you, you may trust me.'

In the flickering light, Saranna saw that he was smiling again. She went to him readily, and settled down in his arms with the great cloak wrapped around them both. As the fire died and the moon rose, they fell asleep.

Saranna awoke to bright leaf-dappled sunlight, and found she was alone by a cold dead fire. She washed herself and drank from the stream; as she leaned over the chattering water, the rune-disk on its leather cord slipped from her gown and she knelt transfixed, watching it turn and sway. Then she heard footsteps behind her and Kor-Sen stepped out of the trees. He bowed to her.

'Greetings, fair lady. You look like dawn itself, bright among the trees. See, I have brought breakfast, fresh clothing, and other good things. Sit you down and eat. We must be on our way to Dor as soon as we may.'

When they had eaten, Kor-Sen cleared up the remains of their food and gear while Saranna retired behind a bush. Here she changed into the plain gown and stout shoes that Kor-Sen had brought from the village. When she came back, Kor-Sen looked with interest at the Ord-rune that she now wore outside her gown.

'That is a curious ornament, Saranna. Was it a gift from your husband?'

'No—I have had it since I was a child. But I would prefer not to discuss it, if you please.'

He nodded thoughtfully, and led the way back to the road.

They made good time, and came into the Gap of Imm by early evening. Footsore but happy, they strolled towards the little port of Dor. Saranna looked up at the great rock-faces on either hand.

'It is as if some giant had chopped through the rock with a huge axe,' she said.

'The people of Dor believe that the gap was made in the time of the Grief of Iranor, when she cast the moon into the heavens and wept for her lost children.'

Saranna stood still with a gasp.

'These cliffs are so old, Kor-Sen!'

'Indeed. And immeasurably old is the tale of the Grief of Iranor. In the time before time her children were lost to her, and cast away on the sea, they say.'

She stared at him. 'But... then I do not understand the workings of time, Kor-Sen.'

'Does anyone?' He spoke lightly, but seeing that she was really puzzled he leaned closer and put a gentle arm about her.

'Saranna, do not be distressed. You have years ahead of you to live, miles to wander in the world. I have found some things clearer, and many less clear, as I have grown older. There is so much we shall never understand. But now—it is supper-time, and there is a good inn by the harbour; I can hear the ale calling to me from here!'

Soon they were walking through the narrow streets of Dor, where the smell of fish permeated the air and the sound of the waves could always be heard. Kor-Sen headed straight for the harbour, where Saranna had no more than a glimpse of water sparkling in the evening sun, before Kor-Sen pulled her through a low doorway.

The inn was dark, and at first Saranna could see little; but she could hear, and to her surprise a chorus of greeting arose about them.

'Kor-Sen! You old devil, what brings you back this way? '

'Hello, Kor-Sen, where you been so long, dear!'

'Who's your friend, then?'

'Very nice too; as usual!'

As a roar of laughter followed this last remark, Saranna found that she could see. The low, long room was crowded, and Kor-Sen, who gripped her hand firmly, was steering her toward seats on a bench against the further wall. By the time they arrived there the innkeeper, a handsome woman of forty, was close behind them with a foaming jug of ale and two mugs.

'Here you are, Kor-Sen; our best brew. My, it is good to see you—and you too, young lady.'

'Good to be back, Enna; this is the Lady Saranna, a friend of mine.'

Saranna sat quietly while Kor-Sen ordered food, and a room for the night. Soon the servant brought a splendid meal of fish, straight from the sea by its flavour, and the travellers ate hungrily.

After supper, Kor-Sen was soon drawn into a circle of men who settled down to serious drinking. Saranna sat on for a while, but no-one took notice of her, so she called a servant-girl over and asked to be shown to her room, where she soon slipped into the big soft bed. But in the still of night she was woken by a muffled noise. Turning over in bed, she saw that the fire had been built up, and on the rug in front of it sat Kor-Sen, hunched over with his head on his knees.

What she had heard was the sound of Kor-Sen weeping. She slipped out of bed and crossed the room, circled his taut shoulders with her arm and tried to comfort him; after a while he looked up.

'I am sorry. I did not want you to wake—to see me like this.'

'It is all right, Kor-Sen. I only want to help.'

He nodded, and stared into the fire, tears still staining his face.

'Where have you been?' Saranna asked.

'I have been—visiting.' He turned to face her, and raised

his voice defiantly. 'I have been with Enna. We are old friends.'

'Good. But why should that make you unhappy?'

'Are you not shocked?'

'Shocked? Why should I be... Oh, I see. What right have I to be shocked?'

They sat in silence for some moments, then Saranna said,

'Kor-Sen, you know all about me—will you not tell me something of your life, and how you came to live here on Imman. For I believe that, like me, you have travelled far—and suffered much.'

He shook his head; but then, at her insistence, began to speak; 'I was born forty-nine years ago in the city of Sen-Mar, by the Northern shores of Isskar. There the Lord Jaren is worshipped, Lord of the desert. He has small love for his people; most of the land is dry and fruitless, and life is hard.'

'Where did you live? What was your family like?'

'There was only my mother. She was a weaver, and as a baby I played at her feet with old shuttles and scraps of rough goat-wool. As I grew older I began to play in the streets with other children, and from them I learned the word, 'father'. I learned that each of them had a father, while I had not, and I learned that my mother and I were much to blame for this, and that neither Jaren—may his name be ever praised—nor his priests would ever bless us.'

'What a strange country yours must be, to treat a lonely woman and a little child so harshly! What became of you both?'

'Too much to tell now—but my mother married, and had some years of happiness with her husband.'

'I am glad of that.'

'But when she was dead and I was grown I came here. I

knew from my mother that my lost father was a merchant of Imman. I talked my way into their Academy—though they laughed at my speech and my desert robe and my rough ways— for I was cleverer than them all; and I have stayed and learnt all they know, and more. And now they all acknowledge that I am the most learned among them. But I am lonely, Saranna. I am very lonely.'

At this he broke down and sobbed while Saranna rocked him back and forth, trying to calm him. When at last he was quiet, she helped him to his feet, and over to the bed, where he fell heavily onto the pillows. She covered him as best she could, and climbing in beside him took him in her arms and held him through the rest of the night.

'Poor thing', she whispered into his hair. 'I will try to care for you.'

The next day, however, Kor-Sen seemed to have no more need of her care. He was brightly cheerful while they breakfasted, kissing Enna goodbye, shouldering his bundle, and leading Saranna down to the quayside all in a brief flurry of activity that left her quite bewildered. Soon they were tossing in a small coastal trading vessel, bound for Drelk around the west coast of Imman, and Saranna was seated alone while Kor-Sen chatted amiably and knowledgeably with the captain and crew. She could hardly believe that this was the same man who had wept in her arms a few hours before.

Eventually she settled down to watch the sea, and the high cliffs, a little hurt and lonely. But from time to time she watched Kor-Sen as he talked and joked with the sailors. Gradually she sensed a warm but shaky feeling creeping over her whenever she looked at him. She turned away to look at the sea, but then his voice rang out again and her head snapped round before she could stop it; she gazed at him. She whispered his name. Tears filled her eyes, and she felt the West Wind caressing her face as they began to spill softly down her cheeks.

After a while Saranna became aware of a burst of activity among the crew. She looked around her and saw that they were guiding the boat with great care between some small islands and the main coast of Imman. To her right now she could see the low coastline, and even the dust of travellers on the coast road. Ahead was the harbour of Drelk; Saranna stood up to see better, and as she did so Kor-Sen hurried back to her. She found herself trembling with her new awareness of him, with the shock of his closeness. He put an arm around her to steady her, and she almost cried out.

'See, Saranna, now we are coming into the harbour; see how calm it is, and what great numbers of small boats and big ships can lie safe here? There is no other harbour so fine in all the Islands.'

'Yes, it is splendid. And what are those great buildings up on the hills?'

'There are three hills, and on that one directly ahead of us now is the temple of Iranor—Irnor, they call her. Over to the left is the House of Knowing; the Academy. On the hill to the right are many great houses belonging to the rich and powerful merchants; below, around the harbour, are the houses of more humble folk, and south a little are the docks and shipyards and warehouses.'

'And where will I find an inn?'

He turned and looked directly at her for the first time that day. 'Why do you want to find an inn?'

'I must sleep somewhere tonight, Kor-Sen; I cannot walk the streets.'

'Well, of course not. But you will come and stay with me. '

She shook her head, and he leaned closer to her, trying to look into the eyes she did not want him to read. 'What is wrong, Saranna? Surely you will not leave me now?'

'You are very kind', she said, and burst into tears.

Kor-Sen put his arms around her gently and she let herself weep on his shoulder for a while.

'Come now; there is no need for such extravagant behaviour; we are about to dock, and must gather up our belongings and look for some conveyance. I have told you already that you make too much of what you call my kindness.'

'Yes, Kor-Sen', she said meekly; and got ready to follow him ashore. Kor-Sen insisted on hiring a donkey to carry Saranna up the long, steep hill to the House of Knowing. She clung on tightly until the road gave a final twist, and led them out onto a wide, level space, cobbled and planted with fair trees to give patches of shade.

Across the square loomed a solid, heavy building, thick-walled and grim, with a great gate set into the middle of the wall and rather small windows giving out onto the plaza. When they came under the shadow of the gate a door-keeper came out to inspect them. Seeing Kor-Sen he became cordial and welcoming at once.

'Welcome back, Sir! I trust you are refreshed and fit after your travels?'

'Well enough, thank you, Grenal. But look to the lady.'

The man hurried forward and helped Saranna down. 'Welcome to the House of Knowing, My Lady,' Grenal began;

but Kor-Sen hurried Saranna in through the gates and under a great vaulted archway into an inner courtyard, exactly square and surrounded on all four sides by identical buildings, with rows and rows of the same small windows that Saranna had seen on the outer facade. All the windows were regularly arranged, and at each corner, where the buildings joined, there stood a huge cuboid tower, each one exactly like the others. From the top of each tower a vast rectangular flag strained in the wind from the sea, and on each was a design of four squares, arranged so that they sat separately in the four corners of the flag. Dull red was the colour of the flags, and the sections were outlined in silver. 'What does the pattern on the flag mean?'

Kor-Sen stopped in surprise. 'Oh! Well, each silver square stands for one branch of learning, and the red field is for the mind that encompasses them.'

'What are the four branches?'

'They are Number; Language; Form; and Thought.'

'And are they all separate, like the squares?'

Kor-Sen had come back to stand before Saranna, and by his smile he was amused at her questions. 'So the Masters of learning here believe, anyway. Each one must choose one discipline and specialise in it if he or she wishes to become a Master. But there is one exception to that rule.'

'And who is that?'

Kor-Sen bowed. 'It is myself—Kor-Sen the foreigner. I have mastered all their silly Branches, and by rights should be Convenor of the Academy.'

'Why are you not, then?'

He spun round on his heel, gesturing at all the neat, quiet buildings, shouting so that the doves on the rooftops flapped startled away;

'Because they hate me! Because they cannot bear me! I should not know so much, should l, you small-minded island law-writers? I don't fit your tidy, tidy patterns—do I?'

By now several of the identical windows had opened to reveal shocked faces. One or two voices were raised in protest, but Kor-Sen went on yelling.

'Thin-blooded theorisers, the lot of you! Can't hold your wine and all you do with love is talk about it! Damn you all—I wish Jaren would frazzle you in the deep, hot desert!'

He seemed very upset, and Saranna grew alarmed. She went closer and took his arm. 'Kor-Sen; come, you were taking me to your rooms.'

He stopped shouting, nodded, and led her on towards the far side of the courtyard. At precise intervals, dark green trees, with thin, tidy leaves, were set in stone tubs; they had a dusty look. In the exact centre of the square, they passed a fountain. It also was cubic in form, consisting of progressively diminishing rectangles of stone, each exactly two feet deep, so that the highest one was some way above Saranna's head. From the centre of the topmost stone, a gentle stream came trickling, and the thin veil of water that ran over the surface of the stones disappeared into drains set about the base.

Soon they went in through one of the identical doors and up a stair-case that was all right-angled turnings, passing more identical doors on the way. At the top of the stair, Kor-Sen threw open the last door and Saranna stepped inside. She gave a gasp of delight, and stood gazing for a while. Then she trod lightly over the woollen floor-coverings of warm red and russet shades, to finger the wall hangings. They were rich with gold and silver thread.

'It is wonderful! Like a part of a far southern land inside this grey building.'

'You like it, then?'

Kor-Sen had followed her in and shut the door.

'Oh, it is beautiful! I expected a grey, cold cell after what I have seen of the outside—but this... ?'

'This, dear lady, is a reproduction of the inside of a tent of the desert wanderers of my own land. They trade far and wide, and love these rich hangings which they get from northern lands—silk and wool far finer than our own flocks can produce. I am glad that it pleases you.'

He crossed the room to her, and took her in his arms. Returning his kiss, she trembled.

'I hope that I shall please you too,' he said.

As the days of autumn began to take the place of summer, Saranna's life slipped into a new pattern, and she scarcely thought of the past. Kor-Sen was kind and caring; she delighted in looking after his home and cooking for him; and sometimes he would cook for her, exotic dishes from IssKor. They fell into a way of spoiling each other, spending all their spare time together, either at home or out in the busy streets and market-places of Drelk.

Some weeks passed quietly in this way; then one evening when Saranna came home from the market, Kor-Sen was not there. She went through to the kitchen and put all her purchases carefully away. Then she came back to the main room, sat down by the window, and waited, staring out across the courtyard. The setting sun was reddening the slow trickle of the fountain; and though Saranna sat watching while the dusk fell thicker and thicker into the square, and the sky above grew black, and the first stars began to shine; still Kor-Sen did not come. She grew stiff and cold and tired; so she got up and walked once about the room, then twice. She lit a fire in the brazier and drank a little milk. Then she went back to her seat at the window, shivering in the cold night air; but still he did not come.

As the grey dawn filled the courtyard, Kor-Sen came creeping up the stairs. He opened the door, and slipped in, tripping over a footstool which fell with a muffled sound on the rich carpet. It was enough to wake Saranna, who sat up in her chair and stared at him.

"Kor-Sen; oh, where have you been?'

He took two steps more into the room, and fell over a low table. Grinning up at Saranna from the carpet, he replied, 'Drinking!'

She moved quickly to help him up, and tried to kiss him, but he turned his head away.

'What is it? What is wrong?'

'I must leave you for a while—I must spend some time alone. Please, Saranna, do not try to stop me.'

'But Kor-Sen, where are you going?'

He turned towards the door, and was gone before she understood that he meant to go at once. Saranna ran down the stairs and across the square, but when she came out under the great archway, there was no sign of Kor-Sen. She stood helplessly, shivering in the cold morning air, and began to cry.

'My Lady?' Grenal the gatekeeper was standing beside Saranna, looking anxious. She began to sob even more loudly. Grenal took her by the hand and led her into his tiny dwelling, a single room hollowed out into the side of the archway of the gate. He seated her on a wooden stool by the fire and draped a blanket about her shoulders; then set milk to warm on the hob.

He said quietly, 'Master Kor-Sen has upset you, I fear.'

'Where has he gone, Grenal? Do you know?'

'Why, yes. He's off to his tower, out on the island—some boatman will take him out there, and then row out once a week with supplies, until the Master takes it into his head to come home, and then there'll he be at the gate, right as a rainbow.'

'Did you say island? What island?'

'Here, My Lady. Keep that blanket round you against the cold. I'll show you.'

Grenal led her back into the courtyard, where he turned left and made for the south-west tower. Here they climbed up and up until they came out onto the parapeted roof.

'Look there, My Lady, to the west,' said Grenal.

Saranna saw a small island beyond the outer line of hills that guarded the harbour of Drelk. In the midst of it she could just make out a grim tower, squat and rounded.

'There?'

'Yes, My Lady. Master Kor-Sen owns that island, and the tower—which is meant to be no end of years old, so they say. And that's where he goes to be alone.'

'Grenal, before next week, can you find out for me the name of the boatman who is going out to the island?'

'Why, easily, Lady Saranna.'

'Good. Then we'll see what Master Kor-Sen makes of his supplies when they are delivered.'

The sun had not yet woken the true colours of land or sea; both channel and island were a deep slate-purple, the water overlaid with a rippling sheen of reflected dawn-light, the island massed dense and heavy against the minimal brightening of the sky. The tower rose like a dark tree. The light grew, and brought out the grey of the thick stone walls, the rough green of the grass that circled them, the echoing grey of cliffs and shore-rocks, the faint silver of the sandy cove below the tower.

Here the fisherman grounded his boat, leapt out and drew it up over the sand, then helped Saranna ashore. He unloaded Kor-Sen's supplies onto the sand, carried them up the rough path to the tower and left them stacked beside the door. Saranna sat on a flat rock on the beach and looked around at the sea and the sky. The fisherman came over to her before returning to his boat.

"Maybe I should come this way this evening, and see if you are still waiting here on the sands?'

Saranna sighed, wondering why everyone else in Drelk seemed to feel they understood Kor-Sen better than she did. 'I am sure that all will be well. You must go now, the fish and the tides will not wait.'

'Goodbye then, My Lady. I wish you good fortune.'

For a while Saranna sat still, gradually becoming aware of life and movement and sound; the surge of the waves, and the swish as they broke on the shore; the crying of the sea-birds, and the scuttle now and then of a sizeable crab passing close by her feet. The wind swept in from the sea and lifted her long hair. As the sun rose she felt warmer, and decided to get up and explore the whole island before approaching the tower. She saw cropped grass, a little heather and gorse, and half-wild sheep that ran from her in panic.

The western cliffs were high and steep; just a long plunge into lashing waves. There were gulls yelling here, and fulmars coasting, while assorted auks played I'm-falling-off-can't-catch-me in the dizziness below her. Saranna turned towards the east and surveyed the tower at the far end of the island.

Grey, crumbling, immeasurably ancient, its curved walls stretched into the sky like a branchless tree or a solitary pillar left behind after the fall of some mighty building. As Saranna wandered slowly back towards it, it seemed to grow ever more solid, taller, more menacing. She followed the path right up to the heavy wooden door, which had no handle or latch visible from the outside, only a massive keyhole. She looked up and saw that the only windows were narrow slits high in the walls. From one of them, a steady stream of smoke issued.

Saranna moved away from the door and settled herself on a nearby rock to wait. Past noon, the lock sounded abruptly. Slowly the door swung inward, and a slight figure appeared in the frame. She sprang to her feet and stepped forward one pace. The figure moved cautiously into the sunlight. At the first sight of the thick white hair she called out,

'Kor-Sen!'

He recoiled instantly, back into the shadow, but after a moment moved forward again. 'Saranna.'

'Kor-Sen. '

He stood looking at her, then smiled. Without a word, he began to carry his supplies into the tower, quickly clearing them away and locking the great door before Saranna had a chance even to offer her help. Then he turned to her again.

'Come and see my island.'

'Not the tower?'

He shook his head and set off towards the far end of the island. She fell into step beside him, a gap of two or three feet between them.

'People leave me alone here, usually.'

'I am sorry, Kor-Sen.'

She walked on, trying to think of something to say. Kor-Sen never seemed to hold ordinary conversations, never said things like, 'How did you get here?' or 'How are you?' He moved a little closer to her, and her hair blew into his face. They walked to the top of the seaward cliff. Silently they watched the waves, until suddenly he said, 'When I first came to this island, I came up this way.'

'What do you mean?'

'Up this cliff.'

Saranna looked down at the creaming foam of the waves below, and then back at Kor-Sen. She hugged him close, and for a moment he stood unyielding. But then he hugged her in return and kissed her ear.

'Please do not fuss about it, Saranna!'

She looked up at him, shook her head, and led him away from the cliff. They wandered on for a while, then walked together back to the tower. At the door he stopped, kissed her, and said, 'Farewell, for now.'

'May I not come in?'

He turned away without a word, and let himself in. He did not look at her before slamming the door. He had not once asked how she had reached the island, or whether she had any way of getting home.

Saranna trudged down the path to the shore, where she sat until the fisherman came back and stood silently before her.

'I think I must ask you to take me back to Drelk, if you will.'

'Yes, My Lady. I—I am sorry for your trouble, My Lady. '

'Well, you tried to save me from it; but I would come here, and I would make a fool of myself. And now I must go home.'

On a quiet grey evening two weeks later Kor-Sen, too, came home. Saranna was in the kitchen when she heard the familiar creak of the heavy door swinging open. She hurried into the main room, and stood looking across the rich carpet to where he waited, shy and hesitant, just inside the door.

"May I come in?'

'This is your home Kor-Sen.'

'I thought you might be less than glad to see me.'

'I—all I have wanted is to see you, Kor-Sen. You must know that'

'Yes.' He opened his arms, and she crossed the room to him. They held each other quietly for a while. 'I am sorry,' he said.

Then he asked, 'What's for supper?'

Saranna began to laugh. 'How dare you walk in here and ask what's for supper? I'm glad to say there is hardly a thing to eat; but of course you'll make up for that with wine, you disgusting man'ᶜ

And Kor-Sen laughed too, and picked her up in his arms and swung her around in a circle; they were very happy. They shared the supper and wine, then settled down together on the soft couch, close and warm.

'Will you tell me now? About the tower and the island and why you ran away from me?'

Kor-Sen said nothing for a while. Finally he asked, 'What did you think of the island?'

'It is very beautiful; wild and lonely, but why do you go there?'

Saranna got up and fetched Kor-Sen more wine. He took

the goblet from her, and slipped his arm around her shoulders again. 'I love you, Saranna. And so I will tell you what I have told no-one else.'

She nestled close to him, and listened.

'The day I left you, I saw my sister in the streets of Drelk.

'Your sister! I did not know that you had any family still alive.'

'I have two sisters, in fact—one here, and one in Sen-Mar. And then there is my father. I came here to Imman all those years ago thinking I might meet him, and wondering what I would say. How I would tell him that I hated him for what he had done to my mother.'

'And did you?'

'No. I met him, but I said nothing to him of any importance. It was at a grand ball given in one of the big houses, many years ago. I met a lovely young girl—very young, a mere child—and she talked to me and flattered me, and I kissed her many times. I was beginning to fall in love with her, even in that short time.'

He stopped, and sipped his wine.

"Go on.'

'I will—but it is not easy, Saranna. When the evening ended and I escorted her to her father—I found that he was my father too. And for a moment, before I ran away from the house and hid myself in shame—for a moment I looked at him and wanted to kill him. I wanted to put my hands about his throat and choke the life out of him!'

Kor-Sen drew a deep shuddering breath and Saranna laid a gentle hand on his arm. He went on, his voice low and sorrowful. 'And worse than that, I looked upon that lovely young girl, and it came into my mind that I might despoil her life, degrade and shame her and our father at once, ruin her as he had ruined my poor mother. I had only to seduce her, and then tell the world of our relationship. And for a long moment, Saranna, I thought to do just that.'

He leapt up and crossed the room to the window, where he leaned his forehead against the cool stone.

'But you did not.'

'No—I did not. I said something, what I do not remember, and I ran. It was then I bought the island, and the tower. It was then I began to drink, and to hate myself for the dreadful things that I found lurking in my own heart. I, who cursed the Priests of Jaren for their cruelty and violence! I am no better than they.'

Saranna went to him, and took his hand, kissing him gently on the cheek. 'But you did not do all these dreadful things—in your grief and sorrow you imagined them, but you did not do them!'

'No—but bad enough even to think of it! I cannot bear to see Maressa's face now, though I doubt if she ever thinks of me. My sister—and I felt such hatred for her. Only on the island can I find peace, Saranna, when I think of that dreadful day.'

She kissed him again. 'I wish you could turn to me—I would help you to bear it.'

But he shook his head sadly, and looked away from her, out into the dark.

Some days later, Kor-Sen arrived home in the early evening with a gaggle of students, who settled themselves in various corners of the room and began to consume ale, wine and food at an alarming rate, while talking non-stop about everything and nothing. Kor-Sen and Saranna joined in the talk, and Kor-Sen was much in demand to confirm or deny this or that assertion or idea. At last one young man said, 'Tell us about the tower on the island, Master.'

'Fiilan! Sssssh!' cried several anxious voices.

'No, it is all right.' Kor-Sen grinned at Saranna, and settled down into his 'wise old teacher' style. 'That tower was fashioned long ago, in the earliest days of the people of the west. In those days a wanderer came to Imman, a stranger from the South who said his name was Vodorian.'

'But Master, do you mean to say that a stone tower could stand for so long?' objected a young girl in a corner seat.

'Who knows what magic may do?' Kor-Sen's eyes were twinkling.

'Oh, magic!' said the student, an aspirant of Number.

'Shhh. Don't interrupt the Master!' chorused several others.

'Where was I? Oh yes, Vodorian. Well, he was a strange fellow and the people of Imman in those days were simple folk and cautious. They saw that he had some store of wisdom—magic, some of them said—and they did not object to taking advantage of his skills. But they were not quite comfortable with him, and asked if he would mind removing himself to the small island yonder, where his tower still stands; the sorcerer's tower, they call it to this day, and after all these centuries they still fear it. So that is why the island is called Vodor's isle.'

Kor-Sen paused for refreshment.

'What became of this sorcerer, Master?'

'He went away to the north across the sea, hundreds of years ago by all accounts. Some say he flew away on a dragon, some that he changed himself into a swan, some that he swam from island to island until he reached the lands of Akent; still others say that he took passage on a ship in the usual way.'

'And what do you think, Master?'

'I? Oh, I can believe anything if I need to. But do you not wish to know who he was?'

'You said he was a sorcerer.'

'I said people long ago called him that. For although he aged slowly, still he did age, and so they thought of him as just a mortal creature like themselves, with some rather special abilities. But I have researched the matter for many years; and I have found out who Vodorian really was.'

'Who?' asked everyone at once.

'He was one of the Great Ones, a child of Iranor, Lady of the West Wind. For not all the children of Iranor are Immortals like her.'

Saranna jumped, and stared at Kor-Sen.

'But... ' she said. He interrupted quickly, gesturing at her that she should be silent.

'Yes, I know. Most scholars believe that Iranor had only two mortal children, a son and a daughter; and that the name of the son was—not Vodorian.'

Saranna and several of the students nodded.

'The boy was Drune, or some such name. I don't know what the girl was called,' put in Fiilan.

'Nevertheless, I am telling the truth. Vodorian was the last-born child of Iranor. There is no time now to tell you of his father, and of how Vodorian became mortal and lived in Time so long ago.'

'Oh, Master, please!'

'No, for it is time you all stopped quaffing my good wine,

and went to your own rooms. But I assure you it was so, and that was how the tower was built where your mad old tutor goes to drink himself silly when you all become too much for me.'

Laughing and chattering, the students took their leave and went away. Saranna sat still and quiet until all had departed and Kor-Sen came back to sit beside her. He took her hand, raised it to his lips, and kissed it.

'Well?'

'Well what, learned Master?'

'What did you think of my tale, woman?'

'I thought it very interesting, Master. But it makes me wonder how many more things you know, that you have not told.'

'Well—I know who you are, My Lady Saranna.'

'Do you indeed?'

'Oh, yes, indeed' I began to guess who you were when I first saw your wooden amulet; and at the Gap of Imm most of my suspicion was confirmed. The final test was tonight. Oh, Saranna—I have read the story of your exile in sheets of parchment so old that they almost crumble at the touch; and yet here you are with me, warm and alive and lovely!'

He leaned over to kiss her cheek, but she evaded him.

'It seems I have been very simple. I thought that no-one in the world— except Drewin, wherever he is—knew who I was.'

'Are you angry with me, Saranna?'

'No—you have told me secrets that you have entrusted to no-one else, and I am glad that you know all about me. But I wish I understood it all. It happened to me, yet sometimes it feels like a dream, or something that happened to another person long ago. Can you help me to understand?'

'I will try, but it is difficult. All the children born to the Lady were born in the place outside of Time that we call Eternity. And there she and her immortal children dwell, coming into our Time when they are pleased to, but not subject to age or change.

But you, Saranna; and Drewin; and Vodorian the outcast, you were sent into Time to live out your mortal lives. Do you understand?'

'But if this Vodorian was born after me and Drewin, how can he have been here all that time ago? And why do people think that Drewin and I lived long ago?'

'Because the stories are confused. Look at the moon—because the moon has always been here, because Iranor cast it into the sky at the Beginning, people assume you must have come into Time at the Beginning. So you are an old, old story, and many little girls are named after you. That is why no-one cries out in amazement when you say you are called Saranna.'

'Do you know, I was so puzzled by the moon. They all thought I was mad when I asked what it was and how it had got into the sky. But who was Vodorian's father? Why did you not want to tell us?'

'Ah! That is simple—I do not really know. Enough to say that I liked the idea of dwelling in Vodorian's tower because he and I are both outcasts.'

'So am I, come to that. But Kor-Sen, do you know nothing about Drewin—whether he is still alive?'

'No, nothing; I wish I did, for your sake. If ever I discover anything, I will tell you at once.'

'I still do not understand.'

'No matter, Saranna—as long as you and I understand each other.'

They sat together in comfortable silence, holding hands. At last Saranna said, 'The Spring Festival will soon be here. Would you come with me to the temple? I should like to see if I can find some sign or word from my mother.'

'Of course, my love—but may we go on the eve of the Festival, at night?'

'Why at night?'

'Because I cannot bear the great crowds—and because Maressa and my father may be there.'

'Very well then—we shall go at night.'

Twelve days later, through a soft dark night that filled the sleepy streets of Drelk, Saranna and Kor-Sen made their way to the Temple of Irnor the Lady. Down the winding cobbles of the hill from the Academy, away from its heavy shadow that crouched square against the deep blue of the sky; through the narrow twisted streets behind the dock area, and up again along paths that Saranna had never trodden since she came to Drelk. At first they climbed between the tumbled, crowded houses of the poor; then the walls drew back a little as they passed through the quarter where the priestesses and priests of the Lady dwelt.

There was a solemn stillness here, a hush that made them both nervous, and they drew close together on the broad empty street, each clinging to the other's hand for comfort. At last they came out from the built-up places, and were under the open stretch of the sky whose remote stars were fading towards dawn. Still on they went, up the hill, until they came to the level place where the House of the Seasons, Temple of

Irnor, stands open to the sky; a broad circle, crossed by paths that met at the centre of the hilltop.

Saranna and Kor-Sen followed the nearest path until they reached the sanctuary. They found that they were both whispering, yet their voices sounded clear in the utter silence.

'I cannot make out anything in the blackness. What is the Temple like, Kor-Sen? Is it very old?'

'Yes—some say that Vodorian had a hand in its making.'

'What are these great arches?'

'They form a circle of stone, wondrously fashioned—as if a living fountain has been—crystallised—into solidity.'

'I want to see it—will the light come soon.'

'I think dawn is near now. Shall I tell you more?'

'Please.'

'At the centre a great column rises from the ground and divides at the top into eleven streams of stone. They curve over and bend to the ground to form the outer boundary of the holiest place.'

'Is anyone allowed to walk there?'

'Only the High Priestess at the great festivals. Can you see anything yet?'

'A bit—what is that dark area around the central column?

'A still dark pool of polished black marble that stands for Ellanna, who is the origin and the beginning of all things. The column itself represents Akana, the act of creation or process of coming into being, while the head of the column is for Iranor.'

'Because she was born from Ellanna?'

'Exactly! And the eleven streams of stone are for the children of Iranor.'

Saranna and Kor-Sen stood gazing up at the great height of the temple; they were dwarfed by the soaring stone. 'One of these columns,' Kor-Sen whispered, 'stands here for you, daughter of Iranor.'

'And one for Drewin,' she answered sadly.

Dawn was glimmering in the east, but their eyes were drawn to the great central pillar. Kor-Sen laughed awkwardly, and released Saranna's hand. 'I cannot bear this place,' he said. 'I must stand further off, my dear.'

Saranna turned to watch him as he walked little way off and seated himself on one of the marble benches that circled the temple. He sighed heavily as he sat down, then remained silent and still, his gaze directed away from the sanctuary toward his own linked hands. She turned back to look at the pillar again.

The sun was just visible upon the eastern horizon, and it seemed to Saranna to be awakening a silver light within the central pillar. She stared at it for a long time, until the light dazzled her and shone like alabaster that encloses a candle. Shading her eyes with her hand, Saranna felt she could discern a faint shape within the pillar, a woman-shape of great stature. At the same time, behind her, a gentle morning breeze awoke and flowed over her from the west. Peering at the figure she whispered, 'Mother?'

Stretching out her arms towards the centre of the circle she repeated softly, 'Mother, is that you? Have you a message for me?' The flickering shape might have been bowing its head, Saranna thought, or maybe reaching out a hand of its own in response. A quiet music arose that seemed to come from the playing of the breeze between and around the arching columns. Yet it very soon grew fainter, and the shape of light grew dimmer as the sky lightened. Saranna found that tears were sliding down her cheeks. She said once more, 'Mother, will you not speak to me?' Her voice was less than a whisper, and the shining shape less than a shadow; Saranna turned away and walked slowly to where Kor-Sen waited.

She sat down beside him and reached for his hand. He jumped at her touch, and looked up at her.

'Sorry, I was thinking, or half-asleep maybe. This is a terrible place, Saranna!'

'But I think it is beautiful, Kor-Sen. Did you not see the shining light, and hear the sweet music? I thought I heard my mother and saw her reaching toward me lovingly.'

He stared at her, shaking his head. 'No, I heard and saw nothing, certainly not such a presence. My dear, you may have seen only what you wanted to see.'

They sat for sometime without speaking. Gradually, imperceptibly, each released the other's hand, and turned away; Saranna looked back at the Temple, and Kor-Sen looked past her to where the sea was beginning to sparkle in the growing daylight. Turning back to her, he said 'It may be time to think of leaving, my dear.'

The temple light had vanished; they found themselves standing in the full light of day. Once more hand in hand, they retraced their steps through the waking city.

For the next few days, Saranna and Kor-Sen stayed quietly at home together, except during the times when Kor-Sen was teaching. The one evening as they sat down to their meal, Saranna said, 'I have been thinking.'

'Yes, my dear? And what have you decided?'

"I did not say that I had decided anything.'

'No, but you have a look in your eye – a look that speaks to me of decisions and change. When are you leaving? And where will you go?'

Saranna sat open-mouthed for several moments, then spluttered a bit before saying, 'Sometimes I could believe that you truly are a magician! How can you read my thoughts, Kor-Sen?'

'No magic – I know you well and care for you deeply. Ever since we visited the temple, you have been struggling to decide your course. I know your restlessness. I sense you have resolved to leave.'

'And you say so very calmly. I have been afraid to speak for fear of causing you pain.'

Kor-Sen reached for the flagon on the table. 'This is one of those occasions when more wine will be needed.'

She smiled. 'All occasions are so with you, my dear.'

'So you are leaving because of my drunken habits?'

Saranna leaned across the table and kissed him. 'You,' she said, 'are always at your silliest when your feelings are deep and serious and true. I do not know whether I find it endearing or infuriating.'

'It prevents my becoming sentimental, which you would not like, my sweet. Where shall you go?'

'To Telan. I am not sure why, but that island calls to me.'

Kor-Sen sighed. 'So many places and voices seem to call you. I knew you would not stay, Saranna. But we shall meet again, I am certain of it. And when we do, I suspect that it may be I who am given the blame for our parting.'

Saranna threw a bread-roll at him.

Two mornings on, Saranna stood on the deck of a ship

bound for Telan, leaning over the rail to say her last goodbyes to Kor-Sen.

'Remember me!' she called.

'Always,' he answered. And one of these days, I shall find you again.'

'What will you do, when I am gone, Kor-Sen?'

He jumped back hastily as the gangplank beside his feet was pulled aboard.

'Oh, can you not guess? I am off to see my father, this very minute.'

At once he turned and slipped lightly away; Saranna hardly saw him go.

Vodorian

*D*rewin was lying on coarse sand, half covered in seawater. He was cold and stiff and tired, as if he had been on a long hard journey. He sat up with difficulty and looked around him. There was just enough light to allow him to see that he was in a narrow, smooth-sided cave. One end was flooded with black water, and the other sloped gently upwards. The ceiling was just high enough to allow Drewin stand upright, but sloped down towards the flooded end and into the water: it was as though a corridor was leading out of the water into the air. Drewin stood up and walked with difficulty up the slope and along the passage.

The light grew brighter as he walked along, and after some time he came to its source: there was a burning torch, like those in the Cavern, fixed to the cave wall at about head height. Drewin stopped and looked at it curiously for a while, then peered about him for other signs of life. There were none: the cave was completely bare. He continued on his path, away from the light and into increasing gloom. Before he had moved far, Drewin found the sand underfoot gradually diminishing until there was only a thin layer on the solid rock floor. He shuffled forward, staring ahead intently, unable to see anything more than a few paces ahead: beyond that there was only darkness. The sound of his uncertain footsteps echoed from the rock and seemed to disappear into the gloom. There was no other sound.

The darkness became deeper as he moved slowly forward, and he was forced to feel his way along the rock. The air was stale and Drewin's clothes were soon cold and damp. It was now so dark that he could not see at all and he reached his hand out in front of his face fearfully. He talked to himself as he walked along.

'What are you doing, Drewin? Where are you going?'

'I don't know, but I might as well carry on: there's not much else to do. Have you got any better ideas?'

'No, I haven't got any ideas at all. I think you are right you might as well carry on.'

'I quite agree.'

'So do I.'

'Well, that's settled then.'

He laughed at himself, and he started to sing:

'Once there was a traveller,
Who travelled out one day.
But this silly traveller,
He did not know his way.
Oh I don't know where I'm going to,
And I don't know where I've been.
I don't know what I've listened to,
And I don't know what I've seen.
Once there was a traveller,
The big wide sea he crossed
But this silly traveller,
He got completely lost.
Oh I don't know where I'm going to,
And I don't know where I've been.
I don't know what I've listened to,
And I don't know what I've seen.
Once there was a traveller,
His way was hard and long.

So this silly traveller,
He sang a silly song.
Oh I don't know where I'm going to,
And I don't know where I've been.
I don't know what I've listened to,
And I don't know what I've seen.

The sound of his voice echoed around the cave, until it was sucked into the silence. Then there was another sound, faint and distant: a rhythmic cracking sound like branches breaking. Then Drewin thought he heard something else: he stopped and listened. The cracking sound continued its slow beat, but there was the sound of a man's voice too. 'Bravo!' it cried, 'Bravely sung!' And the cracking noise was the sound of hands clapping.

Drewin called out and hurried forward as fast as he dared. The clapping and shouting continued, and as he advanced it became louder and clearer, and he became aware of a dim light ahead. Before long, the voice became so clear that Drewin knew that he must be nearing its owner. He stopped.

'Where are you? Can you hear me?' he said loudly.

The reply came from nearby. 'No need to shout. I am over here.'

Drewin looked towards the sound, and realised that he was now in an open chamber several times the width that the tunnel had been. Over to his right he could just make out a squat dark shape on the cavern floor. He started to move towards it, but was stopped by an urgent shout.

'Don't come any closer! This is some sort of trap: I don't know how I sprang it, or how to get out of it, but I don't think it would help for you to fall into it too.'

Drewin could dimly see what looked like a very short fat man. As his eyes adjusted to the light he realised that the man was of a normal size, but was buried up to the waist in the floor of the cave and had a huge pack attached to his back. The stranger said nothing as Drewin lowered himself to the ground and crawled slowly forward, feeling the ground as he went. He gradually approached the trapped man, but the rock stayed firm and he found no cracks or loose stones: it was solid rock.

Now that he was closer, Drewin could see the other's face quite clearly. The two men smiled at each other. Neither said anything for a moment, then the stranger shrugged and spoke. 'It looks as though this trap is just for me. But be careful, it may yet catch you.'

Drewin felt the rock floor with his hands: it was still hard and firm. He sat down facing the smiling man. 'How did this happen? How long have you been trapped here?'

'As to the first, I was walking along this passage, doing no harm to anyone, when the rock beneath my feet turned to porridge and I sank in it up to my waist. Then the porridge turned back to rock and here I am. As to the second, I don't know how long I have been here, but it must be at least a hundred years.'

'A hundred years! Is that not a long time in a mortal life?'

The man shrugged, making the gigantic pack on his back jerk. 'Who said anything about mortals? My name is Vodorian. What's yours?'

'I'm Drewin.'

'Wonderful!' laughed Vodorian, 'It could not be better. Of all the people in all the world that might come to my aid, I cannot imagine that I could find a more perfect rescuer!'

'But I have not rescued you.'

'You will. You will, I am sure. There might have been some doubt in my mind, but since your name is Drewin, all doubts are forgotten.'

Drewin ignored this remark and started moving about the cave looking for some clue to how to release Vodorian, who continued to talk.

'I am afraid I can be of little help. I have pondered for many hours on the question of how I came to be in this predicament, and I regret that I have come to no firm conclusion, beyond the strong belief that we are dealing with malign magic. I can imagine no normal mechanical device which could bring about the regrettable state of affairs in which I find myself. Do you have any knowledge of magic?'

'No, none at all. And I can find no sign of a means to release you. I fear your confidence in me is misplaced. We might try to dig you out, but it would take years, and I would probably hurt you in doing it. Can you move your legs?'

'No, not at all. Do not fear, Drewin, you will release me. I know you will. I'll tell you why, after you have done it.'

Drewin stood at some distance, deep in thought, while Vodorian watched him in silence. Neither said a word: there was only the sound of air sighing through the cave.

Then Drewin came to himself and, with a look of pity and sorrow on his face, he slowly approached the trapped man. 'I'm sorry. I have no ideas. I can do nothing.'

As he spoke, the rock beneath his feet became like wet earth, and his feet started to sink into it. He fell back onto the firm rock, pulling himself free, and as he did so he shouted.

'Quick, Vodorian! Reach out to me and take my hand. I will

pull you out!'

The cave floor around Vodorian had become like quicksand, and with a swimming motion he pushed himself towards Drewin and stretched to grasp his hand. The large pack on his back hampered his movements and weighed him down. By keeping his lower half on the firm ground and getting what support he could from the watery swamp, Drewin was able to reach out and gain a hold on Vodorian's arm. He strained backwards, pulling Vodorian out as he went. Slowly, they struggled and scrambled to get away from the swamp, and finally they succeeded. They watched as the soft floor turned back to unyielding rock.

Vodorian started rubbing his legs and tidying his clothes. He took the pack off his back, examined it carefully, then grinned at Drewin.

'There! What did I tell you? I knew you would do it.'

'Yes, but I did nothing. I nearly joined you in the trap.'

'Well, I will not argue with my benefactor: let's just say that if you had not been here I would still be stuck, and now I am free. In any case, you pulled me out. Thank you.'

Drewin shrugged. 'I'm glad I was able to be of some help. Now will you tell me why you were so sure that I would be able to rescue you?'

'First, would you do one more thing for me? I seem to be numb from the waist down: would you help me to my feet?' Vodorian slipped the pack from his shoulders and at the third attempt Drewin managed to lift him up and prop him against the side of the cave. Vodorian laughed, bowed to Drewin and nearly fell over again.

'Thank you again. I am apparently fated to be in your debt.'

'I hope not! But in any case you can make some repayment by answering the question that you so carefully avoided just now. Why were you so certain that I would succeed?'

'Isn't it obvious?'

'Not to me. No, it's not at all obvious.'

'Consider this: ask yourself why would my brother come to me, if not to rescue me?'

'Your brother!' Drewin staggered backwards until he collided with Vodorian's pack, almost falling over it. He stood staring at Vodorian, who went on cheerfully;

'Well, half-brother to be precise. You are Drewin, brother to Saranna, and son of Iranor?'

Drewin nodded, speechless, and Vodorian continued with hardly a pause. 'Then I am indeed your brother, since Iranor is my mother too. Of course, I am considerably younger than you, but it hardly shows, does it?'

'What!'

Drewin rushed back to where Vodorian stood, and grabbed his shoulders. 'Stop! What do you mean? You said you had been here for a hundred years. The builders of the stairway—was it you—the one who visited them many generations ago? Or are you a madman? You can't be my younger brother, how can you?'

Vodorian patted his cheek soothingly. 'Calm down, Drewin. What are you so upset about? When you appeared and said your name was Drewin, who else could you be but my big brother, come to rescue me?' He laughed again, collected his pack and set off up the sloping passage, followed by Drewin. Darkness was threatening to swallow them up, when Vodorian suddenly took something from the pack, and fixed it to the wall. By the time Drewin came up to him, he had set the object alight, and Drewin saw it was a torch.

'That should lighten this stretch of the path for some time—if any other travellers come this way, they will be gladdened by its brightness.'

Drewin did not answer, so Vodorian set off again.

'Wait! Stop!'

'What is it?'

'I cannot understand how you could be my brother at all. You can't have been born after me, because you've been here in this cavern since before I was born—haven't you? But if you were my older brother, then Mother would have told me about you.'

Vodorian was nodding and desperately trying to speak. Finally he interrupted Drewin. 'I was born after you and Saranna left the Isle, and so I am younger than you. But you have not been in the world long and your body is young, while I have been in the world many years and my hair is going grey, so I am older than you. But I still think of you as my older brother, and Saranna as my big sister.'

He laughed, and waited for Drewin's response.

'Why did you leave the Island? That perfect place!'

'Ah! I too was banished from my home, as you were. But my crime was far greater than yours for I stole away often from the Isle and mingled with the people, speaking to them of things that our Mother believed they should not know.'

'What things?'

'Mostly stories of the Immortals that Mother said would disturb the people and make them envious, and resentful of their mortality and their brief lives. But she became really furious when I taught some people to read, using the runes. Though I did not speak to them of the hidden lore of the runes, she was angry beyond all measure.'

'What did she do?'

'She sent me to a time long ago, and these were her last words to me: 'You will live far longer than mortals do, long enough to see them learn that they are mortal. You will be with them as they strive for immortality and you will see them fail, and die.' And she sent me away, and for nearly two thousand years I have wandered over land and sea. I have made enemies and friends, and seen both grow old and wither and die. For the mortal life is as a wave breaking on the shore. Yet I now have great comfort in meeting my brother, and soon I hope I shall meet my sister Saranna, too. Where is she, Drewin?'

Drewin said nothing. He walked across to the far side of the passage, where he leaned his forehead against the rock. He spoke, but Vodorian could not catch what he said. He went to him and laid a hand on his shoulder. Drewin turned to face him, and Vodorian saw that tears were streaming down his brother's face.

'She is dead. I know that she is dead. I saw her image, cold and lifeless stone, in the land below the waves. I know that Saranna is dead.'

Drewin began to weep bitterly, and Vodorian held him in a close embrace. 'Drewin, my brother, my heart is torn in two: one part rejoices in finding my brother, the other feels nearly dead of grief; that the first tidings of Saranna are ill tidings; that my only gift to her is my sorrow.'

And Vodorian wept with Drewin and the brothers held each other for a long time. Gradually the sobbing subsided and they became calm. Vodorian gently released Drewin and spoke firmly. 'Come, let us look to the future. We must be on our way.'

They sorted out their bags and travelling garments and set off, walking together in silence. From time to time, when the way became dark, Vodorian would stop, light a torch, and fix it to the wall. At last Vodorian asked a question.

''The land below the waves?' You said 'the land below the waves': have you visited Leartenda?'

'Yes, I was there. But I found that I could not stay.'

Vodorian nodded. 'So the legends say!'Few reach Leartenda, fewer are welcome, and fewer still remain.' You must tell me the truth of it.'

'It is a place of colours and shapes that are unimaginable. I cannot describe it: it is as though my memory fails whenever I think of it. I do remember one person who dwells there, but I cannot share that memory with you.'

'I have no wish to pry, and in any case, I'm feeling very tired. Let's settle down and get some rest.'

Casting their burdens down on the rocky floor, the brothers stretched their tired limbs and set about making a camp. Vodorian lit a torch while Drewin unpacked the bags. They had no blankets, but the air was less cold than it had been in the lower reaches of the passage. After a light meal they settled down back-to-back for comfort, and both soon fell asleep.

When Drewin woke, the first thing he heard was a loud snoring from Vodorian, who had rolled over in his sleep and was sprawled halfway across the passage. Drewin shook him awake.

'Come on; time for breakfast!'

'How do you know it's breakfast?' Vodorian grumbled. But

soon he was fully awake. They made ready to continue their journey and set off.

'And now we are on our way, towards the future, Vodorian, can you tell me where we are going?'

'No.'

'Why are we going this way then?'

'It is the only way to go. Upwards: towards the light.'

'You seem so certain my brother: have you no doubts? Why do we not go down?'

Vodorian stopped and turned to Drewin fixing him with a hard look. 'Once when I was young, when I was first sent into the world of time, I tried to return. I tried to go back and find my home, my island. I searched for many years over all the seas of Skorn and I could not find it. When it was my home it was always there: I knew where it was and could find it whenever I wanted to return. But when I returned as a mortal it was not there.'

'I would not wish to return: all my memories would be of Saranna there with me, and it would make me sad.'

'You do not understand: what you wish is not important. It is not your choice: that has been taken from you. You cannot go back, so you must go forward. Let us go forward together.'

So they marched side by side along the tunnel, each of them lost in his own thoughts, until suddenly Drewin said, 'Is it my imagination, or is there more light now than when we started out?'

'Well brother, if it is imagination, then we are both imagining the same thing. Either our eyes are getting used to the dark or there is indeed more light here.'

Whatever the truth of it, they were able to see some way

ahead and, as they rounded a bend in the passage, they saw something out of the ordinary in the distance. There was some obstacle blocking their path. At first it was just a vague darkness, but, as they approached, they could make out its form. It was a gridwork of iron bars, each as thick as a fat man's arm. It stretched from roof to floor, and across the whole width of the passage. There was a small gate set into it, just big enough for one person to crawl through, but it was held shut by a thick iron chain. Vodorian came to it first, and rattled the gate, making a great clanking sound, but failing to make any impression on the massive barrier, apart from dislodging some rust and dust. But, as if in answer to the noise, a loud shout echoed in the cave.

'Who goes there?'

There was a pause as the deep roar rolled up and down the passageway, then it came again, but louder.

'Who goes there?'

Again a pause, and again the challenge, still louder.

'WHO GOES THERE?'

Drewin and Vodorian were struck rigid, and did not answer.

There was no sign of the owner of the voice, apart from the voice itself. There was another, longer pause, then the speaker spoke again, a little quieter, but not much. 'Thrice I have challenged, but there is no reply. I have done my duty, that nobody can deny. Did someone rattle my gate, or was it just a dream? Sometimes, I know, things are not what they seem.'

This was followed by a shuffling sound, accompanied by a weary groaning, and gradually, from an invisible aperture in the cave wall on the other side of the barrier, there emerged a monstrous figure. It was almost human in form, with massive shoulders, long thick hairy arms and short thick hairy legs. As it moved along on all fours, its back brushed the roof of the cave and its elbows brushed the sides. The great head was bent down so that it looked through a tangle of bushy eyebrows. It came to the barrier, breathing heavily, and peered through the bars at the two brothers.

'Thrice I challenged, but there was no reply. Two callers at the gate, but no reply. What kind of way is that to go on? I've done my duty, you should do yours. You should answer my challenge, when I challenge. What kind of way is that to go on?'

Vodorian was the first to respond. 'We are sorry we did not answer, but we did not know where the challenge came from until we saw you here.'

The creature twisted its head to one side and started to scratch its neck vigorously. It did this for some time while Drewin and Vodorian watched and waited.

'Sorry, are you? Didn't know where the challenge came from, didn't you? Well, let me ask you. Let me ask you fair. Where would the challenge come from, if not from me? I am the challenger. Me. Groddin, the gate guard.'

Vodorian took over the conversation.

'Greetings, Groddin, gate guard. It is a pleasure to meet you. My name is Vodorian, and my companion here is Drewin, my brother.'

Groddin eyed them both suspiciously, then scratched its neck again, more thoroughly than before. 'Brothers ay? Vodorian and Drewin ay? What do you want then, ay, hm, ay?'

'Well,' said Vodorian, 'we were travelling along here, hoping to reach daylight, when we came to this barrier. We were hoping that we might be able to pass through it. Is that possible?'

Groddin scratched its armpit for a while, and looked

puzzled. 'Er, yes. It is possible. But I must play fair with you, as you are being so civil to me. There is a payment to be made.'

The creature paused, apparently embarrassed. Drewin took up the conversation.

'And what is the payment?'

'Er, well, usually it is well within most travellers' ability to pay, but usually they are reluctant. In fact, I would say that I have yet to meet a traveller willing to pay it. So usually, if I'm feeling hungry, which I usually am, I don't tell them.'

'What payment are you talking about?' Drewin snapped.

'Now, now. There's no need to become impolite. I was just coming to that. Usually, and I say usually, the price is life. I have to eat after all, and nobody brings me food any more. Haven't done for three hundred years or so.'

'You mean that if we come through the barrier you will eat us?'

'Usually, that would happen, yes. But since you are brothers, and very civil, as I said, then even though I'm pretty hungry at the moment, I'll just eat one of you. That's fair isn't it? And to be doubly fair I'll let you choose which one.'

Drewin was speechless, so Vodorian stepped in. 'You are very kind, Groddin. Excuse us while we discuss this matter.'

The brothers moved away from the barrier and put their heads together. Vodorian spoke first. 'Which is it going to be, then? I would volunteer to be eaten, but I have much to do before I die. Do you feel like becoming a meal for Groddin? It would be a kindness.'

'I, too, am too young to die. Since neither of us is inclined to make the sacrifice, I suggest that we attempt to overcome the monster.'

'I used to be quite good at wrestling, but I have a feeling that those large hairy arms would rip me in two before I could gain a decent hold,' Vodorian laughed.

'There's more than one way to gut a fish, as they say in the islands. It seems to me that our opponent is not very quick of wit. We should be able to use this to our advantage.'

Drewin softly whispered to his brother, then they returned to the barrier where Groddin had been waiting patiently.

'Have you decided. Which of you is it to be? It makes no difference to me: meat is meat.'

Drewin did all the talking, while Vodorian stood back and watched. 'I'm afraid we have been unable to choose. We need your help.'

Groddin unfastened the little gate in the barrier.

'Why don't you both come through, and I shall take my pick? I promise I'll only eat one of you.'

'That's no good, I'm afraid, Groddin. While we take your word, and trust your good intentions, only one of us can pass through the gate at a time, and both of us fear that, because you are so hungry, you will be unable to restrain yourself, and will eat the first one who comes through the gate. So neither of us will go first. You see our problem?'

Groddin scratched its leg, and frowned. Drewin continued quickly.

'So if you could come to this side of the barrier, you would have both of us to choose from at the same time.'

'But I can't get through the gate. I'm too big.'

Drewin looked surprised. 'You are very astute, Groddin. I can see that you have a good grasp of the situation. What are we to do?'

At this point, Vodorian broke into the discussion. 'I think I may have a solution. If we took down the barrier, Groddin could come to this side quite easily.'

Groddin did not reply, but started to scratch its head and look intently at a spot on the floor between its feet. Drewin and Vodorian exchanged glances, and smiled. At last Groddin spoke. 'That's a good idea. And it's not as difficult as you might think, for I can take the barrier down by pulling these little nails from the rock.'

He immediately started to work at the place where one of the bars met the rock, and, after much effort, he succeeded in removing a long iron spike which was holding the grid in place. He worked on each bar in turn until he had removed all the spikes, and the barrier was loose. Drewin took charge.

'Well done, Groddin! Now, if we push this side and you push that side, the barrier should swing round and you can squeeze through.'

So Groddin pushed, and the brothers pushed, and at first nothing happened. But gradually the barrier started to turn. Drewin shouted instructions. 'Keep pushing! We have nearly succeeded.'

They all pushed, and the barrier turned completely round, so that Groddin was now on the brothers' side. But the brothers were on Groddin's side, and they quickly leapt to the spikes and replaced them in their sockets so that the barrier was secure again.

Groddin let go of the bars and looked puzzled. 'We seem to have done something wrong.'

Drewin looked puzzled too, and scratched his head. 'Yes, I seem to have made a mistake. How foolish of me! But while we were working I had another idea. Now that we are on this side and you are on that side, you need not eat either of us. So we'll be on our way. Farewell, Groddin. It has been a pleasure meeting you.'

With that the two brothers walked on along the tunnel, while Groddin sat looking at the barrier with a puzzled expression on its face.

On the seventh day of their journey, they rounded a sharp bend in the tunnel and suddenly found themselves in a large cavern. There had been no warning of its presence until they emerged from the darkness of the tunnel. And it was light. For the first time since they had met, Drewin and Vodorian could see clearly. Although the light was not very bright, at first they were dazzled. Then they looked at each other and laughed.

'Isn't it odd, Vodorian, that we have spent all this time together, yet only now can we see each other clearly,' said Drewin.

'You are as I knew you would be,' said Vodorian. 'Your eyes are like your voice: young, fearless, and honest.'

They embraced briefly, then looked about them. The cavern was about a hundred paces across, and as high as it was wide. The floor was uneven and strewn with boulders: the walls were broken by jagged outcrops and crevices. The light was coming from one of these small openings on the far side, and it seemed unbearably bright to the brothers. Their eyes were still adjusting to the light when they heard the voice.

Arel

*L*ate one summer evening Saranna sat down by the hearth, staring into the glowing depths of the peat and wishing for company. Memories filled her head, visions of other islands and of people she had left behind; she was filled with sorrow and began to sing:

'Over the wide sea, alone I came here;
In the quiet vale, alone I dwell here.
By my lonely hearth, I dream of you love;
Through my empty days of you my lost one.
To the evening stars...'

She stopped, startled. Someone had trodden on the lintel-stone behind her, and as she turned a man's voice, slow and gentle, said,

'May I come in, Mistress? I am sorry to disturb your song.'

'Come in, Arel; you are welcome. I have been wishing all day for some company.'

The shepherd crossed to the hearth in two long strides and sat down opposite Saranna.

'Will you take some ale? Or I have wine from the mainland?'

'Ale, please.'

Saranna fetched his drink and sat down again. 'Now, Arel; what brings you here this evening?'

'I have been visiting farms through the vale today, reporting on the sheep—the lambs are growing well and the flock is healthy for the most part, mistress.'

'Arel, my name is Saranna, and I am no more your mistress than anyone else whose flocks you guard. Not so long ago I was only a farmworker in the household of Aleen and Gannel.'

'If you wish, I will call you Saranna; I should like to think that we could be friends. Life on the hills is lonely, for I should not leave the sheep often during the summer. Perhaps you might come and visit me. I should like to hear tales of Imman and the other islands.'

'Perhaps I might.'

'Good-night, then, miss- Saranna.'

'Goodnight, Arel.'

For three days after Arel's visit, Saranna kept close to the house because of a thick, misty rain that came down over Telan and seemed determined to soak the island, like a giant green sponge, until it was saturated. When the fourth day dawned clear and bright Saranna's thoughts turned to open spaces and fresh air. She whisked through her morning chores and shortly before noon set off towards the hills carrying a basket laden with food and wine.

The day was growing hot as Saranna climbed slowly up the path that led to the highest part of Telan. To her right she had a gradually more and more extensive view of the sea, while on her left the hills rose green and smooth until a few masses of tumbled rock broke through the turf at their crests. Soon she was high above the sea on a level stretch of ground, where the path divided again. A narrow footpath led along the cliff edge, and a broader track wound up into the hilltops. Saranna sat and rested on a rock before starting to climb again. For the rest of her journey, she climbed very slowly, the basket weighing heavier as she got higher; it was a great relief to pass between two rocky heights and see the summer pastures below her on a small, irregular plateau.

Towards the far side of this expanse she could see the little turf bothy that was Arel's summer sheiling. Sheep were dotted about the green, cropping grass determinedly, with here and there a growing lamb kicking up its heels. She could not see Arel, so began to descend the track towards the sheiling. She was about halfway there when Arel ducked out of the low doorway; Saranna called out and waved.

'Arel! AREL!'

He looked up, waved back, and set out to meet her; Saranna, watching his pale-gold hair blowing in the breeze, remembered the first time she had seen him, in the market-place. She and Aleen had been buying linen from Kiril to make sheets for Saranna's new home.

'Who is that tall handsome man?'

'Where? Oh, Arel: he is one of the shepherds. I suppose he is good-looking. But then...' Aleen lowered her voice '... his father was one of the Forest People!'

'Forest people? What forest—there is scarcely a single tree on Telan!'

Then Aleen had told Saranna about the Kirenoi, who lived in the deep forest below the Ragged Mountains of Akent, a beautiful and mysterious people who sometimes visited Telan, but never stayed for long.

'They leave us gifts, wonderful and magical; and sometimes after they have gone, one of the women gives birth to a fair child, like Arel.'

Remembering, Saranna came face to face with Arel on the narrow path, and once more thought how handsome he was.

He smiled at her. 'Greetings, Saranna. Let me carry that basket.'

Nothing more was said until they had reached the bothy and were seated on two low stools that Arel brought out into the sunshine. Saranna began to unpack her basket.

'Welcome to my summer home; you are good to come all this way, carrying that great heavy basket.'

'It is nothing, Arel. Your visit to me was such a pleasant change from my usual lonely evenings; why should I not do what I can in return?'

'That is kind, indeed. I thought when I heard you singing, that you would understand loneliness; that you would understand me.'

He looked down, and hesitated. 'My mother was lonely too; indeed, I believe she died of it, of sorrow for my father. And as a child I was often alone, for as you see I am different from most of the people here. I never knew my father, the stranger from the forest over the sea.'

'Then I do understand; for my father is only a faint memory to me, fading more and more as the years pass; and I too remember my mother's sorrow. Arel, I hope we shall be friends. I—when I lived on Imman, I had a dear friend; but we parted.'

'To your sorrow, it seems.'

'Yes—I thought he would stay with me; but he said our time had come to part.'

'And so he left you?'

'I left him, in fairness, and we parted as friends. But now I miss him.'

Arel patted her shoulder in gentle sympathy, and they started to eat the food in silence.

From this day on, Saranna was usually to be seen on warm and sunny days, climbing the hill-track to the grazing ground, carrying a basket of food to share with Arel. They would talk while they picnicked, of everything that came into their heads, sometimes deep and stimulating talk, sometimes silly and friendly, bringing them gradually closer until they were good friends. Saranna watched Arel at work, and marvelled at the way the sheep followed and trusted him.

'It is simply a matter of patience. They have known me all their lives, and I am a slow sort of person, I never hurry them into things or make a lot of noise, and I have handled them as they were growing up. They probably think of me as an odd sort of sheep.'

This idea reduced Saranna to helpless laughter.

'It is not funny, woman. Where would all you farmers be, I should like to know, if your sheep did not trust me? It is very fine for you, sitting by your fires on chilly spring evenings when the daft things are dropping lambs all over the place and expecting me to look after them!'

'Yes. Of course, Arel. I am very sorry, of course you can be a sheep if you wish, it was very wrong of me to laugh.'

He chased her back to the sheiling, where they flopped down exhausted on the dry turf and sat for a while recovering their breath. Neither of them spoke for some time, as they watched the grazing sheep and swooping sea-birds, the high clouds in the light-blue sky.

Saranna looked across at Arel and saw that he was lying propped up on one elbow, his gaze faraway and abstracted. She watched him for a while, then without thinking what she was doing, moved closer to him, leaned over, and reached out her hand to lift his face towards her. Before he had time to do more than look mildly surprised, she kissed him lightly on the mouth, then more fiercely so that the force of her kiss pushed him back onto the grass. Her body came down across his and his arms went around her. The kiss lasted a long time, and when it ended she lay happily in his arms, her face pressed into his shoulder, her nose burrowing into the rough-spun material of his tunic. Then suddenly she sat up, and looked into his face. He smiled at her.

'Oh, Arel, I am sorry!'

'Sorry? Whyever should you be sorry? Did you not enjoy it? I liked it very much.'

'So did I; but it was a bit—sudden of me.'

'Saranna, you are a rather sudden person. Indeed, compared to me you are like a summer storm that flashes by the island. I have been wanting to kiss you for days. But I might have taken days more to do it. So I thank you for your suddenness.'

There was no answer to this except another kiss – and then another. And Saranna was late home to her disgruntled livestock that evening.

A week or so later Saranna's cat Sinna gave birth to six fat squirming kittens, and when they were weaned Saranna took two of them up into the hills for Arel.

'And what will I do with them?'

'Keep them as friends to ease your loneliness.'

'What loneliness? Haven't I scores of sheep to talk to, as well as this woman from the valley who keeps coming up here and pestering me with her company? And what if they have more kittens?'

'They won't, for both are female.'

'Oh, wonderful! I am to be surrounded by women—ouch, it scratched me!'

'She was only playing. You ungrateful man, I shall not bring you presents or come and see you at all if all you do is complain.'

'Complain? Me? Would I do that? I am simply unused to cats—they are uncanny creatures.'

'Yes, like you—strange and wild and beautiful.'

She snuggled close and kissed him. 'Think how they will play about on the grass to amuse you, and snuggle up to you in the night...'

'I should prefer you to do that.'

'I will. I do. Oh Arel, please do not sound so cross—you are spoiling my pleasure in giving you a gift!'

'I am sorry, Saranna, they are delightful and I thank you very much, and they will be wonderful company for me. There, is that right?'

She slapped his arm gently. 'Yes, better. What will you call them?'

'Cats?'

'No, they must have proper names—see how elegant they are, the little brindled one and the grey and white – I chose the two prettiest for you.'

'Kirenoi names, then. Kirelorena for the grey, and Kirekinala for the brindle. Then I need only cry out 'Kire, Kire!' and they will both come running.'

Soon Saranna had the satisfaction of seeing Arel, asleep on the grass after his mid-day meal, with two small fluffy bundles curled up, one on each side of his chest, with a tiny pink nose and a tiny black one buried in his neck.

'And you were all purring together,' she said when he awoke. 'Or rather, they were purring and you were snoring.'

'I do not snore!'

'Yes you do.'

He took her into his arms and kissed her gently and slowly. 'Stay with me, Saranna. Stay tonight.'

'Yes. Yes, I will, Arel. But first I must go home and tend the animals.'

'Oh, you can't—you must go, I mean, but you cannot walk all that way twice in one evening. No, come and see me tomorrow if it is fine.'

'I can manage perfectly well, Arel. It is early yet, and the evenings are long and warm. I will be back with you when the stars are shining. Cook some supper for me.'

So Saranna returned to the summer valley just as Arel closed the night-fold with a stout hurdle, and walked back to the bothy to stir the cooking pot that was suspended above the fire outside it. The smell of rabbit stew rose temptingly on the evening air.

By the time they had eaten the sky was dark and the stars shone like crystal in its heaviness. A crescent moon had risen; Saranna gazed at it sadly, and could not explain her sadness when Arel spoke of it. For the first time for many months she drew from inside her gown the carved rune-disc, and fingered it.

'Ord', said Arel. 'I have been meaning to ask about that, but the time has never seemed right. Is it a lost lover, Saranna? Is that what makes you sad?'

He drew closer to her. 'Would you rather be with him than with me?'

She turned to him, surprised. 'No, oh Arel, no, you do not understand.' She took both his hands and clung to him.

'I have never known anyone like you, Arel. I have never felt for anyone what I feel for you. You make me so happy.' She burrowed into his arms, and he held her close.

'Keep me safe, Arel, nothing feels as safe and warm as your arms holding me.'

He said nothing, but tightened his embrace. For a while they sat by the fire, and then he turned her face up to his own and kissed her. Soon they went inside, leaving the fire to the drowsy kittens and the remote stars.

When the great storm came, no-one was prepared for it. The days were shortening, but still it was summer, and many flowers still bloomed in the grasslands of the valley. Milk-cows grazed contentedly on the crofts, the birds sang each morning, and up on the hills Arel watched his flock in peace. Then late one evening, drowsing by his fire, he felt suddenly cold. Looking up, he saw that the sky was darkening, not with the clear blackness of a summer night but with the thick menace of deep, heavy clouds. The wind was rising out of the western ocean, sweeping across the waves and over the cliffs of Telan to rush down into his valley. In the pen the sheep were beginning to stir, and as Arel looked around fearfully, the two little cats awoke, sat up and sniffed the air, then bolted into the hut like rabbits down a hole. Even as he decided that he must go to the sheep, the skies flung down upon the island a mass of water almost too solid to be called rain; Arel was drenched in seconds.

The wind rose still further, screaming and moaning around the rocky hills, and the rain settled down into a steady torrent that he could barely see through. Terrified 'baas' floated up to him through the noise of the wind, and he set off, struggling to stay upright on the slippery ground, towards the pen below.

Down in the valley the wind was less, but the fury of the driving rain had everyone up and alert, looking out for their livestock and their possessions. Less than half an hour after the darkening of the sky, the valley began to flood; streams that normally tumbled gently down the hillsides grew into torrents like mountain waterfalls, and rushed down to swell the rivers of the plain. Water spread rapidly across the farmlands, and those who had lofts or sleeping platforms in their cottages hurried to drag stores of food, light furniture and clothing, children and old folk, up the stairs and ladders before the waters broke into the lower floors. In the barns, cats and hens, goats and calves, straw and grain, were bundled up into the storage lofts. Those who had no upper floors tied what they could to the rafters and then perched up aloft themselves. As the flood spread, panic grew, and the night was full of the noise of crying children, frightened animals, shouts of men and women trying to salvage what they could.

Boats began to appear, rushing along at the whim of the flood over what had been fields and tracks and farmyards. Soon animals, and then people, began to fall into the raging water, tumbling away out of sight of their owners and families and the cries of terror and distress grew louder. Still the rain fell, and the wind tore at the island, and now the bodies of cows and goats and people were tumbling about in the dark lake that covered the centre of Telan.

Saranna's little house stood on gently rising ground towards the southern heights. As the rain flung its first attack down onto the wooden roof of the barn, she thought it would fall in on her; but it held, and she looked out through the door in fear and amazement at the power of the storm. Fighting against increasing panic as she thought of all the things that needed to be done, she tried to work methodically. As the streams began to rise, and flowed away past her land to afflict her neighbours lower down, Saranna struggled up and down the barn ladder with sack after sack of grain and as much straw as she could manage; almost all her stock before she heard a yet angrier note in the voice of the wind.

Grandy the cow was lowing in terror, and the hens were squawking. Without stopping to soothe or calm them Saranna began to stuff the birds into a sack, all of them fluttering and pecking and scratching. When half of the hens were inside, the sack was full and Saranna made the hazardous journey from barn to cottage, fighting her way in through the door and banging it shut behind her. Up the narrow stairs she went to the attic store-room, where she let the hens out and fastened the stout wooden door. In the room below she found five frightened cats, Sinna and her remaining kittens.

'Oh! Where can I keep you safe? I can't put you with the hens!'

Desperately Saranna looked around, and her eye fell on the great sturdy cupboard built against the wall; she gathered up the cats one by one and shoved them into the topmost shelf of the cupboard. Protesting and struggling, they at once tried to get down again, but Saranna slammed the door of the cupboard shut and fastened it with the bar on the outside. Loud mews of protest were added to the other hideous noises of the night.

She went out again and the wind flung her down into the thick mud of the yard. In the barn Grandy was screaming, and Saranna saw that the water was lapping against the rear wall. She got herself to her feet and back into the stall, gathered up the rest of the hens and wondered what on earth she was to do with the cow. By the time all the hens were secure, water was flowing into the barn, and Grandy's grunting cries were pitiful to hear. Saranna set off once more across the yard. Untethering the frightened cow was dangerous and difficult; trying to persuade her to move out through the ankle-deep water that filled the barn was almost impossible. Twice Saranna slipped and fell, and once the cow trod heavily on her foot. Slowly she persuaded Grandy to plod through the flood, up the yard and out of the water. Saranna looked up at the hills, wondering whether she could let the cow go free to seek higher ground. Grandy nosed at her trustingly, and she patted the wet head.

'No, poor old girl, you'd be swept off the hills by the wind.'

And then for the first time since the storm began, she remembered Arel. She stood, horrified, in the teeming rain, clutching Grandy's halter and staring into the night. 'Oh Grandy—what will happen to him!'

'Mmmrrrrr!' said the cow.

Saranna turned her attention back to the farm, where the water rose slowly and surely, creeping up the yard towards the house. She pulled and coaxed the surprised cow into the cottage, where it shuddered and dripped hugely onto the earthen floor.

Upstairs the hens were cackling as if to rival the screeching wind, and yowls of fury came from the cupboard. Slamming the door shut and barring it, Saranna came over to the fire-place and found to her surprise that the turf fire was still alight. She poked it into a little more life, found a thick cloth and draped it over the cow to dry her, then went to the sleeping-room to find dry clothes for herself.

The wet clothes and the cloth she tossed over the lines stretched above the hearth. Squeezing past the stolid cow, Saranna bustled about putting everything moveable up into the highest places she could reach. After another hour the water began to seep under the door; but by then only the table still stood on the floor. Saranna retreated with the cow to the highest part of the room, and sat on the step up to the bed-place. Slowly, slowly the muddy water advanced, and Grandy put her ears down and grumbled. It was another full hour before the water reached her restless hooves, and Saranna coaxed her up the step, where she filled all the space that was not occupied by the bed. Across the room, the fire fizzled and went out; and at that moment the rain stopped so abruptly that Saranna was startled by the sudden ceasing of its noise against the roof-slates. And then the wind dropped too, and for a while the sounds of indignant cats and panicking hens seemed as loud as thunder. Finally they too calmed down, and Grandy, with a lumbering sigh, folded herself up into the bed-place as if it were a cosy stall.

'The Lady be thanked!' Saranna wrapped herself in her quilt and settled down onto her bed.' 'But how can I sleep? Grandy, what has become of Arel?'

Saranna awoke in the morning to the sound of bird-song, the screech of furious cats, the squawking of hens and a strong smell of cow. Flinging open the shutters, she saw blue sky and felt the warmth of the sun. Grandy was lumbering about on the muddy floor of the main room, and had added to the mess by splattering her droppings all over the place. Saranna wrinkled up her nose in disgust and fetched down a pair of wooden pattens from the shelf above her bed. As she stepped into them she winced in pain; her foot was sore and swollen where Grandy has trodden on it.

Picking her way across the treacherous floor, she opened

the main door and looked out. The yard was a sea of mud, but the flood waters had retreated down the hill, far below her buildings. Apart from the wooden gate, which lay on its side in the middle of the farmyard, everything seemed secure. With great difficulty Saranna dragged the gate to its proper place and propped it up across the opening in the wall, lodging it as securely as she could with stones. Then she was able to let Grandy out into the yard, and set the cottage door wide open. Next she opened the cupboard door; Sinna and the kittens streaked yowling out into the yard, where they complained loudly about the mud and tried to walk about without getting their feet dirty. Saranna ignored them and limped up the stairs to let the hens out. Then she relit the fire with some turfs from the basket she had stored on a high shelf, realising with a pang that she had forgotten about the stack at the end of the cottage and that it would now be saturated at best, or swept away at worst. This made her feel very sorry for herself, and she began to sniffle. But she struggled on, sweeping out the cottage and feeding all the livestock, by which time it was past noon. Changing the clumsy pattens for stout shoes, she clambered over the wall and set off along the track.

'Saranna! Wait!'

She turned and saw her neighbour Gannel hurrying towards her; he looked dishevelled and anxious.

'Where are you off to, Saranna? You're hurt, it seems. Aleen asked me to come over and see how you did. We're not too bad at our house, thank the Lady, but there's terrible troubles further down. Can I help you at all? Anything you need?'

'Gannel, I thank you, but I shall do quite well for now. I must get up to the hills, I must see what has become of Arel.'

'By the Lady's name! You are right. But you must wait until I get a party together, you cannot go alone.'

'I must, I must, I have wasted too much time already! Don't stop me, Gannel.'

'Well, the man means a lot to you, by what Aleen tells me. But I must come with you, then, you with a bad leg and everything—you will need help.'

'You are very kind. I have a little bread and wine in my bag—perhaps you could fetch some more from my house and follow me?'

'Yes, I will do that—you'll not get far ahead of me. And take care!'

The journey seemed to last forever. Gannel very soon caught up with Saranna, bearing quite a sizeable bundle including bread, cheese, wine and a thick blanket from the cupboard. He shouldered this easily and also relieved her of the satchel; but they were forced to stop frequently and rest, once soaking Saranna's foot in a cold hill-stream and binding it up with her scarf. This helped a little, but on the last steep ascent away from the sea, Saranna was leaning heavily on her neighbour.

Dusk was beginning as they came through the final gap between the rocks, and looked down on the devastation below. The green sheltered valley that had been Arel's home was now a wasteland. A lake filled the central hollow where the pen had stood. The grass was littered with debris; fallen rocks, uprooted trees and bushes. Bedraggled white shapes lay everywhere.

Slowly they made their way down the slope towards the site of the bothy. The path had been washed away and the going was treacherous. When they had almost reached the heap of debris that marked the place where the hut had stood, they found a small sodden bundle that looked like a grey garment.

'It's Kirelorena, Arel's kitten. She is dead, Gannel.'

A few yards further on the way was blocked by a fallen tree, a small twisted thorn washed down from the heights. Caught in its branches was the limp body of the brindled cat, Kirekinala. They came at last to the hut, or what was left of it. Gannel pushed his way into the wreckage and came out to report no sign of the shepherd. Saranna tried to think calmly.

'No, Gannel, of course. He would have gone to the sheep. Arel would never hide away in the hut while he could help his sheep. Of course he is not inside.'

They began to look about them, peering down towards the lake. Gannel gave a shout.

'I see him! I see him there, Saranna, all tumbled on the ground! Come!'

Clutching at Gannel for support, Saranna edged her way down the slope towards the still figure. She called his name over and over again, but he did not stir.

Gannel and Saranna reached the spot where Arel lay. He was face down on the soaking wet grass, his body twisted awkwardly and one of his legs bent under him. Saranna knelt beside him, shaking with fear. The back of his neck felt cold.

'Gannel, he lies so still. Is he dead?'

The farmer knelt too and with gentle hands reached under Arel to feel inside his shirt. 'A heartbeat; so he's not gone yet. But we dare not try to move him, not just the two of us. We might do some terrible harm to him. Well, no time to lose.'

Gannel took the blanket from his bundle and covered Arel with it. He unpacked the food and wine and set them out tidily on the nearest flat rock. Next he produced a small cushion which he placed on a smaller stone close to Arel's head, motioning Saranna to sit on it. Then from the seemingly bottomless pack there came Saranna's winter cloak, which he slung around her shoulders. And finally he placed the pack beside her, saying, 'Some dry kindling, a peat or two, and my tinder-box. Most of the wood lying here is damp, of course, but if you dig down into the peat stack by the hut, there ought to be some dry bits. I'll just take a bit to eat and drink that I can be swallowing on the way. And I'll have a party back here as soon as may be, by dawn for sure.'

'But...' said Saranna.

'Don't fret about it—no time.'

Then he was gone. Saranna watched him climbing stolidly up towards the gap in the rocks, then turned back to Arel. She gently pulled the tangled hair back from his face, and cautiously moved his head into what looked like an easier position. His face was pale and looked as if he were in a very deep sleep. Saranna looked around again at the unnatural lake and the dead sheep; only one or two were moving about and grazing. Tears began to slide down her cheeks. She grasped the wooden disc that hung about her neck. As she drew it out into the fading sunlight, a gentle breeze arose from the west and brought the freshness of the sea air into the shattered valley.

Saranna thought she heard the faintest whisper of a voice, the hint of a lullaby from her childhood. Then the voice faded and became again a murmuring evening breeze. Saranna looked down at Arel and saw that the wind playing about his head was stirring his hair. When she touched it, the hair felt dry and soft again. As she watched he began to move and quite suddenly he opened his eyes and tried to push himself up from the ground.

The wind dropped abruptly and the valley was still.

'Lie there, my love. You have been hurt, you must not try to move. Help is coming.'

'Saranna. What has happened?'

'There has been a great storm. I think you must have fallen and been hurt last night. I came as soon as I could, and Gannel with me; he has gone for help now, and you must rest.'

He closed his eyes again and nodded weakly. After a moment he said, 'I was going down the hill, to the sheep. They were frightened. I remember nothing else. Now I hurt all over, and I'm very thirsty.'

Saranna fetched the wine and contrived to get some into Arel's mouth. Then spreading her cloak beside him, she lay down so that they could see each other easily. He smiled.

'I would like to kiss you—but I think I had better not move.'

She leaned over and gently kissed his mouth. For a while they were quiet, hand in hand under the sky. Then Arel opened his eyes and said, 'The sheep are very quiet. Are they all right?'

Saranna could not answer.

'Tell me—what has happened?'

'The valley is flooded; and a lot of the sheep....'

'How many of them?'

'Most of them, Arel. Most of them are dead, or dying. I'm very sorry.'

He let go of her hand and lay still, his eyes closed. Tears rolled down his cheeks, and Saranna watched, not knowing what to say. She moved closer to him, and explained about the fire, thinking it would be best to leave him for a while. He nodded, still weeping silently.

Some of the turfs near the bothy were remarkably dry.

Saranna toiled up and down, bringing them all to another flat rock near where Arel lay. She covered her new stack with the remains of one of Arel's blankets, in case more rain came. She soon had a fire going, close enough to Arel to keep him warm through the night. A thin stream of grey smoke rose above the little camp, and Arel began to look more cheerful again.

As the dusk thickened, two of the surviving sheep drew near, attracted by the glow of the turf-fire and the sound of voices. One of them came close enough to nuzzle at Arel's neck, and Saranna tried to push it away.

'It is all right, she won't trample me. This is Maro, I brought her up. They know when a person is hurt or sick, she will take care.'

The ewe made funny little noises as she pushed gently at Arel; then she lay down beside him, on the side away from the fire, and began chewing contentedly.

'There! Now I shall be cosy all night.'

Saranna smiled, and began to tidy up the campsite for the night. By the time the stars were out in a clear black sky all was well, and she settled down close to Arel. They both began to drift off to sleep; but Arel suddenly woke up and asked,

'What about the cats?'

'Sinna and the others are all right, I shut them up in the cupboard, they were furious... '

'Yes, my dear, but I mean my cats. You know I do.'

'Yes. They are both dead, Arel. I am so sorry.'

'They were only kittens, still. Only babies.'

'I know—and there are children dead in the valley. It was a dreadful storm.'

'Iranor is angry with Telan.'

'No—I do not think it is that simple. I used to think the Great Ones did things like that, to punish us or control us. Now I am not so sure.'

'Why is that?'

'Oh, Arel, only you could lie on the hard ground with a broken leg, and want to talk about the ways of the Immortals and the meaning of life!'

'Well, come and kiss me goodnight and I promise to be quiet.'

They woke to see the first pale light of dawn coming over the eastern hills, and to hear the shouts of the rescue party coming down from the west, led by the apparently indefatigable Gannel. Three youngsters carried large packs, for their job was to stay and deal with the dead sheep and care for those that still lived. They and some of the older men set to at once to restore the bothy, while the stretcher party came down to Arel and Saranna.

While she packed up her own bundle, the others discussed the best way to handle the injured man. Gannel came over to Saranna, who smiled up at him.

'Thank you again—Arel and I can never thank you enough for all you have done.'

'What else are neighbours for?' He lowered his voice. 'What about them cats, Saranna?'

'Ask the people who are staying if they would please bury them and mark the spot.'

'Very well. I have seen to your beasts, there is little amiss at home.'

'What about your own place?'

'We're fair enough. Some of these poor folks have little left to call their own. But they were quick to offer when I told them Arel might be saved.'

Now the rescuers were ready to ease Arel onto the stretcher. Bands of sheeting were carefully passed under his body, and the stretcher laid beside him so that they could slide him across. He smiled weakly at Saranna.

'You'd best steady his head,' someone said to her. She knelt by him, and took his head between her hands.

'Now. When I say 'three'. You must all lift together, and quickly as well as gently. We only want to do this once, right, Arel?'

'Please.'

'One; two; THREE!'

Arel cried out as his injured leg dragged behind him; but he was onto the stretcher, and they let him rest and stood up to stretch their legs and ease their backs. Saranna stayed to soothe Arel and gave him a little more wine. After a while they set off, with a stretcher party of four, four reliefs walking behind, and Gannel carrying Saranna's pack. She kept as close as she could to Arel's head, and tried to cheer him as they went. Nevertheless, by the time they reached the gap and stopped for their first rest, his face was grey and his lips bloodied. He shivered under his blankets.

'Fever,' said Gannel quietly.

The journey took all day, and Saranna's foot began to hurt badly. She was glad of their frequent rests. Arel's fever worsened, and he did not answer Saranna when she spoke to him. His face was burning, and his lips dry. They tried to get water into his mouth, but it was difficult as he did not help them or try to swallow. It seemed like years before the farm came into view, and Sinna came tripping along the road followed by the four kittens, calling out a protest at Saranna's long absence. At last Arel was laid on the bed, and while the rescuers broached Saranna's last cask of ale and found food for themselves, she did her best to make him comfortable. After the rescuers had all left she stayed at Arel's side, wiping his face with a cool, soft cloth soaked in rose-water, holding his hand, and talking to him as calmly as she could.

In the late evening there was a tapping on the door of the cottage. Saranna hurried to open it, and saw on the threshold the diminutive figure of the old wise-woman of Telan, Daloreen. She carried several small bundles, including an iron pot which she proceeded to put over the fire to heat, without even a greeting for Saranna.

'Come,' was all she said, and Saranna followed her into the sleeping-room. Here Daloreen perched herself on the side of the bed, and looked long and hard at Arel.

'A clean basin of warm water, please.'

Saranna fetched it, and came back to find Daloreen opening her mysterious little bundles and setting the contents out on the shelf by the bed-head. Small glass bottles, bunches of dried herbs, little packages wrapped up in waxed paper. Saranna watched quietly while the healer selected some leaves and crumbled them into the water. Then she steeped the cloth in the fragrant liquid, and washed Arel's face and hands carefully. Drawing back the quilt, she began to cut away the cloth of Arel's breeches with a small sharp knife. The leg was swollen and red, lying at an awkward angle to the body. Gently the old woman bathed the injured limb in the same aromatic water, and Arel sighed in his sleep and seemed to relax a little. Daloreen turned to Saranna.

'Do you know exactly how this hurt occurred?'

'No, he cannot remember. But we found him lying in such a way that he must have slipped and fallen on top of it somehow—the leg, I mean.'

'That is what I would have supposed. He has been fortunate, none of these bones are broken.'

As she spoke she was gently but firmly probing the leg as if to make sure of her diagnosis.

'The leg has come out of its proper place, the joint is awry; but it can be put back.'

'How?'

'By old Daloreen's magic, of course! How else? But it is only a trick, a matter of knowing what to pull, what to push and what order to do it in. Though I am old and you are ignorant, we shall contrive it between us.'

From a tiny bottle of thick glass, Daloreen let out a few drops of blue liquid into a cup of water. A strong, sleepy smell filled the room. Saranna supported Arel's head while Daloreen somehow got him to swallow the dose.

'That will not deaden the pain completely, but it will help. Now, let us get this bed away from the wall and begin.'

Saranna had no clear understanding of why she was doing any of the things Daloreen instructed her to do. Obediently she helped arrange Arel in a particular position on the bed, grasped his leg with her hands placed just as Daloreen decreed, pulled while Daloreen pushed or pushed while Daloreen pulled. She heard a loud scream from Arel, a cry of triumph from the old healer, and looked up to see that it was all over. Daloreen stood grinning happily at her, and Arel was lying straight and relaxed on the bed.

'A miracle,' gasped Saranna, drawing the quilt up over him. Even his fever seemed to have vanished.

'Nonsense—that was knowledge and experience. Now I shall take a little wine, while you and I talk by the fire.'

The two women went out of the sleeping room, and Saranna limped over to the cupboard.

'Stop! What is wrong with that foot, young woman?'

'Last night—the cow trod on it. That is strange, many years ago a cow trod on my hand.'

She swayed a little, and leaned her arms against the cupboard. Daloreen came to her side and led her to a chair.

'You stay there—I will see to everything.'

Daloreen bustled about the kitchen, fetching wine, opening a pungent salve from her bundle to smear on Saranna's foot, binding the swelling up in strips of linen, and meanwhile stirring the iron pot from time to time.

'Mutton broth. There's plenty there for that handsome young fellow tomorrow; meanwhile, this bowl is for you.'

Saranna suddenly felt hungry and began to spoon up the broth. Daloreen nodded in approval, seated herself opposite Saranna, and sipped her wine. After a while she suddenly remarked, 'The time may come when you and I will have much to say to each other, Mistress Saranna.'

'What do you mean?'

'Never mind; I am speaking of years to come. But now I must leave you.'

She slipped into the sleeping-room, looked closely at Arel, felt his cheek with the back of her hand, and came out again.

'Now; keep him in that bed until I tell you otherwise. A little broth, a little bread, a drop of wine and plenty of fresh water. Oh, and I daresay a kiss or two would not go amiss. Goodnight to you; may the Lady bring rest to your house.'

'May she walk with you on your path', Saranna responded.

When she had closed the door behind the wise woman she sat for a while staring into the fire; but soon climbed carefully into bed beside Arel and slept.

The next few weeks were busy for Saranna and her neighbours. They worked together to repair the storm damage and to make plans for the following season. A party set sail for Imman to try to buy grain for winter food, and seed for the following spring, to replace the stocks spoilt or washed away. Few cows or sheep were left alive on the island, and no rams at all. The only bull had drowned, and Saranna's cockerel found himself lent out to neighbours who needed their flocks of fowl restored.

'Lucky bird', grumbled Arel, 'they say it is a fell tempest that brings no good. What about the sheep? What is happening?'

'We have eighteen breeding ewes left, a hundred or so good skins to trade, and Telk will send over a fine young ram. We can plant more crops next season instead of grazing milk cows, and there is a plan to buy goats from Nork; they are always ready to trade for fine wool, they cannot raise sheep on that barren rock. I often wonder how the goats survive.'

'I expect they eat gulls, like the people. I wish I could be up and working with the rest of you.'

'You soon will.'

Gradually Arel grew stronger and began to move about. Soon he was doing small jobs around the house, then in the yard, and finally he was out and about with the rest.

Saranna loved working at his side, preparing meals together, sitting and talking in the long evenings. Sometimes they went to a neighbour's house for an evening of songs and stories and eating and drinking. It was good to sit with him, to hold his hand and to know that she would walk home with him.

One bright cold afternoon, as they were working in the farmyard, Arel and Saranna heard Gannel's voice calling across the fields.

'Such news, neighbours! Nothing like this has happened for years and years.'

Arel opened the gate and the farmer hurried in, obviously bursting to tell all. Once they were seated by the fire, he began.

'They came this morning, in their beautiful boats and their shining clothes, fair as the Great Ones themselves. And such gifts as they brought, I've never seen nothing to match them!'

'Who, Gannel; who came?'

'Sorry, Arel; I'm a bit overcome. The forest folk, that's who, the people from beyond the sea, the fair ones. It seems they heard of our troubles, for they've brought food and wine and ale, blankets and clothing, as well as silver money that we can use to buy ourselves a fine new bull for the heifers—do you wonder if I cannot get my words together?'

Saranna was eager to hear more; but Arel sat back in his chair and grew quiet; until Gannel turned to him some time later.

'Arel, I have something for you. One of them, a noble lord dressed all in green like an oak-tree in spring, asked did anyone know whether Arel the shepherd was alive and well, and I said yes, and he called me to him... '

'What did he say?' Arel's voice shook.

'Well, he made me learn his name, he particularly wanted you to know that this gift was from him, from Kirokerannin, there's a mouthful, but I know that's right.'

'And the gift?'

'Yes, it is here, all safely wrapped, I came straight away after they sailed, no harm has come to it.'

Beaming, he fished in his belt-pouch and brought out a small bundle wrapped in dark-green silk. Arel took it, and sat staring down at it; then sighed heavily, and began to unwrap the parcel very slowly. After a moment or two he held up to the light a finely-wrought silver chain, and suspended from it a pendant fashioned like two triangles that overlapped so that part of one was concealed by the other. They were also of silver, and engraved with patterns of leaves and flowers, and the rune Aer in the midst of them.

'It is beautiful,' said Saranna.

'I've never seen the like—so delicate, and so strong—you could anchor a ship on that chain, I'll warrant.'

'Did he say anything else?'

Arel's voice was strained, and he stared at the amulet turning on the end of its chain.

'Well, yes, he did—he said; 'Say to Kirarelaken that I have not forgotten.' I asked who he meant, and he said you, Arel.'

The shepherd nodded, and clutched the pendant in his hand. 'I thank you, neighbour.'

Gannel went off, with a cheery wave. Saranna turned back from the door to Arel. He was standing, staring down into the smouldering fire, and he had put the chain around his neck; the silver gleamed on his breast. To Saranna he looked like a lord of the forest, standing tall and beautiful among ageless trees. For a moment she was afraid, he seemed so strange; then he turned and smiled at her.

'I will get the supper,' he said.

Saranna came back from the fields one day in early spring to find Arel packing up a bundle.

'Where are you going?'

'Up into the hills. It is warmer now, the lambs are growing strong enough to journey up to the valley.'

'Do you mean that you are going back to the hills?'

'Yes, of course. I am the shepherd, am I not?'

'But I thought that you would stay with me. Oh!'

She burst into tears and sat down heavily on the nearest chair; Arel looked down at her helplessly.

'I have to go, the sheep are gathered—Saranna, why should you think that I would give up being a shepherd?'

'I thought you would stay with me!'

He put down his bundle, and knelt beside her. 'Listen—we will still be together, as we were last summer. You will come and visit me again, and we shall sit together under the stars. We can still be happy, Saranna, but I must live my life as you must live yours.'

She hugged him tight, weeping against his shoulder. 'I don't want to live my own life, I want to be with you. I cannot bear to be alone, Arel, don't leave me!'

Gently he held her away from him and looked into her eyes. 'Saranna, what you are saying is dreadful—that you do not want to live your own life. You and I would not be whole people if we had to be leaning on each other all our days.'

Saranna stared at him. She broke free of his grip and walked away, staring up into the hills for some moments. Then she came back to him, nodding thoughtfully.

'You are very wise, shepherd. Is this the young man I saw dancing in the village, drinking too much wine and singing bawdy songs?'

'The very same! I hope I am wise enough to know when to be foolish.'

'You are—and I am wise enough to know that you are right. But I shall come and see you very soon.'

'Please, my love.'

After a long embrace and many kisses, they walked down to the winter pasture, where the sheep were bleating and the lambs jumping impatiently. One more kiss, and he was away, the little flock following him up the road at a relaxed, ambling pace. Saranna waved and waved until they were out of sight.

Saracoma

*T*he voice echoed around the cave, high-pitched and querulous. 'Who's there? Speak up, speak up. Come on. Come on. What's your business? Healing or wisdom? I'm a busy man. Haven't got all day.'

Only after this string of questions did the brothers see the speaker: he was sitting on a rock in a dark part of the cave, but he was grey, his hair was grey and he was so covered in grime and dust that it was difficult to see where the rock ended and he began. Vodorian spoke first.

'Good day to you, sir. It was not our intention to disturb you, we were just passing through.'

'Passing through? Where from? Where to? This is my cave. Has been for as long as I've been here. My cave. What do you mean by coming here, if not to see me? That's no way to go on. Where from? Where to? That's what I ask, and I expect an answer.'

Drewin took up the conversation. 'We have come from beneath the mountain, and we are going to the world, to the light. May we pass through your cave?'

'From beneath the mountain? No. You could not. What of Groddin?'

Drewin smiled. 'Yes, we met Groddin, and we did not stay to share in his meal. But who are you, to be asking so many questions?'

The grey man grinned and chuckled. 'Ah, I know just too much to give my name to any passing stranger. They call me the Old Man of the Ragged Mountains, but that is because they live down on the plain. My name is for me to know.'

Drewin thought for a moment before responding. 'Then my name is Tendanta; this is my brother Mandanta.'

The old man laughed out loud. 'And you are no fool either, young man: 'From-the-sea' and 'From-the-island' are fine names to travel with. You are right to be cautious. But I sense something strange about you.'

Vodorian frowned and replied. 'No. I can't think of anything strange. We are merely travellers seeking the light of day. May we pass?'

At first, there was no reply: the brothers waited and watched as the old man sat silently on his rock with his eyes closed. Time passed, and there was no movement in the cavern. The light from the opening grew gradually stronger, until at last a bright shaft cut through the gloom and shone on the old man. Motes of dust glittered in the sunbeam and the sage appeared to be surrounded by a shimmering halo. His eyes opened.

'Many years have I been here. Many things have I seen. Many have been the problems and demands brought to me by the people of the plain. I climbed this mountain in search of wisdom, but I got no further than this cavern. I have stayed here, looking down over the plain and felt a great pity for those below. I abandoned my quest, but now ...'

The brothers watched as the old man's confusion passed across his face, and he seemed uncertain what to do. He looked from one to the other as if expecting them to say something, but they were silent.

'Why do you look at me? Why do you not say what you think?'

Eventually he backed away from them and started to pick up items from around the cave, stuffing them into an old canvas bag. As he did so he muttered fretfully. 'What have they seen? What? Something in their eyes. They know! They have been there. I must go. I must go. Now!'

The old man wearily shouldered his bag, and walked past the brothers into the dark passage.

Drewin and Vodorian watched him disappear into the darkness, then turned and looked at each other.

'Do you see something in my eyes?' Drewin asked.

'Only light, and hope.'

Drewin laughed. 'Is that all?'

'Yes, all to an old man who had lost them. Now he can start his quest again.'

'And so can we.'

They turned to the bright opening in the far wall of the cavern, and walked forward together towards the light. The ground was uneven and scattered with rubble, but the brothers did not stumble or deviate from their path: they walked straight across the cavern and scrambled over the larger rocks inside the opening. Together, they emerged from the gloom into the bright light of day.

They found themselves on a narrow ledge, high on a mountainside. On either side they could see rocky crags reaching up towards them. Below a sheer drop fell away to a broad green plain that stretched away into a distant haze. The white sun blazed in a white sky, bleaching the colour from the landscape. The air the brothers breathed was clean and cold and dry. When Vodorian spoke, small clouds of vapour escaped from his mouth and hung briefly in the still air before disappearing.

'I have seen towering waves in a wild storm, and the sun

turn the sea to shimmering gold; I have seen the soaring cliffs of Mil and the green fullness of Ennvale, the Rainbow Rocks on Drent and the black beaches of Pelk. But this stark land moves me more than any other I have seen. Such vastness makes the sea seem small: such stillness almost frightens me.'

Drewin gazed into the distance as if trying to see beyond the horizon. After a while he spoke dreamily. 'My heart tells me that this land is my home.'

Vodorian turned to Drewin with a look of sadness in his eyes. 'Let us go down.'

It was near the middle of the day when they started climbing down the mountainside. For most of the journey they were scrambling down steep slopes of rough rock. In their haste they scratched their arms and bruised their knees, as they slipped and slithered on loose stones. As they descended the air became warmer and their dusty bodies became covered in sweat: the sun beat down on them with a moist burning heat.

As they neared the foothills, the ground became less steep. Soon they were able to walk upright, and by the time evening was falling, their feet were striking not unyielding rock, but stony soil: there were some tufts of thin grass and small ill-nourished bushes. As the sun finally sank behind the towering heights of the Ragged Mountains they came to a narrow rushing stream, and stopped to drink the clean cold water. They washed the dust of their journey from their bodies, then ate a little food from Vodorian's pack. As the dark of night enclosed them, they settled down to sleep in the lee of a rock beside the stream.

The brothers woke to a cool clear morning. They climbed onto the rock that had sheltered them, and, shielding their eyes with their hands, looked towards the rising sun. From where they stood they could make out the course of the little stream from below them to where it flowed out between two rocky hills onto the plain.

'If we follow this stream it will lead us down to the plain. When we reach open country we can decide which way to go.'

'No, Drewin. I think the time has come for us to part. I do not want to travel across that wide expanse: I will stay in the foothills and travel to the north. I feel that is the way for me to go: it is there I will find my father.'

Drewin looked to the north, then at his brother. 'Is that the goal of your journey? I wish that we could travel on together, but we must follow different paths, it seems. Why is your father lost in the North?'

Vodorian shook his head sadly. 'I am not certain; he may be anywhere upon the face of Skorn. Mother would never tell me so much as his name, no matter how often I asked her. But you and I will meet again, I hope. Let peace attend your path 'til then'

'And may our Mother be your protector.'

The brothers embraced and parted. Vodorian leapt over the stream and started towards the north at a brisk pace, and Drewin followed the stream to the east.

As the afternoon wore on, the stream became broader and slower, and led Drewin through a small wood. The shade from the trees was a relief, and as he travelled Drewin listened to the peaceful sounds of the birds' songs and the scurrying of small animals in the undergrowth, to trees rustling in a gentle breeze and the soft burbling of the stream. While the path was level and grass was underfoot, he was often forced to push through tangled bushes and briars in order to stay near the stream. He pressed on until darkness came and he could no longer see where he was going, then he stopped, wrapped himself in his cloak, and fell into an exhausted sleep soothed by the sound of water flowing past.

The next morning he was awakened by a shaft of light slanting between the trees. Before he was fully awake he stumbled towards the light and found himself at the edge of the wood. The sun dazzled him into wakefulness and for the first time he saw what made the plain so green. The ground fell away from where he was standing then stretched into the distance, and it was covered with a vivid green grass growing shoulder high. The flatness was almost unbroken: even the river was hidden by the tall grass. Only one feature broke the monotony of the landscape: a steep-sided hill stood up from the flat land, silhouetted against the pink morning sky. Drewin had seen it from the mountain, but had thought it much smaller; now it was nearer he could see that it dominated the plain around it.

Drewin sat down where he was and ate some bread while gazing across the green expanse. 'That will be my home. I see my future there.'

So saying, he filled his flask with water from the stream and set off across the plain in a straight line towards the hill.

As soon as he reached the level ground of the plain he lost sight of the hill. The tall grass prevented him seeing further than a few paces in any direction, and while he tried to walk in a straight line, he could not be sure that he was going the right way. At first he was guided by the sun, but as the morning wore on and the sun rose higher in the sky, it became more difficult to tell whether he was on the right path.

There was no shelter from the heat of the day and clouds of insects hung in the still air and buzzed around his head as he passed through them. He heard the scuttering of fleeing animals as he pushed through the lush green grass: occasionally a bird would fly up ahead of him screeching a warning of his approach. But he saw nothing larger than a bird and the loudest noise was the sound of his feet trampling down the grass. His body became wet with perspiration: his shirt clung to his back, sweat trickled down his legs into his shoes, dust and seeds stuck to his face and hair.

He carried on until the sun was high overhead, and at midday he paused to take a little food and drink. Refreshed, he pressed on towards the east, walking with a fast regular gait, and only stopping when the sun finally disappeared behind the Ragged Mountains.

Not until the twelfth day of his journey did he see signs of change in his surroundings: the grass was becoming taller and greener, and occasionally he came across clumps of flowers, small bushes, and other plants. Then, as evening approached and the day was growing cooler, he pushed through a thick growth of grass and found that he could see some distance ahead: it was as though a door had opened and he had been released from a small room. The ground fell away, sloping gently down to a broad, slow-moving river. Undisturbed, except by the wake of an otter and a duck dropping down onto the surface, the smooth water reflected the darkening western sky. A thick growth of trees and undergrowth covered its banks in both directions as far as the eye could see, and on the far side the ground rose up again to the level of the plain.

Drewin saw that the steep-sided hill stood near the river not more than a day's walk away downstream: he had come a little too far north. He walked wearily down to the riverside and lay down to sleep beneath the trees.

The following morning Drewin awoke and went to the river's edge. He knelt down and slowly reached into the river beneath the bank and, almost immediately, pulled his arm out of the water, bringing with it a large brown trout. He cleaned the fish, made a fire, and ate a filling breakfast. Then he set out along the river bank on the last stage of his journey to the hill.

The air was cool by the river, and when the sun grew hotter Drewin could walk in the shelter of the trees. Now that he was nearing his goal, he walked more slowly and stopped occasionally to take a drink from the river or to pick fruit from a bush. Even at this leisurely pace, by early afternoon he had reached the foot of the hill and he stood for a moment and looked up at it.

On its east side the hill rose steeply out of the river which curved round its base, and on the west a rocky ridge sloped up from the plain to join it near its summit. It had looked quite small when Drewin had first seen it from the foothills of the Ragged Mountains; but now it seemed immense, towering above him and casting a great shadow across the river.

Drewin went to the river to fill his flask with water, and gathered fruit from the bushes until his bag was full. Then he set off towards the ridge. The slope was steep and covered in a tangle of small bushes: his feet slipped on loose soil as he scrambled up on hands and knees up out of the valley. By the time he reached the rocky outcrop he was already tired, but without pausing he attacked the climb to the top of the ridge. Here he was forced to cling to a wall of hard rock and climb slowly, feeling his way with hands and feet. This took most of the afternoon, and he pulled himself up onto the top as the sun was starting to sink behind the Ragged Mountains. He paused briefly to get his bearings, then set off once more up the gentle slope towards the top of the hill. The way was now easier as Drewin could pick a path between boulders and outcrops, and he reached the summit as the last light was fading from the sky. He sank to the ground and fell immediately into a deep exhausted sleep.

When he awoke, the sun was high in the sky. He stood and found that he could see the whole expanse of the grasslands and the broad river curving away from his viewpoint towards the south-east. He saw the mountain range that stretched like a wall in the west, and the shimmering heat haze lying to the east.

'Good day, sir.'

The voice was gentle, a little hesitant, but it came from just behind him and it made him jump. He turned towards the sound and saw a young woman, dressed in grey, seated on the ground in the shadow of a boulder. She was smiling, almost laughing, and seemed pleased at the effect of her words. In one fluid movement she stood up.

'I did not mean to startle you, sir. I would not do that for all the world.' She smiled again.

Drewin finally pulled himself together and replied. 'Not startled, just a bit surprised: I have been alone for some days and I hardly expected to meet another person here.'

'Oh, I know. I know. I thought it would be fitting to greet you, once you had arrived.'

'You knew I was coming?'

'Oh yes. It has been the only topic of conversation across

The Green for days. I daresay they are discussing it in Velar this very moment.'

'Velar?'

'Downriver. Velar Rivermouth. By the sea.' She waved her arm vaguely towards the south-east, where the river disappeared into the distance.

'And did they know in Velar that I would be coming here, to this hill?'

'That is what the conversations have been about. There were some who said that you were crossing The Green to the desert of Sinor; some said you were heading for Velar and had lost your way. But I thought that you must be the one from outside, the man from the sea, and that you were coming to The Hill. I am Chafrash of the Shakrien: what are you called?'

'You have guessed right: my name is Tendanta, from the sea. But how did you know?'

Chafrash shrugged and laughed. 'I only know what everybody knows: it was foretold.'

'What was foretold? When?'

'Long before I was born it was said that one day a man from the sea would come to The Hill, and would stay here and give names, and help all the peoples of the plain. Are you that man, Tendanta?'

'I do not know. I know only that I have come from the sea, and when I saw this hill I felt that I must come here. And I have come here.'

'Then you are that man: I feel it in my bones. I welcome you, Tendanta, in the name of all the peoples of the plains. From this day you will watch over the plain and all in it. From this day you are to give names to all things. This is a happy day!'

'I am not as sure as you about these things, but I will stay here for the time being: I am tired of travelling.'

'So be it. The reason does not matter: the deed is enough.' She paused, and seemed to be listening.

'Ah!' she exclaimed, 'Here come the Chorien. And the Tarrien with them. How odd!'

Drewin listened; he could hear nothing. But after a long while he heard people approaching the hilltop up the rocky ridge. He could make out a number of voices and the sound of many feet on the stony path. Chafrash heard it too, and they both turned towards the ridge and waited for the newcomers to come into sight.

About twenty people, men and women, some wearing green and some brown, emerged from behind a large boulder. When they appeared, they were all talking loudly to each other, but their voices gradually subsided when they saw Drewin and Chafrash. Two of the strangers, a man wearing green and a woman in brown, stepped forward.

'I am Shorkat, speaker of the Tarrien,' the woman said, 'and I would have a question answered. Tell us, woman of the Shakrien, is he The One, the man from the sea?'

She pointed at Drewin.

'He is called Tendanta: from the sea. I think he is the one foretold,' Chafrash replied.

The man stepped forward and looked Drewin in the eye.

'I am speaker Tarsh, and we, the Chorien, wish to know whether you are the one foretold.'

All were quiet, waiting for Drewin's reply.

'I do not know. I know of no foretelling, nor was my coming ordered or asked for. I am here: I am called Tendanta. That is all I know. Tell me, what is said of The One?'

Shorkat answered. 'It is said that The One will come to the Hill, that all will change across The Green, and even the Hill itself will change, though it has been the same since the beginning of the world. It is said that the coming of the man from the sea will be a time of joy, like the time of the Twins. What do you say?'

The people watched expectantly, as Drewin prepared to speak.

'I say that this land is yours, and this foretelling is yours. I have no powers here: I have no rights here, except what you give me. The cook is judged by the taste of the food. Test me, and if you, according to your traditions, accept me as the one foretold, then I will be the One.'

'Well said.' said Shorkat, 'Let us test your wisdom. Let the speaker of the Chorien present our dispute.'

She turned to Tarsh with a bow, and he started to speak.

'We have come here hoping that you, Tendanta, would lend us wisdom. It is said that the Old Man of the mountain is no longer there, that he has died, and so we have no-one to turn to but you. Here is the cause of our problem: we, the Chorien, are people of the river, we know the river and all its fruits. We use our skill to take the fruits of the river, and we do it well. Bring the fish for Tendanta to see!'

Four of the brown-clad Chorien came forward carrying a large object wrapped in wet cloths. They laid it on the ground and unfolded the wrappings to reveal a plump brown trout.

Tarsh continued.

'This fish is our catch of yesterday. One Chorien family laboured all day to catch it. It is a good catch, worthy of a day of work. But the Tarrien would give only part of their work of a day in exchange for it.'

Tarsh stopped speaking and stood aside for Shorkat.

'We live to the north where we are the best hunters of the plain. This a good time, and yesterday we took five deer.'

The five dead beasts were brought forward and laid on the ground.

'The Chorien say that they should receive those five deer in exchange for one fish, but we say a beast for a beast: one deer for one fish. The Chorien say we are liars, but that is not true: we are always honest.'

There was a murmur of agreement from the Tarrien hunters, then Tarsh took up the challenge.

'But you did not say that two seasons ago, when the deer had gone to the south, and you wanted our fish though you had nothing to trade. Then we said that you had nothing at the end of your day's work and we had many fish, so we exchanged many fish for nothing that you might eat and not starve. You did not say 'one beast for one beast' then. Who is the liar, and who speaks the truth?'

The Chorien shouted their approval, and it looked for a moment as though a fight might break out. But Shorkat silenced them all with a gesture, and addressed Drewin.

'This is not the first time that we have had this dispute, nor are we the only clans to argue over such things: last full moon the Shakrien and the Korsh shed blood over a handful of herbs. Tell us Tendanta, which of us is right?'

Drewin stepped between the two Speakers and turned to Shorkat. 'You have asked me a question; let me ask you one in return: does the sun rise into the sky in the morning?'

'Yes, it does,' she replied.

'And do all the Tarrien say so?'

The Tarrien said they did, and Drewin turned to Tarsh.

'And the Chorien: do they say that the sun rises in the morning?'

'We do,' said Tarsh.

'Good,' said Drewin 'At least you agree about something.'

This brought smiles and laughter from both clans. Drewin continued, 'The sun rises in the morning for all people everywhere, so all people agree that the sun rises in the morning. But hunger and thirst and all desires come at different times to different people, and so all people argue about food, and clothes, and whether a woman, or a man, is beautiful. They have different opinions, and there is no truth to be found. So my answer to you is that neither the Tarrien nor the Chorien is right, and that you must come to some agreement, or keep what you have.'

The people of both clans looked bewildered, and Shorkat voiced their thoughts.

'You are saying that we should do what we know to be wrong, that we should deny what we know to be true?'

'No, I am saying that if you want the fish and, if the Chorien want the deer, then you must find some way to make a trade that seems fair to both of you.'

'But we cannot both be fairly treated,' said Shorkat.

'I think you can,' Drewin replied, 'The Chorien say 'a day's work for a day's work', but some days are better than others. Would the Chorien say 'fourteen days' work for fourteen days' work'?'

The Chorien hesitated, but murmured their agreement.

'A month's work for a month's work?'

Again they agreed.

'A year's work for a year's work?'

'Yes.'

'And in a year do you think that you give fish and receive deer in equal numbers?'

'It may be so,' agreed Tarsh grudgingly.

'Then the Chorien believe in 'a beast for a beast' just as the Tarrien do,' Drewin concluded, but Shorkat quickly intervened.

'But we cannot be sure. It may be that over a year the Chorien will gain, and receive more than they give. How can we trust them?' she said, and the rest of the Tarrien voiced their agreement.

Drewin said nothing, but went to his pack and took out a knife. He then looked among the rocks, found what he was seeking, and came back to the waiting people carrying a stick. He carved one notch at one end of the stick and five at the other, then he split it in half down its whole length so that there were two sticks marked with identical notches. He went to the animals lying on the ground and cut two fins from the fish, and some hairs from the coat of a deer and fixed them to the ends of the sticks. Then he stood before the people of the plain holding up the two sticks.

'There is no need to trust one another, although, in time, you will. If you exchange the five deer for the one fish you can each take away a record of the trade. These two rods of wood are the same: at the end marked with a fin is one mark saying that one fish was exchanged, and at the end marked with the hair of the deer are five marks saying that five deer were exchanged. You can each bring the rods when you trade, and make more marks, and when the marks at one end are the same number as the marks at the other you can throw away the rods, because you will have exchanged 'one beast for one beast', and the Tarrien will be happy. And when you trade again you can make a new rod.'

The people crowded round Drewin and examined the sticks. They talked together, Chorien with Tarrien, and they agreed that the recording rods were good. Shorkat of the Tarrien and Tarsh of the Chorien came to Drewin and the crowd became quiet. Shorkat raised her arms above her head and spoke.

'We, the Tarrien will agree to this, and in future we will use these rods of Tendanta. I say that Tendanta is the one foretold; he has shown us wisdom in this matter.'

Then Tarsh spoke. 'We, the Chorien, agree, and I say that Tendanta has proved his worth. I will spread the good news of the coming of the One to the Hill. But first let us all, Chorien and Tarrien, build a shelter for the man from the sea, and let us build it of stone so that it will stand for a long time, so that he will stay among us for a long time. '

Word was sent, and all the people of the two clans came to help in the work of making a home for Drewin. They cleared the rocks and boulders from the ridge and levelled its surface, making it a causeway leading from the plain up to the hilltop. Then they took the rocks they had gathered and built a house with thick walls and a roof of reeds that would be cool in the heat of summer and warm against the cold winter winds that blew across the plain. And they made the hilltop level and took the rocks from it to make a wall round its edge and with the rest of the rocks they built a storehouse next to Drewin's new home.

When the work was finished, meat and fish, wine and fruit were brought to the hill and a great feast was held. All the Chorien and the Tarrien were there, Chafrash of the Shakrien had stayed, and some members of the other clans came, but none of the Korsh. Tarsh and Shorkat made long speeches praising the wisdom of Tendanta, story-tellers sang the old songs of the plain, and there was much laughter and joy, and drinking of strong wine. As the feasting came to an end, and the sky showed the first light of morning, Drewin rose to speak.

'I thank you for your kindness, for your welcome, and for giving me a home. It has been said that I will be the giver of names, and I have been thinking of what this might mean. I would like to name this place, and the river that runs below here: this hill I name Saracoma, and the river Sarannen, both in memory of one who was lost to me. That is all I have to say, so let the songs go on and the music play until the sun is high in the sky!'

Then a new song was sung, of the coming of Tendanta, and the journey across The Green, and the making of Saracoma. There was much laughter at Tendanta's loss of direction, much cheering and jeering at the exploits of the builders in moving massive stones, and a great shout for the description of the feast and the naming. While this was going on, Chafrash came to Drewin and spoke to him.

'I am of the Shakrien, but I am not with them. For some time I have roamed The Green and dwelt with other clans, as is the custom, but I have not found a home, a man, a family. It is as though I do not belong.'

Here she paused and a sadness came over her. She took a deep breath and continued. 'Here I have found a kind of peace.

It was not in my mind that I should come to The Hill, but now it is Saracoma it seems different, and I feel peace here. I am well and healthy: I do not think that I am too young, or too old. What do you think Tendanta?'

'I think I do not know what you are saying. Why are you telling me these things?'

'Tell me if you think I am not fit, that I am not suitable. In your wisdom give me your opinion.'

'You seem well enough to me, but what does that matter? I feel you want something, but you have not told me what. What are you saying, Chafrash?'

'I have a favour to ask. You must refuse me if you do not feel that it is fitting, if you think I am unworthy. I will accept your judgment, and go away without another word.'

'Please, Chafrash, will you say what you mean. You keep asking for my opinion, and expecting me to be unkind, but I still do not know what you are asking. What are you talking about?'

The young woman took another deep breath. 'May I stay here? I would be no trouble to you: I might be of some help to you. May I stay with you on Saracoma and learn your wisdom?'

Drewin was taken aback. 'Is that what all this mystery is about? You act as though I would be granting some great favour. I have said this is not my land, nor is Saracoma my hill. You can stay here if you will, and as for wisdom, you may learn all you can from me, but that is not much. You may have more to teach than to learn, for I am likely to get lost on the plain and not be able to find my way home. And I have never hunted deer.'

When the Tarrien and the Chorien went away after the feast,

Chafrash stayed at Saracoma with Drewin.

In the days that followed, Drewin helped Chafrash to build a shelter on the hilltop. While they worked he taught her the skills of shaping stone and wood that he had learnt in the Cavern; and she told him the ways of The Green, how to steer a straight path through the grass and where the animals of the plain were to be found.

The people of the plain started to come to Saracoma seeking advice on their disputes and problems. Each time they came they brought gifts of food or useful tools, so that by the time winter came Drewin's storehouse was well supplied and his home had all the comforts that he needed. So it was that when a group of Puchellian women came for advice about a family dispute, there was no food or tool that they could give that Drewin did not already possess.

They pondered this problem for some time, as was the way with the Puchellian, and finally decided that, instead of making a gift, they would give work. They built a device on the hilltop for lowering a pot into the river below, so that Drewin would not have to climb down to the river to get his water. It became the custom of those who came to seek the advice of Tendanta to make a gift, or to add to the comfort of Saracoma.

When the men of the Ranapalien came to Saracoma to learn how to watch the sky and predict the seasons, they built a guest house on the hill for the peoples of the plain. The Fien, who lived nearby, brought fruits in season and would bring rushes for the floors of the houses. And occasionally travellers would rest at Saracoma and give some foreign luxury in payment.

As winter passed and the next year came and went, Saracoma grew bigger: more people followed Chafrash and stayed on the Hill to learn from Drewin, and, in time, each clan built its own guest house there; others stayed nearby and supplied food to Drewin and his guests, and a settlement grew up on the river bank below the hill. Within a few years, it had become the custom for all trading between the clans to take place close to Saracoma, so that Drewin could be called upon in case of a dispute. An area at the lower end of the causeway became a market place, and for most of the year it was occupied by traders, seated in tents or on carpets, selling all kinds of goods. In time, merchants came from Velar in the south-east, from Karressinon in the east, and even from beyond the Ragged Mountains, and houses clustered around the market. And Saracoma grew: it now stretched from the jetties of Bankside by the river up the slope to Market Place and was starting to spread out onto the plain. The Hill itself was completely covered with the stone buildings of Tendanta's Home.

Healing

'*I* do not believe it!' Saranna looked up, startled, and tried to see where the voice was coming from.

'Once in a lifetime, yes—but twice? It is too much.'

She scrambled up from her ungainly position, kneeling amongst the herb-beds to plant out seedlings. Turning, she saw a face peering over the garden hedge; a face crowned and aureoled by a wild mass of white hair.

'Kor-Sen!' She rushed towards the hedge. 'Kor-Sen—to see you again after so many years—Oh, come in, here, the gate is over here.'

He smiled broadly. 'Saranna, my dear lady, I know where the gate is. But how do you know, and what are you doing here?'

They trailed along the hedge, one on either side, towards the wooden gate. Reaching it, they paused and stood looking at each other.

'You are as beautiful as ever,' he said.

'And you as smooth-tongued as ever. Never mind that, what do you mean, what am I doing here? I live here, this is my house.'

Kor-Sen scratched his head. 'I cannot imagine how that could be; we must pursue the matter further. In spite of dangerous precedents, will you let me through this gate?'

She laughed, and unlatched the gate. 'You have not changed a bit. Yes, you may come in. Indeed it is dangerous to admit you through any gateway, but nevertheless, oh wise Master, you may enter.'

She stood aside and curtseyed. He swept through the gate with an air of mock-grandeur, and bowed formally. Saranna collapsed into giggles.

'You dear, dear man, it is so good to see you. Come and give me a kiss.'

He raised his eyebrows at her. 'Really? Are you sure, now? There is no large young man within the house just waiting to come and set about me for taking liberties?'

'Kor-Sen.' She held out her arms to him, and he came and held her, kissing her long and deeply, resting his head on her shoulder at last with a sigh.

'Saranna. It is good to see you, my dear one.'

For a moment they stood together, still and quiet. Then he stepped back and looked quizzically at her.

'Now, woman, will you answer my questions instead of asking me things in exchange—you used always to complain if I did that. Why is this your house, when it should be Daloreen's? Where is the old charlatan? What has been happening to you, and are you happy? Those will do for now, I think.'

'Kor-Sen, did you know Daloreen?'

He looked at her sharply. 'Did I? Why, of course I do. We are old, old friends. Charlatan was merely a joke, I learned much from her in my youth. Where is she?'

'Oh, my dear, I am sorry—but she is dead.'

He staggered a little, and for a moment looked old and tired. Saranna took his arm and led him to a seat on the wooden bench by the door of the house. He covered his face with his hands.

'I have sat here with her so often. We were lovers once, in the distant spring-time of our lives. I had hoped to see her once more, before—'.

'Before what?' Saranna sat beside him and took his hand.

'Never mind, there will be time for that later. Tell me about Daloreen—how long ago was it?'

'It must be more than three years now. I have lived here for five years, here in this house I mean. She trained me in all her herb-lore and healing skills, or as much as she could before her death. Since then I have been teaching myself. I was a farmer before that, out on the hills over there, but Daloreen wanted me to come into town and live with her. She knew that she was dying; she talked of how the people would need a healer when she was gone; so I came. She never mentioned you.'

'No. Her private life was always—private. I did so want to see her. And now, who knows—do people ever meet again when this life is done?' Again he sighed deeply, and Saranna leaned over and kissed the top of his head. He looked up at her.

'But see, you are here to comfort me; we at least have met again, and that is good. Maybe we should drink to our reunion?'

'You wicked old man, you are beyond redemption!' Saranna brought out a flask of mellow pale-green wine, and two goblets. Solemnly Kor-Sen poured a little into one goblet, then swirled it round and cast the wine into the air.

'For the Lady of the West Wind; and in memory of Daloreen; and with thanks for our meeting.'

She touched her goblet to his. 'To you, my dear; you are very welcome.'

When they had drunk together, Saranna went back to her gardening. As the afternoon grew hotter, she saw that Kor-Sen was drowsing on the bench; he had finished up the flask while he watched her. Declining all offers of food, he clambered up the narrow stairs to the sleeping-chamber, and lay down on the bed. He was asleep before Saranna left the room. She went down to put away the gardening tools and start preparing something special for the evening meal.

'Something nourishing, and that good red wine from Imman to go with it,' she thought.

As she worked, she sang softly to herself, enjoying the unusual sensation of cooking for someone else, the awareness of his presence in the house. Once or twice she was interrupted, as was usual. A small boy came, anxiously clutching a puppy with a sore patch on its side. Saranna brought out a healing ointment from her store, and in exchange took the child's offering of a root of moon-rose, one of the rarest and most useful of the healing herbs. The boy must have searched long and hard for it, and she planted it immediately in a dark, cool corner of the garden. Next there came the carpenter with a cut across his hand, which she dressed with spider-web and moss, binding it up for him and receiving a nicely-turned wooden platter in payment. Then it was dusk, and the village grew quiet as the time for the evening meal drew on. Saranna checked her preparations; all was well in the kitchen, the table ready and the food cooking. She went up the stairs as quietly as she could, but found that Kor-Sen was awake, lying on his back and looking at the ceiling. Saranna sat down beside him.

'I hope you are rested, Kor-Sen. Supper will soon be ready, and good strong wine of Imman to wash it down.'

'You are very kind to me—as ever. It will be good to talk with you once more.'

During supper and for a long time afterwards, as they sat close together before the fire, they talked and talked of all the things that had happened since their parting. Saranna told of the great storm and of her years as a farmer. But when she spoke of Arel, her voice faltered, and tears came to her eyes.

'What is this? Did this shepherd cause you pain, Saranna?'

'Oh yes, Kor-Sen, he did. But you need not sound so indignant, for you too caused me pain.'

Kor-Sen drew nearer, and put his arm about Saranna's shoulders. Speaking very gently, he said, 'Tell me what happened.'

'He went away. He went off to his precious Forest Lands to look for his father; and I wanted him to stay with me. Oh!'

She put her head down on Kor-Sen's shoulder, and wept. He stroked her hair and murmured soothingly until suddenly she sat up and moved away.

'A fine comforter you are, Kor-Sen. Do you know, the very first time Arel and I spoke together, I told him about you. About our parting, which pained me although I too felt I must go; it hurt me to see you hurry away to your father without even waving me farewell. And Arel spoke kindly, and comforted me. Now it seems I have travelled around in a great circle, for he too has left me.'

'Saranna; listen to me. Please do not weep. It is the way of mortal life that friends and lovers meet and then part; sometimes to meet again as we have done. There is no special failing in you, my dear.'

'But people always leave me!'

Kor-Sen handed her a splendid silken kerchief that he brought out from the sleeve of his robe, and while she mopped her damp face he said, 'But you too have left people behind, my dear. What of Kerren of Esmil? What of Drenn, your husband? Did you not depart from them without a backward glance? Did you not tell me in Drelk that you had decided you must move on?'

'But that... that was...'

'Was what? Different? I think not, Saranna. Do not be so eager to think there is something special about the things that happen to you. Life brings these sorrows upon all of us, day by day and year by year. Why must you always see the hand of Iranor wreaking punishment upon you, in every turn of chance?'

Saranna carefully folded the kerchief, sat up straight, and looked silently into the fire, while Kor-Sen watched. At last she turned back to him and said,

'Now tell me of yourself—what you have done, where you have travelled.'

Kor-Sen leaned towards her, one hand stretched out, about to speak; then he smiled, nodded his head slowly, and relaxed into his place. 'Let me first tell you about my father; for after you and I had said our farewells—all right, some farewells!—upon the quay at Drelk, I went at once to his house.'

'And did you see him? What happened?'

'Well, first I had to get past the guard on the gate, past the servant at the heavy door, and up the stairs to his chamber. There was another servant there who asked me my business, but I pushed him aside and threw the door open.'

'That must have made a grand impression on your father!'

'Unfortunately it did not, for the room was empty.'

Saranna tried to stifle her laughter.

'Now who is making fun of serious matters!'

'I am sorry—what happened next?'

'All the servants were rushing about making a fuss, which came to Mannen's ears. He came puffing along the corridor to see what the matter was. So I walked into his room and sat down. He spluttered his way in after me, demanding to know by what right, and how, and so forth.'

'And?'

'And I stood up again and said to him, 'Mannen the Merchant, you are my father, and in my mother's name I curse you; but for myself, I pardon you.' He gasped like a beached whale and went on saying, 'What? How? Who?' for some moments. But gradually I made him understand, and he began to weep, especially when he heard of my mother's death. And he told me... -'

Kor-Sen stopped speaking, and Saranna saw the glint of tears in his eyes.

'What did he tell you?'

'He said that he had loved my mother all his life, but that on his return from Sen-Mar he was forced to marry the woman his family had chosen. 'Why did you not come to me before? Why did you not tell me you were my child? You are the son of my love, the son of my heart, my first-born—all that I have should go to you.''

'Oh, the poor man!'

'Yes, indeed. He was weeping harder and harder, and he hugged me, and showed me a small picture of my mother, painted by a miniaturist in the market-place of Drelk from his description—he had kept it hidden all those years.'

Saranna got up to fetch Kor-Sen more wine. 'And now? Have you become friends?'

'Yes, I think so. We met several times before I set out on my travels. But it is late now, Saranna; we must speak of my journeyings tomorrow.'

Healing

In fact there was little time for talking on the following day;
Saranna was besought for help by a frantic husband whose wife
was struggling to give birth, and had been so for two days.
Saranna was furious at the sight of the woman, hardly more
than a child herself, lying grey and exhausted upon the bed, her
body wracked with convulsive pain, too worn out to scream.

'Why did you not call me before?'

'Oh Mistress—will she live? Will all be well with the child?'

'No thanks to you if she does.'

Saranna turned him out to fetch the wife's mother, and set
to work herself. The child was trying to be born the wrong way
round, as she suspected, and though she struggled all that day
for its life, and though the mother endured much pain, Saranna
was not able to save the little one. While the girl sobbed weakly
in her mother's arms, and the young man wept bitterly in the
next room, Saranna wrapped the still, cooling form in the
clean linen that would have swaddled it. She kissed the little
forehead, and said, 'The Lady has taken you to herself; go with
our blessing.'

Then she laid the body in the newly-made cradle, and went
out. She walked home through the early evening, weary and
sad. As she opened her gate, Kor-Sen came out of the house.

'What is it, dear one?'

'A baby—a first-born daughter. And she is dead, Kor-Sen, I
could not save her.'

As she began to cry, he took her hand and led her into the
house. There he seated her by the fire, drew off her shoes and
washed her tired feet and hands. He brought her wine and
food, urging her to eat and drink, feeding her himself when
she tried to refuse.

Afterwards he half-carried her up the stairs, and put her to bed. She clutched at his hand.

'I should have liked a daughter.'

'Perhaps you will have one, one day.'

'No. No, I shall soon be too old. And Arel will not return. Nor will you stay with me.'

He lay on the bed beside her, and held her gently while she fell into a troubled sleep. All night he held her, kissing her tenderly when she cried out in distress. Towards morning, they both slept soundly.

The next day, Kor-Sen refused to allow Saranna to work. When people came looking for her he asked them to return the following day. The more urgent cases he treated himself, out of Saranna's store of medicines. She sat by the fire, until he coaxed her out into the sun and brought her a light mid-day meal on a tray. He settled down beside her with a large flagon of wine, and began to talk again of his years of travelling.

'Once more I passed through the Gap of Imm, and drank at the Saltfish on the quay. Then I took a boat to Imm, and walked through the long grass and inhaled the fresh sea air. Off to Pelk and Nork, where I struck up an acquaintance with a wise old bard, almost ninety years old, and gleaned much useful lore from his songs. It is astonishing what ancient memories are preserved upon these isolated islands. He sang to me of the Grief of Iranor and the Birth of the Moon, fuller versions than I have found anywhere—and yet none of those people can read, nor have they even heard of the Runes!'

Saranna got up and began to walk slowly about her quiet, deep-hedged garden. Kor-Sen followed, still talking, watching the lines of stress and tiredness on her face ease gradually away as she became absorbed in his traveller's tales.

'Then I went to Telk, where they needed a general healer-cum-teacher, and settled there in a pleasant little house.'

'Why did you not come to Telan? You knew that I was here.'

'That is why I did not come. My heart told me it would not do. And I was right, for what would your Arel have said if I had come whistling in through the farmhouse door one day?'

She smiled. 'He would have looked down upon you from a great height, said, 'Welcome, Old One', in respectful tones, and poured you a flagon of ale.'

'I see! A fearsome prospect; I am glad that I stayed on Telk, where life was quiet! After a year or so I drifted down through Ipple and Drent; on Drent I heard something that interested me greatly.'

Saranna stooped to examine a flowering primrose.

'There is an Academy of sorts on Drent, nothing like Imman of course, but a dwelling of learned women and men who teach those willing to come and learn. I thought seriously of settling there, but they were all full of a tale brought back by a wandering trader of some great new centre of learning in the north. Saracoma, they called it.'

Saranna looked up, hearing a noise at the gate. An old woman stood there, fumbling at the latch.

'Excuse me, my dear, this is old Saneen, she is almost blind and needs salves to ease the irritation in her eyes.'

She moved towards the gate, but stopped. 'Perhaps you might be of help, Kor-Sen. I can ease the pain, but nothing I have tried has any effect on Saneen's vision. The world grows dimmer for her month by month.'

'I am willing to try.'

Together they welcomed the old woman.

'Saneen, this is my good friend. Master Kor-Sen. Should you mind his examining your eyes, while I prepare the salve? It may be that he can think of something that will help.'

'Oh, good-day, master. Look away, if you will. It is kind of you, I'm sure. But unless the Lady herself deigns to touch these poor old eyes, I doubt that I shall see for much longer. Still, look, look.'

Kor-Sen seated the old woman on the garden bench, and turned her face towards the sun. The eyelids were reddened and sore, and there was a cloudy discharge lying thickly across the eyes themselves. Kor-Sen peered at this carefully.

'I have seen this before, in Ipple. Saneen, where does the water you drink come from?'

'From my own little spring, Sir. In my garden.'

'Yes. And no-one else drinks from it?'

'No, not since my husband died and my children left my house for their own homes. Most folk in the village draw water from the stream that flows down to the sea.'

Kor-Sen turned to Saranna. 'This main drinking supply is clean and fast-flowing, I take it?'

'Yes, it is—it comes down from the hills.'

'Saneen, did anyone else in your family suffer from soreness of the eyes?'

'Why, yes, a little. Now you come to mention it, the children have not been troubled since they left home.'

'Ah! I thought so. Let us take your new supply of ointment and come to your home, and I will look at this spring.'

Slowly, with the old woman leaning on their arms, Saranna and Kor-Sen passed through the main cluster of houses and down into a hollow near the sand-dunes that bordered the beach. Here was Saneen's small cottage, and she led them around it to where a sluggish spring welled up through the rough grass to form a shallow pool.

Kor-Sen knelt down beside it, sniffed it, tasted it, and peered at it, while the women leaned over him curiously. At last he looked up. 'Saranna, have you never examined this spring before?'

She shook her head.

'Well, look. Saneen will not be able to see this, but you look.'

She knelt beside him, and cried out when she saw the tiny, tiny black insects that skipped on the surface of the pool.

'What are they?'

'A kind of sand-fly, I would guess. And their eggs, which will be too small to see, will be in every drop of water that Saneen drinks. And that is the source of your blindness, my dear.'

The old woman clutched at his arm as he stood up.

'Oh, Sir! But what does that mean? Can it be made well?'

'I think so. If you stop drinking this water at once and get some strong youngster to bring you pure water instead.'

Saneen was incoherent with delight, and hugged them both many times. At last she tottered off towards her daughter's house in the village, to spread the good news, and Saranna turned back towards home. Kor-Sen followed her.

'Why so quiet. Lady?'

She shrugged her shoulders, and walked on. Kor-Sen plodded silently beside her, and at last she stopped and turned to him. 'I feel so—stupid, sorry, careless—I should have discovered this for myself, and saved Saneen from years of suffering. Why did I not see it?'

Kor-Sen took her hand.

'Come. Let us go down to the sea, and sit together, and talk.' He led her down through the village to the beach. Arm in arm they crossed the sand and settled in a warm and sheltered spot. Saranna leaned back against a rock, and Kor-Sen sprawled on the sand with his head on her lap. They could see, beyond the sea to the north-east, the dim outline of the Ragged Mountains and the darker line of the Forest Lands.

'I wonder where Arel is now.'

'He is by now King of all the Kirenoi, I have no doubt; I wonder how you could bear to let him go away.'

Saranna stared out to sea for some minutes, and Kor-Sen sat waiting in silence. At last she said, 'He wanted to go, to find his father. That is surely something that you can comprehend, Kor-Sen. And at about the same time Daloreen asked me to come and live with her. It simply—came about.'

'When I was younger, Saranna, I used to believe that things could just 'happen' to me. But now I doubt if life is quite so simple. Perhaps nothing happens to us without some degree of contrivance; or intention; or simply consent, on our own part.'

'I do not understand.'

'Probably not. I am not stating it very clearly. Let me tell you a story about when I was a little boy; when my teacher, Karenoran, wanted me to win a place in the Temple School in Sen-Mar. I had to go on the appointed day and be submitted to many harsh tests and trials. And at first it was like that. I was submitted to all these things, sent into the temple by my mother, left there by Karenoran and Dal-Nen, my guardian, pushed around and bullied by priests and novices and rich boys. But then something changed. I took control. I decided that I would have my place in their school, and I would have it on my own terms. And since that time, I have never let anything 'just happen' to me.'

'No. I can see that. Indeed, you seem rather to be one of the things that happen to other people, or so you have been to me.'

'Saranna—how can you be like this? How can you sit and let things flow over you, engulf you, carry you along with them? Do you never ask yourself 'Why should I do that?' or 'How did I come to be here?''

Again Saranna was silent for some while before answering. 'Not often. Sometimes I have wondered whether I should be different. But life has been good to me, by and large.'

Kor-Sen sat up abruptly, and slammed his fists down into the sand.

'Rubbish!' he shouted. 'What utter foolishness, woman! How can you speak so of a life full of loss and pain and wandering?'

'How dare you speak to me like this!'

Saranna sprang to her feet and turned to run away. Kor-Sen grabbed her by the ankle and she fell over into the sand.

'Let me go! What madness has come upon you? Let me go!'

'No, I will not let you go—stop running away, Saranna, for once in your life be still and think!'

She wriggled free of his grasp, raised herself up onto her knees, and aimed a fierce blow at his head, catching him across the face.

'Ouch! That is better.' He smiled at her. Saranna became suddenly still.

'Better! Better? Now I know you have run mad!'

'Now; shall we continue our talk?'

'I have no wish to speak of this; it distresses me.'

'Sometimes we must become distressed in order to achieve anything. I asked you to think. Do you know what you should be thinking about?'

She shook her head. 'But no doubt you do, wise Master.'

'Oh, my dear, do not be angry with me, but listen. Before we came onto the beach, you were annoyed with yourself because you had never noticed the reason for Saneen's blindness. And the question you should be thinking about is this—why did you never inspect the spring? Why did you rest content with treating those sore eyes? Why, Saranna?'

They knelt on the sand, looking into each other's eyes, for a long silent moment. Then Saranna said,

'I do not understand. You were speaking of Arel going away. What has this to do with Arel?'

'Sit down again with me, Saranna, hold my hand and let us talk about this slowly and carefully. There is a link, you see. If I were to ask you again, 'Why did you let Arel go away?' that would be very much the same question.'

'Would it?'

'Yes, my dear. I have thought about you a good deal while we have been apart, and come back to this again and again. Why, my dear lady, do you let bad things happen to you over and over and over again?'

'I do not! I don't, Kor-Sen—why are you being so cruel to me?' Saranna began to sniffle, and Kor-Sen handed her his kerchief once more.

'I am not being cruel, or I do not mean to be. Listen to me just a little longer, I beg you.'

She shook her head; but stayed beside him, listening.

Over and over again he questioned her, his voice lilting

gently like the chant of a temple singer. At first Saranna was slow to answer his questions, but gradually began to respond as if hers were the second voice at some great ritual, not quite an echo, not quite a response.

'Why did you leave the Island of the West Wind?'

'Because Mother sent me away.'

'Why did you leave Kerren?'

'Because I heard Mother's voice in the wind, telling me to leave.'

'Why did you marry Drenn?'

'Because he wanted me to.'

'Why did you leave him?'

'Because you made me.'

'Why did you part from me?'

'Because you said it was time.'

'Why did you part from Arel?'

'He wanted to go away.'

'Why did you become a Healer?'

'Because Daloreen wanted me to.'

'Why did you not inspect Saneen's well?'

She looked up at him, the rhythm of question and answer broken, and anguish spread over her face. And then she burst into tears. She sobbed and sobbed, falling into Kor-Sen's arms and drenching his tunic. She gulped and sniffed and shuddered in her despair, and Kor-Sen held onto her tightly and said nothing.

After a long time, the sobs grew quieter and Saranna tried to mop her face with the kerchief. Kor-Sen helped her.

'I am sorry,' she said.

'You have no need to be so. Now, I have done with being

cruel for today. It is your turn now.'

'I have no desire to be cruel!'

'I mean it is your turn to speak. And I will stop this pretence of being wise, and listen to you.'

Saranna took a deep breath, then another. 'I do know why I never inspected the spring of water.'

Kor-Sen was silent, but nodded encouragingly.

'It is because it never occurred to me to look behind what was happening, and see whether something else might be making it happen.'

Kor-Sen nodded.

'I know why that is like the rest of my life, but I do not like to think of such things.'

'But now you can, quite safely, you know, for I am here. Tell me.'

'I never have bothered to ask whether I had to do the thing that was in front of me, or whether I might choose to do something different. Even when I decided to leave Drelk, that was mostly because I believed that you wanted me to move on.'

He nodded again.

'I think you are right, Kor-Sen, about letting bad things happen. I think that is what I have always done.'

She paused for a while, looking up at the sky. 'But I do not think I can answer the biggest question of all.'

'And what is that?'

'Why? Why have I lived in this way?'

'Well—that is the big question. But I do not believe I should answer it for you. Instead I will ask you it and see if you can find the answer.'

Saranna looked away fearfully; as she did so a cloud passed

over the sun and a wind arose from the sea.

Kor-Sen spoke in a gentle but firm voice. 'Saranna, why do you think you have no other recourse than to let bad things happen to you?'

Saranna stood up and looked out over the waves, as if she were listening. She walked towards the water's edge where the waves tumbled onto the sand and stopped when the sea was washing over her feet. Kor-Sen followed her.

'Why, Saranna? Tell me why.'

She turned to face him, but could not look him in the eye. She mumbled something, as if to herself.

'Say it to me, Saranna. Tell me.'

Saranna lifted her eyes to his. 'I must be made wrongly in some way. There must be a flaw inside me that works for bad, like the invisible creatures working to destroy Saneen's eyes.' She sat down plop in the water, rested her head on her knees and wrapped her arms over it. There she sat silently while the waves rushed in and soaked her.

Kor-Sen stooped, lifted her up, and carried her back to the rocks. He sat down, cradling Saranna in his arms, and rocked her gently, softly humming a tune. Tears ran down her cheeks and onto her wet clothes. When the tears stopped he spoke softly into her ear.

'And now it is my turn again. Now I will tell you something. Listen: you must always remember this. You are not bad; you are not weak; you are strong and good. And you must—you must—live as if you were strong and good.'

They sat for some time hand in hand until the tide went out.

The next day passed quietly. Saranna worked all day, with people who came seeking her skills, weeding the garden, cooking. Kor-Sen worked with her, but they said very little to each other. There was a warm closeness between them, and often they would exchange a smile.

Towards evening Kor-Sen suggested a walk, and they strolled together back to the beach, stopping only to buy some wine from the little inn on the way. This time they walked further along the shore, sitting side by side on the marram-topped dunes and looking out to the south-west across the wide sea.

'Now, Mistress Healer; let us return if we may to the subject of my great discovery, which I had thought would interest you. I was just going to tell you all about it when Saneen came to the gate.'

'It does interest me. You have heard of some place in the frozen north where something or other has happened.'

'No, not the frozen north, but north certainly. The northern part of Akent is a broad continent, and there are wide lands between the Ragged Mountains and the East Sea. Deserts there are, and great expanses of grassland where nomadic peoples roam. It is there, far off across these grasslands, that a city has been built, a place dedicated to wisdom and learning and healing, to the study of the stars and the earth, of mortals and Immortals.'

'Then I see why you are so excited. But who lives there, so far across the wild lands?'

'The ruler of the city is called Tendanta, and his followers are many. The people of the nomadic tribes have welcomed him as their predestined lord, and the wise and the seekers of wisdom are flocking to him from all lands; from IssKor, from Mardara, from Imman and the islands, even from Sharn the dissolute, and even, they say, from the Forest Lands. And that is where I want to go. That is where I want to end my days. That is why I came to Telan, to see Daloreen once more, and to find you if I could.'

'You came to say goodbye to me, then.'

He drew her towards him and kissed her mouth tenderly. 'Yes. Though that is not as easy as I try to make it seem, Saranna. Yes. But I came also to tell you of my journeying, and especially of two of the visits I made.'

He paused again, sat up and stared out to sea. 'One of my first journeys after we parted was a walking-tour around Imman, just wandering slowly from place to place as the fancy took me.'

'From Inn to Inn, no doubt.'

'What a harsh opinion you have of me! I was about to say, that one of my stopping-points was Salk.'

'Oh. I see. And did you go to the farm? Did you see Drenn— and Raðenn?'

'No, but I picked up all the gossip. Drenn had married again, a local woman who took no notice whatever of Essk and had put her nose out of joint. The old woman tried to spoil 'young master Raðenn' but he went his own way. The finest child there had ever been in the vale, they said—a fearless rider, the swiftest runner, the sweetest singer, that anyone has ever seen. Tall and fair, so beautiful that you would think he had the blood of the Immortals in him. Drenn was very proud of him. There is also a daughter by the second wife.'

Saranna, between grief and delight, could hardly speak.

'Poor Essk!' she said at last. 'She drove me away so that she might have Drenn and Raðenn all to herself; but they have flown beyond her reach.'

'That is very generous of you, Saranna, to show such pity for the woman who did you great harm.'

Saranna squeezed Kor-Sen's hand. 'I have learned something over the years, you know. Some of what you helped me to speak of yesterday. I need not have been Essk's victim. With a little effort and care we might have been friends. And I might have been a true mother to my little boy. Now I wonder if I shall ever see him again.'

Kor-Sen coughed huskily, but said nothing.

'I am glad to have news of them, Kor-Sen. Thank you. What was the other matter you wished to speak of?'

'Years later, on my last journey before I came here, I sailed to Sen-Mar—to my mother's city. I wanted to see that once more, too, before turning my back on the southland forever. And I stayed there some months. There were many ghosts to be set at rest. I disputed theological points with those dreadful priests of Jaren; winning hands down, of course. I impressed the courtly and the rich with my vast learning. It was greatly enjoyable. At last I was invited even to the court, to make my humble bow before the most puissant King, His Majesty Jor-Kan V, Scourge of the Desert, Living Breath of Jaren, Lord of all that lives between the mountains and the sea.'

'Before the King! Was he very splendid and terrible?'

'Well, in truth he was a fat old man wheezing on a cushioned couch and dressed in velvet. Impressive no doubt, but somewhat hot for the climate. He is a nice enough old fellow, although of no great intelligence. He has no sons, and there in Jaren's land they insist upon a son to inherit the throne. So he is to marry his eldest daughter to the splendid young Vizier, Tel-Kor, Right Hand of the King, Swordbearer of Jaren, Lord of Sen-Mar, etc. etc. It is he of whom I wish to tell you.'

'Why is that? Do get on, Kor-Sen, you drag your tales out so much.'

'I am hesitating, dear one, because you are going to be angry with me.'

'I? Angry? Why should I be?'

'Well, because of young Tel-Kor. He is not a native of IssKor, you see. He comes from the islands.'

'Yes?'

'From Imman.'

'Yes?'

'Saranna—Tel-Kor is—he is Raðenn.'

She sprang to her feet, knocking over the wine bottle in the process. Kor-Sen instinctively grabbed it and set it upright again. Then he looked up, saw the expression on Saranna's face, and took a deep draught of wine. 'I knew that you would be angry.'

'Why did you not tell me at once?'

'I knew you would say that.'

'I must go. I must go to IssKor and see my son.'

'I knew you would say that, too. And I wanted you to myself for a few days before you flew off in a burst of maternal fury. I am sorry, Saranna.'

She walked away towards the sea, as if she intended to wade in and swim to IssKor. Abruptly she stopped, and turned back. She sat down again, took the wine bottle from Kor-Sen, and drank slowly. 'Go on. Did you speak to him?'

'Yes, I did. I said I was an old friend of the family, but I did not mention you for fear of distressing him. We cannot know what Drenn has told him about his mother.'

'Or what Essk has told him.'

'Essk is dead. He told me that. He left the farm only a few years ago and came to IssKor, proving himself a brave soldier in one of their innumerable 'holy' wars against the barbarians of The Neck, as they call them. Then the princess took a fancy to him in his panoply of war, and the King liked his manners, and there you are.'

'My son? My son will be King of IssKor?'

'The Breath of Jaren, no less. Maybe you had better go to him, Saranna, and suggest ways in which he might mitigate the heat of that breath—he'll need his wits about him if he is truly to rule that land, rather than be ruled by the Priests.'

'How could I help him? What do I know of priests and rulers?'

'You know a great deal about people, and about caring. Listen, and I will tell you what IssKor is like. Listen carefully.'

She saw that his face was set in a grim expression. Taking his hand, she drew nearer to him and said gently, 'Go on, my dear—tell me.'

'I—when I was a scholar in the temple, I was not allowed to see my family. I did receive a little news; I heard that my mother had married Karenoran, my tutor, and that they had a daughter, Tamnet. That pleased me, for I knew how lonely my mother had been. But that was all, I knew nothing more until I was eighteen, old enough to choose whether to stay on and train for the priesthood, or to leave for some other life. Then they called me before the Voice of Jaren, and told me... told me... I can't, I cannot say it!'

'Kor-Sen! My dear, dear Kor-Sen—come here to me, there, there, it's all right, don't tell me if it is too awful, it's all right,

I've got you, there, there... '

He dragged the back of his sleeve across his face like a child, and sniffed loudly. 'You must know this; and I need to tell you. Hold me, Saranna.'

'Yes. Yes.'

'They told me that two years before, Karenoran had been arrested on a charge of teaching false and pernicious doctrines in his school, of teaching children that there was a great Lady who dwelt far off in the west, who ruled the world and created everything in it, even the Lord Jaren himself.'

'But...'

'Ssssh! Listen! They dragged him from his home into the market-place, and there they cut him slowly to pieces with swords. They did not kill him first. My mother... my mother was forced to watch. She was pregnant, and when she collapsed of the shock, it was too much for her and for the child. They both died. My little sister had been living alone with poor old Dal-Nen for two years. That is how things are managed in IssKor, Saranna, and that is why your son will need your help.'

She held him tight as he wept on her shoulder. 'Kor-Sen; Kor-Sen—why did you never tell me?'

'I have never told anyone before.'

'What happened? What did you do?'

'I left the temple and went to take care of the little family I had left. They dared not touch me, not even the highest of the priests, for I had a reputation throughout the city. The common people had got it into their heads that I was the Son of Jaren – never mind why—but that was useful and I played it for all that it was worth. When I came away, I knew Tamnet would be safe; she is married now, and I saw her on my last visit. She is as happy as anyone can be in that dreadful country. Dal-Nen died just before I left to go to Drelk Academy.'

'It is all too much to comprehend. You were wise, Kor-Sen, to wait before telling me this. Let us go home now. We must eat, and talk about it all. There are many plans to make. Come.'

Chafrash

W hile Saracoma grew, Drewin spent most of his time
talking with the people who came to seek his advice,
and those who came simply to learn. The space in front of his
house became a court of law and a place of learning, and he
would spend day after day on the hill, receiving visitors from all
across the Green and beyond. Some came to ask one question,
whether about some family problem, or about justice and the
right way to order matters, and some came to stay and study the
ways of thought that Drewin had learnt in the Cavern. Many
remarkable people came to Saracoma to be near Tendanta
the wise and he learnt as he taught. Drewin respected all who
came to learn, but he held Chafrash in the highest regard as his
teacher. Whenever there was an opportunity, he would go out
onto the plain with her and she would teach him the lore of
the clans.

The lessons would start early in the morning before the
sun rose. The Shakrien were renowned for their knowledge
of herbs and healing, and Chafrash first taught Drewin the
names of all the useful plants that grew around Saracoma. She
showed him how to gather roots and leaves, flowers and seeds,
and explained what their uses were and how they should he
prepared. At the end of the day they would go back to his
house and dry the plants they had found, or make lotions and
infusions from them for future use. Sometimes they would go
on long journeys, lasting several days: she took him along the
river and out across the plain to find the rarest medicines. They
travelled to the foothills of the Ragged Mountains in the west
and the fringes of the desert of Sinor in the east, and even as

far south as the headwaters of Ranap River, and north to the lands of the Tarrien.

While they travelled, Chafrash taught Drewin how to hunt and where to find the best plants to eat, and they lived off the land. They would carry bows for hunting and a fine light deerskin tent to sleep in, but usually, as if by chance, they would meet with other travellers towards evening, and would be given food and shelter for the night. All the people of the plain gave hospitality to strangers, no matter what their clan.

Drewin learnt quickly, just as he had done in the Cavern, but he failed to master one skill: he could not find his way through the grass unaided. Chafrash tried to teach him: she drew maps on the ground to show where they were going; she explained how he should watch his shadow to adjust for the movement of the sun; she showed him how to keep to a straight line by feeling the wind on his face and watching the way the grass leaned. But to her it was second nature, something she had been able to do since childhood, and she could not really explain it to Drewin. Sometimes she would let him lead the way and try to let him learn by his mistakes, but he soon veered from the true direction, and she would have to correct him or face a very long journey. When they met other travellers she would sometimes discuss the problem with them, but usually they thought it was very funny. Before long, all the peoples of the plain knew of his affliction, and he became known as 'Tendanta the wise, who does not know his way home.'

Drewin also lacked a talent that seemed natural to the clans: knowing when other people were nearby. When he had first come to the Hill, Chafrash had demonstrated this, and since then he had noticed that everybody except him seemed to know when someone was approaching. They would say, 'Here come some Fien' or 'Those Tarrien are passing by again.' But when Drewin went to look, he could see no sign of the people until they emerged into the open. He had asked his companions how they did it, but they just shrugged and laughed.

So when one day, while there was a gathering on the Hill at Saracoma, someone shouted 'The Korsh are coming!' he took no notice, until Chafrash led him by the arm to the parapet and told him to look to the east. He looked and saw travellers moving towards Saracoma: it looked as though a group of very tall people was approaching, their heads and shoulders clearly visible as they pushed their way through the grass. Drewin turned to Chafrash for an explanation, but she just laughed. 'Wait. You will see for yourself when they arrive.'

When the Korsh finally emerged from the grass, he saw that each of them was riding on the back of a large four-legged animal. He had not seen such creatures before and he turned again to Chafrash.

'Horses,' she said, and walked with him to the top of the causeway to await the arrival of the visitors.

The Korsh came slowly up the slope towards them. There were six men in the group, the last one leading an un-mounted horse by leather reins. When they reached the hill top they dismounted and approached. At their head was a tall man with long black hair who smiled and addressed Drewin.

'Greetings to Tendanta, from the Korsh. I am called Pikrin, and I speak for my clan.'

'Welcome Pikrin, and welcome to your companions. Is there some way that I can be of service to you, or your clan?'

'No, today we will be of service to you, I think. It is said that you have great wisdom in many matters, but in one thing you have some difficulty: it is said that you lose yourself in the Green, and do not know your way home.'

At this the Korsh grinned broadly, barely able to contain themselves, but when Drewin started to laugh out loud, they laughed too. Drewin replied, 'What is said is true. I was not raised in the Green, nor am I as wise as people say, and I am reminded every day of these things by not being able to do what the smallest child of the clans can do. Perhaps it will prevent me from becoming too proud.'

Pikrin looked into Drewin's eyes and answered, 'It is not said that Tendanta is proud, and you do not seem proud to me. Put we have not come to laugh at you or to remind you of your failings: we have come to make you a gift of welcome.'

He waved an arm to his companions and they brought the extra horse to where Drewin stood. 'This is our gift to you. He is called Gar, and is from Lassian itself. It is said that Lassian horses are descended from the Immortals and only the great may ride them. I think you may ride Gar.'

Drewin approached the horse and stroked its massive head. He spoke quietly into its ear then took the reins and in one smooth movement mounted. He proved to be a natural horseman, and in a few days the Korsh had taught him all they knew of horse-riding. Now he was able to ride out onto the plain without fear of getting lost, as long as he stayed within sight of Saracoma.

No-one but Tendanta rode a horse in Saracoma. The people would stop what they were doing when he rode by on his way onto the plain, and sometimes someone would shout a greeting: 'Now don't get lost!' or 'Come safely back!' and everybody would laugh. And Drewin world whisper to Gar, 'As long as I have you with me, my friend, I will be safe from pride.'

If Chafrash was to go with him on an expedition they would pass through the town together, and nobody laughed when Chafrash walked with Tendanta. The two would stride through the street deep in conversation, planning their trip or debating some question of law or nature, and those who saw them became quiet, so that the pursuit of knowledge should not be interrupted. The wealth of Saracoma grew from its fame, and the fame of Saracoma rested on the wisdom of Tendanta. But it was not merely the understanding of their own interest that restrained the people of the town, it was the beauty and dignity of the man and woman walking in their midst. Nobody laughed when Chafrash walked with Tendanta.

On his trips in search of herbs and minerals Drewin always took some sticks of charcoal and a small sheet of white canvas so that he could write down what he had learnt. When he returned to his house he would copy his notes onto parchment scrolls using black ink and a pen made from a feather. He had not taught the runes to his students, not even Chafrash, and those who were aware of his scrolls sometimes wondered what the mysterious marks were. Some thought that they were magical and the source of the wisdom of Tendanta, but others felt that this was a mystery that would be revealed to them when they were worthy. Chafrash was the only person who had seen Drewin making his charcoal notes, and for a long time she restrained herself and did not ask any questions. But, one day, after many trips, she finally asked the question that all the seekers of knowledge wanted to ask. She and Drewin were camped by the river after a day of investigating the plants and animals of the reed beds, and Drewin was writing on his canvas sheet.

'Tendanta, will you tell me what you are doing, and what the purpose of those marks is?'

Drewin did not reply at first, as he was concentrating on his task, and Chafrash thought that she might have offended him. But, when he had finished what he was doing, he put down his charcoal, folded the cloth and smiled. 'I will tell you a little about the runes, but there are some matters that no mortal should know, and I must keep them hidden. What I tell you now is not secret, and may be shared with all who seek knowledge. Come here.'

Chafrash knelt beside Drewin, and watched as he traced the fourteen runes in the dust with a stick. 'These are the runes: there are fourteen, and each one makes a different sound.'

Chafrash bent her head down to the marks in the dust, and listened. 'I cannot hear them!' she said, and when Drewin laughed she frowned at him.

'Why do you laugh? I hear no sound, and my hearing is better than yours!'

Drewin controlled his laughter and took Chafrash's hand. 'I am sorry, my friend: I did not explain properly. It is my fault. What I should have said is that each rune represents a sound: when I see a rune I can imagine the sound it stands for. And when I see the right group of runes I can imagine a word. Runes can make pictures of words. Look.'

Drewin scratched a pattern of runes in the dust.

'That says 'Chafrash'. Well, it really says 'Javrath': there are no runes for the speech of the clans. The runes speak with the sounds of sea breezes and flutes, but the peoples of the Green have coarse words and harsh sounds.'

Chafrash looked at the symbol in amazement, and Drewin showed her how each of the runes appeared in its proper place, and how the different sounds combined together. Soon she had learnt the fourteen sounds, and was able to write her own name in the dust. Before long, she was writing other words.

'But the sounds are wrong. Why are there fourteen runes, Tendanta, and why do they look like that?'

'There must be fourteen, they must look as they do, and they must make the sounds they do, or they lose their power. For they are not just a means of recording words – but I may not speak further of that to you, Chafrash. You must trust me when I say that no more runes can be made'

'Why? Why shouldn't we make new runes for the sounds of the Green? Look.' Chafrash took the stick and scratched the rune Jaer in the dust.

'You say I must make my name begin with a Jaer sound, but why shouldn't I say that this—' she added a line to the rune

'makes the sound 'ch' that is the real beginning of my name.'

Drewin stared at the shape that Chafrash had drawn, and frowned. 'But that can't be right: it would not be a proper rune. The runes were made before time, and are eternal: we cannot change them.'

'Yes we can. I just did. It may not be a real rune, but let it be an imitation. Let it be my rune. I mean no offence to the Immortal Ones: it is but three lines in the dust.'

Drewin frowned at the new rune again, as if he could erase it by concentrating. 'You make it sound so simple.'

'It is: I do no harm if I make a mark on the ground and say that for me it stands for a sound, or a word. It may not be eternal or magical but it does no harm. And why not make runes for the other sounds that the clans use; the coarse rough sounds of coarse rough people.'

'I did not mean that! I love the talk of the Green: it has a music of its own, but it is not as melodious as the Old Tongue that I learnt from my mother. But I think you are right: we can make signs and symbols to mean what we want them to mean, so let us make runes for the sounds of the Green.'

On their return to Saracoma Drewin and Chafrash locked themselves away for several days and made six new runes to go with the one that Chafrash had devised. The number of the runes increased to twenty-one and Drewin started to teach them to all the peoples of the Green and all his students.

From the time that the new runes were made Chafrash stayed with Drewin in his house, and they lived and worked together. Their study of the runes became the centre of their lives, and Chafrash soon mastered all their intricacies. This work brought them closer to each other: they thought as one and their friendship deepened.

Secretly Drewin carved a wooden amulet decorated with leaves and bearing the new rune that Chafrash had invented: he attached it to a thong to make a necklace and gave it to her. 'I have a surprise for you. Here is the rune 'Chaer': it is doubly yours, for you made it and it is the first sound of your name.'

Chafrash took the amulet and examined it. Then she handed it back to Drewin.

'It is lovely, Tendanta! Let the hands that made it place it round my neck.' As Drewin looped the thong over her head, Chafrash put her arms around him and kissed him gently on the mouth. He jumped back in surprise, and she laughed.

'That was my surprise for you in return!"

Drewin became serious. 'This is not a matter for games and laughter: it is the first rune made by a mortal, and so it is very special. Keep this amulet always; it is part of you.'

Chafrash took it and examined it closely.

'But why all the solemn warnings? I would not willingly lose such a thing: I will keep it always because you made it, and because you gave it to me, and because I love you.'

'Do not ignore the power of runes: they can be the means of bringing great good or great harm. My life was devastated by runes so that I was taken near to death, and it was built again through them so that now I am raised up high in the eyes of the people I care for. But none of this has been my doing: I have been subject to other powers.'

As Drewin became the teacher, so Chafrash became his student and she pondered and frowned while examining the amulet.

'If I am to look for meaning in this sign beyond just the sound that it stands for, how should I understand this carved disk? Why have you made it for me? Is this gift of wood more than a gift?'

'No. It is your rune: it was always yours, and so the rune is not really a gift. But the wood and its decoration is a gift from me to you, my little sister.'

'I am a sister to you?'

'Yes, that is how I have come to think of you. We seem so alike sometimes; it is as if we had known each other before, all our lives. I had a little sister once—long ago—but I lost her. You are like her, in some ways: you trust me as she used to trust me. But she was taken away from me – it wasn't my fault. Will you be my sister?'

Chafrash laughed, but she was not amused: when she replied her voice was angry.

'Your sister! And you will be my brother? No, Tendanta. I have four brothers, and that is quite enough: I do not need another brother.'

Drewin was taken aback and said nothing. Chafrash glared at him in silence for a moment, before walking to the door. 'There is something here I do not understand: it is as if you only see what is far away, as if you are not really here, cannot see what is near at hand. This is something I must consider. I must talk to my mother. I will leave early tomorrow and seek my clan in the west.'

Chafrash was away for eight days, and Drewin missed her, but continued with his work. When she returned she brought her mother Frashni with her. Frashni was thin and dry, with brown weathered skin and clear sharp eyes that darted this way and that, missing nothing. Chafrash presented her to Drewin with due formality, but as soon as greetings had been exchanged, the mother sent her daughter away as if she were a little girl.

'Go away Chafrash and find something useful to do. I wish to talk alone with this man.'

To Drewin's surprise, Chafrash crept meekly away without comment or gesture. Frashni watched her go then turned to Drewin. 'Well!'

She looked him up and down and he felt like a naughty child. 'Too old to race with the deer, as they say, but you look fit enough. Some say you are wise...' She paused, looked Drewin up and down again and grunted.

'Say something wise, man from the sea.'

'You have travelled some distance to be here. My wisdom tells me two things: you have come for some reason, and you would welcome a drink and perhaps some food. Sit down here and I will fetch some.'

Frashni grunted again, sat down, and watched Drewin prepare food and drink. As they ate she looked steadily at him but said nothing. When they had finished, Drewin sat back and addressed Frashni respectfully.

'You have some anxiety that I can help you with. Please tell me what it is, and I will try to help.'

The old woman looked more kindly now. 'You speak well enough. You are polite and not completely stupid. You'll do.'

'I'll do as what?'

'As husband for my eldest daughter, of course. Why else do you think I am here? For my health?' Frashni chuckled quietly while Drewin sat with his mouth open, speechless for a moment.

'Husband? I have not asked... She ... This has not been

discussed: Chafrash is a student, a seeker after wisdom, we seek together: we are like brother and sister.'

At this, Frashni snorted loudly. 'Did I say you were not completely stupid? Have you not seen the way she looks at you? I knew how she felt the first time she spoke your name to me. Do you not know how you look at her? Brother and sister! Pfah!'

'No. You do not understand. I'm not going to marry: I have too much to do. There is so much to find out.'

'Don't avoid the question. This is your home, and into your home you must bring your wife and make your children. This is how it has always been, how it always will be. Who is to be your wife if not Chafrash? Who is to be your children's mother if not Chafrash?'

Frashni was standing now with her hands on her hips, looking down at Drewin. He avoided her eyes and seemed to be talking as much to himself as to her.

'No. This is not my home. I thought it was, but it isn't. My home is far from here, and Chafrash cannot go there. Neither can I.'

Drewin spoke with such finality that Frashni turned and left in silence. She spoke a few words to Chafrash, then left Saracoma at once and returned to her people.

That evening Chafrash came to Drewin's room and found him writing in one of his books. He looked up and smiled, but she did not smile in return.

'We must talk. There are things that need to be said, Tendanta, and they are not being said.'

Drewin put his quill down on the table and went to pour some wine, but Chafrash stopped him.

'No wine: we need clear heads. What we say and do tonight will be of great import to us both.'

Drewin put down the jug and sat by the fire. Chafrash sat opposite him. For a moment there was complete silence. Drewin smiled at Chafrash, but her face was expressionless. Slowly the smile faded from his face and he spoke. 'This is serious, isn't it?' She nodded. 'To do with your mother's visit?'

'Is that how you see it? To do with my mother?'

Drewin looked perplexed and doubtful. 'Do you know what she said to me?'

Chafrash smiled. 'Not exactly, but I can imagine.'

'She said that we ought to get married. Can you believe it? I can understand how things must look to her, and I know that the pursuit of knowledge is not of concern to most people of the plain, but have you not explained now we work together? She seemed a little confused.'

Chafrash looked into Drewin's eyes, with an almost cold expression. 'Did she seem to be confused? Are you sure it is not you who are confused?'

'I don't understand.'

'The truth!' Chafrash almost shouted. 'At last you have spoken the truth. You do not understand: and I do not understand why you do not understand. How old are you?

Thirty high summers? Forty? I cannot tell. But you are not a child: you are full grown. Why do you not understand what any man of the clans knows? Why do you not understand love?'

'Love? Ah...love: yes I know about love. You may not realise it but I have spent some considerable time studying love. It seems to me to be the essence of any community that the people within it care for each other in a network of mutual relationships. Love seems to me to be the single most important emotion that mortal beings entertain. It is my opinion that animals do not have the ability to love, in the sense that we understand the term, and of course neither do the Immortals. It is my opinion that love is the exclusive

preserve of human beings.'

Drewin paused for breath and glanced at Chafrash, who, instead of sitting in rapt attention as she usually did, was laughing.

'Oh Tendanta, my teacher, I don't want a lecture. Just tell me how you feel. Have you ever loved? Have you ever felt the madness of the hares in spring, and run about demented?'

'What?'

Chafrash stopped smiling. 'You don't know what I'm talking about, do you? You really don't know!'

'What is there to know? I have seen these things you are talking about, but I do not always do what others do. That is not my way. I am not as other men: I am different.'

'Different? You were born as other men are, and you will die as other men do. And between the one and the other you will feel joy and pain, hate and love. But perhaps I am mistaken? You do not seem as other men. Tell me, where do you keep your feelings, where is your heart?'

The fire crackled in the silence until Drewin replied. 'It has not been given to me to love as others do: I have no home here. I cannot explain these things to you.'

Chafrash reached out and took Tendanta's hand. 'When we first met here on this hill, all those years ago, before it was a city, you were travelling, searching. You had a light in your eyes: you were bright, like a flame. But now that light has faded and your eyes are dull.'

"I was young then: now my hair is going grey, and I am tired.'

He sank back into his chair and sighed. Chafrash took his hands in hers and became fierce. 'No! You talk as if you were an old man, frail and toothless; hut you are not! You are not! You are at the height of your powers: you are strong and wise and good. Yet you seem sad, as though there was something yet to do. Something left undone.'

'It is you who say I am wise and good. Since first I came here the people of the Green have told me that I am these things, when I arrived you all welcomed me as the one

foretold. You saw me as an answer to a need, but I have never really been what you thought I was. It is a deception: you wanted me to be someone that I never was, and I pretended that I was that person. Tendanta is not my true name: it is the name of what you wanted me to be.'

Chafrash sank back, her eyes downcast. 'I do not know what you were before you came, but here, on the Green, in Saracoma, you are a bringer of harmony. Before you, for generations there was discord and distrust, and now there is peace and plenty. Look at Saracoma: a prosperous city, where before there was a barren hill; a place of learning, famous in far lands. You have done this, no-one else.'

'No! You are wrong. I have done nothing. All that has happened here has happened because the people of the plain longed for it.'

Drewin stood and went to the fire. He picked up a stick and poked the spitting logs. Chafrash watched him and waited, and after a long silence he spoke hesitantly.

'When I first came here I thought I had come home. But this is not my home: my home lies far away, a long journey and too many years to count. I am a stranger here, and I may not go to my true home. I am far from the sea, far from where I belong, and I cannot go back.'

'You have followed a path to here: why do you not retrace your steps?'

'Because I am mortal. Only through death can a mortal being return to the time beyond time, and I am not ready to take that journey yet. It is difficult to explain.' He opened the front of his tunic to reveal the wooden amulet on its plaited leather cord. Chafrash looked at it curiously, entranced by the play of the firelight on its smooth surface.

'I made this many years ago, at a time of joy in my true home. But because I made it I was cast from that place into this world of change and mortality. And I may not go back.'

'It is like the one you made for me. Why is Orth carved on it and not Ord?'

'Orth is the rune of my sister Saranna. For my amulet I carved her rune, and on hers I carved mine. But now the other is lost: my sister is lost.'

A shade of sadness came over Drewin, and he gazed into the fire. The light of the flames played over his still face. Chafrash spoke gently. 'Now I see: Saracoma and Sarannen are named in memory of your sister: Saracoma—Saranna of long ago. Does that mean that she is in the past, gone, or that she still lives in your memory? What has become of her?'

'I do not know. The sea took Saranna from me when I was little more than a boy, and since then I have been lost. I have been taken away from home, from the sea, and I fear to be near the restless waves: I am afraid to face the salty wind and the sound of my mother's angry voice. Saracoma is not my home, but I am safe here, far from the cold sea and the fierce wind, far from the eternal isle.'

Chafrash did not answer, and for a long while all that was heard was the sound of the logs in the fire settling. At last she stood and looked at Drewin sadly. 'So be it. We shall be brother and sister only, and neither of us is to find a home.'

She hurried to her room, where she sat on her bed, and wept.

Drewin rose and went out into the cold clear night and looked out over the city of Saracoma, and the plain beyond. He listened to the sounds of people closing up their shutters and calling their children in to bed; he smelled the mixed aromas of many evening meals: Saracoma was at peace. He watched thin clouds scud across the sky and listened to the gentle sound of windblown waves pass over the moonlit grass. He spoke quietly to himself.

'Where are you Saranna? Where have you taken my rune? Where is my heart?'

The Forest Lands

*T*owards the middle of a fair autumn morning, the sailing vessel Kiren brought down her sails and made fast to the quay at Kiril. Here the forest river ran deep and wide, and ships could sail up from the sea into the heart of the busy little town that lay on the south bank. To the north, the dark forests of the Kirenoi marched right down to the shore; some of the massive old trees had roots projecting into the water, as if they had set out to make the crossing but had stopped in mid-stride. From the deck of the ship, Saranna and Kor-Sen peered across into the green gloom.

'Do you expect to see Arel standing there, waiting for you?'

'No, of course not. But how ancient and secret the forest looks even from here. I think I can see a wooden landing-stage across there.' She pointed, but while Kor-Sen was still trying to make out the spot, one of the sailors broke in.

'That's right, My Lady, that's where they set sail from if they come over to our side—the People from over the river.'

Kor-Sen scribbled on a scrap of parchment with a smudgy end of charcoal. 'A fascinating circumlocution. Do the people of Kiril fear their neighbours, would you say? I would have thought they would be used to them, indeed they must have— well, 'other' blood in their veins themselves after all this time.'

The sailor shrugged. 'Search me. I'm from Pelk meself, no nonsense about Pelk. Not that I'd know, would I, knots is more my line. A good-day to you both, and the Lady protect you.'

Saranna and Kor-Sen left the Kiren and set out across the town, through busy winding streets and crowded market-squares where fish sparkled on piles of ice and marvellous toys and gadgets of Kirenoi make were offered for sale alongside humble wooden plates and everyday necessities like lentils and butter.

'I like this place, we have already passed at least six Inns,' said Kor-Sen.

'But we need somewhere that has rooms to let. Do you know of anywhere we could stay?' Saranna asked a stallholder.

'Yes, indeed. My own sister runs the finest place in Kiril, the Towering Tree, a short walk up that way. Good clean bedrooms, My Lady, and an excellent home-brewed ale, Sir.'

'Splendid! Then let us make haste, Saranna.'

'One moment, Kor-Sen. Would you go ahead just a little, and I will catch you up. Please.' Obligingly he shouldered his bundle and set off. Saranna and the stall keeper went into a huddle, and eventually exchanged a small parcel for a rather large coin of Imman. Then Saranna hastened after her companion, and found him seated at his ease on the veranda of a handsome building on the very edge of the town, with a view across lush green meadows to the river, and the forest beyond. Close to the Inn stood the mighty oak tree that gave it its name.

'This ale is indeed excellent. The girl will bring you some forthwith.'

Saranna smiled. 'When I am a very old woman, and I remember you, the first thing I will think of is the two of us drinking together, toasting this and that, and passing severe judgement on the quality of the ale or wine!'

'And when you are a very old woman, I trust you will remember also that I loved you, Saranna, as much as it lies in my heart to love. I wish you many years of happiness, wherever your journey ends.'

They sat together hand in hand, quiet and thoughtful.

After a noon-meal so excellent and so large that they could not finish it, they took their things to a pleasant room under the eaves of the house, with a small window that looked towards the forest. Kor-Sen went out to see about buying a horse, and Saranna sat looking at the trees until she fell asleep in her chair.

Many hours later she was woken by the touch of a gentle kiss upon her brow. Kor-Sen was bending over her, and outside the window the sky to the west was reddening.

'Supper will be ready soon. And you must come and see my splendid steed, a prince among horses. Well, perhaps not quite. But a nice beast. Come and meet him.'

Down in the stable of the inn, Saranna was introduced to a quiet, middle-aged, sturdy looking horse, not very high at the shoulder but looking as if he would plod a long way before seeking rest. He was chestnut brown with one white foot, and an irregular white blaze on his nose. His name was Oakapple.

'What a handsome animal—you should not be in much danger of falling off, he looks very steady.'

'Such insolence! I am not, I would have you know, given to falling off horses. Now come and have supper, My Lady.'

Over fresh white bread and a savoury stew of pork and apples ('They grow the pigs on trees too, no doubt', Kor-Sen muttered), the two friends lingered and talked, enjoying the evening that they knew would be their last time together. Towards the end of the meal, Saranna drew from her pocket the little bundle she had purchased in the market-place.

'This is for you.'

Kor-Sen picked it up and held it, looking at Saranna. 'I have no gift for you, dear.'

'That is no matter. I wanted you to have this. Please open it.'

He unwrapped a small box of plain sandalwood, and opened it to reveal a ring of shining gold resting upon a scrap of velvet. 'Saranna! This is magnificent—it must be the work of 'the people across the river', don't you think?'

He slipped the ring onto his middle finger, and held out his hand to show Saranna. The design was of apples, round golden apples side by side forming a ring around the finger.

'Never before have I worn a ring on my finger, not for any lady.'

'Well, then wear this for yourself, and not for me. Much sorrow can come of wearing someone else's token.' Saranna drew out the polished wooden rune-disc that she wore still, and fingered the Ord-Rune. Kor-Sen stretched out a hand to touch the wood gently.

'To think of the immeasurably distant time and place in which your brother shaped that disc. Those ancient trees beyond the river here were seeds in the ground when some tree fell, and was borne hither and thither by the tides until one fragment was cast up onto that timeless shore. My Lady Saranna, what a long way you have journeyed, and what wonders you have seen.'

'All that seems so remote now. Wonders are not what I remember, but the ordinary things I have done, the days of hard work, the love and friendship I have shared, the cool mornings on the farm, sounds of sheep and the falling waves; I remember all that, Kor-Sen, and that is what really matters.'

In their last night together there was warmth, and closeness, and joy. But the next morning sorrow overcame them, and they both wept bitter tears as they clung together in their room, feeling the strangeness of knowing that they might never meet again. At last Saranna said, 'I thought you had taught me how to bear parting and grief. But this is hard to bear.'

'My dear lady, we will endure this and other sorrows still to come.'

'How? How and why do mortals bear so much grief?'

'As for why, that is out of my knowledge. But how—well, we move on because we have somewhere to go; and because it is never possible for mortals to move backwards. Time does not allow it, Saranna. We cannot go back and we cannot stay still—so we go on. And our love for each other, which brings this pain, will give us also the strength to bear it. For we must go, my dear, I to my destiny and you to yours.'

'You to study the stars and I to find my lost child. Yes, you are right. And we will be strong.'

They carried Kor-Sen's bundles down the stairs and loaded them onto the broad back of Oakapple. One long last embrace, and then Saranna stood at the door of the Inn to watch Kor-Sen ride away towards the south, through the town to the coast road. He did not look back.

As soon as he was out of sight Saranna wandered down to the riverbank, and stood looking across the deep-flowing waters. The trees were still and heavy in the morning sun, and there was no sign of life. Saranna stood looking at the forest for some time, then set off back to the inn to prepare for her journey the next day. She had decided to cross the river to the Forest Lands in search of Arel.

Waking in the grey of early dawn, Saranna slipped downstairs through the sleeping inn, and went out onto the porch for some fresh air. Here she almost tripped over a dark huddled form on the wooden floor.

'Oh!'

The form grew taller, and revealed itself to be a young woman, wrapped in a brown cloak and clutching a small bundle.

'I am sorry to startle you.... '

'Who are you? What are you doing?'

They both spoke at once; Saranna turned away and sat down on one of the benches, heedless of the dew-damp surface. Her heart was still racing from the shock.

'I am called Willowood. I want to cross the river with you.'

'With me? But why—and how did you know I was going to the forest?'

'I asked Rowanflower, the maid here. We were friends, when we were little girls. Before she knew that I was one of those who—who want to go away, want to go to the forest to find the people of the trees.'

'But what of your family?'

'They wish me to stay; but they know they cannot prevent me. Those who are called by the forest, must go. Please let me come with you, My Lady.'

'Very well—it will be pleasant to have a companion. My name is Saranna—and first we will breakfast together.'

As the sun rose the two women walked together away from the inn and into the centre of Kiril. Here they searched for a long time for someone willing to ferry them across the river to the forest; at last they found an old woman, bent and toothless, who said that she would take them in return for two gold pieces.

'I'm too old to worry, my dears, what those Others might do to me. Besides, I'll not set foot on shore, you must just get yourselfs on land as best you can. I've no wish to linger under them shadows, not I.'

The boat she led them to was battered, leaky and very small. It also stank of ancient fish. Prattling away, its owner hauled on the mooring rope and drew her craft alongside. 'Crab I call her and crabby she is; like to toss us into the river as easy as take us over. But don't you worry, pretty ladies, Marla will get you there. If you'd just oblige by baling her out, my dears.'

She thrust into their hands a couple of dented and rusty tin basins, which they began to wield straight away, in the hope of making a dry patch for their feet. It was an awkward business, clutching their bundles on their laps to keep them out of the disgusting oily water. The hems of their skirts and their leather sandals were soon soaked; more water came in almost as fast as they could bale.

'How will you get back, Marla, without us to bale?'

'Don't fret, my dear, I shall manage. Crab's no awkwarder than me, we understands each other well.'

Marla sniffed hugely and went on with her rhythmic pull; pull; pull; at the oars. Saranna urged Willowood back to the baling, and steadily they drew nearer to the green, dark shore of the Forest Lands.

Soon they were under the shadows of the trees, and at last came alongside the little wooden jetty.

'Quick, quick now, out with you, out!'

Saranna tossed both the bundles onto the jetty, scrambled up, and turned to pull Willowood after her. The girl was scarcely on the landing stage before Marla was away, head down and rowing as hard as she could for the other shore. They looked after her, and saw how bright and busy and colourful the town looked in the afternoon sun. They stooped to pick up their bundles, and Saranna cried out. The jetty, far from being the simple structure it had seemed from across the water, was a work of art. It was carved and decorated along its edges, and the corners embellished with laughing faces.

'How beautiful!' Willowood was charmed, and ran about the jetty exclaiming at each new wonder she discovered. Saranna made no reply.

'What is wrong? Why don't you come and look? What are you staring at?'

Saranna was gazing upwards. 'I am looking at the trees,' she said.

Willowood too looked up, and grew still and quiet. Far above them the trees towered, so tall that they could not see the topmost branches, though they heard the faint trembling sound of the breezes from the sea stirring the distant leaves. Massive trunks stretched up into the canopy of green, and the two women were tiny figures at their feet. They both looked down and tried to see into the forest; but only a few paces in front of them there was thick darkness, green-and-brown shadows where the trees clustered together as if to defend their land from intruders.

Saranna picked up her bundle and stepped into the wood, seeming to Willowood to vanish almost at once in the deep shadow.

'Wait!' she shrieked, and plunged after her companion.

She found her just a pace or two into the forest, and seized her hand. 'Saranna, we must keep together, please, I thought you were gone!'

So they held hands as they walked on into the depths of the Forest Lands, like two children adrift among the trees. Far, far above their heads a glimmer of golden light penetrated into the topmost branches, but soon died away into greenness, hardly illuminating the forest floor. It was cool, almost chilly, and there were no pathways, no sign that anyone might have passed that way before, and no sounds at all. They walked on and on between the trees, losing all sense of direction. Gradually the darkness grew completely impenetrable, and they halted.

'We had better camp; it must be night,' said Saranna.

Willowood shivered. 'I'm cold, Saranna—and I'm frightened. Should we go back?'

Saranna looked around, seeing nothing but blackness in all directions. 'I have no means of knowing where 'back' is. Sit down and wrap your blanket around you; some food will make you feel better. But I do not that think a fire would be wise.'

The word 'fire' leaped from Saranna's lips and boomed through the trees, growing louder and echoing among the invisible throngs of branches and leaves.

'Fire. Fire! FIRE! FIIRRE!'

Willowood screamed, and grabbed Saranna, who held her tight. Saranna raised her head and called out to the thick, menacing darkness that pressed against them.

'Trees of the Forest Lands, pardon me. I will not bring fire into your land, I swear it. I will not speak of it again, only forgive me. We want to pass among you in peace. Let us rest now and tomorrow we will go on. I swear never to harm any tree of this land, never by my mother's name.'

The echoing died away, and the women felt a drawing back of the pressure around them. Gradually silence was restored, and they sat down in the cramped space between the roots of the trees, wrapped themselves in blankets, and took their supper. All was peaceful as they fell asleep.

As soon as Saranna woke, she felt a difference in the air; more light came down to her, one shaft of golden sunlight actually reaching the grass where she sat, waking its true green colour out of the pervasive greyness. She sat up, listening and looking; there was movement in the branches, a rustling such as she might hear in the more familiar boughs of an island orchard. And faintly in the distance she heard the morning song of the birds, melodious and sweet as shy brown woodland birds all over the world. Saranna woke Willowood gently.

'It is lighter; and nicer: and I can hear birds!'

'Yes. It seems I said the right things last night. Let us eat breakfast and go on.'

They plodded on for the whole morning without any sense of getting anywhere. They could see further into the forest than on the previous day, but still all that they could see were trees and trees and trees; great sturdy trees that looked as if they had stood there unchanging since Skorn was shaped.

'It makes me feel so small; so—unimportant,' said Willowood. 'I wish we could meet someone; I wish something different would happen. I feel as if we shall walk on and on and on through these terrible trees until we die!'

'Oh!' cried Saranna. For at this point something different did happen.

They came into a small clearing, the first they had seen; when they stood together in the middle and looked up, they could see high above them a glimpse of blue sky, laced across with bright green leaves that tossed about in the breeze. Then suddenly a squirrel scampered up a tree-trunk, chattering loudly. High above them, it stopped and threw down twigs and leaves that hit Willowood's head and made her jump.

Meanwhile on another tree a woodpecker landed with a flurry of green wings, and began a loud drilling that echoed about them. Straight away they heard a screeching call from above, and saw another bird, so brightly coloured and so magnificently plumed that both women cried out in admiration.

'What is it, Saranna? What kind of bird? I have never seen anything so lovely!'

'Skrawwwk!' said the bird, and seemed to bow in acknowledgment. They both laughed. At once it plunged down, dropping until it was just over their heads, where it hovered like a kestrel, its long tail and broad wings shimmering like cloth of gold even down in the glade; it seemed to bring the sunlight with it.

'Skrawk!' it said again, and began to fly in a circle, while Saranna and Willowood whirled about trying to watch it. When they were thoroughly giddy, the bird shrieked again and vanished among the trees, diminishing rapidly to a distant speck of light in the shadows.

The travellers sank down exhausted, and looking round they realised that the woodpecker and the squirrel were gone too; all was quiet again. For a while they sat gasping and recovering their breath. Then Saranna stood up and picked up her bundle. Willowood looked up at her.

'Perhaps we should follow the beautiful bird?'

'But which way did it go?'

'That way, I am sure of it.' Willowood pointed into the forest. 'There, I see it far off on a branch, I see it shining, Saranna!'

'I see nothing; but I will follow you. Lead on then, and we

shall see where this bird is taking us.'

For many hours they trailed after the golden bird; the forest darkened again around them. Time and again it fluttered off again into the darkness, while they tried to hurry after it through the treacherous undergrowth and over the vast gnarled roots of the trees. Miles and miles they covered, and were sobbing with exhaustion when Willowood cried, 'It's gone, it's gone, I cannot see it! Saranna, what shall we do, we are lost!'

'Ssh, ssh, be calm, Willowood. It is evening now and we must rest. Perhaps the bird will come back to us tomorrow.'

'Perhaps it won't. But you never know,' said a totally strange voice.

Both travellers whirled around, standing back to back and looking frantically about for the source of the voice.

'Over here!' it said.

They turned.

'No, over here!'

They looked over their shoulders. Willowood began to cry.

'Show yourself, stranger,' cried Saranna. 'Are you a coward or a fool, to frighten a young girl in this way? Come out and show yourself! We have done you no harm.'

'What! Traipsing through the forest and pursuing the Kingsbird until it drops! No harm!' The voice came from yet another direction, but Saranna refused to turn around.

'We are travellers, strangers, and do not know your customs; yet we had hoped for some courtesy and hospitality from the Kirenoi. If we have offended, it was in ignorance; yet you torment us and mock us. You should be ashamed.'

'My, how serious and solemn you are, lovely lady.'

This time the voice sounded closer. Saranna looked up, and

Willowood dried her tears. A tall, slender young man, hardly more than a boy, stood before them. Fair and dressed all in green, he carried a bow, a quiverful of arrows, and a knapsack of soft deerhide. He swept them a low bow. Saranna inclined her head in reply, and Willowood curtseyed. 'Kirenkaloken, at your service. And who may you be, fair travellers?'

'I am Willowood!'

'Are you indeed? In our tongue that is Kirilokala, and I see that you will be in need of a name in our tongue, for you will stay with us. And you, stern one?'

'I am Saranna of Telan.'

He stood absolutely still for a moment; still and silent. Then he bowed his head. 'Then for you, My Lady, there is no name in our tongue, and you will not stay in the Forest Lands. Nevertheless, I am honoured that it should fall to me to greet you. There! Was that courteous enough, ladies?'

They both laughed at him, and he joined in.

'Most high courtesy, my lord Kirenkaloken. But can you tell us where we should go from here?'

'Me? No! And I must be off. Here, take this.'

He thrust his knapsack into Willowood's arms, dashed behind a tree, and was gone. They searched around all the nearest trees, but could find no trace of him. Bewildered, they sat down, huddling into their blankets and opening their bundles.

'There is very little food left.'

'And no water. Let us see what he has left us.'

Willowood unfastened the knapsack, and smiled with delight. 'Cold meats and fruit and wine and water; enough for both of us.'

The food was as fresh and delicate as if it had come from the table of a king.

'So that was the Kingsbird. I wonder what strange things tomorrow will bring.'

But Willowood was too happy eating and drinking to reply. Soon they settled down for the night, and fell deeply asleep. They woke in the morning to bright sunlight and the noise of rushing water.

'What has happened? Where are we?'

Saranna did not reply. Wordlessly she stared at the wide path that had appeared while they slept. It cut a broad swathe through the trees, and their campsite was on its verge. To their left and to their right, it stretched away into a gold-green dimness, immeasurably far off. Above, a strip of clear blue sky was visible, and the lacy green treetops swayed overhead.

'What is that water sound?'

Willowood listened for a moment, then ran across the pathway and into the trees on the other side. Saranna started after her, and heard her calling out,

'Look, come and look!'

She caught up with Willowood, who was standing looking at a steep slope that suddenly plunged down ahead of her. A stream came leaping out of the rocks just below them, rushing and tumbling down through the forest, in and out around the trees, over stones and under ancient roots.

'A pool, a pool!' shrieked Willowood.

She set off down the slope at precipitous speed. Sighing, Saranna went back to collect their things from the campsite, and then followed at a more sedate pace until she came to the deep brown pool where Willowood was already splashing happily. It was beautiful. A small willow tree leaned over the pool, moss covered rocks edged it, and the water rushed in from above, spilling out more slowly on the lower side.

'This is wonderful; come in!'

Saranna shed her clothes, dropping them on top of Willowood's, and slipped into the water. It did feel wonderful after all those hot miles of walking, and she revelled in it. Above them a green light grew stronger, and they began to feel some warmth in the air on their faces.

'Why does this forest keep changing? And how?' asked Willowood.

Saranna ducked under the water and came up again spluttering. 'I don't know. It is supposed to be an uncanny place, according to all the stories.'

'But I did not dream that so much magic could really happen. Next we shall be seeing the White Doe, the one with the black ear and four black feet, that—OH!'

There she was, lightly running up the slope, the white doe of the Forest Lands who gave her milk to the Twins when they first came to the land beyond the mountains. At the edge of the pool she paused, one black foot in the air, and her deep golden gaze rested fleetingly on the women. Then she bent her dainty head, drank, and skipped away into the woods. Saranna found that she was holding her breath. She let it out all in a rush, and beside her Willowood did the same.

'Oh!' she said again.

'Willowood, please be careful what other creatures you name here. If you know of any more fabled beings from the old tales of Kiril, I'll thank you to keep them to yourself.'

They climbed out of the pool at last, dried themselves as

best they could, and set off down the grassy way. It was good to be walking in the light, along a clearly visible road. Yet the journey was monotonous; for the rest of that day they saw nothing and met no-one. They went on and on between the ranks of identical trees, until exhaustion overtook them and the sky above began to darken. Then they halted and settled down at the roadside to rest for the night. As the dusk deepened into true darkness, they saw stars overhead, their first view of the night sky since they had entered the forest. They gazed up at them for a while, then looked down to find a tall figure standing dark and silent, very close to them. Both cried out in alarm, and instantly the figure vanished.

'It must have been a shadow,' said Willowood.

Towards morning Saranna found herself dreaming of Arel. She was talking to him, but he was silent and sad, and did not answer her. Gradually she felt warmth and sunlight breaking into her dream, and opened her eyes to find that she could still see Arel's face. He was standing where the shadow had been on the previous night, looking solemnly down at her.

'Arel!' But as she sat up, he was gone, in a flash of green and gold and silver. Saranna said nothing to Willowood about the strange vision of Arel. Together they breakfasted and then set out again down the long road that stretched ahead as straight and monotonous as ever. About mid-morning they rested, and saw their first sign of life since the previous day. Out of the long grass between the greenway and the forest came a small grey rabbit, that stopped and sat up to look quizzically at them.

'Oh, Saranna, look! Here, rabbit, come and have some bread.' Willowood crawled cautiously towards the rabbit, but it turned away and headed into the forest. She set out after it, but

Saranna called her back.

'It would not be wise to leave the road. We may never find it again and we do not know what enchantments may lurk in the forest. We must be careful.'

The road led them on and on between the endless ranks of trees. Suddenly Saranna looked into the forest, and stopped.

'What is it?'

'I thought I saw—yes, there it is—a flash of light, like a reflection from gold or silver. There, look!'

Saranna rushed to the edge of the road and looked into the forest. A short way off she saw a little glade, its grassy floor sprinkled with white flowers. In the middle of the grass stood Arel, splendid in a suit of silky green, his silver pendant about his neck and the gleam of gold at his wrists and on his fingers. This time he was smiling at her, and holding out his hand towards her. Saranna darted forward, calling his name. Behind her Willowood shouted.

'Saranna! Where are you going? Come back—you said we must not...'

Her voice was cut off, and Saranna, stumbling forward, cried aloud in fear as the vision of the glade vanished. She tripped over a tree-root and fell, and as she fell her hands and face were torn by sharp thorns on the tangled bushes that suddenly filled the small gap between the trees. She struggled to her feet, but the bushes tugged at her hair and her clothes, and she stumbled. Lithe, thorny branches wrapped themselves around her and she struggled, screaming. At last she fell heavily to one side and struck her head against the trunk of the nearest tree; after a moment of fierce pain, everything around her grew dark, and she felt herself falling into the darkness.

Consciousness returned abruptly, and Saranna was surrounded by the sounds and smells of people living and working all around her. Somewhere venison was roasting, and somewhere else a voice was singing. Nearby children laughed and shouted, and a deeper voice called out, 'Over here—put them in the hut at the end!'

Saranna opened her eyes, but could see nothing at first. She lay still, feeling with her fingers—there seemed to be a bed beneath her, and as her eyes grew used to the light she realised that cracks of daylight were visible here and there. She was inside a small building and outside was a crowd of people. Abruptly the door was flung back and a young man entered.

'The King commands your presence, stranger!'

Saranna stepped blinking into bright sunlight. A stern young Kirenoi awaited her, and beside him a tall young woman, looking equally serious and strong. They motioned to her that she should walk between them, and set off. Saranna looked about her with interest. She was in a town, built in a huge clearing within the forest. Over the roofs of the farthest buildings, the tall trees could be seen in every direction. Most of the houses were of modest size, but wonderfully constructed of carven wood. As the little group passed by, beautiful Kirenoi children gazed at Saranna around corners and through windows. She smiled at them, and one or two waved in return.

Soon her escort led her into a wide open space between the houses. A fair green lawn filled it, dotted with small trees, shrubs and flowers, and crossed by a wandering, slow stream. Across the stream was a delicate wooden bridge, and at the far side of the green stood the largest dwelling Saranna had yet seen. The guards led Saranna across the bridge and over the lush grass to the great door. Here stood two very tall men, Kirenoi they seemed but with dark hair and brown skins. They wore splendid body-armour that flashed in the sun, and they crossed their long spears in front of the elaborately carved doors.

'Who comes seeking the King, Lord of the Forest?'

'Here stand Kirelonara and Kirinokalen, bringing the stranger who was found in the forest, to answer to the King.'

The doorwardens stepped back, raising their spears, and hammered three times, in unison, on the mighty doors. Slowly and silently the doors swung open, and Saranna was pushed forward. Still flanked by her guards, she stepped into a panelled room, with doors on every side and a staircase rising against one wall.

Her captors hurried her through another set of double doors straight ahead. These led to a lofty hall, lit by high windows with delicately carved frames and clear glass like crystal. Far off at the end was a raised dais, and upon it stood a vast wooden throne, dark and polished and even more intricately carved than the outer doors. Upon this throne sat a tall man, and as the party made its way towards him Saranna saw that his head was bowed and his face buried in his hands. He was dressed in a suit of deep-green silk and cloak of velvet, with a fillet of gold binding his long fair hair. Bracelets and rings of gold and silver and emeralds sparkled in the shafts of light from the high windows. About his neck hung a long silver chain, and on it gleamed a pendant shaped like two triangles overlapping.

Saranna rushed towards the throne. The King looked up, startled, as she came to a halt at the foot of the dais. It was Arel.

'Saranna! Oh, my dearest Saranna! How came you here?'

The guards had come up behind her, but at a wave of Arel's hand they departed, bowing their way out of the hall. Arel stood up and held out his arms, and Saranna ran lightly up the steps to him; they held each other close, half-laughing and half-crying with delight.

'Arel, my dear—to think that you are the King of the Forest!'

'Oh, that is not important—what matters is to see you again. I have been longing for you, hoping and wishing that you would come to me. For two nights I have dreamed of you, travelling through my forest, but I did not think it could be true. Come with me!'

He led her behind the throne, opened a door, and ushered her into a smaller chamber, modestly furnished and bright with sunlight. It had wide windows reaching almost from the floor to the ceiling along one wall, looking out over an enclosed garden. Here two plump white sheep grazed, their wool as soft and pure as a fluffy summer cloud. Arel crossed to an open window and leaned out, calling them by name.

'Marda! Jenna! Come.'

With much baa-ing they trotted fatly over to the window, where they pushed their noses into the King's hand and accepted titbits from a bowl on the wooden sill.

Saranna sat down near the window and waited. At last Arel turned, sighed heavily, and sat opposite her. 'Oh, Saranna, I am so lonely! I wish I could be a shepherd again. They call me 'Shepherd of the Kirenoi' in honour of my early days, but that is only a name. I am also 'Lord of the Greenwood' and 'Spirit of the Trees'; Kirarelaken, King of the Forest Lands. Oh, Saranna no one has called me Arel for so long!'

Saranna went over to him and gently kissed his mouth.

He smiled.

'That is nice. Why don't we do that again?' He took her in his arms and kissed her with more fervour.

'Yes, that is good; and now you look more like the Arel I used to know, with a twinkle in your eyes. Now sit down and tell me what is so terrible about being a King?'

At that point there came a knock at the door, and a young boy dressed all in daffodil-yellow silk came in, bowed, and said,

'My Lord King, the Hour of Audience draws near. Will it please you attend your court?'

Then he bowed and went out. Arel groaned. 'I will tell you, if I am ever granted enough time. But for now you must excuse me.'

When he had gone Saranna sat down again. One of the sheep poked its nose in through the window and bleated at her. Then there came a hesitant knock and two people came through the door; to her surprise Saranna recognised them both.

'Willowood. And the vanishing Kirenkaloken, too. Welcome.'

'Oh, Saranna, the King has sent us to you, to show you your room and everything. Is he not wonderful, so tall and handsome and romantic and remote and kingly...'

Saranna laughed and Kirenkaloken bowed deeply.

'I should like to go to my room very much; please show me.'

Saranna washed herself and rested in her elegant chamber; and soon a page-boy appeared to summon her to the mid-day meal. This was a splendid affair, with many long tables set out in the great hall. Saranna was given a place of honour, seated at Arel's right hand at the high table, which had replaced the throne on the dais. There were endless courses of meat and fish and fruit, and Saranna was glad when the meal at last ended. She and Arel returned to his private room, where he kicked off his high leather boots, dropped his cloak on the floor, pulled off his elegant doublet and unlaced the neck of the exquisite lawn shirt that lay beneath.

'Oh! That's better!'

He sank down onto a couch and held out his hand. 'Come here, Saranna; tell me all that has happened to you since we parted.'

She sat beside him. 'I will, Arel—but first tell me the story of the Forest Lands, and of why the King is so unhappy.'

'Very well, if I must; but I will make it as short as I can. Once, long ago, this was a wild grassland, with no trees at all. The Twins came here, guided by the white doe, and it was they who established the forest and made the Kirenoi to live here, the fair people among the trees and the dark below the earth, where they mined the gold and silver and jewels that they all delight in. It was the dark Kirenoi too, who learned to carve and work in wood, and to build houses and fashion bows and arrows. For many centuries they dwelt together in peace; but then the fair ones grew proud and haughty, and said that they were the lords of this land and that the dark ones were merely their servants, only fit to labour for the benefit of their masters. And there was bitterness and anger between the kindred. They complained to the Twins, but instead of settling the quarrel they themselves fell out, and the whole land was divided against itself. Rivers rose up out of their beds and flung themselves against trees, even rabbits and squirrels attacked each other in the forest, and the Kirenoi went to war.

'Fair and dark, they slaughtered each other, and the fighting went on for hundreds of years. My own father was killed only a year or two before I reached this land. But when I came here it had ended, and they all said that I was 'The One Who Should Come'—that is what Kirarelaken means—and if I would be King then peace would endure forever. And so here I am.'

'I am sorry for your father's death. But how wonderful to be a peace-maker and a King—is it not, Arel?'

He shrugged. 'Not to me—I only wanted to find my father, and since I cannot I would like to go home, Saranna. Back to my sheep and the quiet hills.'

Saranna stood up, and went over to the window. 'Can we go into this garden?'

'Yes, if you like.' He drew back a curtain, opened a door behind it, and followed her out into the sunshine.

'Now, Your Majesty, let us think about all this.'

'Must we?'

'Yes, if you are the king foretold.'

'Oh—what has all that to do with me? With Arel the shepherd of Telan? How can I change myself into a King just because they want me to?'

'But you do not have to change yourself—what were you best at in your old life?'

'Caring for my sheep.'

'How did you do that?'

'Well, you know that, Saranna. I watched them and guarded them and led them and talked to them and got to know them all as well as I could... what?'

'That is it!' Saranna shouted. 'That is how to be a King!'

The sheep fled, startled.

'It is? Is it?'

'Yes, it is. Your job is to draw the two kindreds together, to lead them forward in peace—who better than a shepherd to do that?'

Arel's face brightened and he took two great strides towards Saranna, caught her up in his arms and whirled her round and round.

'Oh, my love, this is why you have come to me, to show me what to do and give me back my happiness.'

He put her down and began to kiss her warmly. 'And you will stay with me, Saranna, and be my Queen and we shall lead the Kirenoi together—why are you looking like that?'

'I—cannot stay here, Arel.'

'Why not? You came to be with me—did you not?'

Saranna shook her head. Arel turned away and walked slowly across the grass and into the palace, carefully closing the door behind him. Saranna looked after him helplessly, until the two sheep came up to her and gently butted their heads against her.

'Baaaaa!'

'Yes, I know. And what am I to do now?'

She followed Arel into the house and the two sheep stared after her for a while. Then they went back to cropping the sweet green grass.

The next morning the cheery face of Arel's page-boy appeared around Saranna's door.

'Good morning, Mistress! His Majesty sends you greeting, and asks you to take breakfast with him in his private parlour.'

Saranna was soon knocking on the door of Arel's room by the garden. He took her hand and said quietly, 'I was very rude and cross and angry yesterday. Will you forgive me?'

'No—it was my fault.'

'No—I should not have....'

They both began to laugh, then hugged each other. At last Saranna said, 'Arel, it is wonderful to be with you again. But there is a journey I must make, a place where I have to go.'

'And where is that? What place could possibly be better than my forest realm?'

'I am going to IssKor.'

'IssKor—I see. To meet your old friend Kor-Sen?'

'No, Kor-Sen has gone far away and I do not expect to see him again. I am going to IssKor because Raðenn is there, my son Raðenn.'

Arel fell silent, and got up from the bench. He went over to the sheep and started scratching one of them behind the ear. Finally he came back and stood in front of Saranna.

'Then of course you will have to go. But no-one comes to this land without some good reason. I wonder what my forest has in store for you? You must stay long enough to find out.'

'Yes—I will. And we are friends again, are we not?'

'We have never stopped being friends. Be welcome to my kingdom, Saranna.'

Three days passed pleasantly in the quiet Forest lands. On the fourth, Saranna woke in the dead of night to pitch-blackness and the sound of someone opening the door of her room. She sat up and felt for something, anything, that might serve as a weapon of defence. Then the door swung open and the gleam of a candle spilled golden into the room, lighting up the anxious face of Arel, who was pushing the door open.

'I am sorry—did I startle you?' He came a little further into the room, and she saw that he was dressed in a very regal nightshirt, all lace and frills and sweeping folds. For a moment she thought he looked silly, and then when she looked again into his eyes it seemed that instead he looked rather magnificent.

'Quickly, you must come with me into the forest. The moon is rising outside your shutters and curtains, and it is time.'

'Why? Time for what?'

'Because the moon is rising, and because I tell you that you must. Saranna, do as I say and come, there is no time to lose.'

He held out an imperious hand, and she got hastily out of bed. Before she could reach for any garments to put over her own night-gown, he had seized her hand and was leading her from the room. The unshielded candle guttered and flickered as they went along the silent corridors and down the grand staircase. Here Arel blew out the candle, released Saranna's hand, and left her standing dazed in the blackness while he unbarred the heavy main doors and flung them effortlessly back. Into the sleeping palace flooded the silver light of the full moon; Saranna stepped to the door and peered out to see the heavy roundness of it hanging low over the tall trees around the clearing. She was about to speak, but Arel seized her hand again and pulled her though the doorway. As they headed for the bridge across the stream, Saranna looked back and saw the two doorwardens lying in a deep slumber, one on each side of the door. Arel pulled her on, almost roughly, until they reached the very brink of the forest, where he stopped. She stood panting; Arel seemed to tower over her, and his eyes flashed in the moonlight.

'Saranna, now you must choose. Will you go alone into my forest, or shall I guide you?'

'Alone? Oh, please come with me, Arel, do not leave me

alone.'

He looked down at her and smiled, saying in a more normal voice, 'Do not look so frightened. It is not an evil forest.'

He leaned down and kissed her softly on the forehead. 'Come.'

They stepped into the shadow of the trees. Arel led Saranna on and on into the wood, never speaking. At last she thought she heard something, a rushing sound that broke faintly through the silence and the curious silver-dappled light.

'What is that sound?' She found that she was whispering.

'Wait and see.' Arel went on, more rapidly now, drawing Saranna after him. The rushing sound grew louder and louder and Saranna began to think that it might be running water. Then abruptly she and Arel were out of the trees and standing on the edge of a glade, broad and level and awash with moonlight. The rushing noise became a roaring of water, and beyond the smooth silvery grass Saranna saw the tumbling, sparkling column of a waterfall that plunged endlessly into a wide black pool.

'Where are we, Arel?'

'Kingsfall. The heart of my forest. Here the White Doe drank when she first came to the land. Here the first trees were set by the Twins. Here the realm of the Forest Lands had its beginning. Welcome, Saranna.'

'What must I do here, lord King?'

'You must stand here alone, and see what is shown to you.'

He kissed her lightly and moved away. Saranna stood desolate near the edge of the water. She looked down and swayed giddily. By some trick of the full moon, the silver light penetrated the depths, and the pool showed deepness beyond imagining, deeper it seemed than all the oceans she had crossed on her journeyings. She took a step backwards, but felt her way blocked by something soft and solid. A little scream of pure terror burst from her, and she looked round. The white doe, silvered by the moonlight, stood behind her, pushing her to the brink of the pool. Kingsfall spread its clear veil across the face of the rock like a mirror of polished silver. Saranna thought she saw in this mirror a white form, flowing and indistinct, at times becoming clearer and then breaking up again in the shifting flow of the lucid water against the ancient stone. It resembled the image of a woman, and straining to see the face she stepped so close to the water's edge that her bare toes were wetted. The doe vanished as silently as she had come.

'Mother? Lady Iranor, is that you?' Saranna sank to her knees on the grass, clutching the rim of the pool with cold fingers. As she stared, the image shifted again, and she stood up to see better. The wavering woman-shape sparkled, steadied, and then faded away completely. Saranna gasped. She looked down and saw that there was no reflection of her face in the pool. As she gazed, her image shimmered slowly into view, with the moon above her head and stars all about her—and Arel, smiling, reflected beside her.

'What did you see, Saranna?'

'What I saw in the orchard long ago.'

'And are you pleased with what my forest has told you?'

'Yes, Arel—I am content.'

Joining hands, they bowed before the falling water, and walked away between the silent trees.

Leaving

*E*ven though autumn was approaching the weather was fine, and by early afternoon the Saracoma market place was too warm for work. The traders were resting, eating, and talking in small groups and there was little activity. Kor-Sen, grey with dust, strode between the stalls towards a group who were swapping jokes and travellers' tales.

'... so this fellow who calls himself a horse-trader, he says, 'Well, it's got four legs hasn't it?' And I says—this'll make you laugh—I. says, 'If you say it's got four legs, I think I'd better count them,' and he didn't say another word—no answer to that.'

As Kor-Sen approached, the laughter died out and the traders looked him over. The humorous horse-trader stepped forward and, standing beside Kor-Sen, addressed the group. 'Now I'll show you what trading, is all about: it's about observation. Now what do we have here?'

He walked round Kor-Sen, examining him closely. The group started to chuckle in expectation. Kor-Sen watched the performance, but said nothing.

'What we have here,' continued the trader, 'is a dusty individual'—laughter—'But why is it dusty? Because it has walked across the Green in the middle of the day. And why has it done that? Because it doesn't know any better, that's why. But why has it come here? It ain't a trader: it hasn't got no goods. It can't have come to study with Tendanta the Wise up in the Citadel on the hill: it's too old and tatty for that game. It must be a beggar.'

The speaker bowed as his audience laughed and applauded.

Kor-Sen smiled and held up his hand for silence. 'May I add a comment to this learned discourse? Observation is indeed important, but so is the art of asking the right questions: if you had asked, I would have informed you that, contrary to appearances, I am immensely rich and would have rewarded politeness and hospitality with great munificence: since you have been both rude and offensive, my generous inclinations have been thwarted. The lesson for you is: if you seek wealth and happiness, look beneath the surface of things. I thank you for your welcome, and for providing me with what I required.'

He bowed low in the elaborate manner of the court of Sen-Mar, smiled sweetly at the open-mouthed traders, and walked on towards the causeway and the hill top. When he was half way up the causeway he stopped and looked out over the city. Buildings of dried red clay sprawled out over the plain to east and west and a number of bridges arched gracefully over the river. Everywhere there were signs of quiet prosperity: the people were clean and well dressed, the animals fat and contented, and most of the houses looked comfortable and spacious. Kor-Sen laughed and continued to the hilltop.

When he reached the end of the causeway he stopped to take in the scene. The top of the hill was taken up by a muddle of stone buildings around a central courtyard, but dominating the view was a tall house with large unshuttered windows and an imposing, heavy wooden door. The thick walls rose up from the ground in an unbroken line to form a parapet: the whole building was faced with polished green stone which reflected the golden sunlight down into the courtyard. The place was deserted except for a single deer delicately nibbling at a bundle of hay between two of the buildings. This was the only sign of life until the door of the house opened and a young man dressed in an elegant robe of finely woven wool emerged into the light and advanced towards Kor-Sen. 'Welcome to Saracoma. You look tired and dusty: come and sit for a while and I will bring you some refreshment.'

He led the older man to a bench, and then brought a pitcher of wine and two cups from the house. They drank as they talked. 'I am Garian,' the young man said, 'and I have the honour of staying in the house of the Lord Tendanta and assisting him.'

'The 'Lord' Tendanta? I was told of a seeker after wisdom who lived here, not one of noble blood.'

Garian looked shocked. 'Tendanta may not nave noble blood, but he has a noble heart and is beloved of the people of the Green. No man has questioned his worth for many years: it is proved and attested by many noble deeds. Many noble deeds.'

Laughter crinkled the corners of Kor-Sen's eyes at the young man's earnestness.

'Forgive me. I meant no slight to the honour of your 'lord'. In most lands that I have travelled, and I have travelled many, a 'Lord' is one surrounded by sycophants and fools, one who, if he ever thought an original thought, gave up the practice in his youth. I am sure that Tendanta is the exception: if it were not so, his fame would not have spread across all the lands of Skorn.

'But let me introduce myself: my name is Kor-Sen, and I am a voracious seeker after wisdom. I have exhausted the storehouses of so-called knowledge in the Temple of Sen-Mar and the Academy of Drelk, and now I have come here to pillage the learning of Saracoma, to learn from Tendanta the teacher. Is the lord a teacher? Is he willing to take students?'

Kor-Sen poured himself some wine and watched Garian try to frame a response to this oddly worded request.

'I will have to speak to him.' He rose and scuttled into the house to find his master. Kor-Sen waited patiently, making good use of the wine pitcher and gazing contentedly over the town and the green plain beyond.

Before long, another man emerged from the house and approached Kor-Sen. He was wearing a golden-yellow silk tunic and a rich red surcoat: his sandals were of finely crafted leather and his fingers bore jewelled rings of precious metals.

'Good day, sir. You appear to have confused my young friend: can I help you in any way?'

'I hope so. I have come some distance to find a man called Tendanta, known as Tendanta the wise. I wish to ask him to take me as a student. My name is Kor-Sen.'

The newcomer sat down beside the older man, poured what was left of the wine into a goblet, and took a sip. 'I am Tendanta, and people call me wise. But I regret that my answer to your question is no: I am not a teacher and I have no students, though I am always willing to join with others in the pursuit of wisdom, provided they are sincere and are prepared to work.'

Kor-Sen jumped up and laughed and clapped his hands. 'An excellent answer! The best I have heard for many years. I am sick of old grey men who declaim their truth with voices full of certainty: give me the quest, the challenge of seeking to understand.'

Drewin smiled at these words. 'Well said. Perhaps after we have studied together for some time we will find out which of us is the teacher and which the student.'

From that day Kor-Sen lived in the fine house in the Citadel of Saracoma and studied every day with Drewin and Chafrash. He revelled in the thinking and talking, but he was not merely a seeker of wisdom; he sought other pleasures wherever he could find them. In the town he found wine, women and late-night revelry: on the Hill he found hard work and its rewards. Kor-Sen moved up and down the causeway with equal ease: his wit and his charm enabled him to drift through the life of Saracoma like a breath of spring.

These were times of gaiety and light hearts: not since the clans had come together to celebrate the coming of Tendanta had there been so much laughter on the Hill.

During the day Kor-Sen spent most of his time with Tendanta, on the flat roof if the weather was fine or in Tendanta's room when it was too cold or wet. They would sit facing each other for hours at a time talking: sometimes Tendanta would discourse interrupted occasionally by questions from Kor-Sen, sometimes it would be other way round.

Occasionally voices would be raised when a point was being disputed, and a single argument could continue for days.

One subject they returned to again and again was the origin of the runes: finally they decided to bring, the issue to a conclusion, and they climbed up the steep outside stairs to the roof together and settled themselves on cushions. Kor-Sen spoke first.

'Now let us settle this once and for all, or agree to differ. For some reason you always express reservations when I argue that the runes were made by our ancestors for convenience, and if there are things we do not know about them, that is because the knowledge has been lost to us. But you never say why you disagree, or by what evidence or authority you stand in this matter. In fact, I often have the feeling that you have some source of knowledge that you are not sharing—some secret that you fear to reveal."

Kor-Sen accompanied his last statement with a penetrating stare that demanded a frank reply. Tendanta smiled.

'Sometimes I feel that very thing about you: while the rest of us feel our way in the dark, you make wild leaps of imagination and always land on firm ground. You are right, of course: I do have reasons for doubting your view, and they are not the result of deep thought or research: they came from a chance encounter long ago—a man I met In the dark under the Ragged Mountains: he had studied ancient writings for many years, and he gave me some of his learning. He told me of the power of the runes that were made before the beginning of time and before the coming of mortal beings to the world.'

Kor-Sen laughed. 'I have heard these things too, but they are tales of market-place magicians and charlatans—stories to charm children to sleep—spells to turn lead to gold. Who was this teacher under the ground? Did he wear a golden cloak embroidered with strange devices? Did he carry an oaken staff?'

'No, he dressed and spoke plainly. His name was Vodorian.'

Kor-Sen's laughter stopped abruptly. 'Vodorian! You have met Vodorian? He is still alive? No, it cannot be: he was some impostor who had heard the name, a mountebank, a fraudster.'

Tendanta took offence. 'What are you talking about? Impostor? Fraudster? His name was Vodorian, I am certain of it. Why should he lie? Why should I?

"I can see that you are sincere; but when I tell you that I have spent years studying the writings of this Vodorian, and that those writings were in books hundreds of years old- so old that some pages crumbled to dust in my hands – you must agree that it is remarkable that he should be alive. I estimate that some of the books were written over a thousand years ago. If you did not meet a ghost, you talked with a very ancient being.'

'He did not seem very old: he was full of life, and he had fewer grey hairs than you.'

Kor-Sen laughed. 'Ah, then he cannot have suffered as I have. Do you realise that he is almost one of the immortals, a child of Iranor, the mother of all beings, mortal and immortal. But he was truly her child.'

'I know.'

'He told, you did he? But before we return to our discussion, will you answer me this? Did he tell you anything about his father?'

Tendanta thought for moment before answering, trying to recall what Vodorian had told him.

'No. He told me nothing: only that he was searching for him. When I last saw him he was heading to the north, hoping to find him. I felt that he did not know who he was looking: for.'

'If I am right in my guess he will not find him in the north, and it might be better if he did not find him at all. But that is not for me to say. Let us return to the point at issue. If Vodorian is the authority for your views on runes, they must be taken seriously. What exactly did he say?'

'This is a matter of the utmost seriousness: I have discussed it with no-one but Vodorian himself. It must not go beyond we two.'

Tendanta waited for Kor-Sen's nod of agreement before continuing. 'Vodorian always maintained that the runes provided the true names of all things, and by their true names all things are known, and through this knowledge they could be commanded: only through the Old Tongue and the true runes could all things and beings in the world, be commanded. I have taken this to heart and sought to find the true names of all things: at the same time I do not go by my true name, lest I be enslaved to the will of another. All that I teach the people is that the runes may be used to write down words, to record and to remember.'

Kor-Sen, who had listened intently, rose to his feet, walked to the parapet surrounding the roof and gazed out over the plain. After a while he returned to sit opposite Tendanta.

'I think I see. This reveals some things that have been hidden from me. I don't know what to say. For the time being I will accept that this idea must not be spread abroad: there are those who would seek power over both objects and things, though often enough they have little control over themselves. But for people of good will it offers a path to immeasurable wisdom. Let us leave it for now and talk of it later, when I have had time to think deeply on what you have said.'

Some say that it was from this time that Saracoma became the home of wizards.

Some days later, Kor-Sen was discoursing on maturity, wisdom and adulthood. He strode up and down in front of the window of Tendanta's chamber, emphasising each point with a beat of his finger.

'We must all grow up and leave home sooner or later. The young owl grows its full plumage and hunts alone when it is time: young men and women must find their own way. We can see it in the life of the people of the Green: in the end all the young people find their mates and their homes in one clan or another. It is the way of nature.'

Tendanta had listened to these remarks with growing agitation and at last he spoke. 'But what if you have no home?' he demanded. 'What if you have never known your father and have been cast out by your mother? What if you have no home to leave and no home to go to? Where is home then?'

Kor-Sen looked puzzled. 'Are you saying that you have no family—that you came from nowhere? This is impossible – a riddle: you must have come here from east or west north or south. Let me guess: I am a student of names, and yours is rare. Tendanta – from the sea: a strange name for a mother to give her child. Ah, but you told me once that this was not your true name: you named yourself to hide the truth. But why that name? Why 'Tendanta'? It sounds as though it might belong in a legend. I say you are from the far south.'

Tendanta laughed out loud. ''No, neither the south nor the north. I must confess to being unfair to you: you could not guess where I came from, and I am not going to tell you. The past is past: my life started when I came to Saracoma nearly twenty years ago.'

'Did it? That is an interesting way to talk.' Kor-Sen started to walk back and forth, paying no attention to his surroundings and talking to himself.

'A man without a past, with no home and no name? It all sounds somehow familiar, but I can't place it. Let me think. Let me think. This Saracoma, this creation, is named as a memory, a remnant of the past—so he has a past. What does it say?

'Coma' means past, but what does 'Sara' mean? 'Saravella', or 'Saraff', or Sara ...'

Kor-Sen stopped abruptly and looked at Tendanta, awestruck. He fixed him with the fierce look that had often terrified students in Drelk. He flung a question at Tendanta.

'Do you have a wooden disc on a leather thong about your neck, and does it have a rune carved on it, and is that rune 'orth'?'

Now Tendanta was staring at Kor-Sen with a look of fear and disbelief. 'How do you know that? Have you been spying on me?'

Kor-Sen chuckled. "No, I have seen one just like it – only the rune was 'ord' and it was worn round the neck of a young woman.'

'Young woman? What young woman? Where could she have found the disc?'

Kor-Sen was puzzled by Tendanta's response. 'I have been right in what I have said so far? And I am right when I say that your name is not Tendanta, but begins with 'ord'? Then who do you think this young woman is? It is your sister whose name begins with 'orth'.

'My sister? But she is dead. She is only a memory.'

'Then I must be very mistaken. I am on the best of terms with the lady who wears that amulet, and when she looks on the rune her tears are real. Yes, her tears are real: I have no reason to doubt her. She does not go about under a false name.'

Tendanta became angry: he jumped up and looked as though he might strike Kor-Sen.

'Who is this woman? Who does she pretend to be? What are you saying?'

Kor-Sen became exasperated. 'I am saying that I have met your sister, Drewin. Your sister Saranna.'

'No, my sister is dead. She is dead. You have met an impostor who has the rune: anyone might have found it, or stolen it.'

'Do you really believe that? Could anyone have stolen an object of such power? One that Saranna kept always close to her heart, just as you do yours.'

'I do not know. What you say sounds true, but I do know that my sister is dead: she was lost at sea.'

'No: she lives, and I spoke with her not a year ago."

Drewin became quiet and sat down in his chair. He started talking, but quietly, so that Kor-Sen could hardly make out the words.

'Spoke with her? You spoke with S—Sa... S—Saranna? Listen to me; I can hardly say the name. I have not spoken that word in a lifetime. Alive? No. It could not be so. I would have known, I would have sought her out, protected her. Little Saranna. I would have loved and cared for her, dried her tears and kissed her pains away. I would have given her back her amulet, and she would give me mine. Then we could go home and mother would kiss us both and forgive us. And we would all be happy again on the Isle. But I left her and she died alone at sea, and she will never have her rune. And I will never have mine.'

He stopped and sat up, suddenly alert. 'But I can have mine!'

He sprang to his feet, and ran from the room, crying out, 'Where is this woman? Bring horses. I must find her and take back my rune. Where is she?'

Saranna's Journey

*A*fter another week had passed, and hints of Spring could be seen in the Forest, Saranna spoke to Arel about her plans to travel on towards IssKor. Arel nodded, a little sadly. 'Spring is good for journeys; and I will make a grand progress through the land to escort you fittingly to the borders and see you over the River.'

That afternoon they pored over maps, and decided to travel southeast through the forest, almost to the foothills of the Ragged Mountains. Here the Kirenoi might easily ferry Saranna across the River, and she would be able to follow an ancient track down to the coast road that led south-east around the mountains' southernmost spur.

'They say that path is the way the twins walked when the white doe led them here. The country people call it Twinstrack—a good omen, Saranna.'

Two days later, in warm spring sunshine, a magnificent procession set out from the palace. All were on foot, for the King had declared that he would walk the length and breadth of his realm to show his kinship with the earth and all that grows in it. All the people gathered to cheer and to wave banners of green silk. As they reached the edge of the forest, a sudden wavering shimmer rippled across the trees, and Saranna found herself looking down the broad road that she and Willowood had travelled.

'Oh! So it is a magic road. I wondered why it was not visible on the maps. Where does it lead?'

'Wherever you are going,' replied Arel. 'It will take us to the riverbank at the point we seek.'

As they made ready to go into the wood, a voice called them.

'Wait, wait! Your Majesty, My Lady.' Willowood came panting up to them, her arms heaped with spring flowers. Curtseying hastily, she draped garlands around their necks and said,

'May peace attend your path, Saranna, and may you come safe to journey's end.'

'Willowood, I shall miss you. I hope one day I will return, and see you and Arel again.' The two women held each other close and wept a little. Arel came to them and said,

'I think we had better depart now, Saranna.'

Willowood curtseyed and turned away, hurrying back over the bridge towards the palace. Saranna turned, and followed Arel into the greenway.

For seven days and more they travelled at a leisurely pace through the forest, stopping at small settlements, or solitary dwellings, so that the King could meet and talk with his people. At last they came out of the trees, close by a landing-stage carved and fashioned as elegantly as everything the Kirenoi made. A boat was concealed nearby. Saranna looked around at the forest world again, and across to the bright open lands she must travel through alone. For a moment her resolve almost failed her. Arel held her close and she clung to him. 'Courage, dear one. My love, and the blessing of the Twins, goes with you. You will not fail.'

'Arel—I do not want to leave you. But I must find Raðenn.'

'Yes, you must. And we may yet meet again. Remember that here in my land you will always find a refuge from sorrow and danger.'

'I will never forget you, dear Arel.'

'Of course you will not—nor I you. Go in peace, Saranna.'

After one last kiss he led her to the boat, and the two young Kirenoi who were to row her across helped her carefully down, and loaded the pack she would carry.

As they crossed the River, she waved and waved, while Arel and his attendants waved back. Tears misted her eyes, but she wiped them away, looking steadily for her last glimpse of him.

Scrambling out onto the bank, she waved once more, and turned away. By the time the boat reached the forest shore, Saranna was out of sight around a bend in the rambling track; she did not see Arel's hand raised in blessing, nor hear his final words for her; 'Go well, and peace attend your path.'

Saranna walked steadily all morning. The land was wild, a rolling country of low hills scattered with scrubby bushes and stunted trees, and coarse grass where rabbits scampered and a few sheep grazed. The track was narrow and broken, but clear to follow, and she plodded on easily enough up and over the gentle folds of the foothills. From time to time she had to cross one of the streams that came down from the Ragged Mountains, but they were either narrow enough to jump across, or shallow enough to wade through. At length, feeling thirsty, she stopped. Looking up at the sun, she realised it was mid-afternoon, and just as suddenly felt hungry. She halted by the next stream, a clear rushing torrent between tumbled stones. Here she found a little shade under a clump of bushes, and after drinking some water from her cupped hands, she settled down to open her pack and see what the Kirenoi had given her.

The satchel was of doeskin, with broad straps that sat easily across the shoulders. Inside it Saranna found a smaller pouch of the same soft leather, and inside that some gold, silver and bronze coins such as were used in IssKor, and along the Neck.

'How kind—I never thought about that.'

Next she unwrapped packages of fresh bread, fruit and cheese. There was a flask of wine, but she set that aside for later, together with packets of dried meat, dried fruits and biscuits. As she was repacking these, another object fell out of the satchel and landed at her feet. It proved to be a small hinged box of some fragrant, light-coloured wood, fastened with a delicate silver clasp. Saranna opened it carefully, and a folded piece of parchment sprang out. She unfolded it and read;

'Wear this in remembrance of me.' Lifting the scrap of soft white fleece that covered the contents of the box, she discovered a ring of gold, set with pale green gems. It was fashioned in the shape of four running deer, tiny figures linked head to tail and with the gems set for eyes. It was exquisite, and when she slipped it onto the middle finger of her right hand, it fitted perfectly. Carefully she folded the parchment and put it back in the box, which she fastened and hid deep in her pack.

After eating she set off again, following the Twinstrack through the unpeopled land. For four more days Saranna made her way slowly south, sleeping under thickets of thorn or in hollows of the rolling foothills. On the fifth day the going became more difficult. The mountains loomed higher and higher above her as the track wound more closely under their steep sides. Soon Saranna was struggling to pick out the meanderings of the track among broken rocky outcrops. The path was rising now; below, to her right, she could see over the lower land down to the distant coast, a patchwork of green fields and little houses and villages. She struggled on up the ever more precipitous path, until she was clinging desperately to the rock wall on her left for fear of falling. Night came down on her as she climbed. Saranna sat down, exhausted, and pressed her back against the rock.

'Why did I come this way? I hate this horrible path!' She huddled into her cloak miserably, and bowed her head. Dusk deepened around her, and the first stars peeped out. Suddenly she felt a gentle warm breeze that came out of the west and stirred her hair and the hem of her robe; she looked up and saw a great white owl sweeping on the breeze towards her, silent and majestic. As she watched, it plunged down as if hunting, then rose up into the air again and came straight towards her, carrying something in its talons. Swooping low, it dropped a large dead branch beside her, and wheeled away down towards the lower slopes again. Saranna stood up to watch in astonishment as it dived, rose, and came back to her again and again, until it had gathered a huge pile of dry wood. Then it settled on a large rock, folded its wings, and stared at her, its huge eyes reflecting the newly-risen moon.

'Thank you, owl. Is this for a fire?'

It lowered its head as if in a bow of agreement. Saranna gathered some of the wood together in a ring of stones, and stacked the rest a little further off. The bird watched her closely.

'If you please, owl, I do not know how I am to light this fire.'

It began to move rapidly back and forth on the rock, shifting its weight from foot to foot and darting its head here and there as if agitated. Then it took off again in a fluster of white wing, and circled over Saranna's head, looking intently down. Finally it swooped again, picked something up, and came back to drop it at her feet. Then it resumed its perch and began to knock its beak against the surface of the rock in a series of comical little bobs.

Saranna stooped to pick up the owl's latest offering, and found it was a flint of the sort the people called firestone; it would strike a spark when hit against any dry rock. Saranna looked up at the owl, which stopped bobbing and settled into a more dignified pose; Saranna could have sworn it sighed with relief. Kneeling by the fire, she struck the flint repeatedly against another stone, and soon the dry wood caught and blazed up; warmth and cheer transformed the little camp on the side of the mountain. Saranna rummaged in her pack, brought out some of her dried meat, and stood up. The owl was still watching her, and she stepped carefully towards it. It roused uneasily, raising its neck feathers and shuffling its claws against the rock, but it allowed her to draw near.

'Thank you, kind owl of the West Wind. Please will you accept this gift in return?'

She held out a piece of the meat, and the owl blinked at her and made a noise in its throat. It contemplated the meat for a while as if assessing it. Then with a sudden movement it reached out with one foot and delicately grasped the offering with its claw; Saranna let it go, trying not to laugh as the bird stood on one leg and blinked several times at its prize. With dignity it lowered its head, snatched the meat with its beak, and gulped it down in two swallows. Again it stood glaring with its strange moonlike eyes. Saranna bowed to it. 'May the West Wind carry you safely, always.'

The owl stretched out its wings, flexed them a few times, and then rose into the air, effortless and beautiful, sweeping around Saranna's head for the last time before heading away to the south-west, a diminishing silver dot in the moonlight.

Saranna's fire warmed and cheered her; she ate some food, took a little wine, and curled up in her cloak to sleep, her head on the soft doe-skin satchel of the Kirenoi.

When the morning dawned bright and fresh, she felt strong, rested and confident. Packing up her belongings and carefully extinguishing the fire, she set out along the Twinstrack. Soon she came to a place where the track bent round sharply to the right to skirt the sheer rockwall that thrust suddenly out at a right-angle. Now for five hundred yards or so Saranna had this sheer rockface to her left, and the view on her right became the northern country over which she had travelled. She paused for a while to look back. There were the rocky slopes she had clambered up, and beyond them the greener foothills where she could just see the sparkle of the tumbling streams. Beyond that the river, and a green line that marked the Forest Lands. On the edge of sight were the misty heights of the Ragged Mountains, that curved round to the north-west so that they filled the horizon.

Saranna gazed for a long time across that sea of dark green in the middle distance that was Arel's kingdom. Then she sighed, turned away and set off again towards the farther edge of the rockwall. Here the path curved sharply round to the left, and Saranna edged cautiously round it; the sight that met her eyes made her cry aloud in wonder.

She was on a broad ledge, grassy and watered by a little stream that trickled down the mountainside, through a channel in the midst of the grass, and then over the edge to the lower slopes. The Twinstrack crossed this grass, passing through the stream, and at the far side descended to the south-east in a series of steep but naturally-stepped drops that took it rapidly down to gentler and greener lands. Saranna saw tree-tops below the ledge, and meadows lower still. But so amazing was the more distant view that she spent barely a minute taking in these details before turning back to it. Below Saranna the coast road wound through fertile farmlands, and golden sands were visible in coves along the rocky shore. Beyond, the sea sparkled blue in the morning sun, and white caps of waves rippled in the West Wind. Tiny white gulls and terns flashed across the water, and away beyond the stretch of empty sea where, so they said in Telan, the sea-folk lived below the waves, Saranna saw the islands. Telan, Telk, Mil and Ipple, sharply-edged against the blueness; Imman looming more hazily beyond them. Saranna told herself that she could see Esmil, away to the south-west, but if anything was visible beyond Imman it was probably only Drent.

Still, she gazed eagerly across the archipelago for a long time, remembering. At last she roused herself to leave the high green haven, crossed the lush grass and began the descent. As she went down the air grew warmer, and Saranna had to stop and roll up her cloak so that she could carry it in her pack. When she came out of the trees again she found herself in a gently sloping meadow deep with new grass and scattered with spring flowers. She could hear singing somewhere ahead, and she went on slowly and quietly so as not to startle the singers. Then she came over a rise in the ground and found herself looking at a farmhouse and yard that had been hidden by the slope.

The old stone house was built of slabs of the grey mountain granite. There were stone walls around the yard, and a paddock

where a donkey and a couple of draught horses grazed. In the
meadow a small group of children was absorbed in a singing
game.

'Ak to Iror leads and then, she the heat and warmth begins,
She the heat and warmth begins,
She the heat and warmth begins.
After Iror, Skeer does bring long and sunny days to Skorn...'

As they sang their hands moved in the intricate actions that
go with this ancient song, and Saranna watched their serious
faces as she drew slowly closer to the little circle. Suddenly
the smallest child, a tiny girl with a cloud of soft golden hair,
looked up and saw the stranger approaching. She let out one
yell; the singing stopped, and the children froze into stillness.
Saranna stood still too.

For a moment they all watched each other warily; then the
oldest child stood up and spoke politely. This was a girl too,
perhaps eight or nine years old. She dropped a curtsey and said,
'Greetings, stranger; we are pleased to welcome you. Who is it
that we greet?'

Saranna replied with equal gravity. 'Greetings to you, fair
children. I am sorry for spoiling your song, and I thank you for
your welcome. My name is Saranna.'

Courtesy satisfied, they all came close to her.

'I am Alia, and this is Calan and Malan, they're twins, and
that's Hella, she's a baby.'

'I'm FREE!' shrieked the little one indignantly.

'Well, we're six,' announced the twin boys in scornful chorus,
while Alia confided,

'I was nine years old last birthfeast, I am the oldest. Would

335

you like to come in, mother will be pleased, we never see anyone up here she says.'

Saranna was charmed. She had never had much to do with children except as a healer, and this chattering group was very beguiling. The boys dashed towards the house, scrambling over the wall and calling, 'Mother, Mother, a lady in the meadow!'

Alia led the way more sedately towards the gate set in the wall, while little Hella thrust a sticky hand into Saranna's and toddled trustingly beside her. As they crossed the yard a woman came out through the house-door, wiping her hands on a towel and peering at the stranger warily. She was some years younger than Saranna, with a broad, pleasant face that broke into a welcoming smile when Saranna smiled at her.

'Greetings, and blessings on your house.'

'She is called Saranna, mother,' Alia put in, while Hella shouted,

'Pretty lady—Hella's fend—I like the lady!'

'Girls, girls, be quiet. Greetings to you, traveller, and welcome. I am sorry about my noisy brood, they rarely see a visitor as we are so far from the village. I am Darla; do come inside, please.'

Darla settled Saranna comfortably at the kitchen table with milk to drink and cakes, cheese and apples to eat. She chattered away, obviously delighted to have company, and Saranna too enjoyed the talk after her lonely journey.

'Have you travelled far?'

'I came down from the mountain today—I have been many days on the Twinstrack.'

'What—through all those empty lands! You would have done better on the coast road. We never use that track except to fetch back strayed sheep, it is too near the river, too near Them across the river, you know.' Here Darla lowered her voice and gestured significantly with her head towards the wide-eyed children. Saranna smiled to herself.

'Well, I shall be going by the coast road from now on.'

'I'm sure that's very wise. But now I think of it, you would never have come here unless by that road, and it is so good to have company. You are welcome to stay the night, or rest with us a few days before you go on.'

Saranna felt a tug at her skirt. Looking down she saw Hella snuggling up to her, patting her knee with a plump little hand.

'Ess, please, nice lady stay here please.'

Saranna smiled, and lifted her new friend onto her lap. 'Well, I can hardly say no after such a nice invitation. I would be glad to stay.'

Darla looked pleased, and whispered to the children; they led Saranna up a steep staircase that led straight into the first of two sleeping-rooms under the roof.

'This is where mother and father sleep, and that's Holla's crib,' explained Alia. She led the way into the next room, where Calan and Malan were stripping linen from one of the two bedsteads that almost filled the room.

'That's the boys' bed, and this one is mine.'

'But you can have ours,' said Calan.

'We are going to put nice clean sheets on—the very best ones!' added Malan. They scampered out and down the stairs; within minutes they were back with the very best sheets, with which they enthusiastically made up the bed.

'Where will you two sleep?'

'Hayloft!' The grin of delight with which they both

announced this news relieved Saranna of any feeling of guilt about turfing them out of their bed. Everyone trooped downstairs, where good smells came from the oven. Darla was preparing supper while the man of the house, Boren, was setting the table. Saranna was introduced, and Boren bowed to her with a quiet dignity that she liked. The food, the conversation, the comradeship of the evening meal and the quiet hours by the hearth afterwards made her wish that she could have settled in just such a home. Gradually she dropped off to sleep, and was gently woken and led upstairs to the soft bed with the very best sheets. In the carved wooden crib beside her parents' bed, Hella slept with her bottom in the air and her knees drawn up under her. Saranna fell deeply asleep within minutes of climbing into bed.

Saranna spent five restful days on the farm, slipping easily into the family's ways, working alongside Boren and Darla, playing and singing with the children, bathing little Hella and rocking her to sleep in the old wooden rocking chair by the hearth. Boren and Alia seemed to treat her as a sister or a very old friend, while the children simply delighted her, chattering away all day, taking her on long walks, showing her everything they could think of that might interest her, asking endless questions.

'Where do you live?'

'Nowhere, at the moment.'

'That's silly, you must live somewhere!'

'Don't be rude, Calan, Saranna is on a long journey and she will find somewhere to live when she arrives.'

'Well, where did you come from, then?'

'I have had many homes.'

'Why?'

'Why—I cannot answer that. Because I have.'

'Oh.' Calan wandered off to join his twin, and Saranna turned her attention back to Alia, who wanted to learn all about healing and herbs. Hella clung tightly to her 'fend's' neck, stroking her hair, singing to her, and now and then breaking in with comments of her own. Suddenly she said, 'Is you a mummy?'

Saranna was startled, and for a moment could not answer.

'What is the matter, Saranna?' asked Alia.

'Nothing—nothing, Alia, do not worry. Let us take Hella up into the meadow and look for rabbits, shall we?'

The rest of the day passed happily. But later that evening, when all the children were asleep and Boren was drowsing by the fire, Saranna sat down beside Darla.

'I will have to move on, Darla. I must, although I love it here.'

Darla looked up from her work, and spoke gently when she saw the strain in Saranna's face. 'Why is that, my dear?'

'Oh—something Hella asked me today.'

'Has she upset you, Saranna?'

'No—but the question meant more to me than she could have known. She asked if I was a mother—and that is the reason for my journey, Darla. I am a mother, but not as you are. I have never known my child.'

Saranna found that she was crying, and Darla put her arm about the other woman's shoulders. 'Why not tell me all about it?'

The story of Raðenn was a long one, and in the midst of the telling Boren awoke, saw that something was amiss, and moved quietly about preparing warm drinks for them all. Saranna found hers very comforting. Boren sat down with them and heard the end of the tale, and both he and his wife looked at Saranna with sympathy.

'You poor thing. I cannot think how it would be if I were separated from my children.' Boren stopped, because Saranna had begun to cry again.

'Neither could I, until I came here and saw what I have missed. I have been so happy here, but I have been borrowing happiness from you, when I might have had it for myself. Oh—what a mess I have made of everything!'

'Saranna—you are trying to put things right now by going to your son, and you have told us so many wonderful things, healing and travelling—things I have no hope of ever doing. We have led our lives differently, but that does not mean either of us has done wrong.'

'You are right, I know. But it is painful sometimes. And I must be off, tomorrow I think, and get on with making things right.'

'I think you must. Though I am sure that one day you will come back and see us. Now, as it's market day in Erag tomorrow Boren can give you a ride for part of the way. Then you need only walk along the coast road, which is nice and flat. You must remember your condition.'

For a moment there was a total silence as Saranna stared at her friend. Darla smiled back at her. 'Condition? Darla, what do you mean? What condition?'

'Saranna! Can you really not know? I should hope I am right, since I'm in the same way myself.' Darla smiled at Boren, who leaned over and kissed her. Saranna began to laugh. At first the others looked alarmed, but her laugh was so light and infectious that soon they joined in. The sound rose louder and louder, until four sleepy heads appeared around the foot of the staircase, wondering what the grown-ups were up to.

Eventually Saranna quietened, and Boren shooed the children up the stairs. 'It is so foolish of me, Darla. Only twice in my life has this happened to me, and each time someone else had to tell me! What am I to do?'

'Just carry on with your journey, and take good care of yourself. You have time enough to get at least as far as IssKor before the baby comes. And the Lady will protect you.'

'So she will, Darla. So she will.'

A slow, jolting ride in the dark brought Saranna, Boren and Alia into the central market-place of Erag just before dawn the following day. The wide, irregularly-shaped clearing between the houses was thronged with people, setting up stalls and unloading goods for sale, by the light of flickering brushwood torches. By the time Boren found a clear space to tether his horse and unpack his own wares, the light was growing in the sky. The three travellers climbed down and Saranna turned to Alia.

'I will come back, I promise. And then you can show me your new baby brother or sister, and meet my little one—just think of that.'

'Will it be soon, please?'

'I do not know. But I would not break a promise to you, Hella. I think you will be a healer one day, and you and I will study together again. So trust me, and wish me well now like a brave girl.'

Hella nodded flung her arms around Saranna and held her tight. Boren said, 'I wish you well too, Saranna. I hope you find your boy, and you can both forgive the past. May the Lady go with you.'

'Boren, how I shall miss you all. I shall never forget you, and I will come back—tell the others that I promise to come back!'

So at last they parted, and Saranna made her way out of the market-place to quieter streets of cottages and huts where the fishing families lived. Between the houses she could see the sea, tumbling onto the quiet shore of the Inner Mouth. At the very edge of the town she came to a small inn, quiet and clean, too far from the market to be crowded at this hour. Here she rested and took a light second breakfast, before setting out in earnest along the coast road. Although she walked slowly, by mid-morning she could feel the beginnings of an ache in her back. She sat down by the roadside to eat and drink a little from the well-stocked pack Darla had given her. Leaning against a tree and watching the gulls sweeping across the sparkling sea, she fell asleep in the mid-day sun.

When she woke several hours later, the ache in her back was much worse, and the sky was dotted with light-grey clouds coming in from the west. Groaning, Saranna scrambled up, repacked her bag and set off again eastwards. Less than a mile along the road she was forced to stop, get her cloak out of the pack, and wrap it round her against the increasing rain. The soft road was becoming muddy and slippery, and Saranna struggled on, hoping desperately to find some dwelling where she could shelter. But the land stretched away to the north of the road, an endless rolling green landscape that seemed empty of life.

For two or three muddy miles Saranna pressed on, growing

more and more anxious as the sky darkened and the rain settled into a steady downpour that soaked through her clothes. Just as she felt she must collapse from cold and exhaustion, she saw a light ahead, that flickered for a moment and then vanished. Saranna hurried towards it, slipping and sliding in the mud and blinded by the rain that lashed into her face. Across the sea the West Wind swooped, blowing her cloak uselessly about her. The light flashed out again, much nearer now, and in a few moments Saranna was drawing aside a flap of soft leather from the entrance to a tent and calling out, 'Hello! Who's there? May I come in and shelter from the rain?'

A total silence followed; Saranna stooped and went in, blinking in the light of the fire. Gradually she made out two small figures dressed all in green, their hair tied back with leather thongs and their hands resting on bows that lay beside them, with arrows to hand.

'You need not fear me. I am a traveller in these lands, and seek only to escape the fury of the storm. Will you let me rest here? I am wet and cold.'

Slowly the two stood up, and Saranna saw that they were a man and a woman of small stature, dressed alike in green tunics that ended at the knee, and were belted with leather. The woman spoke. 'This is not a storm, but a shower of rain, woman of the south. Yet you are cold and distressed, and none such may be turned away from a tent of the Chorien. Be welcome to our hearth. I am Gresh, fisher of the River, and this is Alesh my husband.'

Saranna bowed solemnly. 'I am Saranna, a healer of the western islands. I thank you for your welcome.'

At this the little people seemed to feel that honour was

satisfied, and became more relaxed. Smiling, they drew Saranna close to the fire, helped her out of her wet clothes and wrapped her in a soft dry blanket.

'You are with child,' remarked Gresh, smiling even more.

'Yes.' And Saranna smiled back.

Fish was cooked for her on the hot stones that edged the little fire, and she was given a drink of what appeared to be sour milk. Her hosts began to talk to her, explaining that they were further from home than they usually travelled. They lived to the north, fishing along 'The River' as they called it.

'What brings you so far south, Alesh?'

'Our Lord came south, the One Foretold, who rules the tribes with wisdom,' explained Gresh. 'Before he came the people did not think about other lands, or other peoples. But he came from beyond our land, and now he travels back beyond our borders for a while, and so we decided to see for ourselves, Gresh and I. We do not like this salt water, and its strange fish, and tomorrow we will go back to our own people.'

'What of your lord?' Saranna asked, but she was already too heavy with sleep and warmth and food to hear Alesh reply, 'He will come back to us. When he has found the bad woman who pretends to be his sister, he will come home.'

Saranna woke next morning into warmth and comfort, the sun climbing up the eastern sky and the waves on the shore swooshing softly against the sand. For a while she lay luxuriating in the softness of her blanket; then opened her eyes wide and stared up at the blue sky.

She sat up. There was no sign of the tent, nor of the little people. Spread on the grass beside her she saw her cloak and other garments. Her pack stood close at hand, looking as if it was more full of food than when she had begun her journey from Erag.

She scrambled out of the blanket, dressed, ate a good breakfast, and gathered up her belongings. All the time she looked about her, north to the plains, east and west along the road, south over the quiet waters of the Mouth, but she could see no trace of her rescuers and in the end, with a shrug, she set out again eastward.

The morning was uneventful, and shortly after her noon-meal Saranna came to a fork in the coast-road. The broader way swept off to the left, a little uphill, while a narrower track branched towards the sea, becoming almost a part of the strand as it made its way below the sand-dunes and above the high-tide line. Away to her right there came a flash of silver, and she saw a pair of terns dipping and rising, plunging into the shallows of the incoming tide in search of fish. Almost without thinking she turned into the right-hand track and followed the line of the beach. The going was soft and wearying in places, but Saranna enjoyed the solitude of the strand. Sometimes rabbits popped up in the sand-dunes; always there were gulls crying on the wind and shore-birds scuttling and peeping; but she saw no other travellers, and walked on until evening.

Just as her back was beginning to ache, the track began to turn into a proper road; rounding a particularly high dune, Saranna saw a village ahead, less than half a mile away. She came among the first houses shortly afterwards, and made her way over an old bridge that crossed the river in the midst of the town. Narrow and precarious, it was built of great natural slabs of stone, resting on uprights built from smaller stones. Saranna paused half-way to look upriver. A little to the north she saw a second bridge, an elaborate affair of shaped and carven stone, set amongst greater houses, shops and inns. 'This must be Twinbridges, as Boren told me,' Saranna thought.

Here the tribes of the plains came, travelling down the river, to trade the spoils of the hunt and sweet freshwater fish for the produce of the farmlands and the more exotic goods ferried across the Mouth from IssKor and Mardara in the south. Already the sky was darkening, and Saranna saw lamps being lighted up in the town, and heard the sound of music and laughter. But she turned away, went on across the old bridge, and sought out a plain and humble inn that was only distinguishable from the cottages surrounding it by its faded sign that swung creakily in the evening breeze; The Flounder.

Saranna was made much of by the landlady and the local people enjoying their evening's relaxation. She was provided with enough stew for six people, with bread and butter and wine and cheese; everyone wanted to ask her questions, which she did her best to answer in spite of her weariness.

'Walking all alone, a lady like you—are you not afraid of robbers and vagabonds?'

'No, indeed- I have made many friends on my journey, and now I have not far to go—only as far as IssKor.'

There was much shaking of heads and buying of fresh ale at this—Saranna tried to turn the talk into other channels.

'I heard music up in the town as I came along; is there some celebration?'

An old man snorted into his beer. 'Bless you, mistress, that's how they rich folks up there always carry on of a night. Though I daresay it's worse than usual, what with this great lord from foreign parts staying at the inn—the best inn, they calls themselves, though they can't brew beer like mistress Cara here – and all his escort and horses and so forth.'

The word 'lord' echoed in Saranna's tired head, and she was quiet for a moment, trying to remember where she had heard it recently. By the time she came back to awareness, the talk in the room had moved on and several of the younger men were boasting about the relative merits of their fishing boats. Saranna excused herself and slipped away to her room, where she burrowed thankfully into the soft, clean bed, and soon slept.

After breakfast the next day, Saranna set off again along the narrow way that led close by the shore; by the end of the morning, Twinbridges was almost out of sight, and she was travelling slowly but steadily southward along the eastern shore of the Mouth. Gradually she drew away from the water, as the shore-road bent slightly east to come back into the main southward road. Saranna sat down near the joining of the lesser road with the greater to take her noon-meal. While she ate, she watched the sea-birds and the falling waves, remembering the far west, and the home of her distant childhood. She reached for the Ord-rune that had travelled with her for so many years, caressing it as it lay against her heart on its cord of silk.

'So many miles. So many islands. So many years, and still I have no rest.'

Saranna sighed and stood up slowly, turning away from the sea to look out across the empty lands to the east, then south, where two roads went rolling away over low, barren hills, one to Sharn the Godless city, one to distant IssKor. Then she looked northward along the main road that stretched silently away into a dim haziness. A flicker of movement was visible in the haze. As she looked, it grew clearer and Saranna thought she could hear a faint sound of hoof beats. Gradually the sound grew louder, and the vague shapes solidified until she saw clearly that a small company of people on horse-back was coming towards her. Dust billowed around them, and they swept down rapidly, nearer and nearer, until they drew level with her. One of the riders saw her, raised one hand, and cried, 'Halt!'

The whole company drew up, not very tidily, and the horses blew and snorted and tossed their heads up and down, while the riders peered at Saranna standing on the lower road and looking at them. Finally a tall man on a particularly splendid grey horse dismounted and handed his reins to someone to hold. Slowly he crossed the rough ground between the two roads; Saranna could not see his face, for he wore a broad-brimmed hat, and was looking down, picking his path among the clumps of marram-grass. As he drew near, he swept off the hat and she saw that he was grey-haired, handsome, and bore himself with dignity. His tunic and hose were of fine materials, and Saranna wondered if this could be the lord who had passed the previous night at Twinbridges.

Soon he stood before her, and bowed. 'Madam; please accept the greetings of a traveller. I am from the north, and am called Tendanta. It seems that you are alone, and I wonder if my company may be of service to you, if you are journeying far in these wild regions.'

He smiled. Saranna smiled back at him, looking up into his face. She was about to speak, but something about the traveller struck her silent. Something about his face.

'Madam?'

'I am sorry—my greetings to you, sir. But—have we not met before?'

He shook his head. 'Surely I should remember such a lovely and charming lady'

But Saranna was not listening. She was staring at the breast of his tunic; he looked down, bewildered, at the polished wooden disc that hung there. Then she looked again at his face and stretched her hand towards him, swaying on her feet. Alarmed, he reached out his own hand to steady her.

Gripping his arm fiercely, Saranna cried, 'Where did you get that disc? Why are you wearing it, it is my brother's, not yours. You said your name was Tendanta.'

'Yes, that is my name. Poor thing, why are you so distressed?'

She looked up into his face again, studying it closely. Then she almost hissed at him, 'What does Tendanta mean? What kind of name is that? Tell me at once.'

Tendanta stepped back, shaking his head. 'It is my name, that's all. It means 'from the sea', but that is not important. Anyone's name may mean anything.'

Saranna let go of his arm, and stepped back. She drew from her gown the disc she had carried for so long, the disc that matched almost exactly the one upon Tendanta's breast.

'Drewin,' she said softly, 'do you not know your sister?'

A Meeting

'No.' The tall traveller stepped back, stumbling on the tufted grass that pierced the sandy soil. The woman followed him, stretching out her hands. He backed away. 'No—you cannot be Saranna—she is dead!'

'Drewin; look, here is my rune that you made for me when we were children.'

He shook his head, opened his mouth to speak, closed it again. Then he said, 'You see before you, lady, Tendanta, Lord of Saracoma, he who was thrown into the sea, wisest of all rulers, he who cannot find his way—that is who I am.'

'Tendanta—your name is Tendanta? Then what has become of my brother, Drewin. That rune you bear is his handiwork—see!' Again she held out the Ord-rune; he stared at it, then peered closely at her face.

'But I was certain that you were dead.' With these words he sat down heavily on the ground, his fine silken hose sprawled carelessly in the dust, and buried his face in his hands.

Timidly, Saranna reached out her hand and laid it on his bowed head; he shrank away. She sat down beside him and said,

'What is it? What is causing you such sorrow, Tendanta?'

'Sorrow! Is that what it is? It is sorrow, is it?'

She laid a hand on his arm, and this time he did not pull away. 'Tendanta— if you insist upon that name—I am Saranna, and long ago when I was a child I lived with my brother, Drewin, on a remote island—far away to the west. But I have not seen him for many years. If you know—oh please, tell me what has become of him.'

He stood up again, and walked away, across the road and

down onto the strand. Startled, Saranna got up and followed him across the dragging shingle and the wet sand. She caught up with him by the waterline, where he stood careless of the creaming wavelets that soaked the toes of his elegant riding-boots. He was wringing his hands, twisting them together around the wooden Orth-rune, and as she reached him he began to speak, still staring out over the sea.

'When I saw the statue, I decided then that you must be dead, and that I must travel on without you. I was so certain, Saranna.' He looked directly at her, his face close to hers, and she looked into his eyes;

'You are Drewin. You are my brother.'

He nodded, and held out his arms. Slowly she drew nearer, and reached for him; he held her very close, but very gently, as if she might dissolve, or drift away. The waves swished about their ankles, and the West Wind stirred the folds of their garments, mingling them and swirling them about their bodies.

'Oh Drewin, Drewin.'

They stood close together for several minutes, and Saranna felt the memories of her childhood creeping close about them, wrapping them round and wiping out the years of separation and grief. Her eyes were closed, her arms tight around her brother, and her face buried in his chest—she could hear nothing but his heartbeat, feel nothing but his presence. She sighed happily, wishing that they could stay like this for ever.

Drewin pulled away roughly, and she saw that tears flowed down his cheeks and glistened in his beard.

'What is it? Oh, do not cry!'

He turned and set off along the beach; Saranna stared after him, then looked around wildly for help. She waved her arm in the general direction of the riding party, and a slender figure began to make its way towards her. Drewin was soon a good way off along the shore.

'My Lady? May I be of service? My name is Garian, and I have the honour to dwell in the household of the lord Tendanta.'

'Greetings, Garian. I am Saranna, and I am sister to Tendanta, who I know as Drewin.'

Garian looked startled.

'He is in great distress—I cannot follow him, I may have caused him pain—please, Garian, go to him and tell him—ask him to come back and talk to me.'

Garian nodded, and set off without further questions— Saranna liked him at once for this. She stood and watched the slim figure sprinting along the beach towards the now distant silhouette of her brother, and saw with astonishment Drewin fling himself to the ground, crying aloud and beating the sand with his fists.

Garian reached the spot, and stooped over Drewin, helping him tenderly to his feet and gesturing back towards Saranna. Drewin shook his head, but Garian persisted and indeed began to pull him bodily along the beach. Saranna watched intently, and was startled when a voice spoke close to her ear.

'May we be of any service, Mistress?'

She jumped, and turned to see that some more of Drewin's companions were close to her, dividing their curious glances equally between her and the distant struggle.

'That is kind—I am Saranna, Tendanta's sister. Let us go back to where you have left the horses, Garian can bring my brother there. I think we would do well to set up camp; this meeting has been a shock to us both.'

Saranna must have sounded more confident than she felt, for as she swept through the group and walked towards the main road, they all fell in obediently behind, and in spite of much murmuring and whispering, set to work at once. By the time a reluctant and heavy-footed Drewin was led up by Garian, the others had pitched a tent, unfolded a lordly chair and table, set out food and drink, and begun to light a fire; some were unsaddling and tethering the horses.

Saranna was impressed; but the object of all this attention was oblivious to it. He simply slumped down on the chair—leaving his sister standing – and seized a goblet of wine, which he drained rapidly, and refilled from the flask that stood there. Garian, disapproval written all over his features, unearthed a stool from the baggage and set it for Saranna.

'Will you have some wine, mistress Saranna?'

'Thank you, Garian—you are very kind. Just a little, mixed with water, please, and I should like a little bread.'

Garian supplied these things and withdrew; Drewin meanwhile sat staring into space.

'Drewin.'

He jumped at the sound of her voice.

'Drewin—are you not glad of our meeting?'

For a moment he seemed to be thinking these words over carefully, as if they puzzled him. 'Glad? Yes, of course I am glad. It is a miracle. I thought that you were dead.'

'You have said so, my brother—but as I am not, I would prefer that you now stop repeating it.'

'I am so sorry, Saranna; so sorry... '

Drewin put his goblet down and burst into drenching tears,

353

wiping the back of his hand across his distorted face. Saranna suddenly felt filled with anger, and she stood up and crossed to where he sat, seizing him by the shoulders. He looked up, startled, through his copious tears.

'Sorry! Sorry, Drewin? Yes, sorry for yourself, it seems. What need is there for all this grief and misery? You are my dear lost brother, whom I love, and I have found you again, and it is a great, great joy to me; but not, it appears, to you! Drewin, stop it! I have not waited through the long years for this!' She shook him hard, then released him. He sniffed.

'Have you been waiting, then, Saranna? Have you been looking for me and hoping for me?'

'Yes—yes, of course. I have worked, Drewin, and wandered and loved and suffered and borne a son—I am with child now, though you have not noticed it – but all the time, my dear brother, I have thought of you and wished for you and hoped against hope that you lived!'

He nodded, heavily and slowly. Then he reached for more wine, which the silent Garian poured and handed to him.

'Children? I have no children, Saranna. But I also have remembered. My city is named for you—Saracoma, the memory of Saranna, that is its name. I have never forgotten you. But when he came, and said you were alive, I was angry with him. I knew he must be wrong. So I came seeking this woman he talked of, to prove him wrong, you see. But he was right. I am sorry, Saranna.'

He smiled up at her like a naughty child, and her anger flared until it burst out of her, fierce as the rage of Iranor in the dawn of time, and she struck her brother across the face, once, twice, and screamed at him, 'Sorry! Sorry! I hope you are sorry! How dare you turn me into a memory, how dare you, Drewin! It was your fault, yours, mother told you to care for me and what happened? Your stupid knife hurt my hand! You made the runes, you gave me your rune and made her angry, and you let her turn us out onto the sea, and then you left me, Drewin, left me and forgot me and never tried to find me. How dare you tell me that you are sorry!'

She went on hitting him, still screaming, and all around them the startled company gathered. Drewin stood up and seized Saranna's wrists, calling out to Garian and the others for help.

'Quick, quick, she will hurt herself, help me Garian, hold her. Oh Saranna, Saranna.'

Garian fetched a blanket and helped Drewin to wrap Saranna in it, leading her into the tent where a light bed had been set up.

'Fetch one of the women—the child—oh Saranna, my dear, dear sister, please do not weep.'

'It is better, Tendanta, that she should—she will be calmer when the tears have flowed.'

'You are right, Garian; but fetch Arnat to be with her. May the Lady forgive me for what I have done and said today. Look, my little sister has returned to me.'

The two men looked down at Saranna, who was drifting into exhausted sleep, still clutching Drewin's hand.

When Saranna woke the next morning, the first thing she saw was the smiling face of a young woman. Saranna smiled back at her.

'Who are you?'

'I am Arnat. I am of the Tarrien.'

'Where is my brother?'

Arnat smiled again and laid a slender finger to her lips;

then pointed downwards. Saranna raised herself carefully and looked over the edge of the bed; Drewin was asleep on the floor beside her, wrapped in a deerskin blanket.

'Tendanta has been with you all night, lady Saranna. For many hours he sat where I sit now, and held your hand, and spoke to you of when you were children long ago. But at last I persuaded him to rest, and I have stayed here to watch over you.'

'Thank you, Arnat. I think I must have heard him, for I dreamed of the island, and of how we used to play together. My big brother, Drewin—he took good care of me. '

'I am sure he did, My Lady. I will fetch you some milk, now—you must rest, and think of your baby.'

She slipped out, and Saranna leaned over to run her fingers gently along Drewin's cheek. He opened his eyes and smiled up at her. When Arnat came back Drewin was holding his sister's hand against his cheek and they were talking. She put the milk down quietly, and slipped away again.

For the rest of that day, Drewin and Saranna were together. They walked a little along the shore, hand in hand. They sat together, watching the tranquil sea. They said very little. Over their evening meal, shared with Drewin's friends, they laughed and chatted about everyday things. Only when they kissed each other goodnight did Drewin say hesitantly,

'Saranna—there is so much that I must say to you.'

'And I to you, dear brother. Half a lifetime we have passed apart. Tomorrow let us speak together of what we have seen and heard; of where our lives have taken us—and where we are to go.'

Next day they walked a little way to the north, and sat down in the sunshine beside the quiet sea. Saranna spoke about Drenn, and Raðenn, and once or twice she wept while Drewin squeezed her hand in sympathy.

'So from the moment he was born, Essk came between us. I dread my meeting with him—what can he think of me?'

'She was a wicked woman, Saranna.'

'I think that she was lonely and needed someone to care for. That is beyond mending now. I must hope that Raðenn will receive me and hear what I have to say. I shall not make the same mistake with this child, Drewin—no one shall come between me and my baby.'

'That is good, Saranna. You sound strong and brave when you talk like that. I remember what a sturdy little girl you were. I wish I had children of my own.'

'And have you no lady to share that wish with you?'

'I share my home with Chafrash; but she and I are as brother and sister. I made her an amulet, a rune-disc, with the new rune, Chaer, that she made.'

'Oh Drewin, Drewin! You were wrong to do so.'

'Why? I made one for you, and you are my sister.'

'Yes, but Chafrash is not, though you call her sister. And such a gift from a man who is not a brother – she must have believed you were declaring your love! How could you be so foolish?'

'Do not say I am foolish, Saranna. You said that when you hurt your hand on the island. And when we met again here, when you were angry with me. I am not foolish, though I may not truly deserve to be called Tendanta the wise.'

'I am sorry; of course you are not—but it seems that you can be slow to know your own mind. From the way you speak of her it is clear that you love Chafrash as much as she loves you. I cannot think why you have not married and had those children, many years ago.'

The next day they began to talk again, slowly at first, then rapidly and excitedly, interrupting each other, asking questions, explaining, laughing. Then they began to speak of Iranor, and their talk grew slower, their words quieter. Gradually Drewin fell silent, listening with a frown on his face and his shoulders hunched over. At last he was staring down at the ground, his head clutched between his hands. Suddenly he leapt to his feet. He went away from Saranna, out of the camp and off into the open lands. She did not see him again until the evening. He came and sat beside her at the doorway of the tent.

'Forgive me, Saranna—I could not bear to listen. I have tried not to think of mother since she cast us out from our home; it was like a knife in my heart to speak of her. We have lost her forever through my thoughtlessness.'

'No, Drewin not lost, not truly. Though were not born as mortals, now we know Iranor our mother as mortals know her—in the things we do day by day, in the people who love us, and in those we love. When you return to Saracoma, Drewin, look into the eyes of Chafrash, and you will see how much your mother loves you.'

He sat silently for some moments, watching the red disc of the sun that rested now on the horizon. 'So—it is my little sister who is now the wise one. And I am truly the one who cannot find his way. Saranna, until this moment I believed that my life had ended when I left the island; I have been waiting for it to begin anew. Oh Drewin Tendanta, you are a fool indeed!

Saranna hugged him and began to laugh.

'What is funny?'

She giggled helplessly, and Drewin shook her gently. 'Answer me, you silly little sister, what are you laughing at? How dare you laugh when Tendanta the Wise is speaking his wisdom!'

At this she began to howl with mirth, and Drewin joined in, still not knowing why. They fell into each other's arms, and laughed and laughed and laughed. When they grew quiet again, Saranna said, 'Oh, Drewin, we are both very foolish—think of us walking the world all these years, feeling how tragic it is to be mortal!'

'Yet how lovely are the lands of Skorn. Who would go back to a lonely island?'

'Iranor is alone there; as the Immortals are always alone.'

Drewin nodded; and hand in hand they gazed into the west, until darkness covered the sky.

Early next morning Drewin took his sister's hand and led her again towards the beach, where they walked along close to the waves, their hair blowing in the gentle westerly wind.

'Well, Saranna—we must choose our future path.'

'I think you must return to Chafrash, Drewin. And I must go to Raðenn.'

Drewin looked out over the waves, and sighed. 'I know that you are right; but it is hard to part again so soon.'

They stood still, and hugged each other tightly.

'What must we do, Saranna? Surely at the parting of the children of Iranor some sign or portent should be seen? Should not the sky darken or the waves rise up?'

She looked up at him and smiled. 'Come here, Drewin; no, closer; and bend your head.'

'What are you doing? My disc! No, Saranna, it was only a

foolish jest—oh, give it back!'

'Ssssh! Now consider, Drewin. For your jest may serve to show us what we should do.'

Drewin stood looking at her, his hand still rubbing at the side of his neck where the mark of the leather thong could be clearly seen. Then he smiled, and reaching out both his hands he lifted the Ord-rune from around Saranna's neck.

'Yes, that is right, Drewin, I know it. For I am no longer only a memory in your keeping, nor you a forlorn hope in my heart. We are ourselves, Drewin and Saranna, children of Iranor, children of Skorn.'

They stood in silence, each clutching now the disc that bore their own rune. Then Saranna asked, 'Where is the link that you made?'

'It is lost, Saranna—I lost it—no, I gave it away, long ago.'

'No matter, my dear. You and I are joined by more than a link of wood. Look.'

She took the two amulets into her own hands, and tied the thongs firmly together. 'Do you see what we must do?'

Drewin looked at the discs that he had made with such toil and care. They were very beautiful and he was proud of them. 'Must we?' he said.

'I think that we must', said Saranna.

'They will simply float in on the tide.'

'No, they will not—Grandmother will not let them.'

Drewin threw his head back and laughed, a deep echoing thrilling laugh that startled the whole world into an expectant stillness; birds hung in the sky, waves paused in the act of breaking. He took the amulets, and whirled them around and around above his head, releasing them at last so that they flew through the air in a mighty arc and splashed into the sea far out from the shore.

They sank at once into the restless water. Drewin and Saranna stared into the west until their eyes began to ache from the brightness of the sun on the water; but no further sign came to them. At last they turned away and began to walk over the sands away from the sea towards the waiting road.

But where is Raðenn?

Look for the further adventures of Saranna in

THE
DRY
WELL

*Coming next in the Skorn series
from*

Eluth Publishing

The Dry Well

Prologue

There was burning sand beneath his feet. Light speared upward from the sand, a blue shimmer obscured the horizon and a yellow glare wavered overhead. He looked down, trying to move rapidly to ease the burning of his feet. But he fell, scorching his hands and knees.

He began to crawl forward, but found no shade. His tears dried up, his lips were cracked and sore. Sand stung his face; he whimpered. He fell into darkness.

Dreaming of coolness beneath island trees, he strove to see the face of the woman who turned away from him. He thought she was weeping. In the dream, water sounds were everywhere; the swooshing of waves upon the shore, the splashing of fountains and waterfalls. He plodded towards a deep brown pool beneath a cliff face straggled with fern. The woman was gone. He could not reach the water.

A rough hand grasped his hair and a warm trickle dampened his stretched lips. A cracked voice hissed in his ear, 'Look at me, destroyer. Look at me.'

He opened his eyes and the sun blazed into them. Turning his head he saw an old woman's face close to his. She laughed softly and tilted against his lips a small glass bottle. He swallowed the precious drops of moisture greedily. He tried to speak, but the old woman was chanting, crooning, closing her eyes and swaying while she pulled his hair viciously with one hand and in the other gripped the ancient bottle.

'I want more,' he whispered.

The old one opened her eyes; her song was ended. Dizziness swept over him and he thought the sky was turning above. The sun dwindled away into the blue, and the face of the old woman was less and less distinct. He made one desperate effort to twist away from her grasp, but found himself falling, falling out of the light and the heat into a place where silence wrapped around him and he lost all memory of day.

Lightning Source UK Ltd.
Milton Keynes UK
UKHW02f0534100118
315875UK00009B/375/P